W9-CBC-024

OTHER LAUREL-LEAF BOOKS YOU WILL ENJOY

ANNA OF BYZANTIUM, Tracy Barrett

BLACK SHIPS BEFORE TROY, Rosemary Sutcliff

DR. FRANKLIN'S ISLAND, Ann Halam

ELDEST, Christopher Paolini

THE HEALER'S KEEP, Victoria Hanley

LADY ILENA: WAY OF THE WARRIOR, Patricia Malone

THE SILVER KISS, Annette Curtis Klause

SNAKECHARM, Amelia Atwater-Rhodes

THE SUBTLE KNIFE, Philip Pullman

Acclaim for Tamora Pierce's

TRICKSTER'S QUEEN

"Pierce concludes the story of Alanna the Lioness' daughter, Aly, spymaster par excellence, in a fantasy thriller that continues the rich and complex tale begun in *Trickster's Choice*. . . . Characterizations are complex and well developed, and the intricate intrigue is compelling as Aly uses her cadre of spies to collect information and manipulate events leading up to revolution. The [love story] . . . adds its own spice to a thoroughly engrossing novel, sure to please." —*Booklist*

"A gripping fantasy, *Trickster's Queen* is hard to put down."
—*Children's Bookwatch*

"Pierce's legion of fans has embraced the Trickster series, especially older teenage girls thirsty for strong young female characters." —*San Antonio Express-News*

"Strong female characters of a totally different kind live in Tamora Pierce's latest novel. . . . Through this fast-paced adventure tinged with romance and humor, Aly tries to protect the rightful heir to the kingdom's throne."
—*Detroit Free Press*

"From her first book, *Alanna: The First Adventure*, to *Trickster's Queen*, her twenty-second, Pierce has crafted smart, brave, kick-butt heroines." —*Des Moines Register*

"Pierce continues the story of brave and clever Aly . . . in this feminist fantasy about conspiracies in an exotic land. [A] complex and rewarding tale." —*KLIATT*

"Infused with spirited action and intrigue, this fantasy moves with lightning speed toward a war for power in the Copper Isles. . . . What ensues is a power struggle involving humans, gods, immortals, and fantastic beings, all of whom must choose a side and fight from their hearts. . . . Boys and girls alike will enjoy this fantasy." —*Voice of Youth Advocates*

"Although magic does play a part . . . Aly manages her problems by thinking through them and also anticipating what could happen. Throughout the novels, she manages to grow and change into a young woman with a definite mission to her life." —*The Pilot* (Raleigh, NC)

"I highly recommend this book, especially to fantasy fans, because it showcases an amazingly well-woven story that gets you hooked from page one with an exciting plot that twists this way and that."—*The Denver Post,* "Colorado Kids"

"Tamora Pierce has outdone herself in *Trickster's Queen*. . . . There's everything in this book from fighting and suspense to romance and adventure." —*The Dallas Morning News*

Tortall Books by Tamora Pierce

BEKA COOPER TRILOGY

Terrier

Trickster's Choice

Trickster's Queen

PROTECTOR OF THE SMALL QUARTET

First Test

Page

Squire

Lady Knight

THE IMMORTALS QUARTET

Wild Magic

Wolf-Speaker

Emperor Mage

The Realms of the Gods

THE SONG OF THE LIONESS QUARTET

Alanna: The First Adventure

In the Hand of the Goddess

The Woman Who Rides Like a Man

Lioness Rampant

TAMORA PIERCE

TRICKSTER'S QUEEN

Published by Laurel-Leaf
an imprint of Random House Children's Books
a division of Random House, Inc., New York

Sale of this book without a front cover may be unauthorized. If the book is coverless, it may have been reported to the publisher as "unsold or destroyed" and neither the author nor the publisher may have received payment for it.

This is a work of fiction. Names, characters, places, and incidents either are the product of the author's imagination or are used fictitiously. Any resemblance to actual persons, living or dead, events, or locales is entirely coincidental.

Copyright © 2004 by Tamora Pierce
All rights reserved.

Originally published in hardcover in the United States by Random House Books for Young Readers, New York, in 2004. This edition published by arrangement with Random House Book for Young Readers.

Laurel-Leaf and colophon are registered trademarks of Random House, Inc.

Visit us on the Web! www.randomhouse.com/teens
Educators and librarians, for a variety of teaching tools,
visit us at www.randomhouse.com/teachers

The Library of Congress has cataloged the hardcover edition of this work as follows:
Pierce, Tamora.
Trickster's queen / Tamora Pierce.
p. cm.
Summary: Aly fails to foresee the dangers that await as she uses her magic to safeguard Dove and her younger siblings, despite knowing that her thirteen-year-old charge might be queen of the Copper Isles when the colonial rulers are defeated.
ISBN: 978-0-375-81467-9 (trade)—ISBN: 978-0-375-82878-2 (tr. pbk.)—
ISBN: 978-0-375-91467-6 (lib. bdg.)
[1. Fantasy.] I. Title. PZ7.P61464Tq 2004 [Fic]—dc22 2004003120

ISBN: 978-0-375-81473-0 (pbk.)

RL: 5.7
October 2008
Printed in the United States of America
10 9 8 7 6 5 4 3 2 1
First Laurel-Leaf Edition

To Bruce Coville,
divinely tricky, magically inspiring—
one of the best men I've ever known,
and
To Mary Lou Pierce,
the best Ma in the world

CONTENTS

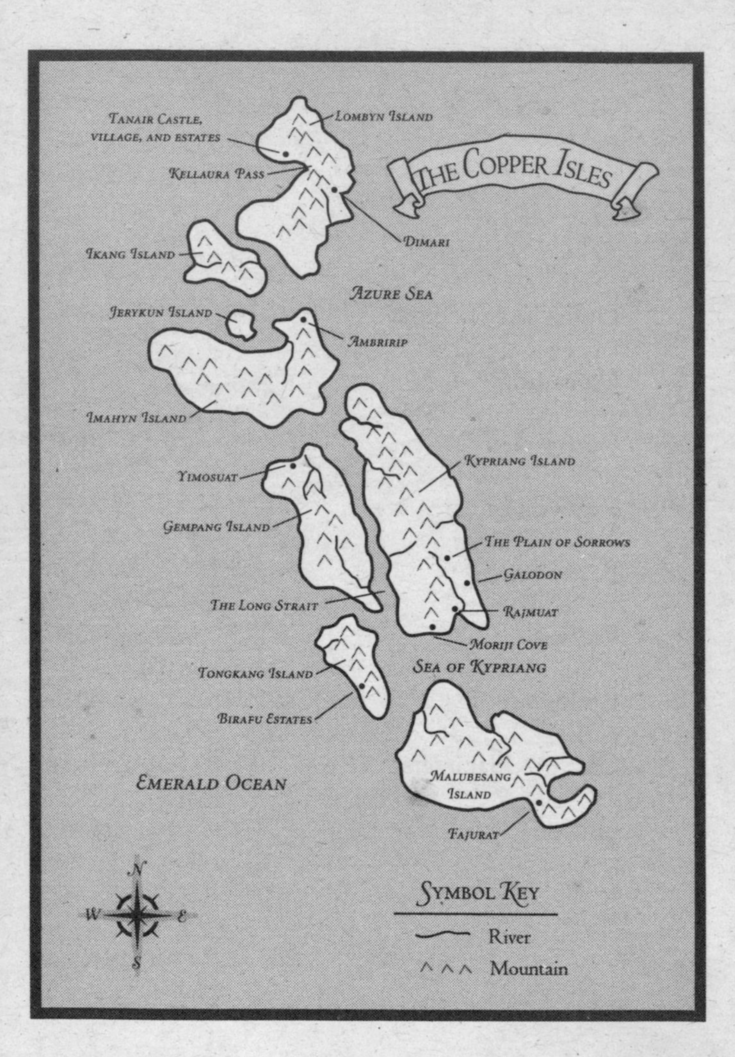
The Copper Isles
Tanair Castle, village, and estates
Lombyn Island
Kellaura Pass
Dimari
Ikang Island
Azure Sea
Jerykun Island
Ambririp
Imahyn Island
Kypriang Island
Yimosuat
Gempang Island
The Plain of Sorrows
Galodon
The Long Strait
Rajmuat
Moriji Cove
Sea of Kypriang
Tongkang Island
Birafu Estates
Emerald Ocean
Malubesang Island
Fajurat
N
W
E
S
Symbol Key
River
Mountain

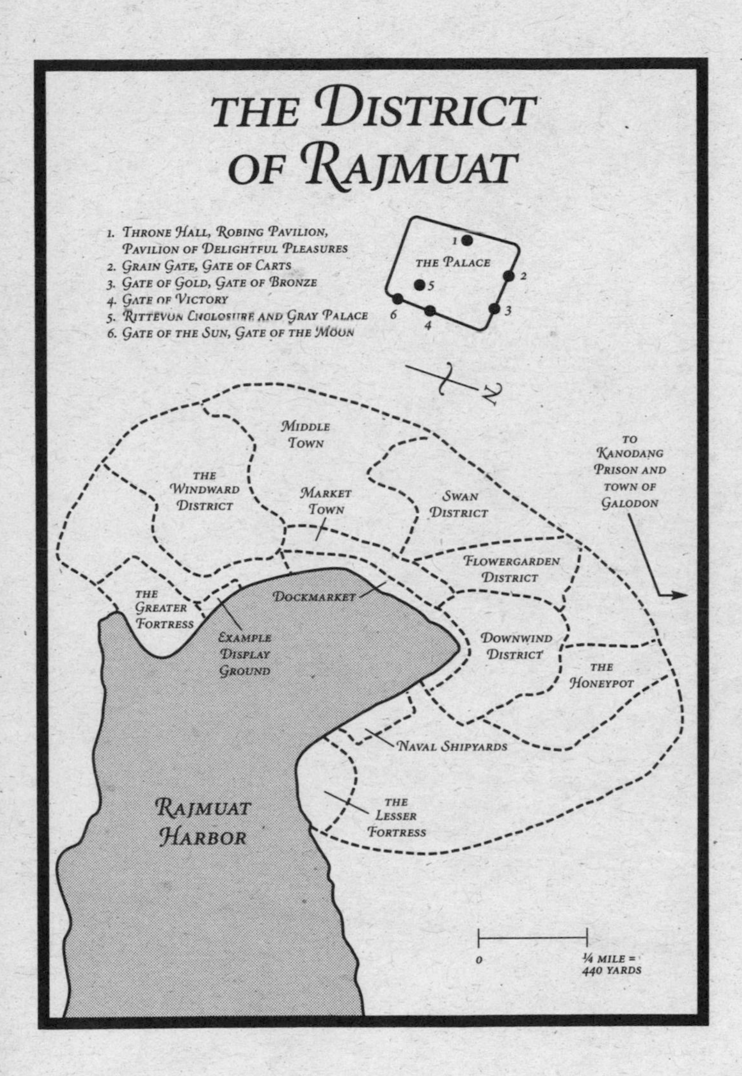
THE DISTRICT OF RAJMUAT
1. Throne Hall, Robing Pavilion, Pavilion of Delightful Pleasures
2. Grain Gate, Gate of Carts
3. Gate of Gold, Gate of Bronze
4. Gate of Victory
5. Rittevon Cholosure and Gray Palace
6. Gate of the Sun, Gate of the Moon
the Palace
1
2
3
4
5
6
N
Middle Town
the Windward District
Market Town
Swan District
To Kanodang Prison and town of Galodon
Flowergarden District
the Greater Fortress
Dockmarket
Example Display Ground
Downwind District
the Honeypot
Naval Shipyards
Rajmuat Harbor
the Lesser Fortress
0
¼ mile = 440 yards

In a time of fear, the One Who I Promised will come to the raka, bearing glory in her train and justice in her hand. She will restore the god to his proper temple and his children to her right hand. She will be twice royal, wise and beloved, a living emblem of truth to her people. She will be attended by a wise one, the cunning one, the strong one, the warrior, and the crows. She will give a home to all, and the kudarung will fly in her honor.

—From the Kyprish Prophecy,
written in the year 200 H.E.

Prologue

The Copper Isles

In the winter of 462–463 H.E., the brown-skinned raka people and their many allies, part-bloods and white-skinned luarin, prepared for revolution against the luarin ruling house, the Rittevons. The raka plan was to replace the Rittevons with one who had the bloodlines of both the raka queens and the luarin rulers, a passionate girl named Saraiyu Balitang.

The leaders of the raka rebel conspiracy did not spend the winter months dozing. Throughout the Isles, Crown tax collectors vanished from their beds, never to be seen again. Even more baffling, all the suspects who were questioned in their disappearances swore under truthspell that they had last seen the missing officials alive and well. Property damage on luarin estates that winter far exceeded that expected from heavy rains. Dams collapsed, sweeping away acres of rice fields. Blackrot invaded grain silos, destroying winter stores. Bridges fell. Overseers and a few nobles were murdered. When the Crown sent soldiers to kill the people of the nearest raka village, as the law required, the troops found that the inhabitants had vanished. Many people reported hearing war gongs sounding from deep within the lowland jungles.

Life for the Balitang family in the highlands of Lombyn Isle had two sides. One was that of a family that had just lost its patriarch and had to get through the winter months before they could return to the capital city of Rajmuat at the behest of the ruling family. Duchess Winnamine Balitang took solace from her two older stepdaughters, Saraiyu and Dovasary, and her own children, six-year-old Petranne and five-year-old Elsren. She conducted lessons, had snowball fights, told stories, and did her best to keep everyone from screaming with boredom. She also helped train Sarai's maid, a twenty-three-year-old raka woman named Boulaj, and Dove's maid, the former slave Aly Homewood from the kingdom of Tortall.

Beneath this comfortable domestic life lay a second, less visible and more directed. Many of the leaders of the hoped-for revolution were servants to the Balitangs. They guarded the two older girls and perfected their plans. They sent and received information through a network of mages called the Chain, who used their powers to pass messages from island to island. The members of the household practiced fighting arts, from unarmed combat to sword and spear work, in the outbuildings at Tanair Castle. They had an unusual teacher for new ways of fighting: Nawat, a young man who had once been a crow. The duchess saw this practice as much-needed exercise, and both she and her daughters joined in. To the raka's regret, Sarai refused to continue her lessons in swordcraft after she and Dove killed her would-be lover, Prince Bronau, the night he slew her father.

Busiest of all the members of the rebel conspiracy was the newest to join, seventeen-year-old Aly Homewood. She was in reality Alianne of Pirate's Swoop, the daughter and granddaughter of Tortall's spymasters, raised from the cradle to compete in the world of international espionage. During the previous summer she had acted as chief bodyguard to the Balitang children. With the arrival of spring and the move to Rajmuat, Aly knew she would become the rebellion's spymaster. Although the Balitangs' former housekeeper, Quedanga, has remained in Rajmuat to collect information from long-standing networks of spies, Aly's specially recruited spies and those they will train have their own unique work ahead. They will collect information for the rebel leaders to use against their enemies, and conduct whatever actions of sabotage and psychological operations required to put the raka's enemies at odds with each other. For sixteen years she studied such work under her father's eye. Now she would do it herself, for the promise of better leadership for the Isles.

In preparation, Aly used the winter to build a cadre of trained spies, people among the household who could learn and use all she had to teach. The lessons of these raka and part-raka in their twenties and thirties included written and spoken codes and code breaking, lock picking, and climbing. She also taught them sign language, thorough searches, medicines and herbs, and the detection of other spies. Because she was younger than many of her trainees, Aly treated them in a teasing, grandmotherly way, while they awarded her the raka nickname of *Duani* or "boss lady." Aly also spent time with the raka mage Ochobu, creating suicide spells and magic detection charms, and with the rebels' armorer, choosing weapons for her pack and for herself.

Aly dared not tell anyone why she was so eager to take up the mantle of spymaster. To do so, she would have to reveal her true parentage. The raka would see her as a tool of the Tortallan Crown, while the forces loyal to the Rittevon king and his regents would see her as a spy. Only one being knew her true history: the deposed god of the Copper

Isles, the trickster Kyprioth. It was he who had brought Aly to the service of the rebellion that would return him to his seat of power. Although responsible for her presence, Kyprioth did not speak to Aly throughout the long winter. She assumed he was hiding from the god brother and goddess sister who had cast him from his Isles: Mithros and the Great Mother Goddess.

Luckily, Aly had the crow fighter Nawat to entertain and delight her through the long months. His courtship grew more passionate throughout the winter, and he finally stopped offering her bugs to eat.

At the beginning of April, most of the household traveled south to ready the family's home in the capital, Rajmuat. The family and the remainder of the servants, including Aly, took the following few weeks to prepare for the move that would change all of their lives completely and irrevocably.

1

RAJMUAT

April 23, 463 H.E.
Rajmuat harbor, Copper Isles

As the ship *Gwenna* glided through the entrance of Rajmuat harbor, a young woman of seventeen years leaned against the bow rail, taking in her surroundings through green-hazel eyes. Despite her white skin, she was dressed like a native raka in sarong, sash, and wrapped jacket. The sarong displayed her neat, if thin, figure—one with the curves that drew male eyes. The calf-length garment also showed muscled legs and trim ankles protected by leather slippers. Her jacket, worn against the chill of the spring air, covered her muscular upper arms, while the loose areas of her clothes hid an assortment of flat knives designed for her needs. She had a small, delicate nose, inherited from her mother, just as her eyes were her father's. The wide mouth, its lower lip fuller than the upper, was all hers, with smiles tucked into the corners. Her reddish gold hair was cut just below her earlobes to fit her head like a helmet.

Aly looked the soul of repose as she lounged against the rail, but her eyes were busy. She swiftly took in the panorama of Rajmuat as the city came into view. It sprawled over half of the C-shaped harbor, arranged on the rising banks like offerings laid on green steps. Steam rose from the greenery as the early-morning sun heated damp jungle earth. Patches of white and rose pink stucco marked newer houses, while the older houses, built of wood and stone, sported roofs that were sharply peaked and sloping, like the wings of some strange sitting bird. The higher the ground, the more complex the roof, with lesser roofs sprouting beneath the main one. The roofs of the wealthier houses blazed with gilt paint in the sun. Strewn among the homes were the domed, gilded towers of Rajmuat's temples.

Above them all stood the main palace of the Kyprin rulers. Its walls, twenty feet thick, patrolled by alert guardsmen day and night, gleamed like alabaster. The rulers of the Isles were not well liked. They required the protection of strong walls.

In the air over the great harbor, winged creatures wheeled and soared, light glancing off their metal-feathered wings. Aly shaded her eyes to look at them. These were Stormwings, harbingers of war and slaughter, creatures with steel feathers and claws whose torsos and heads were made of flesh. They lived on human pain and fear. In the Copper Isles, ruled by the heavy-handed Rittevons and their luarin nobles, the Stormwings were assured of daily meals. Aly hummed to herself. There had been plenty of Stormwings when she and the Balitangs had sailed north a year before. Now there were a great many more. From the news she had gathered on their voyage to Rajmuat, she wasn't surprised. The regents, Prince Rubinyan and Princess Imajane, had spent the winter rains executing anyone who might give them trouble, in the name of their four-year-old king. Aly nodded in silent approval. It was so useful when the people in charge helped her plans along.

The Stormwings reminded her that she was not on deck to sightsee. Aly turned her head to the left. Here a fortress guarded the southern side of the harbor entrance. Beyond it, on a short stone pier, stood the posts called Examples. Each harbor had them, public display areas where those who had vexed the government were executed and left on display. In Rajmuat, the capital of the Isles, the Examples were reserved for the nobility. They were surrounded on land by a stone wall broken by a single gate. Over the gate, a banner flapped on the dawn breeze, a rearing bat-winged horse of metallic copper cloth, posed on a white field with a copper border—the flag of the Rittevon kings of the Copper Isles.

Guards streamed through the gate and onto the pier. At the foot of one of the posts men were arguing, waving their arms and pointing. They wore the red-painted armor of the King's Watch, the force charged with keeping the peace, enforcing the law, and conducting executions. Aly narrowed her eyes to sharpen her magical Sight. The power was her heritage from both parents, and allowed her to read the lips of the men and take note of their insignia. She identified four lieutenants, one captain, and a number of men-at-arms who did their best to pretend they were invisible.

Someone sniffed behind her. "Carrion crows," Lady Sarai Balitang remarked scornfully. "What, are they fighting over who gets the 'honor' of displaying the next wretch? Or just over who does the mopping?" Sarai moved up to stand beside Aly at the rail, her brown eyes blazing with dislike as she watched the men. A year older and an inch taller than Aly, Sarai had creamy gold skin and tumbles of braided and curled black hair under a sheer black veil. An excellent horsewoman, she held herself proudly straight, catching the eye of anyone who saw her.

"They seem to be missing something." Thirteen-year-old Dovasary Balitang moved in to stand on Aly's free side, and pointed. Where the Example pier joined the mainland stood a large wooden sign painted stark white. On that sign were three names and the words *Executed for treason against the Crown, decreed by His Highness Prince Rubinyan Jimajen and Her Highness Princess Imajane Rittevon Jimajen, in the name of His Gracious Majesty King Dunevon Rittevon.* The date was that of the previous day.

"What happened to their poor bodies?" whispered Sarai, brown eyes wide. "They should be here for weeks."

"Perhaps Stormwings dropped down and carried them off," Dove suggested quietly. Aly's mistress was different from her beautiful older sister, shorter and small-boned. She had the self-contained air of someone much older. She had a catlike face and observant black eyes. Like Sarai, her skin was creamy gold, her hair black, and her lips full. She also wore a black gown and veil in mourning for the father who had been killed six months before.

Aly knew exactly what had happened to the dead, because she had created a plan for anyone executed and displayed here. The absence of dead Examples was her declaration, as the rebellion's spymaster, that she would turn the Rittevon Crown and its supporters inside out. The spies she had sent ahead with Ulasim three weeks before the family's departure had been charged with putting her declaration into action.

Body thieves were expected to attack from the land. No one would expect people to swim to the pier in the foul harbor water. Her people had done just that, to remove the bodies, weigh them down with chains, and sink them in the harbor. The plan worked on many levels. The Crown officials lost the Examples they had made, and the Kings' Watch was left with a mystery. Aly knew quite well that mysteries frightened people, particularly those people who were not supposed to allow them to happen. Sooner or later word of the vanishing Examples would leak out. People would start to see that the Crown was not as powerful as it claimed to be.

"Last autumn Prince Rubinyan told Winna that there would be no more unnecessary executions," Sarai commented.

"Maybe he thinks these *are* necessary," said Dove, grim-faced. "Or Imajane does."

"Hunod Ibadun? Dravinna?" The soft voice spoke the names painted on the announcement board. The voice belonged to Sarai and Dove's stepmother, Duchess Winnamine Balitang. The girls made space for her at the rail. "They wouldn't harm a fly if it were biting them." She was a tall, slender woman, elegant in deep black mourning. "Hunod is—was—Prince Rubinyan's friend!"

"I would guess they are not friends now," remarked Dove, her voice steady.

"Winna, I don't recognize the names," Sarai told her stepmother. "They aren't the same Ibaduns who own those rice plantations on the southern coast of Lombyn, are they?"

"No," replied the duchess, wiping her eyes. "Hunod and Dravinna were cousins to those Ibaduns. They have—had—their own estates on Gempang. They grew *orchids*. Has that become treasonous?"

"It depends on what they grew along with them, I suppose," Dove said, squeezing her stepmother's free hand. "Or what *Topabaw* thought they were growing."

Aly twiddled her thumbs, as she often did when thinking. She was not supposed to protect the family this year.

She was here to gather information and, through exquisite planning, destroy the people's belief in the Rittevon Crown and promote the longing for a young, sane, raka queen. Aly looked forward to crossing swords with the Crown's official spymaster, who'd held that post for thirty bloody years. She knew Prince Rubinyan had personal spies, because she had caught some of them the year before, but the master of the crown's spies, Duke Lohearn Mantawu, called Topabaw by all, was the man who bred fear. The downfall of Topabaw was to be one of her special projects now that she was back in the capital.

She was envisioning her plans for him when she heard a change in the Stormwings' shrieks overhead, from normal taunts to rage. Seagulls fled the harbor in silence, and the city's myriad of parrots stopped their raucous morning conversations. The clatter of shipping and the shouts of sailors rang overloud in the air. Aly waited, listening. Goose bumps prickled their way up her arms. Gradually she heard it more clearly, a rough sound, harsh and bawling.

She straightened with a grin. "Crows," she announced.

The crows burst into the air above the heights west of the harbor in a squalling, quarreling, soaring ebony cloud. They turned the sky above Rajmuat's palace black as activity around the harbor came to a halt. The Stormwings grabbed for height with their immense steel-feathered wings, snarling with outrage at the invaders. They darted at the crows, bladed wings sweeping out to hack them to pieces. The crows, smaller and nimbler, scattered. Wheeling, they dropped, then flew up among the Stormwings to peck at the exposed tender human flesh of their enemies. The racket was indescribable.

I wonder how many of these people know that the crows are sacred to Kyprioth the Trickster? Aly wondered. The raka full-bloods know, but how many part-bloods, and how many full-blood luarin? Are they going to take this as an omen? I hope not. We really *don't* need omens soaring all over the city.

Aly sighed. "I had so wished that our return would be *quiet*," she said wistfully.

"I don't believe the crows care, Aly," Dove replied.

Sarai added, "I like anything that gives those disgusting Stormwings a hard time."

The duchess took a deep breath. "Come, ladies. We'll be landing soon. Let's make sure we've packed everything." She led her stepdaughters below.

Aly stayed where she was, her eyes on the city. Things would start to move fast now. All the way here, she had picked up stories of the unrest in the Isles that had begun over the winter and still continued. Soon actual fighting would begin. The fighting, at least, was not her concern, but that of the rebel leaders who served Balitang House. Her biggest task was to make sure they had the most current information available. For this she had access to the network of informants built up by the raka, a network that drew from every skin color and every social category. She also had her own pack, the spies she herself had trained intensively over the winter. They had come south with Ulasim three weeks earlier to start training their allies in Rajmuat. They and their own recruits would gather still more information for her. Most importantly, Aly would collect information from inside the palace, to give the raka as much news of possible allies and the regents' movements as she could. Aly would then bring all the information together, study it, find connections, and get the boiled-down intelligence to the people who needed it.

She thought the odds of the rebellion's success were good. She respected the raka leaders in the household.

Coming south, she had glimpsed how far their reach extended, and was pleased. They had a strong, beloved candidate for the throne in Sarai. Her attractiveness and charm would win the hearts of the more reluctant citizens of the Isles. A child sat on the Rittevon throne, governed by heavy-handed regents who were despised by many. And the rebels had been whittling away at the luarin confidence all winter. Only this morning they had dealt the King's Watch a hard slap with the disappearances of the Crown's Examples. Aly even had a god on her side, if he would ever show up.

Aly's nerves buzzed. As if he had read her mind, Kyprioth the Trickster appeared at her side. It was Kyprioth who had brought Aly to the Isles, though he was not the reason that she had stayed. Three hundred years earlier his brother, the sun and war god Mithros, and his sister, the moon and fertility Great Mother Goddess, had accompanied the luarin to the Isles and ousted Kyprioth from his throne. Now the Trickster hoped to retake what was his.

"Hello, you rascal," Aly greeted him cheerfully. "Why didn't you ask the crows to behave?"

"If I cared to clack my teeth in a supremely useless exercise, I *would* have tried to tell them to behave," retorted the god lightly, his black eyes dancing with mischief. "You'll find that not all of your allies are under your control, my dear."

The god was lean and muscled, straight-backed like a dancer. For reasons best known to him, he wore a salt-and-pepper beard and hair, both cropped short. He'd once told Aly he thought this style gave him the look of an elder statesman. Today his coat was a bright mass of yellow, pink, lavender, and pale blue squares. He jingled with a multitude of charms and bits of jewelry. His sarong, a skirtlike garment that men kilted up between their legs, was patterned in black and white diagonal stripes. He wore leather sandals studded with copper, as well as toe and finger rings made of copper and gems. For once he wore no copper earring, only a single blue drop.

Aly made a face at him. "Where were you all winter? You left me to yearn. I yearned for months, but you never so much as sent a messenger pigeon." She kept her voice quiet but teasing. The sailors looked too busy to notice her and her companion, even if they could see the god, but she liked to be careful in all she did.

Kyprioth beamed at her. "I was someplace warmer than the highlands of Lombyn," he replied. "Don't complain to me. You were having all kinds of fun, training your little spies. All *I* could do was wait. I did so in a place where I had plenty to amuse me." His gaze was fixed on the city. A will of stone showed as the corners of his mouth tightened. "I've waited a long time for this spring to come."

Aly stayed where she was, though her body wanted to flee. It unnerved her to see that depth of emotion in the dethroned god. "Well, you don't need *me,* then," she joked weakly. "I'll just take the next ship for Corus, get home in time for my mother's birthday."

Kyprioth turned to look at her. "You're just as eager to see this through as any of my raka. Don't even pretend that you aren't. Which reminds me." He reached out and pressed the ball of his thumb against the middle of Aly's forehead. Gold fire swamped her mind, making her sway.

She braced herself against the rail and waited for her normal vision to return. She dug into the folds of her sarong for the bit of mirror she kept there for emergencies. Her forehead looked much as it normally did, pale after the winter and chapped by the sea air and wind. She grimaced and reminded herself to filch Sarai's facial balm, then put the mirror away.

"What was that?" she asked him. "I thought you'd at least leave a beauty mark or something."

"I would not touch your beauty, my dear," said the god with his flashing smile. "And I would be bereft if you chose to commit suicide rather than be tortured or questioned under truthspell. No one will be able to force knowledge from your lips or your hands."

Aly raised an eyebrow at him. "Oh. So they can torture me, they just can't make me tell the truth. An enchanting prospect, sir."

His smile broadened to a grin. "I love it when you call me sir. It makes me feel all . . ." He hesitated, then found the words he wanted. "All godlike. So there's no need to commit suicide. You won't ever surrender what you know."

"Have you granted the others this splendid favor?" she asked, curious. "I wouldn't want them to be jealous."

Kyprioth leaned against the rail, his expression wry. "No one else in the rebellion has put together as much of the complete picture as you have done over this winter, gathering bits and pieces. You simply had to ferret it all out, didn't you? Ulasim can give perhaps a hundred names. Ochobu can give the names of the Chain and the main conspirators among the Balitang servants. If my other leaders die, they can be replaced."

Aly showed him no sign of the chill that crawled down her spine over that matter-of-fact "they can be replaced." He's a god, she told herself. It's different for them.

Kyprioth sighed. "But you, my dear, have learned nearly the entire thing—not the foot soldiers, but those in command and where they are, the members of the Chain. . . . You couldn't help it. It's your nature to poke and pry and gather. Even your fellow rebels are ignorant of the extent of your knowledge, which makes me chuckle."

Aly fanned her hand at him, like a beauty who brushed off a compliment.

"Besides, I've grown attached to you," Kyprioth said, capturing her hand. He kissed the back of her fingers and released her. "I would hate it if you used the suicide spell and left me for the Black God's realm. You know how brothers are—we hate to share."

"You'll have to let me go to him sometime," Aly reminded the god. "*I'm* not immortal."

"That is 'sometime.' I am talking about this summer," Kyprioth replied. His eyes darkened. "Make sure you see this through. Once battle is joined in the Divine Realms, we gods draw strength from the success of our worshippers. If you and I fail, the luarin will exterminate the raka. And I will be unable to help them, because my brother and sister will kick me to the outermost edge of the universe." He brightened. "But there, why be gloomy? We're going to have a wonderful year, I'm sure of it!"

He was gone.

For a moment Aly hoped the god was not placing more trust in her abilities than she deserved. Then she shrugged. There was one way to find out if she was as good at her task as she and Kyprioth hoped, and that was to pull off a war. "What's a little thing like revolution between friends?" she wondered, and looked ahead.

Yards of dirty water lay between the moving ship and the dock, where a welcoming party stood. "So we begin," said Fesgao Yibenu as he came to stand with Aly. The raka sergeant-at-arms swept the docks with his narrow eyes. "No royal welcome, despite Elsren's being the heir," he remarked, settling a helmet over his prematurely silver hair. With a wave he ordered the men-at-arms who had sailed with the family to flank the rail where the gangplank would be lowered. "We are definitely the poor country cousins of the royal house." Fesgao was in charge of the household men-at-arms and the rebellion's war leader. He'd spent his life guarding Sarai and Dove, keeping the last descendants of the old raka queens safe. Now he looked at the man who commanded the twenty extra Balitang men-at-arms waiting on the dock, and saluted him. The man saluted in return, a hand signal that meant all was quiet there.

"They've added checkpoints where the docks meet the land, do you see?" Fesgao murmured to Aly. "They want to know who comes and who goes."

Aly shrugged. Soldiers could not possibly watch every inch of ground between the fortresses that flanked the harbor mouths. In the dark, a hundred raka swimmers could enter the water and no one would know. "If they're watching the docks, they're worried," she murmured. "Let's go and give them more to worry about."

Duchess Winnamine had returned to the deck, leading the two children she had borne Duke Mequen. Petranne, a six-year-old girl with silky black curls and long-lashed eyes, danced in place, excited to come home to Rajmuat. Five-year-old Elsren was his father's son, brown-haired and stoic. He hid his face shyly in his mother's skirts.

Winnamine shook her head as she looked at the dock. "This is not good," she murmured, frowning.

Ochobu, the old raka who was the household mage and healer, came up beside her. She, too, was a leader in the rebellion, responsible for the mage network known as the Chain. They had been the source of the rebels' information all winter. "What is not good?" Ochobu asked. She had a hand against her forehead to shade her brown eyes as she inspected the people on the dock. "You are a duchess, and a woman of property. You cannot walk into the city like a commoner. You must have a proper escort."

"We *have* a proper escort aboard with us," Winnamine said quietly. "Forty men-at-arms looks as if we consider ourselves important. We aren't important until the regents say we are. And half of those men are new. We can't pay more guards," Winnamine said. "I told Ulasim before he left not to hire anyone!"

"Your Grace," Aly said politely. Winnamine looked at her. "Ulasim always has good reasons for what he does, you know that. See the checkpoints? There's been trouble in the city—they didn't have checkpoints at the docks last year. Maybe Ulasim found a way to pay these men-at-arms. Or maybe they're just rented for the hour, like actors who mourn at funerals. You know, to add to your consequence."

The thought of her consequence made Winnamine chuckle as Sarai and Dove came to join them. Overhead the Stormwings glided, shrieking like gulls.

Once the ship docked and the passengers disembarked, Fesgao and the guards circled the Balitang family and helped them into litters. Servants loaded the family's belongings into a handful of carts. Only when everything was stowed and the litters surrounded by armed men did Fesgao move the party out. The litter bearers set off into the tangle of streets that ended at the dockside.

Colors, sounds, and smells assaulted Aly, making her shrink against the litter that held Sarai and Dove. She had gotten used to the long silences of winter nights at Tanair. Street vendors shouted news of their wares, bellowing their praises of jackfruit, sweet cakes, and cheap copper and silver bracelets. Bird sellers walked among them, carrying poles laden with dozens of species of loud, unhappy winged creatures. Shops displaying goods for passersby lined the streets near the docks. Perfumes and spices filled the air with scents.

The pedestrians came in all races and colors, shrieking at those who got in the way and bargaining at the tops of their lungs. They were dressed in all kinds of styles, from luarin shirts and hose to the robes of Carthakis. Many people lined their eyes in kohl as protection against sun glare and the evil eye. Slaves and deep-jungle raka in sarongs or loincloths sported tattoos on arms, backs, and chests.

Aly took it in as she walked beside the litter that held Sarai and Dove. She had picked out a couple of watchers—people who paid close attention to their group. She also recognized a couple of her own trainee spies from Tanair. She smiled, proud as a mother whose child had taken her first steps, then glanced up to see how Winnamine and the two younger children did in the litter ahead of them. Fesgao walked beside them, talking quietly with the duchess. Rihani, the raka mage who looked after Petranne and Elsren, walked on the other side of the litter, pointing out sights of interest. Slowly they moved into the quieter, wider streets of Market Town, the city's merchant district.

There were signs of trouble in Market Town, shuttered stores with Crown seals on the doors to show they'd been seized by the law, chipped paint and splintered wood showing where people had hurled rocks. Aly saw a charred open spot where, if she remembered correctly, a temple to Ushjur, the god of the east wind, had stood. This was most certainly a slap at the luarin, who came from the east. Aly made a note to ask about it.

She had no sense of armed watchers, but she felt observed. Aly looked up. In the houses above the shops, people filled each window, their eyes fixed on the open-sided litters. Aly bit the corner of her lip. Ulasim had gotten the word out that people were not supposed to gather in the street to greet their prophesied queen, but he could not stop them from trying to get a look at her. They were drawing the attention of the spies who followed their procession. She could see them noting the audience. Topabaw and prince-regent Rubinyan would have word of this before noon.

"Busy already, Aly?" Fesgao asked. He'd walked back to her. "Your glance darts like dragonflies on the water."

Aly fluttered her lashes at Fesgao. "I never figured you for a poet," she joked.

He smiled. "We can control the common folk only so much," he continued in his softest tones.

"Oh, I know," she replied lightly. "Her Grace was excited to see all these new warriors of ours. Did we rent them, or may we keep them? That tall one with the scar on his chin might actually be able to keep up with me for all of a day."

"You are too gracious," Fesgao replied, face straight. "You would break the poor boy by noon, and I would have to keep him in the infirmary for two weeks." He returned to the duchess at the head of the column.

"It's dangerous," Dove remarked softly from inside the litter. "They shouldn't stare so openly. Someone will notice their interest."

"Perhaps they've never seen disgraced nobility return to Rajmuat before," suggested Aly. "They could just be looking at Elsren. He *is* Dunevon's heir."

"Not officially," Dove said, meticulous as always about points of law. "The regents have to make Elsren the official heir by decree. They should—it's customary—but they may choose not to, if they think the nobles won't insist. Until then, if people know what's good for them, they won't pay any attention to Elsren at all."

Aly noted more signs of trouble as they entered the wealthier residential neighborhood of Windward: burn marks on stone, and hastily whitewashed stucco. Here no one could watch the streets from the windows of their homes, because these were set back behind walls ten feet high. Instead, people lined the street on both sides.

"The regents will hear of this," Dove added quietly. "They won't like it."

Aly patted the younger girl's thin shoulder. "Now, if they got everything they liked, they would be spoiled," she told Dove. "And nobody likes spoiled regents."

"Spoiled regents kill people and leave them at the harbor mouth," Dove said gloomily.

Aly smiled slyly and told her young mistress, "Yes, but they don't seem to be able to keep them there very long."

Dove glanced at Aly sharply, then eyed her sister. Sarai leaned against the side of the litter, watching the street. "*She* thinks the twice-royal queen is a fairy tale, you know," Dove told Aly. "Made up by Mithros and the Goddess to keep the raka quiet under luarin rule. If there is something going on, she will take a lot of convincing."

"If there was anything for her or you to know, you'd have been told, surely," Aly said. As the raka general, Ulasim had ordered that Sarai and Dove not be told of the plans being made on their behalf. "Worry about prophecies another time. Once we've unpacked and had baths, for instance."

Dove sighed. "All right, keep changing the subject," she said as she sank back against the cushions. "But I'm not fooled. You know something. You're harder to work out than Sarai, but I know you too well by now."

Aly was about to reply "Don't ask me, I have brothers," but she caught herself. Over the winter she had nearly told Winnamine, Sarai, and Dove the truth about her own background. Aly wanted to trust them. She would trust them with her life if she had to, as they had trusted her with theirs. But she could not trust them with her past, and her ties to the rival kingdom of Tortall.

She continued to watch the crowd.

There were spells written deep within the walls that surrounded the Balitang home. They appeared as a shimmering silver blaze in Aly's Sight. As the procession passed through the gate, she saw magic sunk below the stones, wood, and carvings. It was partially covered by the silvery gleam of common magical signs for protection and health that any house possessed. Unless someone else in Rajmuat had the Sight in the strength Aly had it, no one would see or sense anything but the everyday spells. Raka mages were very good at keeping their work hidden.

Ornately carved pillars lined the long front porch and framed the front door of Balitang House. The roof was layered, each lesser roof sporting upturned ends. After the summer's heat and rains, and the winter's cold and rains, with no staff to keep the place up, the house should have looked rundown. But this house gleamed. Not one clay tile was missing from the roof. The stucco was the color of fresh milk. Gold and silver leaf glimmered on the eaves and on the carved wood above the posts.

The staff was lined up on either side of the flagstone road. They wore luarin tunics and breeches or hose, raka wrapped jackets and sarongs, or combinations of styles in an explosion of colors that made Aly blink. Housemaids wore white headcloths; the men wore round white caps. They all looked to be wearing every piece of jewelry they owned.

Aly counted. Nearly sixty people were here, not including the men-at-arms. Balitang House was as fully staffed as it had been the previous spring.

The duchess could not afford this. When King Oron

had exiled them, he had made them show their loyalty with gold, emptying Duke Mequen's coffers. Winnamine had drawn on her dowry to pay household costs. If Prince Rubinyan had not virtually commanded her to return to court, she would have remained at Tanair, which was affordable.

"Fesgao," Aly murmured. The man had come to stand by her elbow. "Who's paying for this?"

"Don't worry," the raka man told her. "Ulasim will explain." He went to help the duchess out of the litter.

Aly looked at the steps. Ulasim waited there, smiling. He was a hard-muscled man in his forties with the brown skin of a full-blood raka. His nose had been mashed against his face on several occasions by someone not kindly disposed toward him. A tightness in Aly's heart loosened at the sight of the head footman. He was the leader of the far-flung raka conspiracy, wise and strong at every trial. He had turned Aly's suspicion into respect. Back under Ulasim's wing, the Balitang family seemed much less exposed. Back under Ulasim's eye, Aly could turn to her specialty and leave him to deal with assassins and alliances.

The big raka bowed to Winnamine. As Aly watched, reading his lips, Ulasim told the duchess that they had not spent money they did not have. He reassured her that all would be explained to her satisfaction once she'd had a chance to eat and rest. As he soothed her, Aly identified a familiar face at Ulasim's elbow. Quedanga, the housekeeper since Sarai was born, had stayed in Rajmuat when the family left the city. She had now returned to Balitang House.

"How did they afford this?" Dove murmured as Aly handed her down from the litter.

"It will be a lovely tale," Aly replied, her voice sweet. "Some parts may even be true."

Dove looked up at Aly, smiling slightly. "You sound as

if you wouldn't put it past them to have raided the royal treasury."

Aly raised an eyebrow at her mistress. "Do you think they wouldn't, my lady?"

Dove sighed. "I hope not. It would complicate things." Dove had understatement down to an art.

Hands folded in front of her, Aly followed Dove toward the house. They did not get far. A tall woman stepped onto the porch. She was a silver-haired luarin with perfect posture. Her luarin-style gown was pale blue with a high collar. Instead of the traditional overrobe, she wore a stole like the raka wrapped jacket, made of shimmering white lawn.

Sarai and Dove looked at each other. *"Aunt Nuritin,"* they whispered in shock.

Aly had heard of Nuritin Balitang—or as Sarai and Dove called her, the Dragon. Though Duke Mequen had been technically the head of the family, it was his aunt who ruled it. When he had sunk into mourning for his first duchess, it was Nuritin who had badgered him into making a new marriage and a new life. Among the Balitangs, her word was law. Among the nobles of her generation, her opinion was the first they sought.

It did not bode well that she looked very comfortable in Balitang House.

Winnamine was the first to recover. She approached the old woman with outstretched hands and an apparently genuine smile on her face. "Aunt Nuritin, it's wonderful to see you. Girls, come greet your great-aunt. Elsren, Petranne, come."

Aly looked at Ulasim and made sure the nobles couldn't see her before she hand-signed: *Does she live here?*

Ulasim nodded slightly.

Again Aly's fingers flew. *Are we safe with her in the house?*

Ulasim came over to whisper, "As safe as anywhere in Rajmuat. We're stuck with the old Stormwing, and that's that. She will learn nothing we do not allow her to."

Aly shook her head. "Well, then," she said, "we'll all just be one happy family. What harm could come of that?"

Once inside, the duchess looked at her late husband's aunt. "Lady Nuritin, may we have some time to settle in before we talk? I'm not at my best so early in the morning, and this is quite a surprise."

"Of course you need rest," the old woman said. "Go. Bathe, change, unpack, take naps if you must. We shall have our talk after lunch, and I can explain everything then."

The family headed for the stairs and the private rooms that opened off the second-floor gallery. The inside of the house was as refurbished as the outside. Teak floors glowed under fresh polish. Seashell inlays along the ceilings and floors gleamed. Frescoes were freshly colored by painstaking hands. The furnishings were influenced by raka, not luarin, taste. Flowers blazed in pottery vases as colorful as the blooms themselves. Hemp rugs with bright borders lay on the floors.

Dove and Sarai had suites of chambers connected by a shared bathing room. Aly looked around Dove's rooms and smiled. There were books on shelves on two sides of the room, books on the bedside table, and candles placed for reading. Dove had covered her walls with maps. Here was every island in the realm, as well as a large map that included the Isles, the Yamani Islands, and the Eastern and Southern Lands. The desk was set with inkwells, quills, and paper.

As Dove bathed, Aly unpacked for them both. She also searched the room, though she expected that her pack of spies had gone over every inch of the house. Mages had renewed all the common spells. She also found more concealed workings against eavesdroppers and watchers, strong ones that made her raise her brows in admiration. Aly had worried that someone might sneak something nastily magical into the house without Ochobu there to supervise, but the old mage had told her the house would be made safe.

Over the winter Ulasim had told Aly that Ysul, the Chain's mage in the Windward District of Rajmuat, where Balitang House stood, was second in rank to Ochobu herself and her equal in power. Aly looked forward to meeting this Ysul. She hoped he would be easier to work with than the cranky, luarin-hating Ochobu. Now, seeing the power in what he had done, Aly prayed he could live in the same house with the fierce old woman.

When she had finished her inspection of Dove's quarters, Ali moved into Sarai's bedchamber and study. Sarai's maid, Boulaj, one of Aly's trainees, had already begun her search of the room for spy magics and bolt-holes where someone could eavesdrop. Aly watched. Security was even more important for Sarai. She was impetuous and hot-tempered, unlike the cool-headed Dove. Since the deaths of her father and his killer, Prince Bronau, Sarai had become hard to handle. She didn't care what she said about the king who had sent them into exile or his family. Aly didn't want any rash words Sarai might let fall in her bedroom to reach palace ears.

"Very good," she told Boulaj when the woman had finished. "You must have had an excellent teacher."

Boulaj grinned, her horsy face lighting up. "She was modest, too."

Once Dove and Sarai had finished their baths, Aly had time for a wash and a change of dress. She then padded down the servants' stair to the work quarters of the Balitang servants and slaves. In the kitchen Chenaol the cook greeted

Aly with a firm hug and kisses on both cheeks, then stuffed a warm meat pasty into Aly's hands and jerked her head toward one of the kitchen exits.

Junai, Aly's former guard, waited there, her face expressionless as usual. Now that Aly was to work with her spies, Junai had been assigned to the post of Dove's bodyguard at Aly's recommendation. As a fighter Junai had a place in the rebellion's inner circle, but she also had an aptitude for spy work, to the surprise of her father, Ulasim. Aly had not been surprised. For someone with no magic, Junai had often been virtually invisible when she had guarded Aly. She was a silent and accomplished tracker, with deft hands, muscles like wire cables, and Ulasim's quick intelligence as well as his sharp brown eyes. Her fine black hair was braided out of her way, and she favored the highland raka's tunic and leggings.

"You missed me so much I can't even have lunch before you sweep me up in a whirlwind of affection," Aly said as she followed the older woman down a hall in the service wing of the house, where the nobles never went. "I knew it was only a matter of time before I won you over."

Junai glanced back at her. "Some of your pack of spies are waiting in the meeting room," she said. "The men will come soon. And this is your personal office." She halted at the last right-hand door in the hall and opened it to reveal a decently sized workroom with maps and slates on the walls. Aly guessed it had formerly been used to store furniture, but now it was ready for her use, complete with a large worktable, chairs, writing supplies, and that glimmer of hidden magical spells for security.

Junai closed the door to Aly's office. "The general meeting room is here." The raka opened the door on the left-hand side of the hall.

2

DRAGONS, CROWS, AND DOVES

Aly walked in to find a much larger room, with a counter along two walls and a series of cupboards along the wall shared with the outside passageway. A number of chairs of all shapes and sizes filled the open floor. Six of them were occupied by the women of Aly's pack. All looked up at her: Boulaj, the plump sisters Atisa and Guchol, pert Kioka, lovely Eyun, and little Jimarn.

Guchol grinned at Aly. "Oh, good! Duani's here."

Atisa slipped to the floor to stretch her legs in a split. "Does that mean we may go home now?" Her black hair tumbled over her face.

Aly plumped herself into a chair. "If you want to go home, you may, my ducks, but you'll miss using the training I beat into you this winter. Where are the lads?"

"Here," a man said as seven of them entered the room. Junai closed the door as they traded greetings with the women and found places to sit.

"Gods bless us," Aly began as they quieted. "Our pack is reunited and the stakes have gone up." All of them nodded. "I trust you've been good lads and lasses and kept up your exercises when you were not under my eye?" She raised a brow as she looked around the room.

"We've been checking the backgrounds of all the new people in the house, those that weren't chosen by Ulasim before our ladies' exile," Yoyox said, smoothing his mustache. He was nearly as fine a pickpocket as Aly. "And using the gossip network set up before the family got exiled. It's good. Quedanga, the housekeeper, she's supposed to just pass messages along, but she's experienced at collecting gossip from the common folk. She gets word from servants, slaves, artisans, priests—and they're everywhere."

"Then we'll leave Quedanga to send messages and manage the people she knows best, since we'll be dealing more with the palace and the military," Aly said. "She knows she's to pass on what she gathers to me?"

"Yes, Duani," Yoyox said so meekly that Aly had to laugh. "To add to *our* ranks"—he waved an arm to include his comrades—"we have fifteen men we've been training the way you want. Most are in this house. Some belong to households on this street, so no one will think anything if they visit us often. And we've the tunnels under the house for when we don't want to draw attention to our comings and goings. Every man has been approved by Quedanga and Ysul, just like everyone who lives here."

"We have another eleven women," Jimarn added. "All in this house for the present. We have started to teach them codes, searches, and theft."

Aly nodded. This was also what she'd trained them for. Each of them had been examined by Ulasim and Ochobu before he or she was allowed to study with Aly, and she had educated them all winter. One of those series of lessons had been about choosing and teaching new recruits. Aly could not constantly look over people's shoulders here in the city, when she would have to spend most of her time gathering and studying information. She had to depend on her trainees' judgment. Now school was done, and her pack had their own work to do.

"How are your recruits doing?" she asked.

"Well," said Yoyox. "Very well."

Everyone nodded. Aly had learned that the raka already understood the demands of being a spy. In a land governed for three hundred bloody years by strangers, they had lived like spies to survive. Aly had simply taught her pack a number of new tricks, while they taught her their old ones.

"And what of Lady Nuritin's servants?" she asked. "How safe are they?"

"Safe," replied Olkey, one of the men. "Her maid is a luarin, a cousin, and devoted to Nuritin. Stays by her side, doesn't snoop. The other woman, Jesi, is more of a clerk, and writes all the lady's letters and notes. She belongs to the conspiracy."

Aly nodded. That was another worry she need not have. "Good," she said. "I'll take reports in here during the afternoon resting time. If you need me to meet one of your recruits, bring her, or him, in." As they nodded, she looked them over. "Playtime's over, children," she said with a grin. "Nice job on the Example pier, by the way. There were soldiers screeching at each other as we sailed by."

Her pack smiled or looked down, depending on their natures. Jimarn met Aly's eyes steadily. She was in charge of the Example operation.

Aly took a deep breath. "What do you have for me?"

Once her people had brought her up to date, Aly ate her cold pasty and went to the kitchen to beg another from Chenaol. As she ate that, the older woman settled in for a good talk. The cook had been Aly's first friend in the household. In her mid-fifties, plump and wickedly humorous, Chenaol had some gray in the black hair she wore in a long braid. She could flip any kind of knife or cleaver and send it straight to the center of a target faster than watchers could see, and could tell good steel from bad at a glance.

They were discussing the missing tax collectors when a messenger boy came into the kitchen. "Her Grace is wishful of you both coming to the ladies' sitting room," he told Aly and Chenaol. "She's got a cloud on her face."

Winnamine must be about to pop, wondering how we paid for all this splendor and why Nuritin is here, Aly thought as she and Chenaol followed the boy.

The room where the family relaxed during their leisure time was light and open, overlooking the flower gardens and the courtyard pool. The cushioned chairs and couches were elegant but comfortable. Nuritin sat in an armchair, facing Winnamine and Sarai, who shared a couch. Dove had taken her usual position, off to one side. Aly slid into her spot behind Dove as Chenaol, with a nod from the duchess, took a chair. Ulasim took his post next to the main door, the consummate footman. Ochobu entered and closed the door behind her.

"Aunt, I don't believe you know Ochobu Dodeka," Winnamine said. "Lady Nuritin Balitang, Ochobu." The two older women looked each other over thoroughly as Winnamine explained, "Ochobu joined the household at Tanair. She is an excellent healer and mage, so we are honored to have her. Ulasim is her son."

Aly crossed her fingers. Ochobu did not always deal well with full-blood luarin, but she would have to if Lady Nuritin was living at Balitang House. Ochobu's stony gaze was not promising. Though barely five feet tall, she gave the impression of being much taller. Her long nose always looked as if it held a sniff, particularly when she looked on luarin.

If Ochobu's stare disconcerted Nuritin, the noblewoman showed no sign of it. Instead she turned her attention to Winnamine. "You will find that many things have changed from last year," Nuritin said. Like Ochobu, her Gift showed in Aly's Sight, though Nuritin's was glowing embers compared to Ochobu's fire. Nuritin continued, "I have explained everything to the people you sent ahead"—she nodded to Chenaol—"and they certainly understood how things will be different." She looked at Sarai. "Stand up and turn around, girl."

Sarai obeyed with a pout. Nuritin looked her over as she might a horse. With satisfaction she said, "We'll have to take in the gowns I've had made. It's just as well I had Ulasim here escort the seamstresses to your rooms during lunch. You lost weight out there in the wilds—very good."

"Aunt!" cried Sarai, fiery roses appearing in her cheeks.

"And black makes you look sallow," Nuritin told her, adding insult to injury.

Aly ducked her head to hide a grin.

"Dovasary," Nuritin said, an actual smile on her thin lips. "Black is not *your* color, either, my dear."

"It *is* mourning, Aunt," Dove explained. "I don't think you're supposed to look becoming in it."

"That is one of the things that has changed," Nuritin said crisply. "Her Royal Highness the princess regent ordained five months ago that full mourning was disrespectful to the Black God, who takes our dead to the Realms of Peace. She ordered that all the court put off full mourning for Kings Oron and Hazarin. The only mourning permitted to any member of the court is a discreet black armband, and perhaps black embroideries or trim. No black gowns. No black tunics. No black veils. We are to wear colors that rejoice for the peace of the dead."

"Meaning Imajane looks dreadful in black and won't wear it if she doesn't have to," Sarai remarked with spite.

Nuritin nodded. "Naturally. But it is a royal decree, with the king's seal attached. You must all put off black at court, or for that matter, anywhere that the regents may appear. It has been suggested that they will regard mourning as a sign of rebellion."

"Aunt," said Winnamine quietly. Everyone looked at her. The duchess stood, arms folded. "You said you had dresses made up. You sent seamstresses up to our family rooms. And there are *these*."

She indicated two open chests. One was filled with money and topped by a clutch of parchments. Aly sharpened her magical vision to read the first of them: it was a letter of credit, issued to the duchess. Next to it was a much smaller chest that bore the crest of the duchess's own family, the Fonfalas. It, too, was open. It held jewelry: gold chains, necklaces, eardrops, and strings of colored pearls. Most were in old-fashioned or broken settings.

"The Fonfalas sent those," explained Ulasim. "They gave their permission for us to melt down the pieces and sell the stones, but we thought we should wait for you to decide."

"And the servants?" asked Winnamine, glaring down at Nuritin. "Where did they come from?"

Ulasim cleared his throat politely. Everyone looked at him. "Many of our new servants come from Lady Sarai and Lady Dove's grandfather, the baron Temaida. The servants are paid by the Temaidas, and clothed by them." He met Winnamine's startled look with a reassuring one of his own. "This is family policy among the raka nobles, Your Grace. When a Temaida girl comes of age at sixteen, she receives a staff of her own, because marriage alliances mean so much to the raka nobility. They want their daughters to appear to advantage."

"Very sensible," said Nuritin with a nod of approval. Slowly Winnamine sat again.

"Your Grace, you were Lady Sarugani's best friend," Chenaol added, referring to Sarai and Dove's mother. "You should remember it is the custom."

Ulasim continued, "They were unable to manage it last year, so they fulfill their duty to their kinswomen this year. The baron sent his regrets that he will not be coming to the city for some time, or he would call on you personally, but he knows that you will treat his granddaughters well."

Meaning last year they were afraid to help the Balitangs when they were out of favor, and this year they don't want to draw attention to their presence, Aly thought. Who can blame them? *I* wouldn't want to belong to the raka nobility of the Isles. It's like living with a knife at your throat. And Ulasim can't tell Her Grace that the Temaidas know Sarai may be queen soon. They're the ones who secretly carried the Haiming royal blood for three centuries, to give it to Sarugani, and then to Sarai and Dove.

Aly hand-signaled Fesgao, out of the Balitang ladies' line of sight: *These new people have been investigated?* Her pack would have checked them, too, but Aly was cautious.

Fesgao replied with a nod and signed, *All hand-picked.* Aly relaxed. Ulasim would have made doubly sure no one suspicious came into Balitang service.

"I can't possibly accept all this," said the duchess, sitting down once more. She was pale. "I can't ever repay it."

"You are not a fool, Winnamine," Nuritin said flatly. "Don't act like one."

The duchess frowned. Her chin came up.

"You will take all this, and you will deck this house and your children in the finest you can buy," Nuritin informed the duchess. "I am sorry—I mourn my nephew's murder, too." She smoothed a braided black armband with fingers that shook. "But politics doesn't wait, and there is work to be done quickly. I had clothes made for all of you, but they must be fitted properly *today.* Tomorrow you are commanded to present yourselves to His Majesty and the regents at court. I believe Her Highness may have intended to humiliate you by summoning you immediately, so she could make fun of your appearance in outmoded clothes. Well! She may be regent, but she cannot be allowed to toy with her nobles in this fashion. I intend for her to fail."

"Who cares if Her Highness plays games with us or not?" Winnamine's gaze was still adamant. "I certainly did not return to accept charity."

Nuritin sniffed. "My dear young woman, has the highland air made you stupid? It is an *investment.*" When no one spoke, Nuritin sighed. "You must build a power base for King Dunevon's heir, goose. Elsren is next in line for the throne. He will need friends and support. Our families agreed that setting you up is worth whatever we might dredge from our coffers." She looked at Sarai. "Men will hare after *you* to forge an alliance with our family. I expect you to *remember* your family, and the interests of your family. Flirt with those men, learn their minds, and promise them nothing."

Sarai's mouth trembled. "I have not done so well in my flirtations lately," she replied softly. "If you haven't heard, my last lover killed Papa. And where were the Balitangs, and the Fonfalas, and the Temaidas, when we were in danger?"

Nuritin's thin eyebrows snapped together. "Your last lover? Do not tell me you forgot what you owe to the family by tumbling Bronau."

Sarai gasped in indignation. Winnamine rose to stand with Sarai. Dove did the same. "Sarai would never disgrace us by bedding a man of whom her father did not approve," said Winnamine, while Sarai's cheeks turned a beet color.

Nuritin's eyes were on Sarai. "Bronau deserved to die," she said, her voice flat. "You and your sister did the realm a service by killing him. You also saved his brother the embarrassment of paying an executioner." She looked at the duchess and at Dove. "Is she a fool? Better to lock her up than have her ruin things for us at court. It is not the place to stumble, not after this winter. The regents have proved to be less than patient."

"She is no fool, Aunt," replied Dove. "She just thinks the family's drawing back from us was wrong. Winna and I understood—Papa understood—the family had to save themselves from the taint of our disgrace. Sarai just hasn't made her peace with it."

"Then make your peace," Nuritin said tartly. "You have a duty to Elsren and to your stepmother, if you don't care for the duty you owe to our royal blood."

"I never had to worry about that before," Sarai retorted, her mouth mulish.

"Before there were several heirs between your family and the throne. Now there is only one. You will marry to your *brother's* advantage, which is the *family's* advantage." Nuritin inspected the faces of those before her. Then she nodded. "Come upstairs. We need to get your new clothes fitted this afternoon. And I want to see Elsren."

The afternoon dissolved in a flurry of fabrics and flashing needles. The Balitang clan had mustered an army of seamstresses to work on the ladies' new wardrobes all winter long, using Nuritin's precise memory for the Tanair Balitangs' height, weight, and measurements. The old woman was surprised to find that everyone, not just Sarai, had to have their clothes taken in. Winter had been lean.

Aly, Boulaj, and even the duchess's personal maid, Pembery, found themselves elbowed out of the way by women who sewed at a speed they could not match. Aly finally slid out and spent the remaining daylight hours inspecting the house and grounds.

Out in the garden an open-sided square pavilion glowed with extra-powerful spells against eavesdropping. Inside it, Aly could hear nothing, not even the artificial waterfall that hissed over rocks beside it. It was perfect for secret conversations.

"Come to me," a familiar voice said behind her. "The air is dead under that roof."

Aly turned and smiled. The new arrival was nearly six feet tall, with skin the color of dark sugar syrup. She hadn't seen Nawat Crow in five days, and as always when they'd been apart, she realized that she had missed him. Everything about him made her happy. He appeared to be about nineteen or twenty, with glossy black hair. His deep-set brown eyes were alert to any movement around him. The young woman who didn't follow him with her eyes when he passed was rare. The women who lingered when they got to know him were even more rare. Nawat's grasp on humanity was light, to say the least. It was perfectly understandable: despite his apparent age, Nawat was three years old as a crow and had spent only a year as a man. More often than not, he acted first as a crow might, then only belatedly and occasionally as a human.

Their friendship had begun when he was a crow teaching her the crows' language at Kyprioth's request. During those lessons Aly had fascinated Nawat so much that he had changed himself into a human, something he told her that all crows could do. Seeing him made her pulse quicken as she left the pavilion. He wore clean clothes and he'd finger-combed his damp, crow-black hair back from his face. His feet were bare. "You forgot shoes," Aly reminded him. Resting her hand on his chest, she stood on tiptoe for his kiss.

Nawat stepped back.

Aly stared at him, her hand dropping to her side. She felt almost as if he'd slapped her. "No kiss?" she asked, keeping her voice light. "I'm crushed."

"You said I must not kiss you in front of people," he reminded her. "You said they will think you are frivolous if we are kissing."

"But we're not in public," she explained patiently. "Listen. No one's outside. We could go behind a tree—Nawat, it's just a *kiss*."

She took a step forward, reaching for his jacket lapel. Nawat took another step back. "I have been thinking," he said. "You will let me kiss you and preen you, but you will not mate with me. I think you are a mixed-up human. You think that mating is not important if you have kisses and preening. If I do not kiss you and preen you, I think you will want to mate with me. To have nestlings. To be with me all our days."

Aly rubbed her temples. Sometimes it was very hard to get a former crow to see things properly. "I didn't say I won't mate with you because we kiss and preen," she said patiently, remembering how close to mating some of that preening had gotten. "I can't be distracted. It's going to be a dangerous spring and summer. This is a horrible time to mate. We can't risk it."

"All life is a risk, Aly," he told her soberly, reaching a hand out to her, then hastily lowering it. "At any moment an archer may shoot you, or a hawk break your neck. A forest fire or a volcano will burn you. A Bronau will stab you. Risk will not end if the god gets his islands back."

Aly sighed. "No, but my task will be done, and then we can mate."

"And what if you are killed?" Nawat wanted to know. "What if I am killed? What if a Bronau steals you away?"

Sometimes a crow cannot be argued with, thought Aly, feeling a little impatient. Sometimes you only give yourself a headache if you try. He'll be stealing kisses again soon enough.

Changing the subject, she asked, "What was that display this morning? It looked as if all the crows in the Isles had decided to draw attention to our arrival."

"The crows came to win our bet with the god," Nawat replied.

Aly raised an eyebrow at him. "I thought that bet was just with the Tanair crows, and just for last summer."

Nawat shook his head. "Not just with my cousins at Tanair," he explained, his dark eyes following a Stormwing high overhead. "He wagered with all the crows of the Isles."

Aly stared at him. "*All* of them?"

Her friend nodded. "While you are here, they will help to guard Sarai and Dove. Only when Kyprioth rules again may we collect the wager, if you are still alive."

"That must be some wager, for you all to risk so much," Aly remarked. "You know, I would be so much more cooperative if I knew what the prize actually *was*."

Nawat gave a bird shrug, a lift of his shoulder blades more than his shoulders. "You would not like it," he said dismissively. "It is for crows."

For the third time that afternoon Aly felt as if she'd been slapped by someone who had never even frowned at her. In a tiny voice she asked, as she had heard girls she despised ask, "Are you angry with me?"

Nawat closed his eyes as if asking for patience. Then he cupped her face in both hands and kissed her mouth softly, lingering, holding them both absolutely still, as if only this connection between them existed. At last he released her. For once Aly could think of nothing to say.

As she stared at him, he answered her. "Never. Never, never, never." Then he turned and walked away.

Slowly everyone settled. The ladies ate with Nuritin, then retired upstairs. Before she joined them, Dove dismissed Aly for the night, reminding her that she could still take off a simple gown herself if she wanted to go to bed. Aly took a last walk around the grounds, knowing that her fellow conspirators would have to wait until most of the household had gone to bed before they could meet.

At last Aly strolled into the kitchen and down the hall to the meeting room. Nawat was there already, as were Chenaol and Ulasim. Except for Nawat, who perched on a countertop, the others had taken comfortable chairs. They shared a pitcher of the liquor called arak and bowls of nuts and fruits. They knew better than to offer the potent arak to Aly. She never drank, fearing liquor would loosen her tongue.

As Aly slumped into a chair, Fesgao arrived, then Ochobu. She brought with her a slender, young part-raka with ears like jug handles. In Aly's magical Sight he, like Ochobu, blazed with his magical Gift. This would be the mage who had laid all the fresh spellwork on the house.

"Aly, this is Ysul," Ulasim told her, pointing to the new man. "Another mage with the Chain. He will live here, to help keep our ladies doubly safe."

"He is mute," Ochobu said tartly as she sat. "King Oron's torturers did that when he was small. So don't go trying to talk his ear off just because he's defenseless."

Aly shook her head. She'd known wolverines with more

diplomacy than Ochobu. Then she grinned. Ysul was using military hand-sign code to say *I'm not defenseless.*

Don't tell Ochobu, Aly hand-signed back, her movements concealed by the arms of her chair. *She's happy because she thinks she just insulted me.*

Ysul nodded gravely and settled on the floor beside one of the cupboards. The room was supposed to be a linen storeroom, but that was only in the daytime.

"Where's Quedanga?" Fesgao asked, looking for the housekeeper. "Now that we're all in Rajmuat again, she ought to join us."

"She's keeping watch," Ulasim replied. "One of us must stand guard for a third of every night, to take reports and deal with the unexpected. I have the time around midnight, and Chenaol gets the time from false dawn to sunrise."

"I'll always take that one," Chenaol said comfortably. "I have to start the bread anyway."

Nawat ate nuts, cracking them with his fingers before devouring them. As Ulasim handed Aly a pitcher of guava juice and a cup, Ochobu spoke a word that set magical signs ablaze throughout the room. They faded slowly until they were all but invisible.

Ulasim leaned in his chair. "It is good to see you all again," he remarked.

"Is it?" snapped Ochobu. "How could you allow that old woman to move in here, Ulasim? She will ruin everything."

Ulasim sighed, running his hand through his long hair. "Mother, one does not *forbid* Lady Nuritin Balitang *anything,*" he explained with resignation. "She is, as far as all Rajmuat is concerned, the head of the Balitang family with the death of His Grace. Technically this is the Balitangs' house, not Her Grace's. It is Nuritin's signature that makes anything to do with this house possible."

"How can we keep anything in this house secret with that woman and her servants at our heart like a luarin tumor?" demanded Ochobu.

Chenaol grinned and poured out two cups of arak. She offered one to Ochobu, who ignored it. The cook gave a "Suit yourself" shrug and drank from her own cup, setting the other within reach. "Just as easily as we keep our secrets with tradesmen and messengers coming in and out all day, old woman," she told the mage. "It's far easier to do in a house like this than it was up in our mountain aerie. You let us worry about Nuritin and her servants. She's good to have on our side—connected to every family of the luarin nobility, and to one in three families among the raka nobles."

"It would draw attention we cannot afford to keep her out, and it would not be easy to arrange," added Ulasim. "Topabaw would think we had something to hide."

"Speaking of hiding . . . ," Aly began. Everyone looked at her. "I admire the way you've concealed the magics on this house. *I* noticed them, but fortunately, the Sight is the rarest aspect of the Gift. You did beautiful work here."

Chenaol looked Aly over. "Since when do you know what's magic and what isn't, mistress?"

Nawat offered Aly a nut. She took it and looked at Ochobu. "You never told them?"

Ulasim snorted. "You spent a winter cooped up with my mother and didn't see it?" he wanted to know. "She never tells anyone anything. She makes clams and oysters look slack-jawed. What is it?"

The old woman grumbled under her breath and tugged her jacket around her shoulders.

Aly popped the nut into her mouth and chewed it thoroughly. "I have the Sight," she told them. "I can see magic, or death, or sickness, or godhood. I can see poisons in food.

If I concentrate a little differently, I can see distant things clearly, and tiny things in complete detail."

"So those liar's signs you told us to look for were not real?" Fesgao asked. "The looking aside, the blinking?"

"Oh, no!" Aly reassured him. "A blink, a fidget, a change in body position, those are all perfectly good measures of a lie told by an amateur." She smiled wickedly. "I just have a little something extra." She looked at Ochobu. "I spent the whole winter thinking you'd told and they didn't care."

"I *don't* care," Ochobu snapped. "It is foolish to rely on magic, any magic, including the Sight. The Rittevons have that much right, at least—they know too many people use magic as a crutch, and they are wary of it."

"So says the mage," grumbled Ulasim.

"And who would know the truth of that, if not a mage?" demanded his mother.

Nawat cracked a nut by slamming it on the counter. Everyone turned to stare at him. "Are we done with all the scoldings?" he wanted to know, his face as open as always. "Because I wish to know what use I will be in this oversized, befouled nest you call a city. I could see plain enough when I came. You have more arrow makers here than you will need." At home in Tanair, he had made arrows with special fletchings, arrows that would kill mages and arrows that flew straight despite the wind.

"But there is need for the crows," Chenaol said.

"No," replied Nawat flatly. "You have your human crows in the palace and the city and the households, picking up whatever news they have. My people cannot enter houses, and there is very little food for us here. We are here to win our wager with the god, not to sit about preening ourselves." He glanced into Aly's upturned face and away. "*I* am here to do more than preen myself."

Ulasim nodded. "He has a point," the big raka admitted. "At Tanair the crows were our watchers and patrols."

"We'll find something for him to do," Aly said impatiently. The thought that Nawat might leave made her chest go tight. "Gods help us, we only arrived today."

No one else commented. Nawat was considered to be under Aly's command. The rebel commander had agreed that winter to make their subordinates and work areas separate for the most part, though they would share any news and special requests at the nightly meetings. On occasion some areas might need to work with different ones, but those cases would be determined as they arose. It was a rebel's way to fight, rather than the way a government would do things. If the Crown captured some of them, the rest of the movement would still be able to continue the rebellion.

Aly looked at Ulasim. She knew it was pathetic to change the subject to get rid of that tight feeling near her heart, but what she had to say *was* important. "In the meantime, may we *now* bring Sarai and Dove in on this? The country is trembling on the sword's edge—we could all feel it on the way here. It's the girls' destiny at play."

Ochobu made a face. "To risk all on the discretion of a pair of girls . . . Not yet."

"I agree," Ulasim replied. "At least, not as regards Lady Sarai's discretion."

Someone rapped on the door. It could not be a stranger to the household, since the servant's wing was kept under watch. Ulasim stood to open the door and admitted Dove.

"Sorry," she said, finding a vacant chair. "It was hard to get away from my chess game. I had to let Aunt Nuritin win. I'll never hear the end of it now."

Ochobu glared at her son. "You could have said she knows."

Aly hid a grin as the big footman shrugged. "She came

to me after supper to tell *me,*" he explained to his mother. "It seemed only reasonable to ask her to come here."

"It's so obvious Petranne could see it," Dove said wearily. "The way the raka watched us all the way to Tanair and back, the crows, a household with all the servants but Aly who are raka full- and part-bloods, servants who used to work for the Temaidas. . . . My mother belonged to some branch of the Haiming clan, didn't she? A small one that escaped the luarin's eyes. It explains a great deal."

Fesgao smiled at her. "You are right, my lady, it does."

"The timing makes sense," Dove continued. "We have only two people with a claim to the Rittevon throne left. Dunevon is a child; his regents make Stormwings look tenderhearted. But do you mean to kill Elsren? Because Sarai and I will never permit that."

"We shall ford that river when we come to it, my lady," Ochobu said. "For the present we gather allies, identify our enemies, and look for the regents' weaknesses. There is unrest all over the Isles. It will be war by summer's end."

"Then don't tell Sarai or Winna," Dove advised. "It's quite possible Winna will have Elsren swear a blood oath not to try for the throne. She hates it at court." Dove looked around at the raka's faces. "You *were* going to tell Winnamine, weren't you? Or is she supposed to die in the fighting?"

"We have made no decision in that area, either, my lady," Fesgao said with grave respect. "Many things must take place before we shall be forced to consider such choices."

Dove leaned back in her chair. "Tell me," she ordered.

Aly watched as the raka straightened, new life and purpose in their eyes, even Ochobu's. One after another they explained how things stood. Dove's arrival had given them something real to look at. She might have been only their future queen's little sister, but she had the same blood in her veins and the same quick wits.

When they had finished, Dove massaged her temples. "It's so much bigger than I could have imagined," she murmured. They all waited for what she would say next. Finally Dove took a deep breath and asked, "Have we a symbol? Some ordinary thing, so the common people and the middle classes will know that our country is changing?"

She's good, thought Aly with appreciation. Right to the heart of the matter. I hope Sarai does half as well.

"A symbol?" inquired Fesgao. "Like a kudarung?"

Dove shook her head. "Something more subtle. Something that looks like a message, that can be put in places where officials won't notice it."

"Something to shake the regents up," murmured Aly.

"If the regents are shaken up," Fesgao pointed out, "they will not take it kindly, I warn you."

"No, I suppose not," Dove acknowledged. "But they're already behaving stupidly. I saw all the new checkpoints in the city. It's the way the Crown chooses to deal with mindless hooligans. You know what the luarin nobility says—the raka get restless every thirty years, and have to be kicked down. We need to tell them this is no clump of restless raka. This is a movement."

"If we make the regents angry," Chenaol said, "they will slam our folk with more laws, more taxes."

"More arrests," added Fesgao. "More punishments. More executions."

"They cannot arrest what they cannot find," Nawat pointed out. "When the People, animals, claim a territory and drive rivals from it, they mark it. What if you find a way to mark your territory for all to recognize?"

Ulasim rubbed his neck as if it ached. "Please do not tell me we must go out and piss on every street corner," he said, a faintly pleading note in his voice.

"Then only the People will know it is your territory, not the Crown," Nawat replied reasonably.

"A symbol," Dove told them. "Scratched into plaster, written on a proclamation that's been nailed up, dug in the dirt, painted on a door or a shutter. Something easy—"

"An open shackle with a few links of chain attached," suggested Chenaol eagerly. "For freedom."

"Harmless enough," Ulasim admitted slowly. "Easy to spread, easy to set folk talking." He looked at Dove. "We'll do it."

"Aly?" Dove whispered in the darkness of her bedroom. Junai was still downstairs with her father.

Aly had not been asleep. She'd been expecting this. "We'll go outside. There's a pavilion the mages fixed in the garden. It's shielded from just about everything inside the walls as well as outside."

Dove and Aly wrapped themselves in robes and padded downstairs. Once outside, Aly led her mistress to the open-sided building where she had talked to Nawat. The girls sat for a moment on the couch, enjoying the cool, damp spring breeze.

At last Dove looked at Aly. "I wish you had told me."

"In all honor, I couldn't," Aly explained. "They expected me to keep my silence, and it is *their* plot. I am a newcomer."

"But the raka, the people not of our household, they know, or they guess," Dove pointed out. "It's why they always turn out to see Sarai and me. Not because our mother was raka, but because they believe Sarai is the promised queen." She rubbed her mouth with her thumb. "I'm surprised the regents haven't tried to kill us already."

"It will come," Aly said. "If they know their business, they will try nothing in the confines of the palace. They'll try in the city, if they can't get inside these walls—"

"And they can't," Dove interrupted, her words half a question.

Aly considered this. At last she said, "Not without a frontal assault, I think. And on the city streets . . . The raka have been planning this rebellion for decades. We have more allies on the streets than the regents suspect. Naturally, I'm going to do my best to make sure of what they suspect and what they don't."

"Alone?" Dove asked.

"Now you're fishing," Aly said, not in the least alarmed. "I have help, and that's all you need to know for the present. When exactly did you put it together?"

Dove began to braid a lock of her hair. "Around Midwinter, I think. Oh, Sarai and I knew the raka believed Sarai might be the promised queen before that, but it took me some weeks penned up in Tanair to see that there was an actual conspiracy among our upper servants, not the usual mutterings of hotheads. Here in the city, it's even more plain."

Aly looked aside for a moment, to do the mind trick that allowed her Sight to work better in the dark. She wanted to see the expression on Dove's face. The younger girl seemed composed, but a corner of her mouth quivered.

It is one thing to guess, and another to *know,* Aly reflected. She's starting to see the cost in blood.

"I *have* been trying to steer them away from a massacre," Aly said, deliberately adopting the tone of an elderly aunt who had convinced the children to behave. "And they have been listening. Even Ochobu, who hates the luarin more than the rest, sees that there's no profit in killing all the full-bloods, let alone anyone who's a part-blood."

"I feel so much better," commented Dove.

"And so you should," Aly replied comfortably, "seeing as how their queen candidate is a part-blood herself."

Dove laughed in spite of herself. "So the luarin's future is just a tiny obstacle, not cause for a bloodbath. You are an optimist."

"I do have a happy nature," Aly replied. "It is often remarked upon." More soberly, she added, "It will be easier with you knowing. They'll listen to you."

"But you and I need to sort out a few things, Aly," Dove told her. "The god you serve isn't really Mithros." She did not say it as a question.

Aly winced. "Um . . . ," she said, her brain racing. She had warned the raka conspirators that Dove was sharp.

"Why would my dear brother care what happens to the raka?" Kyprioth winked into view on the bench opposite them. He lay sidelong on it, his head propped on his hand. His usual motley assembly of jewels, brooches, and charms glittered in the light he cast. "And could we use actual names as little as possible? None of us will rejoice if we catch my family's attention, believe me." He smiled cheerfully at Dove. "Hello, little bird. I'm Kyprioth."

Aly had forgotten the god's effect on those with raka blood. Dove slid out of her chair and onto her knees, where she bowed so deeply her forehead touched the floor. Despite her awe, she muttered to Aly, "We are in *such* trouble."

"Nonsense," said Kyprioth. "We are getting *out* of trouble. Do sit up. You're distressing Aly."

Dove met his eyes. "There are probably dragons who don't distress Aly. Weren't you banished, or some such thing?"

Aly grinned and relaxed. Dove would let no one walk over her, not even a god.

"Details," said Kyprioth, waving away Dove's question. "A mere fluctuation of the balance of power in this part of the world. It's time to amend that."

"Don't you think you should be talking to my sister, then?" inquired Dove, very matter-of-fact for a girl on her knees. "She's the one the people love."

"I need you *both,*" Kyprioth retorted. "She will be charming no matter what. We can leave her to make worshippers of this city. But you, my calculating dear, must be convinced." He threw up his hands. "Question away."

"Actually, your appearance answered the last of my questions, for the time being," Dove told him. "I always was puzzled that your great brother would choose Aly to speak for him. But she's been speaking for you. As *your* choice, she's absolutely perfect."

"Thank you, I think," Aly murmured.

Dove glanced at her. Aly noted the quiver of a barely concealed smile on the younger girl's lips before Dove returned her attention to the god. "You also explain the crows, since they've always been as much your children as the raka. One thing you *don't* explain, though. What happens when someone *does* attract your brother's attention?"

Kyprioth tapped his toe for a moment before he answered. "I will need all the victories my people can gain, to give me the strength to defeat my divine brother and sister. As the raka succeed, so will I."

"And if your brother and sister return early from their little war on the far side of the world, our collective sheep are roasted." Aly inspected her nails.

"Don't say things like that," retorted Kyprioth. "Whose messenger are you?"

Aly smiled brightly at the god who had been making her life interesting for the past year. "Sarai's," she told him.

"Dove's. The duchess's. The raka's. And on down through a great, long, complicated list that ends with you."

"I'm hurt," protested the god. "After all I've done for you, giving you proper scope for your talents."

Dove cocked her head to one side. "For a follower, she's very rude."

"I wasn't even his follower. I was his conscript," Aly told her young mistress. "He press-ganged me from a dreadful pirate ship." She sniffed for effect.

"You may thank me later," Kyprioth said cheerfully. "If you're alive." He vanished.

Dove tried to rise from her knees and squeaked. She had gone stiff. Aly helped her to her feet, then back to the couch, where Dove slumped with a grateful sigh. "Does he come and go like that all the time?"

"Only when he thinks he's losing the argument," said Aly. Lips surrounded by a short, bristly beard brushed her cheek in a kiss.

Behind them Aly heard a tapping sound. She released the sheath for one of the wrist knives she wore even when she slept. The tapping approached Dove from behind. Suddenly a small, young, winged horse, known in the Isles as a kudarung, jumped up into Dove's robed lap.

"Hello," Dove greeted the newcomer softly. There was a tenderness in her voice she reserved only for animals and her immediate family. "Where did you come from?"

The tiny creature fanned his wings, then folded them awkwardly and nibbled at Dove's nightgown where it poked through the front of her robe. "That's not edible," Dove scolded, gently removing the cloth. "Aren't your parents going to wonder where you are?"

A whicker from atop a beam supporting the roof answered that question. The adult pair glided down to the floor with grace and ease. The foal watched with envious eyes.

"You'll be that good one day," Dove reassured the youngster. "You just need practice." Still keeping her voice soft, she said, "Wild kudarung in Rajmuat. *Miniature* wild kudarung. Aly, if the Crown finds out they're here, they may have to kill us."

"Ochobu and Ysul have shielded this house and the air above it. The Crown will have trouble getting a spy inside. Ulasim has cleared Nuritin's servants, and I don't see Nuritin herself sinking to that level." Aly considered this. "They'll *really* want at least one spy in this house," she murmured.

They admired the winged horses in silence until the parents got the foal to return to the beams with them. Brushing horsehair from her robe, Dove asked softly, "What are the rebels' chances to avoid a massacre throughout the Isles? And don't lie to me, please."

"I wasn't going to," Aly replied quietly, shaken from her thoughts about Crown spies. "It depends on how devoted they are to Sarai. If they love her completely, they will respect her wishes not to kill wantonly because they can." Aly bit her lip. She hated to voice unpleasant truths, but Dove would think less of Aly if she tried to give them a sugar coating. "Will there be fighting, and killing? I believe so. The conspiracy can't even control the conduct of the Rajmuat raka, let alone folk all throughout the Isles. We must simply pray that their love for Sarai will make them want to obey her rather than seek revenge. It will be tricky."

"You talk as if this rebellion were already set in stone," Dove pointed out.

"But it is," Aly replied, startled that Dove couldn't see it. "It was set in stone long before I came. With your approval or without it, the raka will rise. They've waited too long, and they are short on queen candidates. They've got the taste of hope in their mouths. That taste is dangerous. The only way we can limit the damage is to keep a firm grip on the rebellion. Even so, we won't be able to control everything."

"That's what I thought," said Dove quietly. "Thank you for telling me the truth."

Aly leaned forward and braced her elbows on her knees. "It is necessary," she explained. "Sarai can command the raka, or enough of them to make a difference, but young as you are, you have influence over Sarai and Winna. They rely on your intelligence. They'll listen to you. If you are to advise them well, someone must advise *you* well, and I think that someone must be me."

Dove sighed. "It was easier at Tanair."

"Oh, yes," said Aly, with a sigh of her own.

3

TOPABAW

The next morning Nuritin assembled the family in the lobby of the house, inspecting them as if she were a general and they her troops. No stray thread or curl escaped her frosty blue eyes, no unfortunate fold or bitten fingernail was not remarked upon. At last she smiled thinly.

"Let us see what Her Highness makes of the impoverished, newly returned Balitangs today," she told the duchess. "If she thinks she can buy you with royal favor, there is no time like the present for her to learn differently."

"Aunt, please," murmured Winnamine. "Topabaw has ears everywhere."

"He may eavesdrop all he likes. At this point, the regents need to keep us happy. They need to keep *you* happy," added Nuritin. "You'll see. Come, ladies, and my young lord," she added with a curtsy to little Elsren.

He looked up at his formidable relative and chuckled.

"Very good," Nuritin said with approval. She took his hand and led them all out to the courtyard.

The ladies had chosen to ride, though Sarai had sulked

over Nuritin's decree that they ride sidesaddle. Elsren and Petranne, along with the maids who served the older ladies, and Rihani, the younger children's nurse, rode in litters; the boxes of ceremonial clothes were in a small wagon at the rear of the procession. Fesgao rode at the head of the double ring of household men-at-arms, every one of them armed and armored. Junai, dressed as a man, walked on one side of Sarai's mount, Boulaj on the other. Aly walked between Dove and the ring of guards, to be on hand in case the Crown decided life would be easier without the older Balitang girls and the rumors that cropped up wherever they went.

Fesgao moved them out into the Windward District. Despite the earliness of the hour, there were people on the streets, and still more atop walls or looking out of windows. Aly found a familiar face in the crowd, handsome Rasaj, one of her pack. The rest of Aly's spies would be watching for anything troublesome or interesting. She saw three other faces she recognized from Balitang House, and she knew her pack had taken some of their own recruits with them. That was fine. The more the merrier.

For the most part it was a quiet ride. Aly saw other signs that the winter had not been a quiet one. The King's Watch kept people from gathering in any one place for long. Aly noticed still more scorch marks and chipped wood, swatches of fresh paint, and an overall atmosphere of tension. At one intersection, shopkeepers washed what looked like blood from the ground, their expressions sullen as they eyed a nearby clutch of Watchmen.

The previous spring, even with mad King Oron on the throne, the city had been a riot of flowers, colors, and movement. Today it was as if Rajmuat held its breath, waiting for something to shatter the stillness of the air. Aly wasn't sure if the place was ready for open revolution, but she guessed it was certainly ready to explode in some fashion.

That pleased her. The people did not seem to appreciate being supervised as if they were children bent on playing pranks against their elders. Not even the luarin acted as if all was right with their worlds.

Their path rose steadily up the terraced sides of the immense crater that was Rajmuat city and harbor. By sharpening her Sight Aly could see there was a soldier posted every ten feet along the palace wall on the heights. There were no marks on the wall, so the city's troubles had yet to reach the palace. She would make sure *that* did not last. The soldiers were alert and sweating under chest and head armor. How many guards did the Rittevons lose to heatstroke? Aly wondered. Summer might be a good time for all-out war.

"I wouldn't want *their* job," she murmured to Dove, pointing at the wall. "They have to be hot up there. Do they always wear armor on duty?"

Dove shaded her eyes. "Usually they wear lighter stuff, metal plates on leather shirts. They're wearing plate armor?"

"Helms and cuirasses at least," Aly replied. "They must be cooking like lobsters."

"Idiots," whispered Dove contemptuously. "Don't they realize the whole city knows what it means when they put men in plate armor on the palace walls? Why not paint a sign that says *We're frightened* and hang it on the gates?"

"Never complain of another's foolishness, my lady," Aly said, her voice just as soft. "Not if there's a chance you might put it to use." She wondered what the city folk had been up to that winter to make their rulers this skittish? She would have to talk to her pack and catch up on the gossip.

The road entered open ground, flanked by emerald lawns perfectly cropped by slave gardeners and populated by peacocks, geese, and more than a few crows. Streams wound across the land in front of the palace walls. Bridges allowed riders to pass over the wide, deep waters where they met the road. The streams held gray and red fish with sharp, protruding teeth.

"What do they feed the fish up here?" Aly asked Dove as they rode over the first bridge. The water on either side churned as the fish swam to the surface, gathering where they heard the sound of hooves.

Sarai heard and answered. "Meat once a day, but just enough to keep them alive," she said, her eyes flashing as she looked at the stream. "For the rest, they eat whoever gets pushed in. The third Rittevon king brought them here from the rivers of Malubesang. They were to help him save money on executions. If you can make it to the far bank and out of the water alive, it's assumed you're innocent."

"How efficient," said Aly, awed in spite of herself.

"That's where the rebel's children go, when the rebel himself, or herself, is made an Example down by the harbor," Winnamine called over her shoulder. "Some years they just throw people off the cliffs into the sea, because the fish are too well fed to eat any more."

So glad I asked, Aly thought with a wince. Then a happier idea made her smile: she would enjoy putting an end to the kind of rulers who would think of such a brutal way to punish their followers, however rebellious.

At last they came in view of the main gate, called the Gate of Victory. It was set behind a deep moat, on the far side of the last of the bridges spelled to collapse if the right command word was spoken. There were no fish in this water-lily-covered moat, but crocodiles eyed the passersby. Beyond lay the gate itself. When it was open, five heavy wagons could enter abreast. Aly could see that the white marble exterior of the walls was only a facade: the core stones were granite.

Traffic here was at its heaviest. They were not the only visitors that day, but the guards bowed low to the duchess and waved her through, while they stopped the merchant who followed them to inspect his wagons. More guards joked with some riders who were leaving the palace.

Once they had clattered down the tunnel in the wall and emerged on the other side, Sarai told Aly, "That was the Luarin Wall. Rittevon Lanman started building it as he put the crown on his head. It took them three generations to finish. Maybe if the raka queens had put up something like that, instead of using softer stone for the Raka Wall, things would be different." She pointed ahead.

Before them lay an open stretch of grass. There was no place for enemies to hide. On the far side rose a wall and a second gate. The stones of the gate were faced in white marble: the rest was a coppery reddish brown sandstone. On the right side stood a giant gold statue of Mithros the Warrior. The crown of the sun blazed on his head. On the right was a giant silver statue of the Great Mother Goddess in her aspect of the Mother, a sheaf of golden grain in one arm. Crows perched atop the statues, squalling without fear of the gods whose images they treated so casually.

"The raka didn't even have statues of the gods here," Sarai told Aly. "They believe it's unwise to draw the gods' attention."

With the Trickster for a patron god, I can see why they feel that way, Aly thought as they passed through the Raka Gate. Its tunnel was fifteen feet long. When they emerged into sunlight again, Aly halted with a gasp.

"I always forget how stunning it is," Dove murmured.

Before them lay a splendor of buildings and gardens that made the Tortallan palace Aly knew so well look like a frumpy old aunt who refused to dress for company. Aly's gaze caught and slid along curved-tipped roofs bright with gilt, pillars capped and footed in brightly polished copper. The doors were intricately carved and polished costly wood. Mother-of-pearl inlays shone on door and shutter panels.

Gardens wrapped around every structure, big and small, studded with ponds and banks of flowers that blazed with color. Trees flourished everywhere. Brightly colored birds darted overhead, the contents of a living jewel box. Aly saw a troop of woolly monkeys race along nearby rooftops and raised an eyebrow: five of them wore collars written over with listening spells. On the ground, crowned azure pigeons strutted along the paths.

As members of the Rittevon Guard came to greet them, one left their number and walked over to Aly. He blazed with a god's borrowed glory in Aly's Sight. He stopped beside Aly and stood looking at it all, hands propped on hips.

"It was the jewel of the Eastern and Southern Lands, once," Kyprioth informed Aly. "And it was *mine*." He flung out an arm, pointing to a stern granite wall in the distance. Atop it Aly saw the crenelations of a luarin fortification, like the castles and the palace she had grown up knowing. "That was the best they could do, my brother and sister," Kyprioth added. She stood with the god in a bubble of silence at the center of the household. "Build themselves and their Rittevon pets a gray stone cave where they may hide from my people. Well, that will change." The god inside the man glanced at Aly. "This is *your* chessboard, I believe, my dear."

Aly beamed at him. "So it is. And the game begins."

With an answering grin, Kyprioth abandoned his guardsman. Sounds from the real world filled Aly's ears. Other guards were helping the Balitang ladies to dismount: after a moment, Kyprioth's guard accepted Dove's reins from her. Dove slid from the saddle; Sarai, with a glare at the guard who had claimed her mount, turned, disentangled herself from the sidesaddle, and jumped down.

Stormwings circled the palace, snarling as crows darted in and out of their reach, calling crow insults. Fesgao rode back down their line, gathering the Balitang men-at-arms in his wake.

"Here we leave our ladies and the young master," he said. His bow had been directed to the Balitang ladies, but his eyes were on Aly. "We will be in the Long House by the Gate of the Moon. Send a runner for us when you are prepared to go."

Winnamine nodded graciously. Fesgao rode off with the men-at-arms and Junai.

Naturally they don't want our warriors staying with us, Aly thought as their small parade moved on. *There's less chance of anyone smuggling in a rebel force that way.* She smiled slyly. *We'll let them find out the hard way that we already have people inside the walls. I do love surprises!*

Nuritin and Winnamine led them down the road called Rittevon's Lance, which stretched from the palace to the royal docks on the harbor. Here it ended at its intersection with the Golden Road. Along the Golden Road sprawled two of the palace's most important areas, the Throne Hall, where the monarchs held audiences, and the Pavilion of Delightful Pleasures, where festivities were often set. Both structures blazed with white paint and gilt against their background of trees.

The Balitangs halted at the entrance of the Robing Pavilion directly across from the Throne Hall. Only the litters and the cart with their clothes had been allowed this far past the inner gate.

Inside the Robing Pavilion, the maids and Rihani led their charges to a small private chamber where they could change into court dress. Aly neatened Dove's many braids and helped her into her gown, shoes, and overrobe. Once the Balitangs were ready, a footman escorted them to the Throne Hall across the Golden Road. Aly followed.

Nuritin's maid; the duchess's maid, Pembery; and Sarai's maid, Boulaj, stayed in the Robing Pavilion. Pembery was to introduce Boulaj to members of the rebellion's network among the servants of the court. Both were ready to glean information from the winter's crop of gossip, news, and whispers. Aly turned down the chance to be introduced now—she wanted a view of the court. Later she would find out who served the rebellion here. Instead she entered the throne room in the wake of her employers.

Meek in her green-on-white printed sarong, her hair covered by a green headcloth, she found a place in the rear to view the proceedings. If questioned, Aly had a reasonable excuse for her presence: she had never been here before. She had come once, as Kyprioth's guest, to view Dunevon's coronation, but that visit had been one of the spirit only. Today she was able to appreciate the realities of the hall: the textures of wood and stone, the scents of flowers, and the whispers and shifting of those in attendance.

The master of ceremonies bowed deeply to the duchess and to Lady Nuritin. He stepped onto the gleaming floor of the throne room and thumped his ebony staff on the brass disk provided for that purpose. Courtiers as colorful as butterflies turned to look at him. His voice rang from the high, arched ceiling and its gilded beams as he proclaimed, "Her Grace, the Duchess Winnamine Balitang. Duke Elsren Balitang. Her Ladyship, Nuritin Balitang. Lady Saraiyu Balitang, Lady Dovasary Balitang, Lady Petranne Balitang."

The family stepped forward when he turned and bowed to them. Slowly, their chins high, they crossed the expanse of floor. Elsren and Petranne, clinging to their half sisters' hands, did their best to act as formal as five- and six-year-olds could look. Their great-aunt, mother, and sisters walked slowly so that the little ones could keep up.

Aly memorized the position of every guardsman in the room. Interestingly, those on duty here did not wear the combined sun and moon that was on the cuirasses of the Rittevon guards who patrolled the palace grounds. These men wore black breeches and chain-mail shirts, covered with an open-sided black tunic. They wore armored caps and carried broad-bladed spears. These men were the King's Guard, the personal bodyguards of the Rittevon rulers. Once more the Rittevon paranoia showed itself. Their kings could not even bring themselves to trust the guards named after them, but relied on the King's Guard instead. Aly glanced up and found black-uniformed archers with crossbows positioned on the beams from which the hall's lamps were suspended.

Aly was impressed. She had heard of the new commander of the King's Guard, a man named Taybur Sibigat. He had certainly smartened them up since Kyprioth had last brought her here. These were not bored or panicky men, as Hazarin's and Oron's guards had been. These were hard professionals, alert and attentive.

At last she turned her eyes to the dais, where the kingdom's rulers awaited the Balitangs. The dais was reached by a number of broad steps. Two steps up from the floor sat the regents, Princess Imajane and Prince Rubinyan, on low-backed chairs. Aly had seen Imajane before, first at the bedside of her dying father, King Oron. At that time she hadn't appreciated just how imposing Oron's only surviving daughter was. She did now.

The princess was an icily beautiful woman who wore her silvering blond hair in a double-domed style. Her chilly blue eyes were placed under commanding arched brows, and she sat with her chin high, like a queen. Her lips were a vivid red against her white skin, which was further set off by a pink gown under a sleeveless overrobe of white silk bordered with silver. She dripped silver jewelry with pink and gray pearls and blue sapphires.

If only someone could teach these people the meaning of restraint in adornment, Aly thought with a silent sigh. They're like newly ennobled merchants. They just *have* to show everyone they have money.

Ten feet to his wife's right sat Prince Rubinyan, the brother of the man who had killed Duke Mequen the year before. A tall, balding man with hard gray eyes and thin lips, he wore a white silk shirt and hose, and a deep blue tunic with figures of dragons in its weave. Like his wife he wore rings on every finger. His were gold set with rubies, onyx, and sapphires.

Their heads were bare even of the modest gold circle they had the right to wear as prince and princess, but they held themselves as if crowned. Aly wondered if it had occurred to them that their lives might be easier if something happened to Dunevon and they simply grabbed the throne for themselves. From the cold, shining pride that flowed from them, she was willing to bet that it had.

Five steps higher on the dais, the source of their power, King Dunevon, sat uncomfortably on an immense teak throne. He was a bit younger than Elsren, and plainly bored. Aly's heart went out to the child, clad in gold and cream silk, a small crown on his head. He was absorbed in something tucked between his side and the arm of the throne. She suspected he had a toy up there.

A man in the chain mail and black tunic of the King's Guard stood at the king's side in a relaxed posture, observing the room. Around his neck hung the gold chain and gold-framed iron disk that marked him as the Guard's captain. This would be the new man, Taybur Sibigat. Aly memorized his face and the way he stood, then turned her gaze back to the child. She wondered how long the boy had been sitting there and how much longer he would do so quietly. Elsren would have thrown a tantrum by now.

Dunevon kicked his soft leather shoes against the throne. Sibigat reached out a gentle hand and placed it on the child's knee. Dunevon's feet went still. His lower lip came out in a pout. This is no life for such a little fellow, Aly thought.

A chill crept up her spine. If the raka had their way, Dunevon would die. Left alive, he would be someone for dissatisfied nobles to rally around. The raka couldn't afford that.

Winnamine and the other Balitangs had stopped three feet from the foot of the dais. The ladies of the group curtsied, seemingly to Dunevon, while Elsren executed a carefully rehearsed bow. Imajane rose and clasped Winnamine's hands in hers. They kissed one another formally on both cheeks as Rubinyan stood.

"Welcome home, Your Grace, my ladies," said the princess. The room was shaped perfectly. Aly could hear the princess as clearly at the rear as if she stood in front. "Welcome to His Majesty's court."

Aly heard the tap of hard-soled boots on the floor behind her. Gloved hands grasped her elbows. One of the two men who had taken hold of her bent down to whisper in her ear, "Come quietly, wench. Draw attention and we'll make you squeak."

Aly made her eyes wide with fright, bit her lip, and nodded. When the men steered her out of the throne room, she trembled just as Aly Homewood, the lady's maid, would surely do. She was being taken captive for some kind of questioning, that was plain. How forceful would the questioning be? She would hate to *need* Kyprioth's protection against her telling the truth under torture. Out onto the Golden Road they went. The silver shimmer of the Gift wrapped around Aly and the men. Whoever had given her captors their orders did not want anyone to know who they had taken. Only one person in the realm would grab the Balitangs' full-blood luarin maid on her first appearance at the palace: Topabaw.

Letting the men half-carry her quivering body, Aly sank deep into her mind, into the liar's palace she had built in her thoughts all through the winter. Most people thought it was impossible for a Giftless human to fool truth drugs or spells, but it was not. Development of a liar's palace had been a game between her and her beloved adopted uncle Numair, Tortall's most powerful mage, a game she had studied until she could fool even him. While he could have broken her if he'd used all of his immense power, he had only tested the strength of her liar's palace against the normal truth spells. The odds were very long that she would ever be questioned by a mage of his stature.

The farther they went, the more nervously Aly behaved, giving her best interpretation of someone who expected nothing good of those in power. She was babbling questions and protests of innocence while her mind weighed her captors. Something was off about them, something that she ought to have identified already. She looked at each from the corners of her eyes, then finally realized what it was: both men were full-blood luarin. It was a sign that she had been in the Isles for some time, that she had come to expect everyone to be some shade of raka brown.

The men guided Aly eastward, followed silently by three

crows. The buildings here were nondescript, despite the gorgeous landscape. These would not be state areas but working ones, where economy was considered before grandeur. When they stopped, she gauged that they were somewhere near the northeast corner of the palace grounds, right beside the Raka Wall. Her guides stopped at a building that showed only a small plaque set in the wall beside the front door: INTELLIGENCE.

Aly went from trembling to shaking in the guards' hold as they took her inside. They didn't appear to notice, but she knew they would spot it quickly if she didn't act like the others who were brought here did. Inside, the walls gleamed in Aly's Sight with spells for silence and fear. Tears began to leak from her eyes as her body was affected by the spells, but her mind worked as coolly as ever. Her father had taken most of her fourteenth year to make her accustomed to all kinds of fear magic. She would be frightened, but it wouldn't swamp her reason if she held her concentration.

This is going to be tricky, she thought.

The guards propelled her through one broad stone corridor and turned down another. Chained men and women hung from the walls. Some of these people were more than halfway to the Peaceful Realms of the Black God of death. Aly cowered from them, as she was expected to do. She wept harder, from pity, and she made certain to count every one. She would add their sum to Topabaw's and the regents' accounts when the time came to bill them.

She understood that she was meant to notice these people's pain. It confirmed the stories of the spymaster's work that had reached her ears that winter and before, at home in Tortall.

"It is just the worst possible combination," her grandfather Myles had said once, shaking his shaggy head. He was

Tortall's official spymaster or, as his son-in-law liked to call him, the Target. "Duke Lohearn is a spymaster as well as a mage, and he has been at his post for thirty years. He thinks he can do everything. If he can't, he'll just kill the problem. No skill, just power."

Aly thought her grandfather might be right. If Topabaw had gotten lazy, secure in his own reputation, Aly would have an opportunity to knock him from his vital position.

The guards turned down a third hall, which ended at an open door. They pushed Aly inside. As she sprawled, they slammed the door, leaving her alone with the room's occupant.

She looked up at Duke Lohearn Mantawu: the ill-famed Topabaw. He sat on a plain chair, one hand braced on his thigh, one resting on a crude table that held a large parchment book, inkpot and quill, a three-throated lamp that smelled of cheap oil, a pitcher, and a pair of cups. Aly closed her eyes and adjusted her Sight so that the blaze of his magical Gift, added to the spells on the charms that bedecked the man, wouldn't blind her. Fumbling at her sash, she drew out a clean handkerchief and blew her nose.

Under the layers of charms, Aly saw a pallid, bony aristocrat in his late fifties. He had a razor cut of a mouth, small brown eyes, and short steel-gray hair. His cheap black cotton tunic and breeches were shabby and stained. Work clothes, thought Aly. Her Sight read the stains as dried blood and other liquids.

Am I supposed to be impressed that a luarin gets his clothes dirty? Aly wondered, lowering her gaze to the man's scuffed boots. She continued to quiver and weep.

"My dear girl, get off that floor." His voice was suspiciously kind. "It's dirty. There's a stool right beside you. Sit on that."

Aly obeyed, still not looking Topabaw in the eye.

"Isn't that better?" he asked. He opened his book to a page that was already marked. "Let's see. Your name is Aly Homewood, correct?"

Aly nodded, then scrambled to say, "Yes, my lord."

"Very good." He smiled mirthlessly, not parting his lips. "Luarin slave, given to House Balitang with the purchase of a cook on April 24, 462. Formerly a maidservant at Fief Tameran in Tortall. No bids were made for your purchase in the slave market." Icy amusement was in his voice as he added, "I think it would be very different if you were to go to the selling block at present. Some would consider you to be most fetching."

That was supposed to frighten her. She whimpered and cringed. "Please don't sell me, sir," she pleaded. "I've a good place, I'm learning to be a lady's maid—"

"Quiet," he ordered gently.

Aly went instantly silent.

"Taken into exile by Duke Mequen Balitang. Served as goatherd, then maid. Fought for your owners during a kidnap and murder attempt by our prince-regent's brother, Bronau Jimajen. Freed as a result. Now serving as maid to Lady Dovasary Balitang. You're a clever girl, Aly Homewood."

Aly bobbed her head. "Thank you, my lord, sir—"

"Your Grace," he said gently. "I have the rank of duke. Look at me when I speak to you, my dear."

Aly raised her eyes as she was commanded to, still shaking. Gazing at him openly, she realized that he did not look like the Crown's stone hammer. There were dark circles under his eyes. His skin was dry and cracked, his lips bitten and peeling. There was the slightest tremor in his hands. His hair looked greasy, as if he had not washed it for a while. This was a man who had been forced to work hard of late.

Topabaw smiled as she met his eyes. "There. Isn't that more friendly?"

She bobbed her head eagerly.

"Do you know, I am surprised they made you only the maid of the younger daughter," he told Aly. "Such a deed as you did for them, they should at least have given you the post of maid to the older girl, or to Her Grace the duchess."

Aly ducked her head. "I couldn't say, Your Grace." Then she met his eyes again, so he would think she lied, that she *had* thought of a better reward, like a higher position.

"They don't appreciate you." He nodded to a pair of cups and a pitcher on his table. "Pour us both a drink," he commanded. "Some wine will do you good."

Aly slowly rose and did as she was told. In Topabaw's position her da or her grandfather would have done the pouring, to make her feel treated almost as an equal, to flatter her. You're supposed to stroke and slap me, so I won't know what's coming, she thought, exasperated with him already. Inspecting the wine with her Sight, she found the signs of truth spells.

Taking her cup, she settled back onto her stool. It was time to call up her liar's palace. Homewood, homewood, homewood I go, she told herself silently, sinking into her own mind as if it were a pool of water. She surrounded herself with the mind of Aly Homewood. Part of her split off to watch and advise. The rest of her awareness filled the liar's palace. She sipped from the cup, pretending she liked the taste of the wine. She also pretended not to notice that while she drank, he did not, though he put his cup to his lips. The spell in the drink went straight to work, making her light-headed and relaxed.

"Does it not irk you, to be at the beck and call of raka?" Topabaw asked softly, more confident. "To be under the orders of that head footman, that cook, those armsmen, when your skin is as white as that of the duchess?"

"It's not my place to say, Your Grace," she said, her voice slurred from the drug.

"You may speak freely here," said Topabaw graciously. "Drink up."

She drank. "I mean, sir, Your Grace—" She giggled, then pressed her arm to her mouth to stop herself. "This is quite nice," she told him, and emptied the cup. He refilled it. Leaning forward as if this bone-pale man were her friend, Aly confided, "It was this way at home, you know. Everyone else gets the good stuff. I get the odds and ends. It wasn't *my* fault my mother left, stupid slut. And now?" She made a disgusted noise and flapped her hand as if driving something away. "Nothing for me again, ever. You know, we have these dark-skinned folk at home. Bazhir, they call themselves. Sand lice, *I* call them. Riding about like lords when *we* own *their* lands. Acting like you're dirt while they eye your bum." She snorted a laugh.

"The Bazhir?" asked the spymaster, folding his hands on his desk.

"These raka, too," she said earnestly. "They're just the same. I want to tell them, Who owns who? Seems to me we luarin beat your lot like drums, miss, so don't you go looking down your nose at me." Her internal distant watcher shook her head over the look on Topabaw's face. His contemptuous smile and satisfied pose told her that she'd said just what he wanted to hear. He didn't even respect her enough to keep it from his face.

"Tell me, where were you born?"

In her liar's palace, a door opened to show her the answer. "Ginine," she said, "north of Port Legann in Tortall. Didn't want to work there. Too many sand lice, if you take my meaning. Then I come here. Sand lice, jungle lice, they're all the same."

He asked the questions she expected. She answered all of them from her liar's palace. The girl who lived there was small and sordid, a petty servant and thief with a raisin for a heart.

"There is a way you may better yourself," Topabaw explained softly. "One that might grant you revenge on those who show you so little respect. If you will perform a small service for me, I will do one for you. Her Highness is always in search of pure-blood luarin girls for her household."

Aly sat up straight, her eyes blazing. "You'd take me from that pen of mongrels?" she asked eagerly.

"You must remain a while longer," Topabaw said, leaning forward to hold her with his eyes. "We believe there is plotting afoot in that household. Our other spies there bring us stories that hardly seem likely. I believe those spies may be compromised, or worse, that they have betrayed me. I count on *you* to find out the truth."

Distant Aly Saw that he lied about spies in the household. She also knew he wanted her to believe him, to keep her from lying to him.

"They'll cut me up if I'm caught," Liar Aly pointed out. "That's a lot of risk for just a promise of 'someday.'"

He smirked and reached into a pocket, drawing out an ordinary leather purse that clinked. "Will this make the risk more bearable?"

Aly seized it greedily and counted the coins—silver and copper, no gold, which might be suspicious if she was searched. There were listening spells on the lot of them. "This is all?" she asked.

Topabaw slammed his fist down onto the table. She jumped. "You overstep!" he barked.

Aly cringed. "Forgive me, Your Grace—I don't know why I'm so loose-tongued," she told him, kneeling on the floor. "Normally I keep my own counsel. I didn't mean any disrespect, I swear. Forgive me, Your Grace!" Distant Aly thought, You ham-handed brute.

Topabaw smiled and sat back. "Mind your place," he ordered. "You will report every third day to Master Grosbeak on Gigit Lane. Depending on what you bring to him, you will receive some manner of payment. And don't try to lie to me, wench," he said coldly, pointing a bony finger at her. "My other spies in your household will be truthful about *your* actions, if about nothing else! Get out."

Aly got out, bowing over and over until she was out of that room, then fled down the hall, bolting past the chained captives on her way to the door. Outside she raced down the path to a clump of trees. She collapsed against one, out of sight, and relaxed, feeling the last traces of the spell vanish from her body. Most such spells were short-lived, so that the person they were used on could return quickly to normal. "Homewood, homewood, homewood I go," she whispered, listening to the shriek of distant Stormwings and the calls of distant crows. Slowly her real self rose from the liar's palace, freeing her mind and concentration.

Waiting, breathing, identifying the scents that met her nose—cumin, roses, jasmine, horse urine, rust—she reassembled herself. Only when that was done did she begin to turn over the interview in her mind. He hadn't made her swear in blood. She assumed Kyprioth would protect her from the penalities for those who broke that magical oath, but Topabaw's omitting it before he'd dismissed her made her even more contemptuous of him than she'd already been.

Ham-handed *and* lazy, she thought with disgust while she stared at the leaves overhead. And sloppy. Maybe he was something once, but no longer.

With a sigh Aly got to her feet, startling a marmoset clan into flight among the trees. "Sorry," she called, and walked down the flagstone path to Golden Road. She ambled down to the Robing Pavilion, sidestepping peacocks and crowned pigeons.

She heard a boisterous call overhead. The three crows who had followed her, seeing through the magical veil over Aly and her captors, were leaving now that she was free and unharmed. She watched as they flew toward a Stormwing that soared overhead, calling insults. The Stormwing jinked in midair, then—with no other Stormwings nearby to watch his back against the crows—fled.

4

The Pavilion of Delightful Pleasures

When Aly looked into the Throne Hall, it was empty. The maids at the Robing Pavilion told her that her ladies and their maids had gone to the Pavilion of Delightful Pleasures. Aly nodded as she tucked Topabaw's purse among their boxes, grateful the Balitang party was still here. She could put off the inevitable questions about where she'd been until tonight. Casually she crossed the Golden Road to the pavilion that lay beside the Throne Hall. Aly knew better than to enter through the porch that opened onto the Golden Road. That was a stage, designed to display the court while important guests presented themselves. With the palace map in her mind's eye, she found a small bridge spanning the creek that cupped the pavilion. A well-trodden path led her to the servants' entrance. As she passed into the building, she walked into an invisible cloud of scent: lotus, rose, sandalwood, and lily as well as cherries, mangoes, and cooked chicken.

Servants pointed Aly to a gallery at the end of a long, narrow hall. Everywhere Aly saw spells for listening and seeing, but their gleam was faint. When was the last time they were renewed? she wondered, seeing glimmers of the spells. Don't they know you have to renew spells every few years? Or are they so sure their spies among the servants will report what is said that they don't bother?

In the servants' gallery the carved screen that served as one of the walls allowed servants to see the nobles beyond. They also allowed the nobles to see their own people, in case they needed something the pavilion did not provide.

Aly took the entire gallery in a second time. The mages of the Chain had been at work here. Pembery, Boulaj, and some other raka servants stood in one corner, talking. Aly heard nothing and could not read their lips. An entire corner of the servants' area was marked out with spells to counter the Crown's magic. These spells were so carefully hidden under other spells that Crown mages might not detect them. The edge of the silent corner was marked out on the floor by a line of boards held in place by a pair of pegs at each end. On this line only, the pegs were perceptibly lighter than the wood in which they were set, the only boards in the floor to show such a marking. It was subtle but effective. Aly approved. It was always nice to see a well-done piece of spy work.

It was also a powerful illustration of how the raka used their magic after the luarin conquest. Raka magic was shaped by subtlety, crafted by mages who spent their lives hiding things from other mages. To those who wielded their Gift as the mages of the Eastern and Southern Lands had been taught, raka magic seemed weak, good only for simple tasks. Its symbols were different, its spells far quieter, shaped for that effect over three hundred years of practice and development, with death for the raka mage who drew a luarin mage's attention.

As she eyed her surroundings, the other servants turned

to look at her. Boulaj waved Aly over to the protected corner. As soon as Aly stepped past those marked boards, she could hear Boulaj speak clearly, when her words had been indistinct outside them. "This is Aly, Lady Dovasary's new maid. She is one of us."

The woman next to Boulaj frowned. "A luarin? She can never be one of us."

"That you must ask the god, if you dare," Boulaj informed her pleasantly. "In our household, we do as he bids us. He chose to make Aly his messenger." To Aly Boulaj said, "This is Vereyu. She represents our folk in the palace." When Vereyu protested the use of her real name and position, Boulaj said, "Ask the god about Aly's faithfulness, if you won't believe me. Go on, ask him."

Aly looked at Vereyu and raised an eyebrow. Most people of sense preferred not to call on specific gods unless matters were dire. There was always the chance the god might not care for the summons.

It seemed Vereyu was a woman of sense. She tightened her broad mouth but did not open it to call on Kyprioth. A stocky part-blood raka, Vereyu looked both intelligent and hard. Her clothing was unremarkable, but her hair drew Aly's eye. The long copper pins that secured her black hair in its coil at the back of her head housed lethally sharp miniature knives.

"You don't go near the throne with those, do you?" she asked, gently tapping one of the pins' copper knobs. "Surely the weapon alarm spells would detect them."

Vereyu swung around almost casually, reaching for the arm Aly had just used, ready to grip it and twist it up behind Aly's back. As Vereyu moved, Aly took just one step to the side, letting Vereyu's hands slide uselessly past. When Vereyu moved straight into another attack, Aly took a second step just out of range, guessing that Vereyu would lunge at her. As Vereyu did, Aly gripped a part of her collarbone that would hurt exquisitely if pressed. Vereyu went still.

"Play nicely, if you please," she murmured in Vereyu's ear. "I'm sorry I'm not to your taste. Do you want everyone to see that we know unarmed combat? Only think of how they would gossip at such undovelike behavior on the part of servants."

Vereyu considered her next move. Aly glanced at Boulaj, who was covering a smile with her hand.

Suddenly Vereyu nodded. Aly waited for a moment, alert for a trick, then let her go.

"If they knew real doves, they'd stop telling us serving-women should act like them," Vereyu said, her voice very dry. "What is it the god uses you for, anyway?"

Aly batted her eyes at the woman. "To guard the ladies," she replied. There was no reason anyone should know her real place in the rebellion if they did not already know. "And a bit of this and that."

Vereyu snorted. "You're the god's, all right," she muttered. "You're just his sort."

Why, thank you, Kyprioth said. The sound of his voice made all the servants in the corner jump, though no one else in the gallery appeared to have heard.

Establishing my credentials with the palace raka? she asked Kyprioth silently as the servants who'd heard him bowed their heads briefly. *I was doing well enough on my own.*

I just wanted to remove any lingering doubts, he said, apparently to her alone. *Better safe than sorry.*

Aly giggled at the thought of the Trickster's ever caring about safety. When she felt his presence fade, she looked around. "I'm famished," she remarked. "Do you people ever feed a girl?"

Vereyu raised a hand and beckoned. A maid came over to them with a tray of fried dumplings and fruit. As Aly ate, she looked around the room. Servants flirted in corners, sat on cushions and chairs and gossiped, or watched their masters in the room beyond. Once she'd cleaned her hands, Aly drifted over to the screen to have a look at the nobility.

Vereyu followed her. "They are not so smug as they were last autumn," she murmured in a voice that dripped venom and satisfaction. "They have lost too many tax collectors and couriers. There have been five riots in the Downwind District of Rajmuat since Midwinter, three of them coming when the Crown sent troops to take raka mages and leaders captive. The Crown's armies have gone without pay for three months."

"I assume this means you take the god's word for me," Aly whispered in return. She had already positioned herself, and thus Vereyu, out of range of two faded listening spells. "How do you know I'm not one of his jokes?"

"Because he needs us too much to joke," replied Vereyu. "Because he needs all the victories we can win for him if he is to retake the Isles. We were great, once." She nodded toward the sprawling chamber on the other side of the screen. "All this splendor was built by *our* people. The world came to these pavilions to discover the true meaning of beauty, when our queens ruled here."

Aly looked into the gallery. Vereyu was right. The Pavilion of Delightful Pleasures was extraordinary. The walls were fashioned of pale marble and lined with arched windows that extended to the floor, the windows magically spelled to keep animals and insects at bay. A tribe of golden lion tamarins sat on the rail of the outer walkway and watched mournfully as servants passed the windows carrying fruit.

Inside, there was a raised dais at the center of the room,

but Aly saw no thrones. Instead the young king sat on a cushion and directed playmates as four boys of his own age, including Elsren, moved toy soldiers and immortals into position all around an intricately carved fortress. Petranne sat beside the king and watched as Dunevon moved the castle's defenders and their weapons along its stone battlements.

Princess Imajane sat in a backless chair in front of the dais, talking to Lady Nuritin. Between them was a small table laden with food and drinks. The ladies chatted, sipped, and nibbled while raka slaves waited on them. Aly read both women's lips: they were talking of Winnamine's "magical transformation" from country lady to noble courtier. The duchess herself sat across the room, talking with other noble mothers as she watched Sarai mingle with a bright cluster of young men and women.

Aly felt Vereyu shift position. "Watch yourself," the raka whispered to Aly, and moved off. Aly could tell that someone else had come up behind her: someone large, because she felt his body heat to the top of her skull. He smelled of soap lightly scented with sandalwood and cinnamon. She pretended she did not notice him, though she kept her ears sharp for any movement that he would make, and continued to survey the large room.

She found Dove near the far rear corner, seated between two older luarin noblemen and engaged in a conversation that was every bit as animated as the ones Sarai was holding. The man on Dove's right had to be in his seventies, bald, the white hair on the sides of his head and of his beard clipped neatly short. His eyes were set in fans of wrinkles. Despite the day's warmth, he was dressed in velvet and wool. Around his neck he wore a heavy chain with a pendant that was half a golden sun face and half a white gold moon face.

"Baron Qovold Engan," a light voice said in Aly's ear.

She gasped, jumped, and spun, as if she had not heard the man come over to speak to her. She stared up into the face of Taybur Sibigat, captain of the King's Guard. He was as tall as her adopted uncle Numair, who stood six feet five inches in his stocking feet. Unlike her uncle, Taybur had a solid build without any of Numair's angular gawkiness. He wore his chain mail as easily as other men wore cloth, despite the growing heat. "He's the royal astronomer, and your young mistress's former tutor in cartography and astronomy. At the moment, he's not the regents' favorite person. He's told them that there will be two lunar eclipses and a solar eclipse this summer, which some people might see as ill omens. That other fellow, next to Lady Dovasary? That's Duke Vurquan Nomru. Old Iron Bum was his nickname when he commanded the army. He was one of your lady's favorite chess partners before she was exiled. They tell me that for a girl of twelve, she played as well as any adult."

Aly could see how Dove's other companion might earn such a nickname. His nose was an eagle's beak set under two sharp brown eyes, his sensuous mouth set in a firm line. His clothing was simple bronze cotton and silk. Like the other male nobles, he wore no sword or dagger in the royal presence, but there were dents in his belt where they normally hung. For a Kyprin noble he showed uncommon restraint in his jewelry, keeping it to a single gold earring, a chain, and gold rings on his index fingers and thumbs.

"Excuse me, my lord, but why do you say such things to me?" Aly inquired, bobbing as much of a curtsy as anyone in a sarong could manage. "I'm just a maid."

"And I am just a friendly fellow," he replied. "I'm Taybur Sibigat, captain of the King's Guard." He smiled at Aly, revealing small, pearly teeth. "I wanted to compliment you on your inspection of the Throne Hall," he added. "You spotted each man I had there, including the ones on the roof beams, where no one else ever looks. And you found every exit." When Aly took a step back, frowning, he shrugged. "Spells around the dais help us to see clearly throughout the hall."

Aly gave him a trembling smile. "I've no idea what you're talking about, my lord," she said nervously, though inwardly she was fascinated. It sounded as if he'd guessed she was a spy of some kind.

"Of course you don't know what I'm talking about," he said agreeably. He was chubby cheeked like a boy. He wore his dark, curly hair cut short over his high forehead. His eyes were brown and observant, and his mouth had smile curves tucked into the corners. "Call me Taybur. We'll see a lot of each other if Their Highnesses have their way."

Aly continued to play the part of the not-very-bright country girl. "I don't know how you can say as much, my lord," she replied, deliberately neglecting to use his name. "My mistress is here today because the whole family was summoned, but she's not of an age to be going to court things. And whyever would a great man like yourself take an interest in a poor little maid like me?"

Taybur's smile lit his face and eyes. "That's very good," he remarked with approval. "I couldn't have done it better myself. Now, if I were being a nice man, one who'd let you believe I'm not suspicious of you, I would say that I like to meet all the very pretty girls who come my way. It would even be true. I'm quite fond of very pretty girls. But we both know that there is far more to you than that."

Aly looked down, the picture of the demure servant. He does suspect me, she thought. He's been trained. "My lord, you talk in riddles, I swear!"

"Very well," he said agreeably, leaning against a corner

post. "You look like a girl who knows her riddles. I understand your name is Aly Homewood, and I know you were once a slave." He pointed to the faint scar around Aly's neck, the mark of a slave collar. "Today you're Lady Dovasary Balitang's maid. Your accent . . ." He cocked his head, studying her with interest. "Tortall, southeastern coast."

"I come from there, my lord," she admitted meekly. She kept her eyes down to hide her growing delight. Somehow Taybur Sibigat had recognized her for a player of the spies' game, but he didn't seem interested in exposing her. She had to try to convince him that he was wrong, but it was lovely to meet someone who spoke the language she had learned in the cradle, the give-and-take between those who sought information. Glancing around the room from the corners of her eyes, she saw that most of the servants watched them warily but without alarm. She even saw liking on some of those faces. This man wasn't as feared as the regents or Topabaw, then.

He tugged on his ringless earlobe. "I'm trying to narrow it down—you're not a Carthaki agent," he murmured, thinking aloud. "They have a, a special whiff about them, don't you agree? A well-polished one. They do unctuous better even than a courtier. Tyrans are a slippery lot. Usually they just ooze around corners. It comes of living in a swamp. But you . . ." He tipped his head from side to side. "The Whisper Man of Tortall. Are you one of his, or have you sold your services elsewhere?"

It would have taken much more than her father's nickname to make Aly twitch. She began to shake her head and continued to shake it as he asked if she served the Marenite, Yamani, Gallan, or Tusaine spy networks.

"You must believe me, I'm just a servant, my lord, just a servant, and I know naught of spying or whispering or anything like that!" she babbled. "I'm just a poor girl from Tortall, making my way in the world!" She glanced up at him from under her brows. "If you suspect me so, why haven't you arrested me or given me over to Topabaw?" she demanded. It was a risky point to make when she was supposed to be terrified out of her wits. She simply could not resist needling him a little in return.

He shrugged. "I won't do the man's work for him. Besides, Topabaw has notified me, through the prince regent, that my assistance and advice are unwelcome."

Hmm, thought Aly, I smell rivalry here. When two powerful men dislike each other, things can slip through the cracks between them.

"Besides," Taybur continued, "I'm sure you'll get to know him soon enough."

Too late, Aly thought, thinking of the purse of coins she had stowed in the Balitang luggage. Inside she grinned broadly. She hadn't realized how much she had yearned for someone who could meet her at her own level. She would be even more careful knowing that Taybur Sibigat had an eye on her. Unlike Topabaw, Sibigat did not hear only what he wished to hear. It would be much more fun to outwit someone who knew what he was doing. She'd only have to worry that the regents might give Taybur Sibigat the spymaster's job if she brought about Topabaw's fall.

Taybur leaned down until his lips were close enough to her ear that the feel of his breath raised goose bumps on her skin. "Whatever game you play at here—and let's just assume you denied it with great vigor and go about our day—please, understand. All I care about is the safety of the king. Conduct whatever games you wish on these palace grounds with my blessing. Topabaw can use the exercise. But sniff around His Majesty, and suddenly I won't like you anymore."

Oh, dear, Aly thought guiltily. He thinks I'm just a regular spy. He doesn't know what the raka are up to, or if he does, he doesn't think it will come to anything.

"You frighten me, my lord," she whispered, keeping her eyes on the ground.

"I told you to call me Tay—"

Whatever else he had meant to say was cut off by a yelp from the dais. Taybur left the servants' gallery at a swift pace. King Dunevon, not liking the way the game of storm the castle was proceeding, had kicked one of the young generals. A seasoned courtier even at that age, the boy he'd kicked knew better than to hit his king. He fell on Elsren instead, pounding the smaller child. The other two "generals" entered the fistfight. Dunevon jumped from his chair, shrieking with glee as all across the room female relatives converged on the dais.

Winnamine got there first, thrusting one boy into his mother's arms and holding another by one arm as she scooped Elsren from the pile. Rubinyan started across the room for the king, but Taybur Sibigat was there ahead of him. Gently the big man hoisted the king onto one hip like an experienced nursemaid.

When Rubinyan reached them, his face dark with anger, Taybur spoke quietly. Aly read his lips as he explained to Rubinyan, His Majesty is wearied. I'm sure Your Highness will forgive him. He missed his nap.

Dunevon, if you can't control yourself . . . , Rubinyan said angrily.

He can when he's had his nap, said Taybur, still the picture of goodwill. He walked toward the hall that led out of the building as Dunevon began to howl. Everywhere men bowed and ladies curtsied to the floor as their king passed.

Taybur walked by the screened-in servants' gallery. "I know, I know, you're tired," he told the boy shrieking in his arms. "Any normal person would be."

Aly pursed her lips. That the king's closest guardian was fond of him was a complication she could not like. Her mind knew that the odds were very good that Dunevon might be killed in the rebellion, Dunevon and maybe even Elsren. She did not want the painful cost of those two young lives on her conscience and heart.

"I hope you weren't looking for romance in that area," Vereyu said as she took Taybur's place next to Aly. "He lets nothing get in the way of his duty to the king. A number of our young ladies have sighed over it repeatedly since he left off courting them."

"I don't sigh very well," Aly replied. "And I've no idea why he singled me out." She continued to scan the room as it quieted and nursemaids came to take charge of the king's young companions. Rihani took Elsren and Petranne back to the Robing Pavilion, chatting with the maid who half carried a still-protesting lordling. Dove had not stirred from her spot between Baron Engan and Duke Nomru. Reading their lips, Aly realized they were talking about the meager winter rice crop. She shook her head. Dove had the strangest interests.

A muttering from the other servants drew Aly's attention to the corridor that led to the main entrance. An immortal made its way into the hall where the regents sat. Aly stared at the unmistakable creature visible through the carved screen as it walked over to Princess Imajane. Even the nobles were turning to stare at the basilisk, some nervously, some in wonder. He was seven feet tall, which was average for a basilisk, with gray skin as pebbly as if it were made of beads. A hint of folds at his chin told the observer that he was young, with only two or three centuries on him. He wore a chain with a loop on it around his belly, to keep his lengthy tail from dragging on the ground. His eyes were gray and wise, with a cat's slit pupils. He bowed gracefully to the princess and the ladies around her.

Aly reminded herself to gape as if she'd never seen a basilisk. This was not just any basilisk. This basilisk Aly knew as well as she knew her family.

"He is a basilisk," one of the other maids told Aly. The smug superiority on her face made it plain that she thought Aly gawped like a country bumpkin. "The monarchs of Tortall sent him with gifts to honor His Majesty's ascension to the throne and the regents' appointment. Wonderful toys that wind up and walk about, and gems for Their Highnesses. You don't see that many basilisks, even here at court." She sighed. "He's leaving soon. A pity. He's much nicer than some of the other special envoys."

"You mean he doesn't pinch your bottom, Mimisem," joked one of the other maids.

Aly watched Tkaa curiously. To uninformed eyes, the basilisk might look plump, as the pouch on his belly bulged. What was Tkaa carrying? wondered Aly. Not weapons. Nobody who can turn folk to stone with a sound needs weapons. Unless he's ill, perhaps?

Imajane smiled up at the immortal, who had deftly stopped just far enough from her that she would not get a crick in her neck as she met his eyes. She chatted with him briefly. When the basilisk went to pay his respects to Prince Rubinyan across the room, Nuritin rose and beckoned to Winnamine. Immediately the duchess walked over to Imajane and curtsied. With a graceful movement of her hand, Imajane invited Winnamine to take the seat Nuritin had just left.

Aly spared a glance for a pudgy man who whispered in Rubinyan's ear until Tkaa reached the prince. Noting how the fellow stood so that no one could see his lips moving, Aly was sure this was Sevmire Ambau, Rubinyan's private spymaster, the one who he'd asked to keep watch on his own brother. After memorizing Sevmire's face, Aly turned her attention back to Winnamine and Imajane.

"And so the Balitangs return to court," the princess said with a smile. A maid glided forward to pour out goblets of wine for the two ladies. Aly looked at Tkaa, then gave a mental shrug. He would know where she was if he needed to find her, and she was certain that he would. She didn't worry about Tkaa giving her identity away. The basilisk was one of her father's best operatives.

She continued to inspect the room. Here and there groups of people sat or stood. They talked, drank, and ate as slaves circulated with trays full of delights. It was obvious that, although they seemed absorbed in their chatter, they were equally observant of both regents. While Imajane and Winnamine talked, Rubinyan stood in a far rear corner. In addition to Tkaa, a group of noblemen attended the prince regent. Rubinyan was a listener, not a talker. He kept a gold cup in one hand, often masking his expression by looking into it.

Aly read the men's lips. They discussed pirate raids along the islands. One man accused another of taking a profit from pirates. The other told him that he would do better to mind his own pirates. The whole thing might have spun out of control had Rubinyan not put a hand on one debater's shoulder and smiled at the other, saying that he would ask the navy to step up its patrols. He handled them like an accomplished diplomat. Aly was impressed.

Forget your pirates, another noble grumbled as Aly read his lips. What I want to know is, what's being done about our missing tax collectors? The flooding this winter swept away three of the bridges in my province, and I have no way to pay for new ones! I need tax money!

You'll be missing more than bridges before the summer's done, thought Aly. A peal of laughter drew her attention to Sarai. She stood at the heart of a group of young men and women, all of whom were applauding some joke. The men's presence did not surprise Aly: Sarai drew men like honey drew bees. Her surprise lay in the number of women of Sarai's age or a little older, women who clearly liked Sarai as well.

Many of the group were luarin who obviously didn't feel, as some of their elders seemed to, that they lowered themselves by association with a half-raka. It was too early yet to tell, but if the younger luarin were more open to friendship with someone of raka blood, they might yet avoid the bloody revolution that Aly feared. It was all too easy to imagine these smug, wealthy people as the dead, the smooth columns and gleaming floor marred with the bloody gouges of swords and the black sooty splashes of magical fire. It was Aly's nightmare. She just hoped and prayed Ulasim and the rebel leaders could keep the rebellion from turning into an all-out massacre.

A brown-skinned man in his twenties was bowing over Sarai's hand. He was dressed like a Carthaki, in a short-sleeved yellow tunic that hung below his knees and sandals that laced up. His black hair was oiled and combed back from his forehead, then held in a horsetail with a gold and amber clasp. He wore heavy gold cuffs inlaid with enamel and a broad gold collar set with amber and lapis. Aly read his lips as he told Sarai to have pity for a man smitten hard by her loveliness when he was far from home. His jewelry wasn't as bright as his lively brown eyes.

Vereyu came to stand beside Aly. "Ah, I see the Carthaki has found our lady. Let's hope he doesn't break her heart."

"I think she's guarding her heart more this year than she

ever did," murmured Aly. "A Carthaki, you say?"

Vereyu smiled. "He's the most amazing flirt. Lord Zaimid Hetnim, the youngest mage to be made head of the Imperial University's Healers' Wing. A close friend of his emperor and some kind of distant cousin to the imperial family. He is taking the chance to learn healing techniques used in other realms before he is made the emperor's chief healer."

"He's a bold one," commented Aly. Zaimid had yet to let go of Sarai's hand.

"That's how you know he isn't from here," Vereyu said, bitterness in her voice. "He'll flirt with raka."

Zaimid released Sarai and let another man move in to greet her. On Sarai's lips Aly read the joke she cast over one shoulder to a female friend, "Have the men here gotten so much more handsome, or am I just unused to it after a year in the hinterlands?"

A young man wearing gold rings on every finger stepped close to Sarai to whisper in her ear.

Vereyu grunted. "Count Ferdolin Tomang. The family holds most of Jerykun Isle, and that means most of the sunset butterfly trade." Aly looked at her and raised her eyebrows in a silent question. Vereyu, understanding, added, "Mages use the butterflies for fair wind and treasure spells. In all the world they are found only on Jerykun."

Against the wall near Sarai's group, a matron with young Ferdolin's eyes and nose snapped her fan open with a crack that drew glances from all over the room. Ferdolin himself never turned away from Sarai to look, even when the fan snap was followed by an intent glare.

"Ah," Vereyu said, amused. "The Dowager Countess Tomang is unhappy. No part-bloods for *her* precious darling!"

Aunt Nuritin hove into Aly's view, like a stately vessel on a cruise, pausing to exchange smiles or a word. Her course brought her to a stop at the empty bench next to Countess Tomang. She eased into the spot and murmured in the countess's ear. Nuritin's hand obscured her mouth, so Aly couldn't tell what her exact words were, but she saw the countess's eyes flick to the dais, where the toy castle still stood, then to Sarai. Her fan quivered. She closed it with a much gentler snap and used it to beckon to a maid with a tray of drinks. The two older women each took one of the delicate crystal glasses and smiled at one another, then drank.

"Well!" said Vereyu, plainly startled. "Apparently Elsren's sister is a better catch than Mequen's half-raka girl child. The year before last she did everything but send him to gather butterflies to separate Ferdy from Sarai."

"May I ask you something?" Aly beckoned Vereyu to follow her to the magically protected corner. Both of them stood with their backs to the room. Boulaj and the other maids and servants were talking casually among themselves. "Have you someone in service here that you *know* is reporting to Topabaw?"

Vereyu's brows knitted together. "How could you—"

Aly smiled. "There is always at least one," she said. "I take it you've isolated him from important information?"

"He knows nothing we do not wish him to know. Now that your ladies have returned to Rajmuat, we were going to eliminate him," Vereyu replied, clearly puzzled. "Most of us voted to dispose of him in one of the streams outside the wall at the dark of the moon."

Aly remembered the flesh-eating fish and shivered. "That would be wasteful," she told Vereyu firmly. "Where does he work?" When the woman hesitated, Aly raised an eyebrow. "The god trusts me," she murmured. "Your general"—the raka code name for Ulasim—"trusts me."

"In the gardens of the Gray Palace," Vereyu said.

Aly smiled, and wondered if Kyprioth was helping to smooth her way. "I need you to do something," she said, her mind flicking through each aspect of her idea. "Two of your people should stop near the place where this spy works. Have you servants who work in the regents' rooms and in the places they take private meals?"

Vereyu nodded, fascinated.

"What your people will whisper, seemingly unaware that he is near, is that they have overheard the regents discuss Topabaw. They couldn't quite tell what was said, but they know Her Highness was unhappy about something, and His Highness mentioned 'new blood.' Don't let him see your people, for the sake of their lives. And then you will let him report to his master. For the present, that will be enough."

She glanced at Vereyu's face and saw astonishment there.

"You may ask your general if it's permissible, but do it quickly, if you please," Aly said. "Before Topabaw finds a way to break through our security."

"Oh, no," Vereyu replied, shaking her head. "No, there's no need to consult the general. You want Topabaw believing the regents are losing confidence in him. And best of all, it will come from one of his own spies." She smiled slowly, the expression putting light in her eyes. "I should have thought of it. I might try a few such rumors myself."

"One or two won't hurt," Aly admitted. "Don't overdo. Topabaw will be hearing more, I'm certain, and not just from the palace."

Vereyu shook her head in bewilderment. "Yes, you belong to the god, all right," she whispered. Looking sidelong at Aly, she asked, "Are you sure you're not him?"

Aly grinned. "No. My sense of fashion is so much better than his."

About to go in search of the privy, Aly halted when Imajane raised her voice. "Am I to believe my ears?" she asked, her voice brittle ice. "I grant to your stepdaughter and your son an honor that any other parent here would love to receive, and you refuse me?"

Winnamine bowed her head. "Your Highness, please. While in your wisdom you have banished mourning dress, the truth is that I still mourn my duke. His children are my mainstay. I am honored beyond all words that you invite my son to live with the king as part of his court, and that you wish Lady Sarai as a lady-in-waiting. I know how many of our friends would love such positions for their children." She swept her arm open to include the other people in the room. "Can you forgive a mother's weakness? Let me keep my children by me for a while longer?"

Imajane drummed elegant nails on the arm of her chair. "They would receive the best care, the best living that a girl and a boy could wish in our household. Sarai would be an ornament to our court and an asset to her half brother. And after all, Elsren *is* His Majesty's heir. Life is uncertain. Dunevon is healthy and strong, but so apparently was King Hazarin. Elsren will not receive the royal education he requires in your house."

Bodies shifted in the outer room. Thinking like her warrior mother, Aly realized that the ranks of nobles were changing their positions. Sarai was the first of the young people to drift over, understandably, since she was under discussion. Aly noted that Prince Rubinyan came up in support of his wife, placing gentle hands on Imajane's shoulders. Dove almost unnoticeably flanked the men who supported the prince regent until she stood at her mother's back. There was plenty of space there. The ladies who formed the princess's court had moved back as if Winnamine had the plague.

Nuritin came up, an army in her own person, to stand next to Dove. Aly was starting to fear that Winnamine had no other support when Dove's friend Duke Nomru walked briskly to stand between Nuritin and Sarai. There was a shift of color: suddenly Countess Tomang and her son glided over as if they meant to join an interesting conversation. They took positions near Winnamine.

Vereyu told Aly and Boulaj the names of other nobles who went to stand with the duchess: Lord and Lady Wesedi, Lady Adona, and Lord and Lady Obemaek. In the end, Winnamine had representatives of fifteen noble houses to support her, even if it was in silence. Baron Engan kept away, Aly noticed, as did Tkaa and about thirty other men and women. Still, those who stood with the duchess were among the most powerful families in the realm; Aly recognized their names from her winter's study. They were telling the regents that they would back Winnamine.

Imajane looked from Winnamine to each of her silent supporters. Times were uncertain enough that Imajane must be thinking hard about whether she could afford to offend these wealthy people. The princess's mouth was a thin, tight line. Aly saw the knuckles of Rubinyan's hands whiten as he pressed his wife's shoulders. She looked back and up at him, then turned and forced a smile onto her lips.

"I fear you subject your son to inconvenience, allowing him to travel to the palace and back each day, instead of dwelling here as the Lelin, Uniunu, and Obeliten lads will, but there." Imajane shook her head. "In my eagerness to have such adornments as your children at court, I forgot your recent bereavement. I hope that the wounds of your heart soon heal." She gave a razor of a smile to Sarai. "Perhaps you will grace us with your presence in the fall, Lady Sarai."

Sarai bobbed a small curtsy, veiling her eyes with her

lashes. "Your Highness honors me," she replied softly. "And I thank you for your kindness to our family."

Imajane graciously inclined her head. "I trust that you, and your stepmother, and your sister Dovasary will join us at the palace the night of the lunar eclipse. Baron Engan, our astronomer, tells us that your sister is quite enamored of such things. It will be an agreeable night's entertainment and a marvel for those of us who worship the Goddess to see her veil her face with a maiden's modesty."

Oh, so that's the tale they're telling, Aly thought. Traditionally lunar eclipses were viewed as unlucky, a blurring of the Goddess's view of her daughters. Imajane was trying to rewrite centuries of belief.

You have to admire her vision, Aly told herself. She thinks big. Or maybe she's just crazy enough to believe it's the Goddess whispering in her mind.

The duchess rose. "We accept your kind invitation, Your Highness. You are too good to exiles. I do fear I am overtired. Our journey was long, and we only arrived yesterday." Her tone was as even and gracious as if she had just complimented the princess's hair, not defied her moments before. "If I may have your leave to withdraw?"

Imajane's eyes glittered like sapphires as they rested on Winnamine. "But only for the moment, Your Grace," she said with another tight smile. "We expect to have your company in the future, too, Winnamine Balitang, at our party and on other occasions. Your presence at court has been missed." She deliberately did not look at the duchess's supporters. "We need to draw you gently from your mourning, and give you other thoughts to occupy your mind."

Prince Rubinyan smiled. "In the meantime, Captain Sibigat will send troops to escort young Elsren to the palace and home each day," he said, his voice smooth as honey. "We shall care for him as if he were our own."

Winnamine curtsied deeply to them both. Nuritin, Sarai, and Dove did the same. Only when the princess nodded did they move to leave.

Aly's mind worked busily as she helped Dove to change for the ride home. That silent assembly of nobles had been most instructive. She had seen it: what might she do with it? Aly knew that everyone in that room had brought away the same lesson she had. The regents needed the luarin nobility to stand with them, united. They could not afford to offend them over something as apparently small as the appointment of a young woman to the princess regent's ladies-in-waiting.

Aly had noticed something else. Very few of the nobles who had moved to shield the duchess's back had hesitated. They had acted as if they'd been prepared to do just that, which meant they had expected something of the kind. In that group that had stood behind Winnamine, Aly had not seen a majority of the court. Those people might be a quarter of the luarin nobility in the Isles, perhaps less. The regents were in so much trouble elsewhere in the Isles that they had to tread lightly rather than punish even this small group of defiant luarin.

As the family met their horses and guards by the Gate of Victory, Aly went through the lists of nobles whose names she had learned from the raka, along with information about their interests, alliances, and political positions. One of them had to have a weakness she could use to turn the regents against him or her, though it might take some doing, particularly if Rubinyan could control his wife's temper.

"It's like rocks," her grandfather Myles had taught her. "Many of them have what the sculptors and quarrymen call cleavage points, spots you may strike with hammer and chisel to break off slabs of stone. Communities and organizations are the same. Find the right cleavage point and you might break them in half, or even into splinters."

If I can divide the luarin nobility by working on the princess regent, I might divide her from her cool-headed prince, Aly thought as their party clattered over the second bridge that crossed the streams outside the Luarin Wall. Slipping between two men-at-arms, she let Topabaw's pouch of coins and the listening spells attached to them drop noiselessly into the water below, which thrashed as the hungry flesh-eating fish fought over the prize.

5

The Demands of Rebellion

All during the ride back to the city the Balitangs could hear the sounds of crows in raucous battle with Stormwings. The birds nagged the Stormwings, pecking them on their sensitive human parts, doing their best to cause the immortals to fly into one another. The crows delighted in the Stormwings' fury and in the fact that being smaller, they could escape harm by flying close to their victims. The moment one Stormwing cut another, even by accident, they turned on each other. People had to dodge falling steel feathers, all of them deadly. Aly spotted three of her pack among the passersby and signaled them to gather as many Stormwing feathers as they could find. Put to an arrow as fletching, they turned ordinary arrows into mage killers.

The only peaceful note showed high over the fray. A pair of kudarung, one chestnut, one bay, soared on columns of hot air rising over the city.

The Balitangs took another route home to avoid late-afternoon market traffic. Aly stumbled and nearly tripped when they passed through Nimegan Square. Someone had made changes to its fountain, one of the city's attractions for its carvings of climbing monkeys on stone trees. Cut into the white marble a foot apart, the open shackle symbol lined the rim all the way around.

By the time the family reached Balitang House, the sun had begun to dip beyond the palace heights. The ladies and children bathed and changed into more comfortable clothing, then took a quiet supper in the smaller family dining room. Once they had finished eating, Winnamine told the maids they were free for the evening. The Balitang ladies adjourned to their sitting room to talk.

Aly retreated to her workroom to read the reports her people had left for her. She noted each new checkpoint they listed on her map of the city; changed the pins that marked allies, enemies, and those still undecided to match her latest information; and placed a green spy marker on Grosbeak's street. Now that she had one of Topabaw's information collectors identified, she would put her people to watch the man, to mark who else reported to him for Topabaw. She meant to turn the spy-master's network of agents inside out, leaving the regents virtually blind to what actually went on in the city.

"Are you coming?" Nawat leaned against the doorway, his arms crossed over his chest. "Everyone's there but you."

Aly put her papers aside. "I wasn't sure if we'd meet early or not." She walked past him, expecting him to kiss her, but he seemed determined to keep to his new hands-off rule. She almost reached out to touch him, only to remember that the raka were waiting. She had some fast talking to do if she meant to finish the night alive.

She poked her head into the meeting room. "Let's go to the Pavilion of Secrets," she suggested pleasantly. "I could do with some evening air."

Chenaol and Ochobu complained, Chenaol because her feet hurt, Ochobu because she just liked to complain, but everyone followed Aly and Nawat outside. Only when they were safely within the pavilion's magical protections, and the miniature kudarung who nested in the roof beams had settled down, did Ulasim look at Aly and raise his eyebrows. "I assume you did not have us troop out here for so much nice, warm, damp air," the big raka said drily. "Even if the spells do keep out the mosquitoes. Do you fear the security spells in our regular meeting place have been breached?"

"No," Aly admitted, "but they won't prevent our people from hearing you shout when I break my news, and I'd hate for them to witness an argument from our wonderful commanders." She beamed at all of them and perched on a railing. From here she could see all their faces despite the twilight shadows.

Dove rolled her eyes. "Aly, just once, forego your love of drama and spill whatever surprise you have. Otherwise I'll go back and listen to Sarai growl about how nobody at court cares about anything that matters anymore."

Aly looked at them, noting suspicion even in Nawat's eyes. Kyprioth, you'd better be ready if they jump me, she thought at the god. "Well, I have good news and better news," she told them. "The good news is that Topabaw has a spy in this household." As they stiffened she quickly added, "The better news is that it's me."

Ulasim had chosen to lean against one of the pillars that supported the roof. "And that's *good*?"

"It's not just good, silly," Aly said affectionately, "it's necessary." She looked at each of their faces. Ysul struggled with silent laughter. Chenaol began to wave a palm fan as Quedanga examined her nails. Fesgao and Dove waited patiently for her to continue, as Nawat looked at Aly and gave his bird shrug. It stands to reason Nawat doesn't understand, Aly told herself. Crows don't sneak into each other's nests and pretend they belong there. "Think about it," she continued. "Topabaw *must* have people in every important household in the city. He's had his job long enough to do it. How do you think he would feel if he kept failing to get someone on the inside here? You've already held him at bay for three weeks. He'd think we were up to something smoky, and he would be right. It's *much* better to have someone report to him regularly, and the fact that he recruited me just makes it easier. As it is, we still need to look for his spies in other households to do the odd search when they visit us. Topabaw will want to be sure I'm telling him everything."

"Doesn't he trust his own spies?" Nawat asked. "Why have them if he can't trust them?"

"Because it's how the shadow world works," Aly explained, her eyes on Ochobu. The old mage was glaring at her. "No spy trusts another. The only thing they expect is a mix of truth and lies. They protect themselves first. Topabaw would be a fool to believe every word I send him; he'll check my reports out of reflex."

"How can you be so certain?" demanded Ochobu. "How can a country maid from Tortall know so much?"

Aly grimaced. "Your god picked me," she reminded the old woman, not for the first time, she thought, and certainly not for the last. "In your shoes, I would expect him to arm me for my post. Do you think the raka could have gotten away with half of what they've done this winter if Topabaw were young and fresh? He believes his own legend. He's been doing this so long that he thinks he can't be tricked. We can use that certainty for many interesting bits of work, and we shall. We will turn his system against him."

"Are you all *mad*?" barked Ochobu. "He could be

listening to every word that's said here at this moment—or she'll tell him what we say when she reports to him!"

"If you weren't so disagreeable, Mother, you'd just put a spell on her and find out right now," Ulasim told Ochobu.

His mother glared at him. "I've worked magic all day," she snapped. "If you're so clever, *you* do it."

"That's very nice, Mother, except I'm no mage," Ulasim retorted.

Ysul shrugged and threw something that blazed like a white veil in Aly's Sight. She let it sink into her skin, though it itched. He inspected Aly, then frowned at Ochobu and shook his head.

"No listening spells?" asked Fesgao.

Ysul hand signaled, *None.*

Aly smiled at Ochobu as if the old mage were a favorite elder who was getting peculiar with age. "Ochobu, if *you* couldn't crack my liar's house, what makes you think Topabaw can? And I doubt his successor will be any better."

That startled them. "Successor?" whispered Chenaol.

Aly nodded. "Well, he'll have one. Too much is slipping through his fingers for him to keep his post much longer. Unless he moves first, of course. Once he knows the regents are losing their faith in him."

Quedanga blinked. "They are?"

"So he will hear," Aly informed them. "As the regents will hear that Topabaw is unhappy with their treatment of him. When people who like control feel that they are not *in* control, they tend to react with a hammer, not a needle. If you keep them feeling things are out of control, believe me, there will be a change in many positions at court. Perhaps even the top positions. Either you trust me, or you do not," Aly reminded them patiently. Her father had taught her that spies spent much of their time explaining themselves to those they worked for, and that any spy must accept such explanations as part of the work. "If you do not," she continued, "then you are already destroyed. I've had ways to send word to Topabaw for nearly a month. Since you are here and breathing, and no member of the family decorates the harbor posts, I suggest that you stop fussing and see to your own projects. We are nowhere near a victory."

"I bet she gives Topabaw even more headaches than she gives me," commented Chenaol. "I could almost feel sorry for him."

Ysul stared at Chenaol, plainly shocked.

"You haven't known her as long as we have, lad," the cook told him kindly. "When you do, you'll understand."

Aly looked at Dove, who smiled crookedly. "I tend to be of Chenaol's mind. Now. What else have we to discuss?" Dove asked, looking at Ulasim.

Later, as their gathering broke up, Aly called, "Nawat? I have something for you to do."

His eyes lit up. "You do? Something real?"

"Something important," Aly assured him. "Come back to my office."

"Did Topabaw hurt you?" Nawat asked as they went inside. "Did he frighten you? I will hurt him if he did."

Aly ushered him into her office and closed the door. "I was as scared as I needed to be," she said, resting a hand on his arm, noting in spite of herself the shift of his wiry muscles under cloth and skin. "You need to be afraid some in a spot like that, or the questioner can tell something isn't right about you." She sat at her desk and produced a sheet of weathered parchment from a drawer. From another drawer she got out ink and an expensive pen. "This will be tricky. I need a crow to drop this in a very specific location."

Nawat sat in one of her chairs, looking at her. Glancing

up at him, Aly couldn't tell what thoughts ran behind his deep-set eyes. "It doesn't seem important to you, perhaps, but trust me, Topabaw won't like it one bit."

"You wish me to send a messenger for you," he repeated, his voice flat. "Or better, maybe, *I* should be your messenger."

Aly beamed at him. "It would be lovely if you did it, if you can. I'm not sure the crows here will understand me like the Tanair ones did."

"They will," Nawat said, still expressionless. "The god wagered with all the crows of the Isles, not just the Tanair flock. We serve you and keep you alive, and we win the wager. They learned to speak with you just as you learned to speak with us."

"That must be some wager, that all the crows of the Isles want to win it," Aly remarked, shaking her head. "What is it—eternal life? Unlimited chances to heckle Stormwings?" She forgot her question almost as soon as she asked it, bending her head over her work. Carefully she wrote in an elegant, properly bred lady's script:

He says he wishes new blood, and new methods, but he also remembers years of service. Still, I think with a bit more discussion, he will appoint you to a post that will certainly restore all *of our family's fortunes.*

Aly waited for the ink to dry, then crushed the weathered parchment several times. Next she ripped pieces off, making sure that none were so large as to destroy the central message. Kneeling on the floor, she briefly rubbed each side of the paper against it, until the parchment looked mauled. She offered it to Nawat.

"It must be dropped near the door of Topabaw's offices, but not too near." She opened a palace map and showed Nawat the spot she meant. "He works and does his torturing there. The reports are that he starts his workday not too long after dawn. He'll be watching the ground out of habit, so don't leave it in the open where anyone can see it. Put it under a bush or something, so he'll just glimpse a corner."

"And stay to be certain he takes it," Nawat added. "I am not a man as Ulasim or Fesgao is, Aly, but I have a mind."

He walked from the room, leaving Aly to stare after him. What had he meant by that? she wondered, baffled. She hadn't said she thought him stupid, or lacking a mind!

He's so touchy anymore, she thought, biting her lower lip when it dared to quiver. He's the only real friend I have here, the only one I can trust not to turn on me if I don't do all the right things. If *he* doesn't like me . . .

She refused to finish the thought. She had work to do. Opening a box, she drew out clothes and put them on: a black hood that left only her eyes uncovered, a black suit that covered her from chin to ankles and wrists, black gloves, and long slippers that laced up over the legs of the suit. The entire thing was made of oiled cloth to repel water and spelled to make anyone who looked at her forget she was there. For the moment she let the hood dangle at her back, so that her own people could see her when they arrived.

They came as the watch called the midnight hour, all dressed as Aly was, carrying robes, gowns, and cloaks. Aly herself had put on the hat, veils, and loose overrobes of a Carthaki woman of noble blood. Small, dark-faced Jimarn wore the same disguise over her own black suit. Fegoro donned a Tortallan Bazhir's robes and headcloth. Lokak wore a southern Carthaki's full-sleeved shirt and billowing trousers under a cloak and turban, posing as Jimarn and Aly's escort. Yoyox dressed in the all-covering black hood and habit of the Black God's priesthood, having sacrificed at the god's shrine that afternoon in repentance, in case the god should decide he was being impious. None of them was worried: of all the gods, the Black God of death was the most forgiving.

From a secret basement under the laundry house, they took a tunnel that led under a block of wealthy houses, emerging in a shed where the slaves who tended the nearby public garden kept their tools. Walking casually, stopping to buy treats from late-night street vendors, the "Carthakis" and the "Bazhir" strolled down to the part of Dockmarket that stayed open late. Yoyox was already there, having taken a different route: a watchman's shack at the landward edge of one of the merchant docks. A soldiers' checkpoint was set at the end of the dock, but it was empty, as were others set to guard the landings. With the harbor's mouth blocked by a protective chain at night, there seemed little point in soldiers' waiting for ships that would not land until after dawn.

The watchman was a friend. He left for a walk as Aly and her people removed and folded their disguises, tied hoods and gloves in place, and checked that measuring cords were wrapped securely around their waists. Once they were ready, Yoyox opened the hidden trapdoor at the rear of the shack, revealing a ladder down to the edge of land under the docks. Silently they all climbed down into the stench and ooze of the harbor's edge. Here the boulders that lay against the earth were covered with a dark slime, which made the footing very tricky. Jimarn, who knew the harbor's reeking edges better than anyone after nearly a month of removing bodies from the Examples pier, led the way. They stayed connected to one another by a length of rope. The spells that kept them safe from observation made it impossible to see each other. Their only lamp was a small crystal globe that threw off enough light to show their path north and east along the shore, under the docks that supplied those who imported and exported goods to and from Rajmuat.

At last they came to a halt under one of three docks separated from the merchant docks by a fine chain net, the farthest edge of which was anchored well past the end of the wooden piers. It did not quite reach the boulders, which meant that Aly and her people could slip into the gap between land and net. Only there did they slide their hoods from their heads so that they could see one another. They didn't have to worry about drunken sailors stumbling through here and catching a glimpse of them. This stretch of the Dockmarket was guarded at street level. The three docks that served the slave markets were set between two nets designed to stop any slave desperate enough to jump ship and try to escape.

Quickly they separated, Yoyox and Jimarn to the farthest of the three docks that supplied the slave markets, Fegoro and Lokak to the second, and Aly to the first, and shortest, of the three: the one where the ship in which she had been a slave had moored. Working quickly and memorizing their results, they took the measurements of the length, width, height, and thickness of all the wood that made up the docks. Once they had mapped the area thoroughly, they gathered on the other side of the net, covered their heads and faces again, and returned to the watchman's shack. There they resumed their disguises for the trip back to Balitang House.

Only after they had all written down their measurements on a map that Aly had made did they return to the laundry house. Guchol, Atisa's sister, waited for them there. Guchol took charge of the stinking suits and thrust them into a large tub of specially treated water to soak, while Aly and Jimarn cleaned up in a second tub filled with soapy water, and the three men scrubbed themselves in a third.

"A good night's work, my lambs," Aly told them as she dried herself. "And a better night to come quite soon, I think."

"Yes, Duani," her pack mates chorused.

Before Aly went to bed, she stopped in the refitted storage room that served Ochobu and Ysul as a workroom. Picking up a slate and chalk, she wrote a request in code for twelve pots of the sticky, flammable paste called blazebalm.

Trotting downstairs the next morning to get more of the soap Ochobu made specially for Dove, Aly discovered a number of servants were already at work, taking bouquets of flowers out into the public areas of the house.

"They know Lady Sarai's back, all right," Boulaj told Aly as she carried a delicate arrangement of orchids up to her mistress's rooms. "Ulasim says it's worse even than the year before they were exiled. And there are some for Her Grace and Lady Dove."

"I know Dove will be pleased," Aly said, straightfaced. "She lives for admirers." As Boulaj snorted and continued up the stairs, Aly went in search of one of her pack. She found plump Atisa arranging a bouquet of bird of paradise flowers in a vase inside the large, formal sitting room.

"Good morning, Duani," Atisa said cheerfully. "Are you still dazzled by the magnificence of the palace?"

"I was more dazzled by the idea of man-eating fish," Aly replied, helping to position greenery around the orange blooms. "Atisa, you help Chenaol with the market shopping, don't you?"

"Every other day," Atisa said with a nod that made her pinned brown curls leap free of her rolled hair. "When she goes to the fish market. She likes to take Hiraos or Rasaj to the meat markets."

Aly grinned. The two men of her pack chosen by Chenaol were the most handsome ones, which Aly suspected was the reason Chenaol requested their help with the heavier meat. "You can't say where you heard it, mind, but tell one or two people Topabaw is cursing the regents for not being firm enough with these rebellions on the outlying islands. Have you identified the best market gossips?"

Atisa pressed a hand to her bosom, shocked. "Duani! The first thing we did was mark out who talks and who is heard around town. We knew you'd never let us forget it if you came and we didn't have sources ready!"

"I feared you'd be so busy beating these city boys off with sticks that you'd forget your old Duani," replied Aly. "But I see how I have wronged you. Pass the message down through your recruits, will you? They should spread some form of rumor that Topabaw is critical of the regents, or their generals, or their laws. Make sure everyone tells a different tale—if it's always the same one—"

"They'll know it's planted," Atisa recited. It was a lesson Aly had taught often over the winter. "Do you want me to pass it to the rest of our pack?"

Aly shook her head. "They'll get their own rumors. We'll ensure the regents and Topabaw have plenty to worry about here at home as well as in the outlying Isles."

"Will talk really bother them?" Atisa asked quietly, her black eyes serious.

Aly patted her on the cheek. "It's hard to ignore talk that's just talk," she said, and smiled. "It's funny, though, how gossip can burrow under the skin. You can't make it go away, and you can't answer it. The target goes frantic, trying to find where it comes from."

"And frantic people make mistakes," Atisa replied, once again quoting Aly. "I'm glad you're on our side, Duani."

Aly grinned at her and went to fetch her mistress's soap.

While the family took breakfast together, Aly ate hers in the servants' mess hall. She was nearly done when Nawat came to sit across from her. "Your message is delivered. I watched him pick it up myself. He did not like what he read."

Aly nodded. "Thank you," she told him. "He'll suspect it was planted, but he'll have other things to consider soon. Do you think the crows will help us send more things like that?"

"They will if you call them," said Nawat quietly. "They will even like being messengers. Talk to them in your dreams, and they will do as you ask. Just as I do as you ask. You don't need me to speak with them."

Aly raised an eyebrow. "Are you vexed about something?" she asked softly.

He was saved from having to answer when Ulasim and Fesgao sat next to him. "Good morning, Nawat," Ulasim greeted him. To Aly he said, "Boulaj says you had quite a conversation with the captain of the King's Guard yesterday."

"Captain Sibigat is interesting," Aly replied. "Sharp." Wanting to needle Nawat for being so distant and contrary, she added, "Handsome and charming, too."

Nawat traced the grain of the wood in the table, not appearing to listen. Fesgao whistled silently, while Ulasim raised his brows.

Aly sniffed, and despised herself for acting like a total lackwit whose nose was out of joint. "He was probably just flirting."

"Don't get attached to him," Fesgao warned. "He is devoted to his little king."

"Ulasim!" Fesgao nudged his friend and pointed at the door. Two of their men-at-arms had arrived, half-carrying a young part-blood who wore only a loincloth. He was caked with dust. Chenaol came over with a pitcher and a cup as the guards helped the youth to sit next to Ulasim; Fesgao moved to the end of the table, where he could see the youth's face. Chenaol filled a cup and handed it to the lad. He gulped as if he'd had nothing liquid in a long time, water streaming from the corners of his mouth. Chenaol refilled the cup as the men-at-arms left. As the boy drank the second cup, Ochobu joined them. Finally the messenger set the cup down.

"I was sent by Inayica, captain of the *Ombak*," he said, thin chest heaving. "She bids me first tell you that the swans are crows."

Ulasim nodded. The phrase was a code to designate that the messenger carried important information. "Go on."

"We're not anchored in the harbor, but in Moriji Cove," said the boy. "The cap'n sent me 'acos I'm the best runner."

Aly folded her hands on the table. Moriji Cove was on the far side of the hills that circled the harbor on the southwestern flank. This boy had run ten miles uphill and down, somehow evading the checkpoints and the city guards. She was impressed.

The boy closed his eyes and spoke as if he recited from memory. "On the Jimajen lands, the Birafu estates on Tongkang," he said. "The raka there have risen. They killed their guards and overseers and have cut the chains from the slaves. Governor Sulion of Tongkang had his mage far-speak to the regents' mages asking for soldiers, but my captain says the first message was caught in the links of the Chain."

From the way he said it, Aly knew that he didn't realize the chain was a human one fashioned of mages. Many of them had been set to watch each isle's governor as protection against this kind of event. She also knew that when no messages came back from the regents, the governors would know their pleas weren't reaching the capital and would try other ways to call for help, ways the Chain couldn't stop. The regents would not be able to ignore the message when they got it—Tongkang was too close to the capital, and the lands the boy had named were Prince Rubinyan's. He had inherited them when his brother Bronau had died.

"How many of our people are on the Birafu estates?" Chenaol asked.

"Two hundred–odd slaves," said Ochobu, "five hundred villagers, and thirty-four upper servants. And it is Jimajen land, has been Jimajen land since the Conquest."

"Is there more?" Ulasim wanted to know.

The youth opened his eyes and shook his head. "That's all the captain said, *duan*," he answered. "They burned the farm, though. We could see the smoke at anchor."

"Come," Chenaol said. "Let's get you a meal and a bed." She helped the youth to his feet.

"I need to get back to the *Ombak*," the youth protested as she led him toward the kitchen. "They'll sail without me!"

"Tongkang hotheads!" whispered Ochobu when he was gone. "We told them to wait!"

Ulasim stroked his small beard, lost in thought.

"It's hard for people to wait when their blood is up," Aly pointed out. "If they've heard of the other revolts, it would be even harder. Everyone says the Jimajens are cruel masters even for luarin."

"It would be good if the rebels simply disappeared," Ulasim remarked calmly. "If they just vanished, under the regents' very noses, so to speak. We need to get word to any of our people close enough to help. We'll take the rebels to Malubesang and let the army hunt them on Tongkang until their feet bleed." He stood. "Let's see who we can shift. Mother, we'll need you to speak with the mages."

Aly also got to her feet. Dove had said she wanted to visit some friends that morning, which meant she would require both her maid and a guard. Nawat remained where he was, hands fisted on the table before him, frowning.

Aly touched his fists. "I miss my cheerful crow man," she whispered.

Nawat refused to look at her. "I miss having a place where I fit."

Aly drew breath to argue, then shook her head and walked away. It was her experience that even the best of men had to indulge themselves with fits of moroseness. She would think of something to cheer him up once he'd had a chance to get bored with gloom.

Dove was ready for her outing. Elsren, too, was ready to go. He sat on the hall bench in his best luarin clothes, scowling as he slumped against the wall. Standing with him was his manservant, Gian. Aly smiled at him. Gian was one of Olkey's trainees. He had brought them interesting tidbits gathered when he attended Elsren at King Dunevon's court.

Dove sat next to her half brother. "Is that the face you show His Majesty?" she teased gently.

Elsren shook his head. "No. I must only show him a smiling face. That's what Aunt Nuritin says. But it's hard. Sometimes he's mean and I can't even hit him."

"Hitting the king would be very bad," Dove said with a nod. "But you could hit pillows instead."

"But pillows don't make me angry," complained Elsren. He looked up at Gian. "If I am good with the king, Gian and the guards let me gallop until we get to the city."

Dove kissed him on the top of his head. "Well, since I know you are always good, with all that practice, you'll be able to outrace Sarai one day soon."

Elsren grinned at her. "She'd be *furious*."

"My lord," Gian said politely, "the guards are here."

Aly glanced through the open front door as Elsren got to his feet. There indeed was a squad of the King's Guard riding into the courtyard. The hostlers waited there with Elsren's pony and Gian's horse.

"Remember, you want to beat Sarai one day," Dove told Elsren as she straightened his tunic.

He flung his arms around her neck in an enthusiastic hug, then trotted outside, Gian at his back.

As soon as Elsren's party had left the house, the number of uniformed guards Aly had commandeered for Dove's trip, led by Junai in men's clothes, assembled there. When Dove saw them, she scowled, very much as Elsren had. "I don't require nursemaids," she snapped.

Junai, inspecting the six men-at-arms, looked at her. "You are the half sister to the king's heir," she said, using more words than she ever did with Aly. "You have your consequence to think of."

Dove glared at the men-at-arms, who stared straight ahead, fighting smiles. "If you scare my friends, I will dismiss you," she told them. "Before, Papa only made me take two guards."

"In those days, you had plenty of people between your menfolk and the throne," Aly said. "Now there aren't. And dismissing them is a choice you don't have."

Dove frowned. "Sarai's the one who likes consequence, not me," she reminded Aly. "Let's go."

As the men formed a loose ring around Dove, with Junai in the lead, Aly took a position on the outside. On their way through the gate they passed the royal messenger with the beribboned copy of the Balitangs' invitation to the eclipse party, which made Dove scowl harder. "I hate parties," she told Aly as they turned down Joshain Street, "but Engan's got this marvelous new spyglass that gives a closer view of the moon, and he'll have it there. Otherwise I'd get vilely ill for the evening."

Few people but servants were out and about yet. Aly spotted three of her pack ranging ahead of and behind them in different disguises. Hiraos was a student, chubby Olkey a toy seller, Kioka a player. The rest of the pack and their recruits would be spread over the city right now, gathering information.

Dove headed straight for the Dockmarket. The guards had to constantly move aside as she was greeted by a story-teller, an herbalist, two fishmongers, and a potter. As they wandered down the lines of stalls, Aly noticed a thing or two: someone had carved the open shackle symbol into a door-post. Four soldiers were posted at each point where a main street opened onto Dockmarket Way, in addition to the soldiers' checkpoints at the docks themselves. All of the soldiers looked bored.

That will change, thought Aly as Dove admired a glass-maker's new baby.

"How do you know all these people?" Aly asked as they waited for a wagon full of kegs to move out of their path.

Dove gave her cat smile. "I'm very quiet," she explained. "Once my nurse thought I was at my lessons, or reading my books, she'd go visit with the staff. I'd make sure she was gone and take one of the tunnels outside our walls. Then I just wandered where I felt like it. Ulasim always managed to find me before I was missed. And I like to know things. It's funny how much people will tell you if they know you're interested. I can blow a glass ball, or I used to be able to. And I can gut and filet fish."

"Did Sarai know?" inquired Aly.

"Yes, but since she liked to sneak off to the stables and

the horses, we worked things out," Dove replied.

"Didn't your father mind?" Aly wanted to know.

"For a long time he was grieving for Mama," Dove explained. "And then he was courting and marrying Winna. I think Winna figured out what I was up to and was trying to decide if she ought to stop me when we got exiled."

The wagon moved out of their way at last. "Don't try anything of the kind on me," Aly told her mistress with a sweet smile. "I won't take it well."

Dove giggled. "I think you'd find me quicker than Ulasim ever did," she replied as they walked on. "Besides," she added softly, "there's more at stake now."

They had come to the poorer end of Dockmarket, where the stalls sold used materials for sarongs and sashes. The sandal and slipper makers were replaced by peddlers who sold used footwear, as well as dented pots, chipped dishes and mugs, and knives that had already been sharpened so often they were just thin strips of metal. Here a few beggars approached them, to be sent along by Dove's guards. Most didn't even try to come near, only watched them with hollow eyes.

"There weren't so many before," Dove whispered to Aly, her thin brows knit in disapproval. "Not nearly so many." She fumbled at her belt-purse. "Have the rest of you coins? I'll pay you from my pocket money when I get home."

The beggars surged out of corners and alleys. Junai put up a hand in warning. "My lady, this is not a good idea."

"Just the children," Dove called, making her voice carry over the racket of the Dockmarket and the pleas of the beggars. "We haven't enough for all of you, I'm sorry!"

The adults fell back, some more readily than others. A few glared at Dove and her guards, all of whom had their hands on their swords. Junai was lazily turning her long staff in a circle in front of her. One twist of the carved grip at the center and long blades would spring from each end of the weapon.

Kioka and Hiraos closed in subtly, until they stood on either side of the opening the guards had left between Dove and the nearest child. The other children came around there, grimy hands outstretched. Aly watched the crowd. Merchants and customers alike turned to look. On their lips she read Dove's name, and Sarai's. Crows descended to perch on stalls, flicking their wings and tails to warn interlopers that this was their territory.

Aly heard the tramp of boots with nailed soles before she saw the wearers. Two squads of soldiers converged on them, knocking people out of the way. Children screeched as adults tried to run, knocking them down. Dove and two men-at-arms grabbed several youngsters, hauling them into the ring of guards as it closed around Dove. Aly slid slender blades from her sash, holding the grips in her palms and lining the blades up against the insides of her wrists so that the soldiers would not see them.

"Go on, get about your business!" snapped a soldier, pushing a slave out of his path. "No assembling, remember, you ignorant swine?"

The lieutenant with the other squad halted in front of Junai. "Let me pass, in the king's name," he ordered her.

Junai stared at him, her dark face without emotion. Aly and Dove traded glances; Dove moved forward, urging the guard at Junai's right to move over so that the officer could see her. "Somehow I doubt the king is concerned with gatherings in Dockmarket," she said icily, drawing herself up to the full height of her five-foot-four-inch frame. "When I saw him yesterday, he was far more interested in playing with toy soldiers, not real ones who strike unarmed people."

The lieutenant stared down his nose at Dove. "And who might you be"—he glanced at Dove's guard and their excellent weapons—"my lady?"

"You address Lady Dovasary Balitang," the guard beside Junai told the man.

"By what right do you knock people about?" Dove wanted to know, her voice quavering slightly.

"The right of the regents to decree that assemblies of more than ten folk are banned, my lady," said the lieutenant. "There have been too many brawls in this part of town of late, and we are charged by the regents to keep order. It would be most helpful for the maintenance of order, *my lady,* if you returned home. They don't get nobility much down this way, and you being here may incite them to rob you."

Dove stared at him briefly, then turned and walked down the street toward the Windward District. Aly lagged behind: the lieutenant had grabbed Junai's arm.

"Mind your place, raka bitch," he told Junai softly. "Before someone cuts your throat in an alley."

Aly rushed forward before Junai forgot herself and showed the man what she was capable of. "Lokeij, please hurry!" she cried, playing the fussy maid, laying hands on Junai's free arm. She had used a dead friend's name so the guard would not have Junai's true identity. "My lady says you have the perfume she bought, and she wants it right away." She looked up at the lieutenant sidelong, fluttering her lashes, making it plain she thought the sallow-faced luarin attractive. "She's that particular, is Lady Dovasary, and I told her to let me carry the perfume, but she says I'm all thumbs. . . ." Talking as frivolously as she could, she managed to draw Junai away from the soldier and down the street. At the first chance Aly turned Junai to face forward properly and said in the softest of whispers, "Don't ever confront them like that again! Ever! You have no right to throw your life away by being disrespectful to some armed lout, not when Lady Sarai needs you. We're not on Tanair anymore, and the regents rule by the fist. Do you want me to tell your father you were stupid, or do you want to promise me you'll never be so foolish again?"

Junai drew her arm out of Aly's grip. "Careful," she said, also keeping her voice low. "People hear you talk like that, and they may start to think you care."

Dove glared up at Junai when they rejoined their group. "Don't ever do that again, Junai. *Ever,* do you understand me? Risking your life in a Dockmarket brawl with a soldier when you owe your life to us!"

Junai looked down at her young mistress, amused. "So it will seem, Mother." She looked at Aly. *"Duani,"* she added with emphasis. "I will be a good girl and try not to get gutted in the market." She moved up into the lead once more.

Dove stalked on, her small face grim. Once they were back at the house, she dismissed everyone, including Aly, and locked herself in the library. Aly waited long enough to hear the crash of a thrown object and Dove's cry of *"Brutes!"* before she left Dove to her rage in peace.

Aly sat on a bench in the main hall, closing her eyes to think. Did the regents understand how much they revealed by ordering their men to break up gatherings? Surely they'd been around government long enough to know it was a bad idea to let people know you feared them in groups that were not even very large.

Ulasim found her there and sat next to her. Aly opened her eyes. "I was plotting," she told him.

The big raka looked uncommonly grim. "I have no doubt that you were," he pointed out. "I believe you plot in your sleep. I have something to tell you. I want you to hear it from me. You may recall that we were trying to think of a way to get quick aid to the people on Tongkang."

Aly frowned, puzzled. Why did he tell her this? That was the military side of their duties, not the spy side. "I'm sure you'll do whatever's right."

"I believe I have," replied Ulasim, resting a hand on her arm. "At his request, I sent Nawat and some of his crows."

For a moment Aly's ears buzzed. Then her entire body went cold, as if she had been dunked in snowmelt. "Nawat?" she whispered through numb lips. "He's no warrior. You can't be serious."

"He and his cousins fought well when Bronau attacked Tanair last year," Ulasim reminded Aly. "He wants to do something, Aly. A man needs something of his own, just as a woman does. And he and his crows can get messages to far more people on and around Tongkang than my mother and all the mages of the Chain. They can watch for warships and soldiers. He thinks he can even divert an armed party. His reasoning is sound. I approved it."

"He's a *crow*," Aly whispered, clenching her hands. "A crow who spends time being a man—that doesn't make him one. You had no right to use him for this!"

"He's not your pet," Ulasim said gently. "It is time that he learns if he is a crow or a man. As long as he sits in your shadow, he cannot be certain. And his stake in this is far higher than yours. He and his people are the raka's cousins. You are only an imported luarin."

Aly flinched. What was wrong with her? She was on the verge of tears. "You should have asked me."

"*He* asked *me*, as was his right," Ulasim replied without mercy. He looked her over with the gaze of a commander who saw a weakness in one of his soldiers. "Must I worry about you? Are you going to pout and mope and ignore our work?"

Aly stiffened at the verbal slap. He'd as much as accused her of not being professional. "No!" she said, outraged.

"Nawat is intelligent. He has the ears and eyes of his fellow crows," Ulasim told Aly, his eyes direct. "This is a chance made for him. He is as safe doing that as any of us are safe." He put a big hand on Aly's shoulder. "This has nothing to do with whatever games you play together, and everything to do with our cause. Have I made myself clear?"

Aly bit her lip. He was treating her as if she were a silly girl who could think only about her sweetheart. Worse, he was right. Just so would her own father speak to her about neglecting her job. Hanging her head, she nodded.

"Then I do not want to hear of this again," instructed Ulasim. "There is work to be done." He got up and strode off down the hall.

6

SPIES

As the family rested and the household prepared for that day's callers, Aly met with her pack. They watched as she tapped the map and the pin that marked Grosbeak's shop. "This is Grosbeak, on Gigit Lane in Middle Town. Topabaw uses him to collect reports from spies in the city. Now we gather information from Grosbeak."

"All of Topabaw's people report to him?" asked Guchol, fascinated.

Aly shook her head. "I doubt it, not with the number of spies Topabaw must have in the city alone. But Grosbeak is a place to start. Guchol, you'll handle this. Put your recruits on him day and night. Everyone who goes there, I want to know who they are and where they live. And don't be surprised when I come there. Topabaw recruited me yesterday."

Unlike the rebellion's leaders, these people had learned their spy craft from Aly, including the tricky work of double agents. If they doubted her ability to protect herself from Topabaw or anyone else, none of them showed it.

"Was it fun?" asked Olkey. "Or did he hurt you?"

"Does the general know?" Kioka inquired.

"Did Topabaw pay you anything?" demanded Lokak.

"He paid me in coin loaded with listening spells, so I got rid of it. The general knows, Topabaw didn't hurt me, and don't get too attached to him," replied Aly. "We'll be dealing with someone new before long, if I have anything to say about it. Once we know who reports to Grosbeak and where they live, we will send them a token of our regard. I was thinking that baskets of rats left beside beds would give our regards that personal touch."

A number of them snorted. Lokak only frowned.

"Yes?" Aly asked.

"Why don't we just nail rats to the door, like the old raka rebels used to do?" Lokak wanted to know. "It's cheaper."

"But not so thoughtful as a basket of them," Aly said. "And leaving the basket in their bedrooms provides an intimate note."

"We're saying we can get at them as they sleep," remarked Eyun, her eyes filled with the discovery of some new twist she had just uncovered.

Aly smiled benevolently while thinking, And this way my aunt Daine doesn't come flying over from Tortall wanting to know why I'm killing animals for no good reason. "Tell me what you have learned from your people so far."

By the time they had finished their reports, the city's bells were chiming the end of the rest period. Aly dismissed them and went to help Dove to dress for the afternoon. The duchess had told Quedanga to open the reflecting pool court and the large sitting room. Afternoon was the usual time for callers, and she expected quite a few.

Aly stood behind a carved screen inside the house to observe the young noble visitors as they flirted, talked to Sarai, accepted treats carried on trays by maids, and gossiped. The younger ladies were watched by their maids, who had taken positions against the walls of the courtyard. Nuritin and Winnamine had chosen to stay indoors, in one of the large, formal sitting rooms, to greet the callers who came to see them. Dove joined them there, after muttering to Aly that she refused to have her brain filled with puffs of scent and flirting, as it would be if she stayed with Sarai.

Talented Eyun made friends among the maids and talked animatedly with them as she gave the men servants sidelong glances. Ukali and Olkey, two of Aly's male agents, were making themselves known to the nobles' servants as well. Pert Kioka was out in the stables, listening to the guards who rode with the noble guests. At some point during the afternoon, talking in strictest confidence with their new friends, all of them would pass on some bit of gossip that would sit ill with those who collected it for the palace. The rest of Aly's pack, and more of the people they had recruited, were out performing the same service. Little of it would go straight to Topabaw or to Rubinyan's spymaster. People who worried about the stability of the government chattered constantly, the threads of gossip twisting as they passed from one person to the next. By the time they reached those who were most interested in holding power, the strands would be so tangled that no one would be able to trace them back to a handful of sources.

Gossip was a realm's lifeblood, Aly's da had told her repeatedly. She intended to make this realm bleed with it.

She let her eyes roam over the crowd, reading snatches of conversation on the lips of their company. Everyone wanted to tell Sarai the winter's news, away from the watchful eyes of their elders. Count Ferdolin Tomang, the Carthaki healer mage Zaimid Hetnim, and the heirs to the Lelin and Obemaek houses wanted to court Sarai. She kept them dancing around her, pouting at one, teasing another, ignoring a third, and urging her female friends to do the same. She seemed cruel to Aly, as if she didn't care if she hurt the feelings of the young men. Was I that bad? Aly wondered, remembering the days when she lived like Sarai. Picking them up and dropping them, whether they deserved it or not, just because I could?

I can't do it anymore, she realized, startled. Even if the god were to dump me into such a gathering at home. It's small to promise a man something, even without words, if you never intend to give it to him, whether it's kisses or your heart.

She didn't like where that trail of thought led her: Nawat. Rather than dwell on him, she looked into the formal sitting room. Here there were older ladies and men alike, deep in conversation with Nuritin, Winnamine, and even Dove. They kept their voices low and watched the maids who served refreshments, talking only when they were out of earshot. Reading the nobles' lips, Aly saw that they spoke of missing officials, uprisings, and the vanished bodies of those executed by the Crown. Dove was engaged in a conversation about copper exports with a noble couple at least three times her age.

Aly eased her way out of the room. She was about to go to the servants' hall when one of the household runners found her. "Chenaol says tell you, one in Her Grace's private study, one in Lady Saraiyu's bedroom. She asks if you have ever been a poacher, since you knew where to set traps."

Aly smiled. "Thank you. Tell Chenaol I'm on my way."

Aly climbed the stairs and entered the ladies' private study. There Winnamine, Sarai, and Dove read and wrote letters and kept their personal accounts. It was one of the first places a spy would look for incriminating correspondence, which was why she had recommended that the raka mages plant a spy trap there. When Aly walked into the well-lit, comfortable room, she saw a part-raka maidservant, locked in place with her hands in a desk drawer. The woman shimmered under the magical net that had captured her. Ysul sat on a chair watching her, his almond-shaped eyes unreadable. Ulasim, too, was present, as was Junai. They nodded as Aly came in.

She went to the chair across the desk from the captive and sat, resting her hands on the chair's arms. The maid glared at her.

Aly eyed her. "Was she searched for death magic?"

Ysul nodded and held up three fingers. He had removed three spells that would have killed the woman if she tried to speak the truth.

"Three?" Aly asked. She looked at the captive. "If someone were to put three death spells on me, I might wonder if they trusted me at all. Such persons would be less than careful about giving you assignments that might cost your life. *I* would not reward service in such a manner."

She inspected the captive. She was a part-raka woman in her late twenties, dressed in a blue gown, probably a mistress's castoff. She wore her brown hair pinned up, with enough hairdressing ointment on it to ensure that no loose hairs would fall on anything she searched. There were white silk gloves on her hands. Through the magic that held the maid captive, Aly could see that the gloves were spelled to keep her essence from sticking to anything she handled. On the desk lay a set of lock picks—good ones, Aly saw with approval.

Aly raised a hand, lifted a finger, then bent it. Ysul lowered the spell, freeing the captive's lips so she could speak.

"I don't understand!" she cried. "I was just looking for a

bit of paper—please don't tell my mistress, she'll be furious, but they always count the paper in our household and I just wanted to write a note to my betrothed. . . ."

Aly held her finger to her lips. The maid's words trailed off.

Ulasim leaned in and sniffed the air around the maid. "You stink of Topabaw," he informed her, his voice thick with scorn. "You were spelled to die before you named your true master—that's spy work." He nudged the lock picks. "These aren't needed to steal paper. If you were a slave, you would pay for these with your life. As it is, you won't look so good with a thief's brand on your forehead."

"I swear, I swear, those were here when I came in!" protested the maid.

"And the gloves?" inquired Aly. "Spelled to leave no trace of you?"

"They belong to my mistress!" cried the woman. "I just borrowed them, you know, to make my hands softer, like hers!" She started to cry.

Aly let Ulasim and Junai question her for a while, listening with appreciation. The woman had been well trained. When Aly judged the time was right, she laid a gentle hand on the desk in front of her. Everyone stopped talking. Aly let the silence linger for a moment, then asked gravely, "What is your name?"

The maid drew breath to speak.

Aly raised the index finger of her hand. So frightened—and so clever—was the maid that she saw even that tiny gesture. She clamped her lips shut.

"I will know if you lie, and I will be displeased," Aly said.

The woman hesitated, apparently considering whether she dared lie in any case. Aly smiled, and the woman reconsidered. "Vitorcine Townsend."

"Very good," Aly replied. "What household employs you?"

Head hanging, Vitorcine murmured, "Obemaek. I am Lady Isalena's maid."

Aly nodded. "Well, then, Vitorcine Townsend. Perhaps we need to summon Lady Isalena. By your own admission, you are a thief." She saw Vitorcine's shoulders relax slightly. She probably has something she can blackmail Isalena with if she should get caught, Aly thought. *I* would, in her place. "Better still, perhaps the young lady will thank us for pointing to Topabaw's spy in her household."

Vitorcine's skin went dead white. She swayed. Only the spell around her hips and legs kept her upright. "I beg you, no," she whispered. "I will do anything you ask. Only do not tell."

"Why should we not?" Ulasim wanted to know. "You have taken advantage of our mistresses' hospitality and defiled this house with your prying." He stepped closer until he loomed over the woman, his eyes fixed on hers. Vitorcine could not escape the fact that he was large, well muscled, and full-raka. In the city, there were feuds based on how much raka blood someone had. Vitorcine had a drop, no more. Used to the city, she would expect full-bloods to be hostile to part-bloods.

Aly leaned forward, drawing everyone's attention. Even Vitorcine looked at her as she cringed from Ulasim. "What has your mistress to fear from Topabaw?" Aly asked softly.

"It may be paltry," the woman babbled, more broken by her own terror than anything the rebels had said. Aly had seen this before with some of her da's agents. She fought to keep her face bland. She knew she had just hit treasure.

"Is it arms?" she asked, her voice gentle. "Or is it correspondence?"

The woman bit her lip. "The Obemaeks will kill me," she said at last. "As Topabaw will kill me if I am found out."

"A moment," Aly interrupted gently. "*Both* of your masters would kill you?"

Vitorcine nodded. "I have not told Topabaw. It could be nothing. What I have gathered is only hints. They write letters in code. It may only be family gossip. I did not wish to inform Topabaw until I have the key to the code. When I find it, I will have to tell him. I have no proof until then, so they are safe from me."

Aly's nerves sang with excitement. Two gifts had dropped into her lap. Vitorcine obviously knew those communications would mean bloody trouble for the Obemaeks should Topabaw learn of them. Yet she was trying to protect her mistress and her family. Whatever Topabaw had used to frighten Vitorcine into spying for him, it wasn't strong enough yet to overcome her loyalty to the Obemaeks.

"You are brave, to take such risks," Aly told Vitorcine kindly, signaling Ysul to free the maid. "A chair, I think." Ulasim brought it over and helped the frightened woman to sit. "Would you like tea?" Aly asked. "Something stronger?"

Vitorcine shook her head. From the sudden grim twist in her mouth, she knew as well as Aly that it was very bad for spies to take spirits.

"I believe we may help each other," Aly continued. This young woman required a velvet touch. Aly would have to be teacher and mother figure. She put an elder's authority into her voice. "Will you do this for me? Copy those coded letters and bring the copies here. We shall see if there is even anything in them that would interest Topabaw." She caught Vitorcine's gaze. "In addition, you report to me what you report to Topabaw. You will also report to me what Topabaw says to you, do you understand?"

"He'll kill me," whispered the woman.

"Then you must be very careful," Aly told her, still kind. "He is not as all-powerful as you may think. I heard somewhere that he is losing his grip on the realm and will soon be replaced."

Vitorcine met Aly's eyes with her own. "Is it true?" she asked breathlessly.

Aly smiled. "Keep it in mind." From the front of her sarong she drew a small, thick book. In it she kept pledges of obedience, signed in blood. Opening it to a clean page, she drew a small dagger she kept in her sash for these occasions. "This is just a formality," she assured Vitorcine. "Write here—you can write, can you not?"

Vitorcine nodded.

"Write that you will serve Balitang House and keep its secrets," Aly explained, setting out an inkpot and pen. She unsheathed the dagger. Its blade was the length of Aly's little finger, and razor sharp. "Then you will sign in blood." As Vitorcine shrank back—the breaking of a blood oath meant the oathbreaker died with the blood boiling in her veins—Aly leaned closer and held Vitorcine's deep-set brown eyes with her own. "You will swear, or they will find you floating in the harbor tomorrow," she whispered.

Vitorcine swore, as Aly knew she would. Everyone thought they could get out of a bad situation if they could just buy some time. Vitorcine was no exception. Besides, Aly had promised to help her with the coded letters.

Once her oath was given and Ysul had put healing balm on the small cut in the maid's finger, Aly went in search of their second captive, another of Topabaw's agents. Ochobu stripped this one, a footman, of any death magics before Aly began her questions. The man had no pearls of news like Vitorcine, but Aly knew better than to expect two such windfalls in one day. Ochobu took the footman's blood vow, giving Aly two agents who would report both on the activities of their noble masters and on Topabaw's orders.

A good day's work, Aly told herself. Da was right. With careful handling, and plans laid in advance, I *can* pluck my enemies' spies like ripe plums from a tree.

While she had worked, new guests had arrived. A glance into the salon where the older men and women met showed her that Duke Nomru sat in quiet conversation with the duchess, Nuritin, and Lord Obemaek, whose daughter Isalena was one of Sarai's friends. Aly's fingers prickled. She would have loved to know what they said, but she was in the wrong position to read their lips.

You can't hear everything all the time, Aly thought as she went to see what was happening with Sarai. But it's so *frustrating*. It occurred to her that she was trying to fill her brain with anything but Nawat. She banished the thought.

There were more new guests in the courtyard. Dove had left the sitting room to speak with two of them. Aly found her mistress seated between Baron Engan, the astronomer, and Tkaa the basilisk.

Aly didn't think Tkaa had come to visit the Balitangs. She gathered up a tray of drinks and circulated, drifting toward Dove and her company. When she reached them, her tray was empty. She placed it on a table and ambled into the house. There she turned down the corridor and out into a separate garden where lovers could talk unseen. She was wondering how often Sarai came here when she heard the click of claws on the flagstones.

Like the rest of the house, the courtyard was spelled to protect it from eavesdroppers. Aly felt no qualms about beaming up at the basilisk as he arrived and saying, "Of all the people I thought to see here, none of them was you!"

She hugged him, careful of his bulging pouch.

"I was fortunate enough to be chosen to bring the monarchs' greetings to the new king and his regents." For so large a creature, Tkaa had a soft, whispery voice. "I also bring greetings from your family. The Scanran War is done. Your mother has returned to court, and your father with her. Your brother Alan is squire to Raoul of the King's Own, your brother Thom continues his mage studies. Your grandparents, your uncle Numair, and your aunt Daine send their love, as does your immediate family. Prince Roald's bride, Princess Shinkokami, awaits her first child. Your aunt Daine expects a second child. And Daine has also sent you a gift."

Tkaa opened his pouch. A glossy black glob about twice the size of Aly's head dropped to the ground with a plop. There it began to wriggle. A round piece broke off, then another, and a third, until thirty-six small blobs sat before her. Despite their similar appearance, many held visible differences inside their bodies: a piece of ribbon or stone, lace and honeycomb patterns, streaks of bright color or light.

The first to break away from the main mass had made its glossy surface resemble Tkaa's beaded hide. Now it produced a neck and a head. "Hello," it squeaked. "I am Trick."

Aly knelt, staring in wonder. "I'd heard of them, but I never saw one," she whispered. "You're darkings, aren't you?"

The blobs produced their own heads to nod. Aly rocked back on her heels. "But I thought you lived with the dragons." One of her favorite Daine stories was about these creatures, made of blood and magic. Aly had always been disappointed that they had stayed in the Divine Realms rather than live in the mortal world with Daine.

"Dragons are boring," announced a darking with a bit of clear quartz at its center. "Dragons study and peer and eat and sleep."

"And talk," Trick added. "For days and days and days."

A number of tiny heads nodded agreement and chorused, "Boring."

"Some stay," said Quartz. "Gold-streak stay. Olders stay. We go."

"Aunt Daine said all but one of you was killed in the Battle of Port Legann," Aly murmured, thinking aloud.

Trick shook its head. "More that Daine not meet in Divine Realms," it told her. "And more born as we split in two."

Aly scratched her head and looked up—far up—at Tkaa. "Why bring them to me?" she asked.

"Daine said to tell you, what one darking knows, all will know," Tkaa explained. "And they are very good at getting into places where humans cannot."

To illustrate, the one patterned like lace flattened itself into a thin sheet on the ground.

"I stay with you," Trick squeaked. "They tell me, I tell you. Sometimes show." Spreading itself thin, it presented a view of the garden where they now stood from the ground.

"Not boring," added one that had blue ribbon inside itself.

"Fun," chorused the others. "Funfunfun."

For once, Aly had nothing to say. In a moment, she knew, her mind would be whirling with ideas, places to send these creatures where the discovery of a human would result in a spy's or Aly's death. And unlike her human spies, these creatures had no tasks they were supposed to be about, so they might hide, and listen, day and night.

"But I'll have to train them so they know what to listen for," Aly mused. "So they can tell what's important or not."

"No," peeped the tiniest of the creatures. "Whisper Man teach us before we come. We know secret. We know trouble. We know rumor. We know fact."

"And murder," added another darking.

"And poison," said a third.

"We know allies and enemies," a fourth darking said. "Between dragons and Whisper Man, we know plenty."

The one called Trick oozed over to Aly. Producing small limbs or tentacles, it began to crawl up her sarong-covered thigh until it reached her sash. Stretching itself cord-thin, it wriggled until only its head showed above the cloth. "Fun," it reassured Aly. "Mortals are always doing things."

After long thought Aly murmured, "Such a delightful gift. And it isn't even my birthday."

After more news from home, she said goodbye to Tkaa and went in search of a covered basket for the darkings. Carrying it, and them, into her workroom, she realized she could tell no one of her new guests. The darkings were too odd. Once Ulasim or the other rebel leaders saw them, they would start to ask questions that Aly dared not answer.

"I'll just say I developed new sources," she decided as she set the basket on her desk. "This will have to do for the present," she told her new spies. "I'll be taking you places later on. Actually, if two of you would join me? I'd like to settle you right away."

The darkings started to bounce like eager children. She chose one that contained a bit of lace in its depth and one that had patterned its skin like bird feathers. "There will be fun enough for all of you," she told the rest as she tucked Lace and Feather into a pouch she could hang from her sash. "Do you need anything? Food? Water?"

The darkings shook their heads. "We get our own," Trick assured her. "No one will see. Mortals don't *look*."

Since Aly had frequently observed that most people didn't pay attention to the details of the world around them, she was inclined to agree. "No one should be able to come here once I lock the door," she explained, "but if someone does, *hide.*"

Every darking nodded. Aly looked at them helplessly. Darkings, she thought. In Tortall she was used to living among legends. After a year in the Isles, she had fallen out of the habit of expecting the extraordinary. As she locked her door and entered the meeting room, she wondered if Kyprioth had anything to do with this.

As if he'd been eavesdropping, the god spoke in her mind. *No, but they are* quite *delightful. Maybe I can recruit them to my service when this is done.*

Lucky darkings, thought Aly as she took Lace from her pouch. "You stay here," she told the darking. Its cocked head managed to convey complete attention. "Some people will come in from time to time. I may be with them, so don't say hello, or nice to see you, or even wait till I tell you what I heard. Just listen, and pass things on to Trick."

Lace nodded, and dropped from Aly's hand to the floor with a plop. Off it rolled, making an inspection of its new quarters.

Aly went out around the house until she came to the window of the room where the older guests had met that afternoon. Most of them were already gone; the rest were preparing to leave. Aly gave Feather the instructions she had given Lace, then held the darking so that it could trickle through a gap in the carved wooden screen and down into the room. The others she meant to place at Grosbeak's and the palace, but she was interested in that group of older luarin nobles who gravitated toward Nuritin and the duchess. Their movement to silently take Winnamine's part at court had been done with such grace and speed that it looked practiced. Something was going on there. With Feather's help, she would learn what it was and if she could use it. As for

Lace and its position in the leaders' meeting room, it never hurt to know what her fellow conspirators were up to. Probably she wouldn't have gotten word of Nawat's commission from even a darking in time to stop him from going, but she wanted no more surprises.

Nawat. The thought of him plunged into a war zone jammed a hot fist of anger and fear under Aly's lungs. Until now she had managed to put off thinking about him. She hurriedly crossed the small garden to one of the lovers' nooks, where she could get her heart under control. She didn't know what to think or say about his departure; she feared so much what she *might* say that she would have to try not to speak of him at all.

She clenched her hands. She knew what damage a sharp tongue could do from her long years with her mother. Aly could not exercise it on Ulasim, or on Nawat if he came home safe. It would be cruel to ask Nawat who he thought he was, to dive into human battles. It would be cruel to point out to him that the household message runners knew more of war than he did. No, she would calm down and get a grip on herself. She would have to handle him properly so that he would stay where he belonged once he returned, if he returned.

That night, when Aly walked into the big meeting room, she found the leaders already present. Ulasim, Fesgao, and Ochobu stood, looking down at a good-sized wooden chest. The others were seated, their chairs pushed well back from the chest as they, too, eyed it.

"There are no spells on it," Ochobu said. She looked at Aly as the girl closed the door behind her.

Ulasim nodded to Aly. "Come have a look," he invited. "This was found on the doorstep of Temaida House this morning, with a label that read *For the Twice-Royal.*"

Aly nodded. In the prophecy that spoke of the freeing

of the Isles, the main person mentioned was the twice-royal queen. The conspirators and the rebels believed that was Sarai, who was Rittevon on her father's side, Haiming on her mother's.

"They had it conveyed secretly to us. Need I say the Temaidas were very frightened?" the big raka asked Aly.

She smiled crookedly. For a house that had secretly raised the last descendants of the Haiming line for three hundred years, the Temaidas as a whole were terrified of their own shadows. Then she reconsidered. Perhaps that very skittishness was what had enabled the Temaidas to survive.

"Ochobu and Ysul say there is no magic on it," Fesgao pointed out. "Yet we are not sure about a box that has come to us from someone unknown."

Aly knelt and inspected it closely. It was a plain chest, banded in iron and locked. She got to her feet and went to her workroom to fetch her lock picks. Little Trick thrust its head out of her sash as she picked up the rolled cloth that held her tools.

"Fun?" it asked.

"Probably not," Aly murmured. "Someone is playing a game, but I'll bet my sarong it's just to send a message. No fun. Back into hiding, you." Trick pulled its head under her sash with what sounded very like a sigh.

In the meeting room, Aly peered into the keyhole of the box and saw no magic. By the time she had inserted three lock picks, she knew the lock's mechanism as well as she knew her own name. Two more picks did the trick. The lock sprang open. Aly tucked it into her sash as a memento and shoved back the lid. Inside were bags, each with a round wax seal on the drawstring. Aly picked one bag up. It was heavy with clinking metal. The thick seal, in bright blue wax, was glossy on one side and dull on the other. Her heart was pounding. She had always loved presents from home.

She reached up under her sarong, where she wore fine cotton breeches to keep the knives strapped to her inner thighs from chafing her bloody. Drawing the right knife, she reversed it in her grip and smashed the pommel onto the glossy side of the wax seal. The top layer shattered, as it was meant to do, laying bare a second seal. A metal emblem was pressed into the blue wax of the true seal: a tin sword thrust through a tin crown. The drawstring loosened, revealing a bag full of silver and gold coins, mixed in age and origin so that they would be impossible to trace.

Aly held out the bag, the seal facing up. Ulasim took it from her with a frown.

"It's the Tortallan national emblem," she told her companions. She smashed the outer seal on each bag to reveal the same hidden seal. "All this money is a love token from the Tortallan king's spymaster." She looked at Ulasim. "They're giving you funding for any mischief you care to concoct. Their spies believe you are preparing to stir this country up. They want to help."

The raka went very still. Finally Chenaol, white under her bronze skin, whispered, "If the Tortallans know, the Crown's spies know. Topabaw knows."

Aly shook her head, busily constructing a story they would believe. She couldn't tell them the truth, that her father, one of Tortall's spymasters, had wanted to be sure his little girl had the coin for whatever she was up to. She got to her feet and stretched, grinning impishly at them. "You may thank the god for this, I think."

They stared at her as if she'd grown a second head. "What do you mean?" Fesgao asked at last.

"The god mentioned once that he was the patron of one of Tortall's highest-ranking spies," Aly told them. It was not completely a lie. Kyprioth had been her father's patron god for years, though George Cooper's family had been unaware of the alliance. "I imagine he whispered a word to that spy that things were unsettled here. There's enough bad blood between the Tortallans and the Rittevon kings that no doubt Tortall would be happy to do the Rittevons and their supporters an ill turn. Promoting rebellion among the raka is a way to do it while still claiming friendship with the Copper Isles." The raka continued to stare at her. Aly shook her head. "You had a princess nearly twenty years back, Josiane. She was being groomed as a future queen of Tortall, except that the heir to the throne didn't wish to marry her. She took it badly. Well, she *was* a Rittevon. She was killed in an attempted takeover, and things have not gone well between your realm and mine ever since. King Oron lost two sons, didn't he, in the attack on Port Legann nine years ago? The god knows the Tortallans would love to pay off an old grudge, and rebellions always need money."

"The god told you this?" Ulasim wanted to know.

"I will ask him," Aly said truthfully. She suspected that her father had pieced together her story during his visit to Tanair the previous autumn, and that he had commissioned Tkaa to deliver the money to the Temaidas without being seen. "But I know he has a connection with Tortall."

"We should send it back," said Fesgao. "I do not like it that they think to buy us."

Aly beamed at him. "Very sweet *and* very silly, Fesgao. They are *buying* mischief. Face it—unrest in the Isles means the regents will be too busy to pay fake pirates to raid Tortall's shores this year. The Tortallans aren't putting any names to it, and they won't expect you to pay them back." She propped her hands on her hips and looked at them one by one. "Countries do this to each other all of the time, you know," she explained. "Meddle in one another's affairs. Look for the tiniest bit of advantage over their neighbors. You don't have to *marry* the Tortallans, just take their money. If I thought you could trust any Carthakis, I'd suggest you approach them for extra funding."

"But we can't trust the Carthakis," said Chenaol.

Aly gathered up the lock picks. "Well, you can't trust anybody, but if the money's all clean of spells, there's no reason for you to refuse it. They've done it this way so it can't be traced back to them. So if someone from here was to accuse the Tortallan monarchs and their spymaster of sending money to support unrest, they can say, 'What money?' and not be caught in a lie." She settled into a chair and began to slide her picks back into their pouches. "Now what else have we to discuss?"

Ulasim shook his head. "You were born a spy, Aly."

She smiled cheerfully. "No, but I'm a *very* fast study."

7

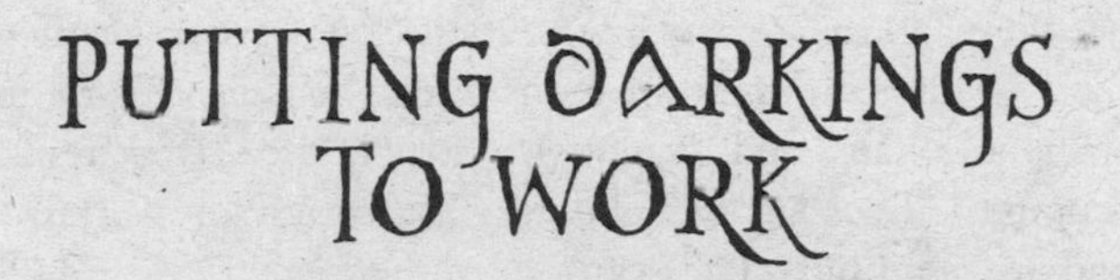

PUTTING DARKINGS TO WORK

The next morning, Aly woke before dawn because her nose itched. She crossed her eyes to see the cause. It was the darking Trick, who had produced a thin tentacle to tickle her with. Aly groaned quietly—Dove was still asleep, Junai gone—and retreated to the privy closet. "What is it?" she whispered.

"Look," the darking told her. It leaped to the shelf that lined the wall and stretched until it formed a thin snake nearly thirty inches long. Then it changed shape until it looked like a long string of black beads. Rising and turning, it made itself into a continuous necklace. Sticking up the bead that seemed to be its head, it told Aly, "Neck more fun than sash."

Aly twiddled her thumbs. Finally she asked, "Where did you get this idea?"

"I snoop," Trick said proudly. "Dove have beads. Sarai have many, many beads. Duchess have beads. Rihani have beads. Chenaol—"

Aly raised a hand for silence. She had the idea that the

enterprising creature would have told her the contents of every jewel box in the house if she had asked. Trick stopped talking. "Do you ever sleep?" Aly asked.

"Sometimes," Trick replied. "After we split to make new darking."

Which could be useful, Aly thought. Spies that seldom need rest. "Have you any information from Lace or Feather?"

"Feather say there weapons under house and barn and stable and dairy and in tunnels under house," Trick replied promptly. "Lace say Ochobu and Ysul magic on workroom and bedroom hurt. Lace can't go in there."

"And the others? What do they say?" Aly wanted to know.

"The others explore Joshain Street. Lord Asembat next door snores in night. Lady Asembat meets young man in room by dock. Spies outside Balitang House from Topabaw and Carthak and Tyra bored. They say nothing happens here. Raka man stabbed soldier and other soldiers kill him. Lady Yendrugi in pink stucco house expects baby. Guards in Kadyet House across street owe Fesgao fifty silver gigits over dice. They tell Fesgao their master say Duke Nomru must watch step with regents. Daughter in Kadyet House is kissing her maid. In Murtebo House—"

Once more Aly raised a hand to halt the flow of information spilling out of her darking necklace. "I have to get some of you into the palace," she murmured. "If you learn all this in just one night, I'll be deluged with what you can learn where it matters."

"Kissing maid not matter?" asked Trick.

"No," Aly said. "But the stabbing and the news about the duke matter." She nibbled her lip, then said, "Once I'm dressed, you go back in my sash. Dove will want to visit the market—I'll find an excuse to break away, report to Master

Grosbeak, and leave one of you with him. When I return, I'll wear you, so everyone will think I bought you at market. While we eat breakfast, get about four of you into that small red pouch I left in my workroom—the place where I put the others. You're all back, aren't you?"

"Yes," replied Trick. Its bead head hung, somewhat forlorn. "No more fun today?"

Aly smiled and stroked the creature's head with a finger. "Don't worry. All of you will be having more fun than you can stand by week's end, I promise."

She gathered up the darking and quietly went into the other room to dress. Junai's pallet was already folded and stowed. Dove slept with her light coverlet over her head. Once clothed, Aly tucked Trick into her sash and went downstairs.

In the stable courtyard, working by the pale early-morning light, all combat-trained members of the household practiced their skills, with Ochobu and Ysul's spells to keep the sounds of their training from escaping into the air outside the walls. Aly joined them and soon found how rusty she had gotten since the family had left Tanair to come south. When Fesgao dumped her on her back in the dirt and leveled a spear at her throat, Aly noticed a trickle of darkness flow away from her sash. It seemed Trick did not care to be smashed. Aly swiveled her legs, twining them around Fesgao's as she gripped his spear, then yanked his feet from under him while gently touching his throat with the spear's butt. She rolled to her feet as Fesgao lay on the ground and cursed, turning to guard herself as Ukali came at her with double daggers.

When the sunrise bell rang out over the city, everyone dusted themselves off and checked one another's bruises. Fesgao tousled Aly's hair with a grin and ambled off with the other men-at-arms to change into uniforms. Aly scrubbed herself and combed her hair in the laundry, then went to her office. Trick was already there, exchanging sniffs with a miniature kudarung on Aly's windowsill.

"There seem to be more of those things every day," she remarked, picking up a sheaf of reports.

"They come careful," said Trick. "They don't all come at once. They can take darkings to other places."

"We might do something with that," Aly said absently, absorbed in her reading. Merchants who dealt in crops were saying that the price of rice would shoot up that summer, which meant poorer folk would be forced to eat millet. It was edible grain, but not by much.

She was halfway through the stack of paper when Junai stuck her head in the door. "You missed breakfast, and Lady Dove wants to go to Market Town," she informed Aly.

"I rejoice," Aly replied, setting her reports aside. "Nobody even saved me a sago cake?" She didn't love the palm-starch cakes, but they were filling.

"I saved two," Junai said, placing them on Aly's desk. "Hurry up. You're supposed to be a lady's maid, remember?"

After she left, Aly hung her red pouch, with its five darkings, from her sash. She then hurried to dress her mistress for an expedition to Market Town. This time Dove and her guards followed Joshain Street to Susashai Way. After three blocks of eyeing the seamstresses' shops that lined Susashai, they turned down Ratechul Avenue. Dove knew many people here, too—flower sellers, door guards, and booksellers. Having learned the day before that Dove could spend an hour chatting with just one person, Aly asked to leave the group for a short time. She knew Dove would be well watched in her absence.

Dove nodded permission as a bookseller came out of his

shop, beaming. Aly nodded to Dove's guards and left.

From here, it was nine blocks to the building that Topabaw's man Grosbeak used as his workplace. Aly walked through his door into a large waiting room, where faded bolts of cloth were displayed on counters.

Seated at a table, with an account book, reeds, and ink before her, was a hard-faced old woman. She glared at Aly but said nothing. Aly looked about as if for a friendlier face, though no one else was there. She wrung her hands to complete the picture of nervousness, then bent down and whispered, "I'm here to see Master Grosbeak. I have messages."

The old woman sniffed. "Don't you all." She got up. "Follow me." She led Aly down a narrow, badly lit hall to an office. There were bundles of paper stacked everywhere, on shelves and on the desk at the center of the room. There was no chair for visitors: Aly suspected that few people would want to linger.

Grosbeak himself was a part-raka with wiry black hair. Aly fumbled with her hands, then her sash, wondering if he'd been trapped into this like Vitorcine or if he liked his work. She noticed the large emerald ring on his left hand as he opened the ledger and decided not to care about Grosbeak. Topabaw had made him rich.

"You're new," he said, his black eyes memorizing her face. "Name?"

"Aly Homewood, your lordship," she said, voice shaking.

"Where do you work? And it's Master Grosbeak, wench. I don't hold with mockery." His voice was as tight and flat as his mouth. He picked up a writing brush, dipped it in ink, and began to copy her particulars into his ledger.

"Please, Master Grosbeak, I'm maid to Lady Dovasary at Balitang House." Aly had tucked a darking with a peony inside it into her sash on the way to Grosbeak's. Now she smoothed her hands over her sash, as if drying her palms. "I wasn't mocking, sir, truly." Rubbing the sash was her cue to Peony. The darking flowed out the back of her sash and down to the floor. Aly stepped closer to the desk so that Grosbeak could not see her below the hips.

"Have you anything to report? Treasonous talk against the regents or His Majesty, letters and messages from mysterious sources, private chats between nobles without the servants to hear? Gossip from the servants about making trouble in the streets? Rumors of unrest, or traitors?" He scowled when she didn't answer right away. "This is Rajmuat, *wench.* Someone always talks loosely."

"Well, but, sir, we've only been back in the city less than a week, and first my ladies had to go to court, and folk are calling, and there's dresses to be made, and my lord Elsren comes and goes from the palace, it's really all very confusing. They were sad when they saw some people from the Ibadun family had been killed when we came, and Lady Dove was scared bad when a fight broke out near us at Dockmarket yesterday. . . ."

She nattered at him until he tired and dismissed her, with orders to listen to more conversations between noble guests. Aly curtsied as much as the sarong allowed, to ensure that Peony was tucked under Grosbeak's desk. When she saw that glint of flower, she knew the darking would manage well, and retreated. The old woman scowled at her in the front room, while a newcomer turned her head so that Aly could not see her face.

Aly was smiling as she turned into an alley two doors down from Grosbeak's. By the time she visited the man again, she would know a great deal more about who was loyal to the regents and who was not. Then she could do her best to direct Grosbeak's—and Topabaw's—suspicious eyes toward their own supporters.

In the alley, she stepped into a dark corner between buildings. "All right, Trick," she murmured. "If you want to spend life as a necklace . . ."

The darking poked its new bead-head out of her sash. "See more," it explained.

"Very true," said Aly. She gently lifted the Trick-bead string from her sash and draped it over her neck. It felt like cool drops of water rolling over her skin as Trick arranged itself in two loops of shiny beads. Under her right ear, one bead joined with another as a kind of clasp, giving Trick a slightly bigger head to speak from, where Aly could easily hear it.

Once she was freshly arrayed, Aly went in search of her mistress. Dove had moved on from the bookseller's where Aly had left her group, so Aly walked along until she saw Dove's unofficial guards. They pointed out the three household guards stationed at the entrance to the largest shop on Dori Way: Herbrand Edgecliff, Bookseller and Importer.

"How long has she been in there?" Aly asked the man-at-arms positioned by the main entrance.

"Long enough for my feet to hurt," drawled the man, an ex-bandit and devoted family servant.

Aly smiled. "Then I believe I'll wait out here. How many books can one person read?" she joked, with only a little, well-hidden wistfulness for long winter afternoons spent curled up, reading until her eyes began to blur.

The man-at-arms grinned. "Don't ask me—I can't read anyway." Then pride dawned on his face. "But my daughter can. Her Grace's maid's been teaching the little ones."

Aly smiled. She understood a father's pride. "She's a clever girl," Aly told him. "With luck she'll go far."

To keep from distracting him, she wandered along the storefront, part of her mind on the talk around her, part on what she had planned for that evening, and part on the bookseller's display. He had a very expensive front window, made of small panes of costly glass, the better to show off his wares. The books looked gorgeous, even through the warps and bubbles in the glass.

Something caught her eye. In the lowest right-hand pane in the corner, someone had scratched a design. Aly sharpened her magical Sight. The emblem of the open shackle was cut into the window. More importantly, it had been done from inside. Someone working in the shop, perhaps Master Edgecliff himself, supported the rebellion.

She yawned. "Maybe I can hint that it's getting toward lunchtime," she told the guard, and ambled into the shop, switching her behind like a lazy servant girl. When the door closed behind her, she reached into the bag that hung from her sash. It was like reaching into a bowl filled with lively cool liquid. A ball of it moved up into her palm. Gently Aly brought out a darking and, while looking at a wall of books, deposited it on a bottom shelf. There was an inch-wide gap between shelf and floor: the darking slid into it and vanished.

Pleased with her morning labor—she would place two more darkings on the way home, one at the checkpoint on Joshain and Trade Winds Street and one near Topabaw's spy outside Balitang House—Aly went to find Dove.

As the household napped, Aly returned to her workroom to talk with her pack and their recruits. They were training more people, teaching them how to gather information and where to send it. And there was news: Vereyu had sent a note from the palace. It seemed that the night before, Topabaw had been forced to interrupt the regents' supper with the news that the luarin governor of Ikang Island had been murdered. Servants had been present to hear both Topabaw's admission that he had no information as yet and Imajane's enraged reply, "Then what good *are* you?"

Aly smiled with pleasure. Already the relationship between the princess-regent and her spymaster was fraying and they had foolishly, or arrogantly, shown it before witnesses. "We must do our best to ensure that Topabaw continues to look unable to manage his work," she murmured, going through new reports on her desk. At the bottom of the stack was a slate with code signs written in chalk: Ysul's notice that her requested pots of blazebalm were ready for use. Before her pack returned to their own jobs, she said, "Those of you who were with me two nights ago, I'll require you at midnight once more." They nodded and left.

Ulasim stuck his head in the door as the last of Aly's pack filed out. "The guests have begun to arrive," he said. "And the young eagles have decided they wish to go riding to Lady Weeps Park."

Aly raised an eyebrow in silent question.

Ulasim answered it. "Her Grace says they will all go, including Lady Dovasary." He gave his thin smile. "Dove is not pleased. She has new books to read. Her Grace says His Grace of Nomru *particularly* requests his young friend's company."

Well, that's that, Aly thought, getting to her feet. It's not as if she can turn down one of the ten most powerful nobles in the realm.

She had asked Dove two nights ago, as she prepared her mistress's hair for bedtime, why she talked so much with a man old enough to be her grandfather. Dove had replied, "He's one of the few people who can keep up with me, and I with him. It's a pleasant change from having to slow down to deal with most people."

Aly, looking at Dove in the mirror, raised an eyebrow.

Dove smiled. "Not *you,* silly. I have trouble keeping up with *you.* Where everyone else sees a straight line, you see a maze, and when I'm done talking to you, the maze starts to make more sense."

"Thank you, I think," Aly had replied then. Now she amended her thought. Dove *would* risk offending one of the realm's most popular nobles if she didn't actually like him.

With Nuritin in command of household social functions, it was less than an hour until they were ready to go. Sarai's court of young men drew straws for the honor of riding at her side. Aly noticed that the Carthaki Zaimid did not choose to compete. Instead he rode with Nuritin, keeping pace with the duchess and her father, Lord Matfrid Fonfala.

Sarai's court supplied all the color and liveliness their parade could want, laughing and joking. At last the park appeared at the end of their road, the entrance graced by curved palm trees. Five wild kudarung soared overhead on the day's heated air. Even the younger riders stopped to watch, awed. When they entered the park, they did so quietly.

Aly and the other servants ended up in a pavilion set near the gate and the stables. Those nobles who chose not to ride left their mounts and wandered among the flower gardens, eating delicacies sold at small pavilions. Sarai and her companions rode on the park's horse paths, racing each other, Sarai determined to beat them all. She lost only to Zaimid.

After the racing, the horses were led to the stables to be cared for by the hands who worked there. The young people then joined the older ones for rest, food, and conversation. Aly wandered into the stables, admiring the horses and flirting with the hostlers, while she slipped a darking each into the saddle blankets of Duke Nomru, Lord Fonfala, and the Dowager Countess Tomang. She had talked to the creatures about what they were to do and questioned them enough to know that they understood her quite well. Though the darkings did not care to be elaborate with spoken language—perhaps because speech was a tricky affair for them—they were very intelligent.

Once the mosquitoes came out, it was time to return. Pembery, Boulaj, and Aly repaired their mistresses' appearances with degrees of success. Pembery and Aly did well enough because their ladies had spent the afternoon talking. As soon as Pembery finished, Winnamine went to see if the horses were ready to go. Boulaj had more of a struggle. Sarai had lost every one of the hairpins that had kept both her straight and her curled locks in place. She shook her long mane free. "Don't pin it, Boulaj," she ordered. "Whose idea was it anyway to make us torture our heads?"

"It's not seemly," protested Boulaj. "Young ladies are supposed to wear their hair up."

"Aly, there's a sheer scarf in my bag," Dove murmured. "Somebody should have thought to tell Boulaj that Sarai's old maid always carried spare pins." She looked at Pembery, eyes narrowed, as Aly searched out the scarf Dove had mentioned. "You were friends with her," Dove told her stepmother's attendant. As senior maid, it was Pembery's job to help Boulaj, as Dove well knew. "Perhaps you might tell Boulaj the different tricks to dressing my sister that she knew."

Pembery recognized a command even when it was phrased as a request. "Yes, Lady Dovasary." Dove didn't look away until Pembery gave a small bow of her head.

Aly produced the scarf, a gold and red length of silk that covered Sarai's hair enough for everyone but sticklers like Nuritin and Countess Tomang, who sniffed at the same time. Aly restrained a giggle and Boulaj covered a grin.

The party was quiet from weariness as they rode back down the stepped rises that lifted the different levels of the city above the harbor. Though it was still spring, the day had been warm and sticky, a hint of summer to come. Nomru and Matfrid Tomang spoke idly of moving to country estates for the summer. Zaimid told his companions, Sarai, Dove, and Sarai's friend Isalena Obemaek, that he wouldn't miss the dampness at all when he returned to hot, dry Carthak.

The closer they went to the heart of the city, the more Aly's skin prickled. The sidewalks were unusually crowded, even for this time of day, and few people on them were moving. Instead they stared at the noble riders. At Sarai.

Aly eased along the line of guards until she found the commander of the Balitang men-at-arms. Junai moved in from the other side of the thin ring of men to listen to Aly. First Aly counted, then wished she hadn't. The Balitangs had sent five soldiers. Most of the other riders had brought one, maybe two, guards, not anticipating trouble on an afternoon's ride to the park.

"You've got your cautious face on," the guards' commander murmured. "What is it?"

"Too many quiet people who are just staring," Aly replied. "And we know who they're staring at, too. Is there any way we can avoid the next army checkpoint?"

"I would think you'd *want* soldiers to handle the crowd," he replied.

Aly and Junai both shook their heads. "Oil on tinder," Junai explained. "The soldiers itching for a fight and the people itching to get at soldiers."

"It might not be too inconvenient to the regents if the very popular Balitang sisters got hurt—or accidentally killed—in a fight between a mob and soldiers. Things get so confused in street fighting—"

"Too late," the commander interrupted, "here's the checkpoint. I'll pass the word for everyone to look sharp."

Ahead, the road crossed with Rittevon's Lance, the street that went from the palace down to the docks. The soldiers at the checkpoint warily eyed the people, who outnumbered them, but did nothing to send them away or to hinder the nobles. It was five blocks farther down that the mob swept out of the side streets to surround the riders. In eerie silence, many of the new arrivals ragged and dirty, they tried to force their way through the guards, reaching for Sarai.

"Whatever you are doing, this is neither the time nor the place." Duke Nomru had a thundering voice when he cared to use it. "You will bring grief upon yourselves with this display. Return to your homes!" He wheeled his mount, forcing the people nearest him to back away.

Ferdy Tomang had stronger feelings. "Raka dogs!" he cried, lashing the nearest member of the crowd with his riding crop. "Back to your kennels!"

Oh, splendid, Aly thought, rolling her eyes. Our hero.

The eerie silence broke with a roar. Half of the mob turned on the young count. Ferdy spurred his horse to rear. The other noblemen and Matfrid Fonfala did the same, urging their mounts to turn on their hind legs, showing everyone the crushing power of those raised front hooves.

Balitang House's people had been trained for this, even if the guards with them had not. Junai and a man-at-arms collected the duchess and Nuritin. They drew them and the other noblewomen onto the sidewalk to put a building at their backs and take them out of the physical movement on the street. Aly gripped Sarai's and Dove's mounts, forcing them toward the same wall.

"Sarai, don't!" cried Dove. Aly looked up.

Sarai had her riding crop raised; her target was Aly. "Let me go!" she ordered. "I have to stop them before they kill people—before we kill more raka!"

Aly held Sarai's eyes with her own. She did not say it, but she thought it: if Sarai hit her, Aly would teach her a lesson Sarai's supporters would not like.

"Don't be a fool!" snapped Dove over Aly's head. "Get the wall at our backs, and get our servants behind us!" Boulaj was already ranging among the maids' horses, drawing them together and moving them to the rear, speaking softly as their riders kept very still. Aly was grateful that maids seldom chose lively mounts.

"This bad," Trick murmured in her ear. "Four-leggers mashing two-leggers bad."

Above the cries of the mob Aly heard the sound she'd been dreading: the tramp of boots. "It's about to get worse," she muttered. Here came the King's Watch, stern, hard men in red-painted breastplates, metal helmets, and boots with nails in the soles and metal pieces that covered the toes, making any kick the soldier gave a bloody one. They were armed with short swords, clubs, and shields, and used all three to drive the mob, cutting their way through to the nobles. A raka woman moved to scoop two children out of the way of their mounted captain, diving between the Balitang guards into the protected inner circle. It was Eyun, one of Aly's pack. She bore a scratch down one creamy cheek. She looked at Aly, who nodded that she'd done well, then turned her attention to the shrieking children. One looked to be a merchant's child. Her gown was luarin-style cotton, unfaded and unmended. She yelled for her nursemaid while the other child screamed over his broken arm. He looked like the worst dregs of the slums, ragged and filthy.

"Here." Winnamine knelt beside Eyun, a flask of water in her hands. To the girl she said, "I'm sure your nurse is fine." She offered the boy a drink from her silver flask. The boy blinked at her, then took the flask and drank. He might have then tried to run with it, but light flashed from Nuritin at Winnamine's side. The boy's eyes rolled up and he collapsed, Nuritin's sturdy old hands catching him before his bad arm hit the stones. Aly had heard that the old lady had been rough and ready in her day. It seemed she could still muster a bit of power at need. "Well, I couldn't leave him feeling all that pain," Nuritin said, meeting Winnamine's look. "And soft-hearted as you are, I suppose we'll need a healer who will tend him."

"That depends on the healer, surely." Zaimid dismounted. He knelt in the street, apparently unaware of the war being fought on the other side of the protective line of men-at-arms and noblemen on horseback. "It's quite a simple break, and luckily, it's not pierced the skin." Gently he wrapped long fingers around the broken limb, his head bent, his brown face closed and thoughtful. In Aly's Sight silvery fire spun a thread from his blazing magical core down through his arm and into the boy's.

He's got wonderful control, thought Aly, impressed. Of course, he would. They wouldn't put a noble idiot in charge of the Carthaki emperor's health.

Zaimid released the boy's arm. The marks of his hands showed pale at first, then faded. The boy stirred, then grabbed his arm. He looked at it, agape, then at Nuritin, who had recovered Winnamine's flask, then at Zaimid.

"You'll do better here until this ends," Zaimid said. "No good sending you out to get something else broken."

Dove nudged Aly and handed over plums that had survived the nobles' meal. Aly gave them to the boy. He began to devour them, his wondering eyes still on Zaimid.

Beyond their circle of safety, the royal soldiers dispersed the mob with brutal speed. Sarai was still trying to fight her way between Ferdy Tomang and Duke Nomru, screaming,

"They weren't hurting anyone! Leave them alone!" She finally gave up when the soldiers had driven the crowd so far down the street that none of them could hear. She glared at Duke Nomru, tears running down her cheeks. "They weren't going to hurt us!"

The older man raised his stern brows. "And do you think that would stop the kind of men they have in the King's Watch? Their orders are to disperse gatherings." He looked down the street, with its litter of bodies. "This one is well and truly dispersed, whatever its intention was." He looked back at the ladies. "I propose we return to Balitang House at all speed, before the animals hired for the Watch return."

Winnamine and Nuritin mounted up.

Aly moved in close to Eyun. "Stay here. Learn what you can, maybe get this little one home?" The little girl had sobbed herself into silence in Eyun's hold.

Eyun nodded and hand-signed, *They wanted to touch the twice-royal. That's all. Just touch her, to know she is real.*

"So much beauty shouldn't be marred," Zaimid said over Aly's shoulder. He brushed Eyun's cheekbone with his fingers. Her cut healed before their eyes, as if the work of several weeks had been put into a breath. There was not even a scar. To Nomru he said apologetically, "Your Grace, my ladies"—he looked at the older women next—"forgive me, but I am needed here. I bid you all farewell." To Sarai he added, "I'll make sure these two children are looked after." He was already unbuckling saddlebags from his horse. Draping them over his shoulder, he asked the boy, "Will you hold my reins?" He passed them into the child's hands. Aly thought he was being overcharitable, giving the reins to a boy who had meant to steal the duchess's silver flask, but it seemed the boy held the healer in too much awe to steal the horse at present.

Aly mounted her pony. Sarai might have pulled away from her group, but her grandfather Matfrid came up beside her as she urged her horse forward, and took the reins. "Granddaughter, you are overwrought," he said quietly, holding her dark eyes with his gray ones. "Allow me to escort you."

They rode off, picking their way around the fallen—Aly was pleased to see a few soldiers groaning in the road—the men and the guards in a ring around the ladies and their maids. Aly looked back between two guards. Zaimid, saddlebags on the ground beside him, was engaged in turning over a woman who resembled a bundle of rags, unaware or uncaring that she'd left a bloody handprint on his white lawn sleeve.

At the house, the gathering broke up quickly. Sarai announced that she had a headache and needed to lie down. Without her to hold them together, the young nobles chose to go home. The gloss had been stripped from the afternoon.

Only when the guests had gone did the Balitang ladies and their maids ascend to the family quarters. They entered their private sitting room to find Sarai and a litter of overturned chairs and decorative tables. Gazing at the mess, Aly thought it was just as well that the second-best furnishings went into this room, which was for comfort, not style.

"Have you taken leave of your senses?" asked Nuritin. Her back was as stiff as a poker, her voice chipped ice. "This is not the behavior of a properly bred young woman, it is the behavior of spider monkeys!"

"After seeing all those 'properly bred' people just sit there while people were being thrashed, I'd *rather* live with spider monkeys!" cried Sarai, eyes swollen with furious weeping. "Every last one of us—every last one—just let it happen! Ferdy was *glad*—he called them raka dogs, I heard him!"

"A riot cannot be controlled, Sarai," Winna said calmly, setting a table upright. "All we could have done was get pulled from our horses and savaged. Soldiers can lose control in those circumstances. They don't care who they batter—and they can always claim they didn't realize we were nobility when we were among the commoners. It's happened before." Dove, Aly, and Pembery began to help the duchess pick things up. Nuritin continued to stare at Sarai as if she were a badly trained housemaid.

"It's happened *here,*" Sarai shouted. "It happens *here,* because soldiers believe the poor are a disease, not people. And they get that attitude honestly—it comes straight from the Throne! It always has and it always will, and people who are supposed to be noble in nature will *let* it happen, for fear of their own lives! Only one of us showed any decency today: Zaimid! The foreigner! He actually cares about people, whether they live in kennels or not!" She stormed out, yanking the door open so hard it chipped the stucco wall.

There was a long silence. At last Nuritin said tartly, "Well! I am not charged with her upbringing, Winnamine, but in your place, I would slap her for addressing elders in such a way."

"She was upset, Aunt," Winnamine replied wearily. "There was blood running in the gutters."

"Screaming and shouting will not change that," snapped Nuritin. "Getting enough power among ourselves to *force* the Crown to change how it rules the people, that is the way to change."

Well, it's one way, thought Aly, collecting the pieces of a broken vase.

What Nuritin had just said sounded very close to treason. If Aly really did belong to Topabaw, she could get all kinds of favors from him for that tidbit alone. She wondered if Countess Tomang—certainly not her son!—Lord Matfrid, Duke Nomru, and Baron Engan, Dove's astronomer friend, held the same view that the Crown must be controlled.

At the conspirators' nightly meeting Aly reported on the fight. Ochobu was not present. The moment she'd heard the news, she had packed her bag of medicines and gone to offer help. No one suggested they would pray for any member of the Watch who made the mistake of trying to stop her.

There were more reports to give and to hear. At last the conspirators separated, most bound for their beds. Aly went to her office. Ysul came in not long after with three packs, setting them on the floor very carefully. He was dressed as an itinerant worker, the kind of fellow people expected to see around the docks. In a cloth bag carried like a bedroll on his back he had his waterproof and sight-proof disguise. Aly dressed in her own suit, then in her Carthaki noble's disguise. Fegoro came again as a Bazhir, Lokak as a southern Carthaki, Jimarn as another Carthaki noble, and Yoyox as Death's priest. Aly, Jimarn, and Yoyox hid Ysul's packs under their flowing clothes.

"Fun?" whispered Trick in Aly's ear. "Meeting not fun. Fight in street and house stupid."

She followed the others to the laundry and down into the tunnel, whispering softly inside her veils, "It depends on what you think is fun. It will be loud."

"Loud maybe fun," said Trick. "You think fight in street and house stupid, too?"

Aly was about to ask how the darking could judge what was stupid for humans when she stopped herself. She had to remember, these creatures were intelligent. They learned ferociously fast. They already knew every member of the household by face and voice. And they had lived nearly ten years among dragons. Surely that counted for something, since Daine had also mentioned dragons were less than patient as a whole. Aly grinned wryly as they emerged from the tunnel.

"Fights were stupid," she said. Then she and Jimarn each took one of Fegoro's arms as the rest of their group cut over to other streets.

As before, the King's Watch had abandoned the checkpoints for the night. The afternoon's unpleasantness had taken place in Middle Town, not at the dock. It was habit among the city's guardians to decide that a violent outburst kept the lower classes quiet for days, which meant they were off their guard now.

Their watchman friend was absent. They entered his shack, removed their disguises, then redistributed the packs. Quietly they descended the ladder to the meeting places of stinking piers, stinking water, and stinking boulders. The noise from the dockside merrymakers was as loud as ever, a jangle of music, singing, debate, and the occasional fight. It covered any slips they made on the rocks. At last they came to the metal net and passed into the slave market piers.

Aly adjusted her Sight as the three teams split up. Beside the piers she could see ships at anchor—seventeen in all. They should be close to empty. Even with the net, slavers didn't like the risk that some desperate swimmer might yet escape. Slaves were always taken to the market's pens as soon as their vessel docked. Aly hoped there would be crew aboard but knew the likelihood was small. They would be out, spending the profits of other slave sales.

She led Ysul out to the farthest left pier of the dock she had kept for herself, the dock where she had disembarked as a slave. As he treaded water, she took a small clay globe from his waterproof sack and jammed it into an opening between boards. Back and forth they went, careful to let no water leak into the sack of globes. At last all six were placed. As they waited, Ysul left the waterproof bag close to the nearest globe. It would be incinerated when the globe was set off. It was always important to get rid of any trace of the mage who did a piece of work like this. If Topabaw's people were good enough, they might track any remnants back to Ysul.

Aly and Ysul returned to the net to wait for their companions. The others arrived, their own bags left behind. Swiftly they made their way back to the watchman's shack and changed out of their waterproof clothes into their disguises. As they left the shack, they took the bundled suits over to one of the many fires that lit Dockmarket and burned them. Then they mingled with the crowds.

They reached the end of the night market, a good four blocks from the slave docks and pens. Wooden barriers were set there, manned by rock-muscled freemen with iron-studded clubs. The slave merchants liked to guard their property.

Aly, Jimarn, and Fegoro reached the barriers, inspected the guards by eye as if they too may be for sale, then turned to look at the fading gaiety of the Dockmarket. Ysul was watching a juggler nearby. When he glanced at Aly, she raised two gloved fingers.

She saw the silver flash of Ysul's magic. At the corner of her eye she noted an orange flicker; fast behind it came the roar as the blazebalm ignited, blowing their cheap clay globes into dust and setting the slave docks on fire. Aly turned when the other merrymakers did, to see a vision that made her shiver in delight. Columns of flame clawed the night sky as fire raced over the docks. Within moments their fire was reaching for the ships. A handful of men threw themselves from a few vessels and swam for shore: watchmen, left behind while their mates toured the city.

Like the rest of the Dockmarket crowds and the guards

on the barriers, Aly and her friends stayed to look on as ship after ship caught fire and alarm bells began to sound in their part of the city. Only when they heard the ominous thump of marching feet did they mingle with the rest of the crowd and flee, splitting up as the crowd did, to find their way home by separate routes.

Aly went to bed feeling drained but pleased. When she had been brought to those docks and the slave markets beyond, she had promised herself that everyone who had fetched her there would come to regret it. It might take her years to find the actual pirates who had captured her, but the docks, and the vessels of some providers of captives for sale, made for a very fine start. She rather thought her mother would approve.

8

PLOTS HATCH

Once again Aly was roused by a tentacle tickling her nose. She cracked one eyelid, to see it wasn't quite dawn. "Trick, I *need* sleep. I know you don't," she croaked after pulling her cover over her head so she wouldn't rouse anyone. "But *I* do."

The darking said, "Sleep or big news? Pick!"

Aly's eyes flew open. She was wide awake. "Big news. And it had better be big."

"Nomru arrested," Trick told her. Aly smothered a gasp of shock. "Nomru at party at palace when messengers come and say docks burn," the darking continued. "When princess say punish many people for this and other trouble they make, Nomru say people afraid. He say, kindness do more than hurting. He say, help to buy food, take less taxes. Princess say, arrest him. Take him to Kanodang. Flame with Nomru still. Flame say Nomru say many bad words. Flame say guards afraid to hurt Nomru."

"I should think so!" Aly whispered. Imajane had misstepped badly. "Why didn't Rubinyan stop her?" she asked.

"Prince try, Flame say. Princess not listen."

I need to get more darkings into the palace, Aly thought. Then she remembered: "Was Quartz there with Countess Tomang?"

Trick nodded. Although the cover shut out the light, such as it was, Aly's Sight still let her see the darking's featureless but somehow expressive face. It had opened up from its necklace shape so that it could watch her—or could it?

"Can you see in the dark?" she asked.

"Nothing dark to darkings," Trick replied, matter-of-fact.

Aly pressed that into her memory, then inquired, "So what does Quartz say? Was the countess there when Imajane ordered the arrest?"

Trick nodded. "Quartz say, countess drink too much rotten grape juice. Countess vomit twice on way home."

Of course she did, thought Aly. Sometimes you don't have to be an oracle to read the omens of your own doom. "Back into place, please, Trick," she whispered. "We're getting up. Tell Flame to try to come home as best as it can. I can learn nothing from Nomru in prison that's useful right away."

As soon as her "bead necklace" was secure around her neck, Aly tossed off her coverlet. As usual, Junai was already gone and Dove was sound asleep. Quickly Aly put her pallet bed away, got dressed, cleaned her teeth, and combed her hair. She raced down to the ground floor and out to the practice ground. Ulasim was exercising his longsword skills with Fesgao, but the moment he saw Aly he put up a hand to stop the match. Fesgao drew up and looked over his shoulder to see what had distracted the big footman. Ulasim handed the practice sword off to Boulaj, then advanced on Aly, his muscled chest sweaty despite the early-morning chill. Aly wondered how long he'd been practicing when he grabbed her by one arm and towed her toward the house. "Lovely to see you this morning," he said, his voice filled with false cheer. "Might I have a moment of your time for a chat? I knew you would agree." Into the house they went, and down the hall to the meeting room.

Aly tried only once to tug her arm from his grip—it was like wearing a shackle on her bicep. "Why the enthusiasm?" she asked, trotting to keep up with his long stride. "I was coming to see you. There's something you ought to know."

He thrust her into the room and followed her in, closing the door behind him. "I'm sure there is a great deal I ought to know, but first, there is something you *will* know," Ulasim said, facing her. "Just *what* were you thinking of last night?"

Aly crossed her arms. "We agreed that, unless it was necessary, we were to keep one another uninformed about exact operations done by our individual groups. It's to everyone's advantage in case we're questioned." He reminds me of someone—who? she wondered.

"Yes, we were to keep one another uninformed about particular operations," Ulasim retorted, scowling. "I do not object in the least to your strategy, your target, or your methods of achieving your goal. I *do* object—gods curse it, woman, must I ask Mother put a watcher spell on you, to let us know where you are if you go off these grounds? What I *do* object to is *you* taking the command yourself."

Aly winced. Suddenly she knew what had puzzled her about his stance and his speech. Just so would her own da chew out the leader who led a raid on his or her own.

"I allowed it because I knew the source of your interest in that area," he informed her. "I can understand it all too well. I also had Fesgao send some of his people out to keep an eye on you, in case things went awry."

Aly had noticed familiar faces in the crowd. She had simply assumed that members of the household had taken a night to enjoy themselves. *Idiot!* she scolded herself. *That's the kind of slipup that can ruin everything! If you hadn't been so fixed on your stupid revenge, you would have asked why our people were out so late!*

"You could have been trampled when the crowd ran," Ulasim went on sternly. "You could have been taken by the King's Watch."

Aly couldn't help it. She snorted.

"Well, even slaves can get lucky once," Ulasim admitted. It was an old Kyprin proverb. "But you endangered your people by being there. You endangered us. And you endangered our ladies. Do you understand me? No more heroics, Aly. I know better than you how frustrating it is to stay behind while others strike a blow. But it's necessary. We know too much, and there are ways to get around suicide spells."

About to explain that the god had made her immune to telling what she knew through torture or magic, Aly changed her mind. Instead she bowed her head. "I'm sorry. You're right. I was foolish."

Ulasim frowned. "Don't toy with me, girl. I'm not in the mood."

Aly shook her head and showed him her real face, which expressed rueful acknowledgment. "I'm not, Ulasim, honestly, for once. You're right." She raised an eyebrow at him. "You knew beforehand?"

Ulasim nodded.

Aly collapsed into one of the cushioned chairs. Since it was impossible for him to loom over her without making himself look silly, Ulasim picked a chair for himself. "And you let me do it anyway," Aly went on.

The big raka smiled crookedly. "I understood. But it

cannot happen again, Aly. You are too valuable to take such chances."

Aly nodded. "But I'll have to do it once more," she pointed out. He scowled. "It'll just be me, a quick job. It's something you really don't want to know about." As if I dared explain about setting darkings to listen inside the Gray Palace, she thought. To Ulasim she added, "I can't trust it to anyone else, and it's vital. After that, I'll move to the rear, just as you do. I swear by the gods." Again she raised an eyebrow at him. "Are you done scolding me?"

Ulasim began to lever himself out of his chair. "I am done," he replied.

Aly put a hand on his arm and pressed down. "I told you I have news of my own, news you'll want to hear."

Ulasim sank back into his seat. "Will you make it quick?" he asked.

"I'll make it quick," she teased, "but once I'm done, you might be caught up for longer than you think. Last night Duke Nomru spoke unwisely to Princess Imajane. He presently enjoys the Crown's hospitality at Kanodang."

Ulasim's jaw dropped. "*Nomru?* Are they mad?"

Aly shrugged. "His Highness, I don't believe so. *Her* Highness? We still await the magistrate's ruling in her case. Now, they've jailed him. The Prince at least will see that if Nomru was an honest critic before he was arrested, he will in all likelihood be an enemy if they let him go."

"They *have* to let him go," whispered Ulasim. "He's the most powerful noble in the realm after Topabaw. And he's one of the wealthiest. . . ."

Aly let him turn the idea of Nomru's wealth over in his mind. After a few moments she said, "Topabaw won't like Nomru as an enemy of the Crown. I doubt Her Highness would ever forgive the duke for implying she rules the Isles badly." She smiled. "And if His Highness is ever said to have a flaw, it is that he desires more wealth than he has. I don't think he's mad, not that I've heard. But greedy . . ." Her eyes sparkled. "I love greedy regents, don't you?"

"Aly, you are a wicked creature," replied Ulasim. The corners of his eyes crinkled. "You are right. Her Highness may have made the mistake, but the prince will not wish to make it worse by freeing Nomru. Even if he considered it, he will not be able to forget the Crown's ability to seize the lands, goods, and wealth from suspected traitors."

Aly traced the edge of a lotus printed on her sarong. "It sorrows me that you think I am wicked," she said wistfully. "I fear you are right. I really must change my ways. Eventually." She sighed, then continued briskly, "Have we people at Kanodang?"

Ulasim gave her a look full of pity. "My dear, we have people everywhere."

Aly scuffed her sandaled foot on the polished floor. "*Inside* Kanodang? Not prisoners, but jailers? Cooks?"

"Everywhere means *everywhere,* Aly Bright Eyes," Ulasim pointed out. "And I will endanger none of our people for a single luarin."

Possibilities raced through Aly's mind as she examined all angles of her idea.

Ulasim waited. "That look in your eyes makes me *very* uncomfortable," he finally said. "You look like the god when he has a horrendous piece of mischief in mind."

This is all I would need, Aly told herself. This would disgrace Topabaw utterly. It would show just how weak the regents really are.

She beamed at Ulasim. "I have an idea, if you're interested. Something no one's prepared for. A fast stroke, it'll have to be. Really fast. But oh, so lovely in the results." She began to whistle a little tune.

"Suddenly I am *very* worried," Ulasim said. "I have visions of islands sinking under the sea because of your 'something.' Spit it out."

Aly looked at the ceiling. "Break out all the prisoners we can, luarin and raka. Use the eclipse. The people think it's unlucky. So use the night when a shadow lies on the Rittevon line"—the ones assisted by Mithros and the moon Goddess, she thought, but did not say, in case the gods were near—"to deal a blow against the ruling family."

Ulasim stared at her.

Aly folded her hands demurely. "We have an opportunity, or so it seems to me."

"What of the risk to folk who know nothing of this? To our own people, to the entire city? The Crown has ordered entire villages slain—what makes you think they'll stop at slaying every raka in the Downwind District? Of all the—"

Aly raised an eyebrow. "Why should they suspect the raka?"

Ulasim took a breath to shout his answer, then stopped.

You have it, thought Aly. Just below her ear she heard a tiny voice say, "Fun."

"They won't suspect the raka," whispered Ulasim. "Nomru's wealthy, he has powerful friends with money and household men-at-arms. The Crown will search the city—they must. But the stroke will fall heaviest on the *luarin*, the very people who are the regents' base of support. Their men will be so busy chasing escaped prisoners and trying to find out how it happened that we will get away with scores of preparations for the actual fighting." Ulasim frowned and stroked his bearded chin. "You are an evil girl child."

Aly ignored this pleasantry. "You'll shake up the luarin nobility. They're already thinking that if the regents will jail

Nomru, who will they turn on next? The duke himself will be in our debt, when the time comes." And you'll force that limp luarin conspiracy to develop a backbone, she thought. Fear for themselves will drive them into planning rebellion instead of just talking.

Ulasim rested his elbows on his knees. "There will be deaths of people who knew nothing about it. They'll torture anyone they think might be involved."

Aly crossed her arms. Knowledge of what she suggested closed over her shoulders like an enemy's arm. She had grown up aware of the deaths of many people her parents had known during an attempt to take the throne. They numbered friends and enemies alike: the uncle her brother Thom was named for; her mother's teacher and companion, the supernatural cat Faithful, for whom her mother still wept; the Shang Dragon, the queen's and her mother's friend; Duke Roger of Conté, the king's cousin; a princess of the Isles, King Oron's daughter, who had been killed in the fighting. Aly's family knew the price of revolution, though she couldn't say as much to Ulasim.

"People died in the street yesterday," she told him. "People who just wanted a look at Sarai. Is this a war or not?"

Ulasim was nodding before she even asked her question. "We free only Kanodang's political prisoners. Unless you mean to loose rapists and murderers on the city?"

Aly shook her head. "They can stay in their cages. I won't mind that. And it will reinforce the idea that it was luarin. They free Nomru, so they figure releasing the other political prisoners will confuse the trail."

Ulasim sat back with a groan. At last he said, "Send me Fesgao and Ochobu. Anything of interest that your people turn up, come straight to me. It's two days until the eclipse—we have to move fast. We'll strike after Her Highness's party."

"It's a good thing you've been sneaking warriors into the city since last autumn, then, isn't it?" Aly inquired.

Ulasim glared at her. "How did you— Never mind."

"Will you be needing my spies?"

Ulasim shook his head. "Where we must go, we have them."

Aly went to find Ochobu and Fesgao. "No fun for us," Trick muttered in her ear.

"Oh, we'll have fun," Aly assured her companion. "I always do." She wandered into the female servants' dormitory. There she hand-signaled to a woman of her pack who was awake: *Bring the girls to the meeting room soonest.* She left and went to the single men's dormitory. Sadly, she encountered Ukali before she could enter the big room. Aly sighed with regret: she knew most of the men slept in loincloths, and she would have enjoyed the sight. Accepting the disappointment, she gave her message to Ukali and went back to the large meeting room.

It wasn't long before every chair was occupied. Some of those without chairs leaned on the walls; others sat on the floor. When they were all settled and the door was closed, Aly said, "My dear ones, I have something for you to do on the night of the lunar eclipse. Alas, it will not include me. I'm afraid our general has told me that I am quite naughty and will no longer be permitted to do such things."

"He's right, Duani," Olkey remarked as he peeled a mango with his knife. "You can't go risking yourself. What if Topabaw had gotten word of last night's celebration? *You're* the one who told *us* if we're caught, it's trouble for everyone else once the torturers and the mages get done with you."

Aly raised an eyebrow, not sure that she liked having her student quote her warnings back to her. "This was personal," she replied.

Guchol was working a comb through her tangled hair. "You told us we can't ever let anything be personal, Duani."

"Sometimes personal is too important for rules," Jimarn said, her cold voice cutting through the room like a blade. "Sometimes personal has to be taken care of." Her flinty eyes met Aly's. They both smiled. Jimarn was a runaway slave.

"Well, I'll be good and not do it again, which means I leave this next bit of deliciousness for those who volunteer," Aly said. She pointed to the map of Rajmuat and its surroundings. On the northeast side of the harbor were the slums of the Downwind District, with the human garbage heap called the Honeypot highest on the slope to the ridge. It was no more than wood cabins on stilts, lean-tos, tents, and shacks. Kanodang was on the far side of the heights. There were only two good things about Kanodang, said the wits. It was upwind of the stench of the Honeypot, and it was a nicer place to live.

At the end of the ridge that split the two was the northeast fortress that guarded the harbor mouth. The Lesser Fortress was two simple towers surrounded by a wall. Aly placed a finger on it, then on the complex that guarded the harbor's far side. The Greater Fortress rose on high ground, dominating the harbor. The display grounds for Examples lay below the fortress's stone ramparts.

"Two nights from this, well after midnight," she explained, "we need fires to start in both fortresses and in the barracks. Ysul will help you with blazebalm. If you set afire all that will burn in both, I will bless you before your ancestors, but I will rest contented if you just keep a large number of soldiers busy for a time. Can you do it?"

"Well, there are the tunnels through the ridge that will get us up into the Lesser Fortress," Rasaj pointed out.

"But they're not safe," objected Hiraos. "They're centuries old, they could collapse any time."

"But they haven't, have they?" asked Lokak. "And the word is they're open still."

"You'll trust 'the *word*'?" demanded Hiraos. "Probably sent in by some old rock rat who wouldn't know if a tunnel dropped on his head, it's happened so many times. . . ."

"So go look for yourselves," Jimarn told them scornfully. "We've got two whole days." She looked at Aly. "There's a pretty big sewer from the Greater Fortress that we can use, if people can stand it. We'd need those special files that cut through iron."

"I know where they're stored," Junai said. To Aly she pointed out, "There's only so much of those things that will burn, you know. They're mostly stone."

"I don't care how much of them burns, only that they burn brightly enough to catch a lot of attention," Aly muttered, rubbing her fingers over her "necklace." She had discovered that Trick vibrated when happy, a sign of contentment as soothing as, and more silent than, a cat's purr.

The room went silent. Aly looked up to see all their eyes on her.

"You want a diversion," Atisa said, grinning. "A big, noisy, attention-getting diversion."

Aly shook her head. "If I'd thought you were stupid, my children, I wouldn't have bothered to train you. Can you do it?" They all nodded. "Well, then, you don't need me. Bring your plans around during the rest period, and we'll have a look. Think it through. I need you all in one piece."

As she walked down the hall on her way back to the kitchen, she asked Trick quietly, "What does Lace report? What are Ulasim, Fesgao, and Ochobu talking about?"

"Getting horses and small sailing boats for escape," replied Trick promptly. "There is cove north of Kanodang where they hide boats. People inside prison will let fighters in. Fesgao must pick out force. They will get word today for people at Kanodang to be ready. We go?" it asked wistfully.

"No," Aly consoled it. "We're going to a party instead."

"Party fun?" asked the darking.

Aly smiled. "It could be."

Once more Dove insisted on a morning walk to see her merchant friends. Elsren was leaving for the palace when they reached the front door. He insisted on hugging his "favorite sister," as he proclaimed to the guards. Aly noted that a number of the black-armored men of the King's Guard turned their heads or brought up their hands to hide smiles.

Once Elsren's party had left, Junai and their escort of men-at-arms emerged from the side courtyard. Dove began to scowl, then sagged. Tacking a proper smile to her face, she greeted everyone by name as they formed up around her. Aly's people slowly collected ahead, to the sides of, and behind their group as they walked down Joshain Street. Today Kioka, Eyun, Hiraos, and Ukali went as secret guards. While Dove visited with her friends, they could deal in rumor.

The walk to the business part of town was not as relaxed as it had been before. Knots of people stood at corners, talking in soft voices, unless soldiers of the King's Watch came to send them on their way. The poorer the gossipers were, the more kicks and blows they got from the soldiers.

"Slime," murmured Dove as they passed one man whose nose was clearly broken and bleeding. Without a word she offered him her handkerchief.

"Stop somewhere and tilt your head back," a man-at-arms advised kindly. "Just wait till the bleeding stops."

The raka muttered his thanks and went into an alley.

"I hope when the time comes things will be done about behavior like that," whispered Dove. "We'll never all live together if the luarin don't accept anyone whose skin is brown."

Her pleasure that day was to stroll down Green Street. Respectable cooks and their assistants shopped here, or they were supposed to. Many stood in tiny groups, whispering. Pairs of men in the scarlet uniform of the Watch paced everywhere, their eyes shifting in the frames made of the face plates of their helmets.

As they passed a small group of civilians, Aly heard a luarin woman with a dusting of flour in her hair whisper to two raka, "Rats, I tell you! My best tenant wakes us all screaming in the dead of night. There was a basketful of rats by his bed! So what does he do but open the door to his room, so they can get out into the house *and* my bakery, if you please! Well, I told him . . ."

Dove and her companions, including Aly, walked out of earshot. Aly smiled. Looking around, she saw the words *Nomru* and *slave docks* on a number of lips. It wouldn't take long for Dove to hear the news.

They halted at a spice seller's stall, with its baskets of seasonings. Dove greeted the woman who was accepting payment from a customer. Aly observed that one seller of garlic, leeks, and onions had hung a decoration at the corner of her booth. Four bulbs were braided together, connected to a broken circle of leeks tied to a wooden frame. It was a very subtle open shackle.

"You're sure?" Dove asked sharply. Aly turned. Her mistress was gripping the spice seller's arm. "There's no doubt?"

The luarin woman shook her head. "My husband was making a delivery to His Grace's house. There's a seal on the gate and everything. The family's inside—they may come and go, but they're terrified."

I should have told the Balitangs this morning, Aly thought, then shook her head. They would have wanted to know where she had gotten her information, and she could not tell them.

A cluster of Mithran priests brushed past their group without so much as an apology. The priest in the lead sported a bite on his cheek. Two acolytes whispered that the temple's master of the flame had been assaulted by rats. Aly rubbed her hands together. People wrote down their secrets, or had a temple scribe write for them, and gave the folded scraps of paper to the master of the flame. It would not be difficult at all for a man in that position to keep the scraps and sell whatever useful information he collected to Topabaw.

They'll be scrambling like an upended basket of rats themselves when Topabaw falls, Aly thought.

"We're going home," Dove said abruptly. "Aly, come along." The guards closed in as Dove said farewell to the spice seller. Once she was ready, they began to hurry back the way they had come. When Aly came up beside her, Dove said quietly, "Duke Nomru was arrested last night, *and* someone blew up the slave docks."

"Did they?" Aly asked innocently. "Fancy that. And we saw His Grace only yesterday. He didn't say he was on the outs with the regents."

"I'm worried about Nomru," said Dove, biting her lip. "He's too mule-headed to beg the regents for anything. And why the slave docks?" she asked with a frown. "Why the ships? There will be more."

"Perhaps as a hint that there should be no more, my lady," suggested one of the guards. "The first thing built after the conquest was a bigger slave market."

Aly glanced at the man. As far as she was aware, he was simply one of Fesgao's warriors, picked for his loyalty and his skill with arms. From his light skin, if he had a slave ancestor or ancestress, it had been some generations ago.

"But we've always had slavery," Dove reminded him. "Even before the conquest."

"They used it as a way to bring the raka to heel," replied the soldier. "Here it became a weapon. Wise as you are, Lady Dovasary, surely you know, if any members of your family are accused of crimes against the Crown, it is the Crown's right to sell any of your household with raka blood. That would include you and the lady Saraiyu."

Dove glanced at Aly. "Not one word," she said.

Aly shrugged. "I wasn't going to say a thing." She put her fingers under her Trick necklace to touch the scar where her slave collar used to be. Dove made a face.

"If the Crown abolished slavery, it would beggar the great nobles," she told the man-at-arms. "They would turn to treason before that."

The man shrugged. "I was just mentioning it as history, my lady. If you please, I am forgetting my duty. I must not converse, or I will be distracted from your safety."

Passing a basketmaker's booth on their way out of Market Town, Aly saw an ornament displayed on the edge of the awning. Palm fronds were woven into the shackle-and-chain design.

They want to join, Aly thought, awed. Not just the raka. The merchant luarin. They want to rid themselves of the Rittevons. But will they fight?

"Trick," she murmured, so quietly that only her necklace darking might hear, "what has Peony to report from Grosbeak? Anything?"

Trick extended a very long neck up until it could loop itself around the back of Aly's ear and dangle its head by her eardrum. "Peony says woman called Lutestring come from palace for daily report from Grosbeak. She takes papers and what Grosbeak says. Grosbeak tells her mysterious new sign of four circles then broken circle appears in more places every day. He say half reports he gets say Topabaw turning against regents. He say other half say regents want to replace Topabaw. Grosbeak is shaking. Grosbeak does not tell Lutestring that he is taking all of his money out of money-changer accounts and packing a bag if he must run. He already send wife and children into country today."

"Thank you," Aly murmured as they walked through the Balitangs' gate. "I'd hate to lose Grosbeak, though. At least, right at present." She stopped, thinking, nibbling her lip as Dove went into the house and the guards returned to their barracks. Aly's unofficial watchers would return to their listening and rumor-spreading throughout the city.

"Why stopping?" Trick inquired.

"Ah," Aly said. The sound of Trick's voice practically inside her head gave her an idea. "Does he take a nap during the rest period?"

Trick waited for a moment, then told Aly, "Every day."

"Peony must wait until he's sound asleep, then whisper that Grosbeak should stay to help Topabaw. Tell him that gods are smiling on Grosbeak." Bless me, I'm starting to talk like them, she thought. Aloud she told Trick, "Ask Peony to tell Grosbeak he will be rich if he stays to help Topabaw. Keep repeating it until he is almost awake. Peony must be careful and speak softly, positioning itself like you are doing. The longer Grosbeak stays and works for Topabaw, the more of his agents we'll catch."

Trick was briefly silent, then said aloud, "Peony say, fun."

Aly smiled. "Well, I did promise *all* of you some fun."

The footman in the front hall told Aly that Dove had headed straight for her stepmother's room. Lady Sarai still lay abed. Aly nodded her thanks and proceeded through the house on the way to her workroom, where she was sure a stack of reports awaited her. They had regular deliveries from the rebellion's other agents, chosen and working long before Aly had even come to the Isles, people like Vereyu at the palace. Like Grosbeak, these people gathered information from their spies and sent it to Quedanga, who made sure that everyone who should see it did, including Aly. There were also reports from those agents Aly's people had recruited and trained, in addition to those of her own packs.

Passing the mages' workroom, she saw that the door was open. She looked inside. A footman who served in Kadyet House across the street was seated on a stool. His breeches were dusty, and he sported a swollen gash over one cheekbone. His shirt was off, revealing a spreading bruise over his ribs. Ochobu worked at the counter behind him, mashing herbs and oils in a mortar as silver wisps of her power rose from it.

"Bacar, what happened?" Aly asked, leaning against the doorframe, turning slightly so that her sarong hugged her curves. She knew this man well enough to flirt with him. "From the look of it, somebody doesn't like you."

He looked at her and winced, trying to cover his face with one hand and his ribs with another. "Bright Eyes, I hate your seeing me when I'm not at my best," he complained. "Couldn't you come back after Duani Ochobu here makes me presentable?"

Aly smiled. "Even bruised, you're a treat with your shirt off. So what happened?"

He let his hands drop into his lap. "I said the wrong thing to one of the King's Watch at the barricade to the slave docks. They burned, you know. The docks and fifteen ships. They might be able to repair the other two ships. *Might.*"

Aly widened her eyes. "Who would be mad enough to do such a thing?" she asked. Since they both knew the other worked for the rebellion in some form, he knew she was joking. "So what did you say to the Watchman?"

"The same thing you asked. What happened? For that I got a double kiss from those cursed clubs they carry, and the threat of Kanodang hospitality if I didn't carry my lazy rump elsewhere." He smiled, his eyes dreamy. "You should see it, Bright Eyes. All three docks and all those ships, burned right down to the waterline. Whoever did it was an artist." Quietly he added, "There's a fifty gold lan reward for information leading to the capture of those who did it."

Ochobu turned with a handful of glop and motioned for Bacar to raise the arm on the side of his bruised ribs. Bacar did so, wincing. Ochobu spread the mixture on the man's torso.

Aly whistled at the reward amount. It was more than any five families in all Middle Town made in a year. "They're dreadfully excited for just a loss of wood."

"Well, the ships' captains are screaming to be paid for their vessels, but that's not it." Bacar lowered his voice. "See, somehow the slaves in the market got wind of the fire. They rioted. Some made it out of Dockmarket before the collars choked them till the catchers found them. And they killed three guards, mauled five more. I got it from some lady friends who work near there." He and Aly smiled at one another. Both knew what kind of "lady friends" Bacar would have near the slave markets. If the information came from them, it was accurate.

"Anyway, the ladies patched me up enough so I could come back here without the Watch arresting me, and I knew my master would have plenty of questions if I came in all battered. Thank the gods for Ochobu here."

The mage spread more of her glop on Bacar's face. Ochobu said, "It'll fall off when it dries, and you'll be good as new. Go beg some food from Chenaol. It'll be dry by the time you're done eating."

Bacar hopped down from the stool. "Thanks, Duani Ochobu," he said. "You just saved me some unpleasantness with my lord Kadyet."

He advanced on Aly, the arm on his undamaged side snaking out for a grab. She let him get just close enough, then swung out of his reach. "Naughty," she teased. "Besides, Lady Dove tore out her hem and I have to mend it before the callers arrive today."

"But what about my being shirtless?" he asked, woebegone, as she sauntered down to her workroom.

Aly looked back over her shoulder at him. "I got an eyeful," she replied, and winked. Strolling into her office, she closed the door and went to her desk. As she'd expected, it was piled with slates and paper.

She picked up a report verifying that there had been a revolt in the slave pens, as Bacar had said. There was more, the writer being employed at the slave pens. The brokers had sent a hysterical delegation to the harbormaster, begging that they be granted ships to carry their current lot of slaves to Carthak. The harbormaster had said he would send the request on to the minister of trade.

Aly smiled, a very different smile from the one she had given Bacar.

9

REPORTS AND CONSPIRACIES

During the afternoon rest, Aly took reports from anyone who came into the meeting room. Between guests, she read the information that was piled on her desk across the hall. She also consulted with Trick, who had news from the darkings. The one Aly had left in the shop of Dove's bookseller friend, Herbrand Edgecliff, revealed that the bookshop was a nest of raka sympathizers, including Herbrand himself, who never had fewer than three fugitives from Crown law in the shop's basement. Edgecliff and his wife, both pure-blood luarin, belonged to the raka conspiracy, which made Aly happy. Every instance that luarin could work with and help the raka was a brick in the wall between quiet coexistence and massacres. All of the darkings buzzed with word of people's reactions to the duke's arrest and the burning of the slave docks. So much of it was the same that Aly asked Trick to tell her only important things she hadn't heard yet.

There was no word from Tongkang or from Nawat. It was much too soon. Even flying, it would take time for him to reach the island and find the rebels. They wouldn't get reports from him for another day or so. Aly tried not to dwell on it. You told him you had to concentrate on the rebellion—well, concentrate on it, her reasonable self said.

The resting time was nearly gone when a recruit who worked for seamstresses in Middle Town came to the meeting room to speak with Aly. She was a slender young raka woman who wore a baby in a sling on her back as she carried a basketful of dye powders. "The cockerel crows at noon," she said, giving the code phrase for the tier of agents recruited by Aly's pack.

"Then it's the cockerel's time to be put in the pot." Aly gave her the counterphrase that meant the recruit could pass information to her safely. She hadn't seen this young woman before. It was possible she didn't even know who Aly was, except that she was in the right room, and she knew the right countersign.

"Late this morning, when the King's Watch came to arrest Duchess Nomru and her family, they were gone," the seamstress said. "There was no sign of them. The servants and slaves were gone, too, every last one. The Watch took what valuables were left, but the lady's jewels and the family coin were all missing."

"Is there anything else?" Aly inquired.

The seamstress nodded. "Five arrests, two of 'em luarin accused of selling books on poisons and death magic to raka, one for taxes, one a printer who had funny pictures of the regents hid away to be placed about the city later, and one of the raka nobles, Meipun Kloulechat. No one knows why. The paper for his arrest has the black seal on it."

Aly knew what that meant: the noble had been arrested on a royal warrant obtained with information from Topabaw. Delivery of such a warrant gave the recipient a chance to kill himself honorably rather than suffer the humiliation of questioning and the execution that usually followed.

Maybe this will teach the raka nobles they might lose everything if they *don't* become involved, she thought. "Is that all?" she asked her informant.

The woman nodded and shifted the sleeping baby. "That I know of. But the city's crawling with King's Watch, all in a vicious mood, and the regents have ordered a company of the Rittevon Lancers to patrol Middle Town and Market Town. Stay out of their way if you see them. They like getting us to move with their riding crops."

Aly had noticed the red welt on the woman's arm. "Two doors on the other side of the hall from me, on your way back, is our mages' workroom," she said. "They'll give you something for that."

The informant shrugged. "I get worse if I fray the material I sew. May your troubles fly away on the wings of crows." She touched her fist to her forehead in a raka salute and left the room.

Aly sat back, considering what she had just learned. Nomru's family and household not only had knowledge of his arrest, but they'd managed to flee the city, or to hide within it in full daylight. They were connected in no way to the raka, so someone else had warned them. She suspected it was a noble who'd been present when the princess had called for Nomru to be locked up, which meant that the warning must have come from a luarin.

The city's bells rang out, signaling the end of the quiet time. Aly went to dress Dove for the afternoon.

Guests descended on Balitang House once again. There were more today, a number of young men and women and their parents. The heirs of three noble families made for Sarai, while their mothers draped themselves between Nuritin and Winnamine.

At first everyone gathered in the big sitting room or at the pool courtyard just outside. Despite the nobles' apparent quiet and lassitude, tension hummed in the air. Every time a young man's voice began to rise, a parent's fan opened with a loud snap of warning, and the errant son went quiet. The girls chattered a little too much, except for Sarai. She remained cool and gracious, as if a man they'd all thought untouchable were not in prison. She had to know as well as anyone that Nomru had helped her mother to resist Imajane's request that Sarai and Elsren move to the palace, but she acted no differently than usual.

Not long after Winnamine's father, Matfrid Fonfala, arrived, the duchess stood. "My friends, I believe the Teak Sitting Room may be somewhat cooler. I am sure our young people would prefer that we were elsewhere. I should think their attendants would be chaperons enough, wouldn't you?"

Idly, as if only the promise of a breeze tempted them, the older members of the gathering followed the duchess. Aly watched as they left. She was fairly certain those people were the core of the luarin conspiracy. In any case, she would soon know for certain, because the darking Feather occupied the Teak Sitting Room.

Aly had expected Dove to follow the older nobles, but she didn't. Instead she talked with Zaimid, who, with a kind man's sharp eye, had noted she sat alone while Sarai's friends jockeyed around her. Once again Aly added a point to the Carthaki healer's score. Zaimid and Dove were soon so deep in a discussion of the emperor's creation of charity hospitals that Aly would have bet that Dove noticed nothing else. She would have lost. When the footman announced Imgehai Qeshi, a priestess of the Black God who served at the city's biggest temple, Dove politely broke off her conversation to introduce her to Zaimid. The priestess wore her habit, but her hood was off, indicating she was not there on spiritual business. After she, Zaimid, and Dove had chatted for a few moments, Dove excused herself and the newcomer to Zaimid and led the priestess away. Aly watched Zaimid's gaze follow them, his brown eyes alert and interested. Then he managed to step out into the pool courtyard in time to be at Sarai's side as she left the sitting room for the garden.

A moment later Trick murmured in Aly's ear, "Feather say Dove and Imgehai have come." Aly twiddled her thumbs. The priestess stood high in the temple hierarchy. She would be a powerful ally.

It was funny. Old King Oron had banished the Balitangs on suspicion of treason. Everyone had thought it was one of his mad ideas. It seemed he'd been right all along. Still, he had to have been mad to consider their group a threat, thought Aly. Obviously they've been talking about this for a while, and they haven't done anything. That will have to change, she decided. If they're to be of any use at all, they'll have to stop talking and start doing.

Ferdy Tomang's raised voice caught her attention. ". . . can't forget who guards their backs!" A number of his friends begged him to lower his voice.

"Don't worry," Sarai told them airily. "There are so many secrecy spells around this place you could start a war in here and the Crown mages would never know."

Aly winced. Apparently it had not occurred to Sarai that secrecy spells were best left secret. If Topabaw had any spies among her friends, he would know by sunset that the place was more than usually well guarded. She reminded herself to warn Ochobu and Ysul and thanked the gods that Sarai did not know about the plans made on her behalf. And Aly was forced to think her more than a little foolish for speaking as she had. Anyone with any sense of self-preservation in the

Isles knew better than to speak so carelessly about the Crown unless that person was *very* sure of the listener's loyalty.

Ferdy lowered his voice, but only slightly. "It's time we taught them a lesson," he said, looking at the young noblemen who stood around him. "I say we wait until tonight and ride to Kanodang. Everyone knows that if you spend enough in bribes you can get inside."

"We can break out Nomru." Druce Adona's cheeks were flushed.

Another young man added, "Show the regents they are nothing without the luarin nobility."

"Teach them a lesson," said another. "And if we have to fight our way out, we will." He set his hand on his sword hilt.

Idiots, thought Aly as she listened to them rant, working themselves into a state of fury. These men were filled with youth's righteous anger, ready to start killing anyone in their path. Only Zaimid said nothing, but stood there, arms crossed over his chest, with the courtier's expression of polite interest. The young noblewomen's faces were a study in contrasts, from those who showed fear to those filled with the men's enthusiasm.

At first Sarai showed polite interest, her expression like Zaimid's. She nodded when comments were addressed to her, smiled when anyone looked at her. Then, as the men began to discuss meeting places and who else they might recruit, a new look crossed her face, one that was half slyness and half contempt. It was replaced by lowered eyelashes, a subtle step on the back hem of her cream-colored gown so that it pulled tight to emphasize her figure, and a pouting lower lip.

"That's all very well and good," she murmured. "But *I* think it's very silly, and useless, and tiresome."

"But we're standing up for one of our own!" protested

Ferdy. "He's a luarin, a noble! They can't treat us this way!"

Sarai pouted even more. "I bet Their Highnesses expect it. I bet they'll have hundreds and hundreds of soldiers inside the walls, waiting for something just like this."

Good point, Aly thought. But Ulasim and Fesgao will make sure of that before they go. They're too sharp to miss something that obvious.

Sarai continued, "You'll all be arrested, and maybe even put on display at the harbor mouth, and *then* who will be my escort to the Summersend Ball?"

"Or mine?" added one of the sillier noblewomen.

The realization of the likely consequences slowly dawned in the young men's faces. When Sarai reminded them of arrest and execution, they began to lose their enthusiasm. It took a little more work, but in the end Sarai had cast their feverish excitement to the four winds.

Out of curiosity's sake, Aly looked at Zaimid. The Carthaki watched Sarai and the noblemen, the tiniest of smiles on his lips. He knows what she's doing, Aly told herself. And he's not surprised by the results.

When talk turned to a riding party the day after the lunar eclipse, Aly ended her watch on the nobles and returned to her workroom. There was more to do, and she had better ways to use her time than by listening to airbrains chasing butterflies. She smiled. *Airbrains chasing butterflies* was a phrase her mother often used.

Aly resumed her walk. "Maybe Mother was more right about such things than I thought," she murmured.

"What such things?" asked Trick.

"Oh—the way those fools were talking, and how quickly they changed their minds," Aly replied.

She could not see if the darking nodded, but she did hear its contempt when it said, "Stupid."

One of the household runners came to Aly's office, bearing a message from Chenaol. Aly's first double agent awaited her in Chenaol's private sitting room—Vitorcine, Isalena Obemaek's maid. Aly went to see her. Vitorcine paced in Chenaol's sitting room, her hands white-knuckled as she clutched a small basket. Once Aly had closed the door, Vitorcine thrust the basket at her. "I made copies of everything," she whispered as Aly leafed through the papers in the basket. "Topabaw has seen none of it."

Aly looked into the maid's worried eyes. "You know Topabaw will reward you well for information he can use against the Obemaeks. And yet you put off telling him, at the risk of your own life, to keep your masters from trouble."

Vitorcine blushed and looked away. "Lord Obemaek has been a father to me. Lady Isalena is a fine mistress. She's never hit me like some of the other ladies do." She wrung her hands. "I don't *want* to betray them, but Topabaw . . ."

A twinge of something like guilt for putting Vitorcine in such a spot pinched Aly's heart. She ignored it. She would do anything to protect the Balitangs. If that meant blackmailing the powerful Obemaek family, Aly would do so. "Is there anything else?" Aly wanted to know.

"No. Not information, but—I must report to Topabaw's man tomorrow night," Vitorcine explained. "What should I say?"

Aly had expected this. "Tell him that there is great unrest over the detention of Duke Nomru, which is true enough," she said. "The hotheads rant, but they fear Topabaw too much to act. Say also that people are afraid they will be next. Tell him you fear Lord Obemaek suspects you, and that you must be very careful until you think your master has decided you are no danger. That should fill his tiny belly for the moment."

"And Topabaw will accept that?" Vitorcine asked, her cheeks pale.

"Practice it in a mirror until you can say it convincingly," Aly told her, just as an elder who cared for Vitorcine might say it. "Topabaw has seen this kind of thing before, after all. The city will be talking of the arrest for days. You're no good to him if your master leaves you dead in an alley somewhere. The excuse will wear thin after a time, but I trust that by then we'll have something else he can gnaw on."

Aly left Vitorcine to collect herself before she rejoined the other servants, and walked down the hall to her office. Stepping inside, she closed the door and whispered, "Trick?"

She felt her necklace stir. "Scared lady," Trick remarked, sticking a head up next to Aly's ear.

"She has every reason to be scared," replied Aly as she sat at her table. "Ask Feather what they're talking about."

Trick instead released itself and trickled down Aly's sarong to pool in her lap. There the darking spread to become a circle with a shiny surface. An image appeared, and with it sounds. It took a few moments for Aly to identify what she looked at, because the angle was extremely odd. She finally realized that Feather must be seated atop a cabinet, looking down at the nobles assembled in the room.

Aly raised an eyebrow, then leaned back and listened to the luarin conspirators. She was still listening when someone rapped hard on her door. "Trick," she whispered. "Sash."

Grumbling softly, the darking folded itself up so Aly could tuck it away.

"Enter," she called.

Atisa stuck in her head, grinning broadly. "Your traps have caught three more spies, Duani," she said. "Do you want to make them our spies yourself, or should one of us convince them?"

Aly got to her feet. "I shall do it," she told Atisa. "But you come and watch. I cannot be everywhere, and things are heating up." She strode down the hall in Atisa's wake, her thoughts flying in a dozen directions. As conspiracies went, she didn't think much of the luarin's, but it gave her something to work with. They might stiffen their spines if they allied themselves with the raka, though getting the two groups to agree would be a trick and a half.

That night, in the conspirators' meeting room, Aly told her companions what she had learned that day. Not once did she look at Dove or mention that Dove had been meeting with the luarin conspirators.

When Aly finished, Chenaol snorted. "That dried-up bunch of twitterpated worrymice!" she said scornfully. "They've been whispering for years, without anything to show for it."

"Maybe it's time to give them something to show," remarked Ulasim.

Quedanga spat on the floor. "Deal with luarin? I'd as soon boil my hands and head."

Aly looked at the ceiling.

"I don't think it's worth it," said Fesgao. "They do not have the best security, if our Aly could ferret them out before she'd been here so much as a week."

"And what will you do with them if we win?" Dove wanted to know. "Kill them? Kill Sarai's friends and their parents? Kill the people she studied dancing and riding with? Kill Winna and her family, and the Balitangs?"

Ysul hand-signed, *Better to be allies. Many old raka houses are gone. Not all luarin are bad luarin.*

"Because I can tell you, just from reading Saren history," Dove said quietly, "once the killing between peoples who share a country begins, it is very hard to stop. The lowland whites and the K'mir tribesmen have been killing one another for centuries. The only way to avoid that fate is to decide we must live together, and then do our best to ensure that we do. We can do as Rittevon Lanman and Ludas Jimajen did when they came here, and reap a bloody harvest of our own, or we can call a halt to it."

"Easier for you than for some of us, Lady Dove," Chenaol pointed out.

Dove's eyes flashed. "I didn't say easy. I said *necessary.*"

The door popped open. Ochobu was there, her gray hair straggling out of its pins, sweat rolling down her face. Ulasim, closest to her, guided his mother into his chair while Chenaol poured a cup of mango juice.

Ochobu gulped it down, then said, "News from the Chain. The people of the Birafu estates are now gone, traveling over land or by ship. The crows managed to bring in some merchant galleys along with fishing boats. There is more." Her face was alight with triumph and malice. "Governor Sulion of Tongkang was found dead on his balcony this morning. He'd been shot with three crow-fletched arrows."

Aly looked down, quivering. She knew, just as surely as if he'd shouted it in her ear, that Nawat had been the archer.

"The Crown will go berserk," Fesgao said, his eyes burning. "The governor of Ikang and the governor of Tongkang killed within a week of each other? Never has such a thing happened, not after the Conquest!"

"And more," said Ochobu. "Just this last, so let me finish. The Velochiru raka on Imahyn have burned the homes of the overseer and of the family. The governor there has sent a call for more troops."

Ulasim rested a hand on her shoulder. "You're done, Mother," he said kindly. "Rest awhile. What did you do, speak with every mage on the Chain tonight?"

She glared up at him. "I'm not senile," she snapped.

Ulasim gave his crooked smile. "Ysul, will you reach the Chain mage closest to Nawat? Ask him to ask Nawat if he will take a look into the situation on Imahyn?"

Ysul nodded and left them.

Dove looked after him, then at Ulasim. "Do all the mages of the Chain know hand signs?"

Quedanga was mending a sarong. "Ysul writes the message and shows it to them. General, if we don't get atop this storm, it's going to roll straight over us," she warned. "I don't know if the god arranged it this way, or if it's just a dam bursting, but we need to take control of it."

Ulasim leaned against the wall. "We'll have a way soon to make contact with the would-be rebels among the luarin," he remarked in an even voice. "I expect more fights in the city over the next week. It seems clear enough to me that the Crown cannot control this city and the outlying islands, too. If the regents send more troops away from here, we may have an opportunity to announce ourselves—we shall see. In the meantime, Aly will continue with her work. Fesgao and I have a project or two, as have Mother and Ysul. Quedanga and Aly, make certain everyone hears of what has taken place on Tongkang and Imahyn. Chenaol—"

"Crow-fletched arrows," said the cook, who was also their armorer. "It would be easy if I had a ready supply."

"I'll ask the crows," Aly said. "I'm sure they know where they've lost feathers. Have they been bringing in Stormwing feathers from their brushes with them? Nawat asked them to before we came here."

"I find a pile of them by the kitchen well every evening," replied Chenaol. "And since we've no longer got Nawat to cut them up and use them on arrows, my girls have found a way to turn them into throwing darts and set the shafts in hilts so they become knives. Pity the beasts aren't cleaner," she mused. "The feathers would be perfect for tissue-cut raw fish, but we don't know where those feathers have been. Even after boiling I don't trust them."

"There will be more," Quedanga said. "They and the crows have been fighting all over the city. I saw the most astounding thing yesterday as I shopped. Stormwings lined up in the air wingtip to wingtip and darted at a group of crows to cut them in half."

Aly snorted, guessing the result.

"The crows split and got them on the backs and chests as they passed," Quedanga said. "One of them even managed to dump a load of dung on their queen's head."

All of them shook their heads over the audacity of crows and the frustrations of Stormwings as their group broke up. Dove waited until she and Aly were climbing the stairs to the family quarters before she made Aly stop.

"If you know what they talked about, you know I was there," she said quietly, looking up at her face. "Why didn't you tell?"

Aly shrugged. "It wasn't my secret to tell. You'll let our group know when you feel it's time." She felt the urge to add something but was not sure it would help. "Your ladyship, I know you're just thirteen and all, but—and don't bite my nose off for it—I trust your judgment more than that of some older people I know." They both knew she meant Sarai; Aly could see the awareness in Dove's eyes. "Others I might question, but I know you're not a fool. We opened the door to the luarin in there tonight, that was the important thing."

When they entered the ladies' sitting room, they found the duchess on the floor with Elsren and Petranne, telling a story, as Sarai read a book. Winnamine used her long, elegant hands as the raka storytellers did, making them form shadows on the wall that looked like figures from the tale. Rihani, Pembery, and Boulaj had sewing in their hands, but they were as entranced as the children, watching each shadow. Even Sarai spent more time watching than she did reading. Dove and Aly sat quietly in their regular spots, Dove folding her hands in her lap, Aly taking up the sewing she kept in a basket by her chair.

The story ended. Pembery and Boulaj began to stitch as Winnamine got to her feet. Elsren was asleep, worn out by another day with Dunevon. Rihani scooped him up and waited as Petranne kissed her mother, Sarai, and Dove good night. Once the children and their nursemaid were gone, Sarai gave up even the pretense of reading.

"Winna, when will they let Nomru out?" Sarai asked. "They can't just keep him in Kanodang forever."

"I doubt it," said the duchess. "I imagine that he will be out—one way or another—by the end of the week. In the meantime, we have the eclipse party tomorrow night. Have you decided what you will wear?"

Sarai ignored this distraction. "If only we knew some men with *spine*," she complained. "You should have heard them this afternoon, planning 'the great rescue of Nomru.'"

"I hope you discouraged them," said Winnamine. "Don't they understand they could die that way?"

Sarai smiled bitterly. "Relax, Winna. All it took was a pout from me and they were happy to give it up. I can't think much of their courage if they care more about escorting me to the Summersend Ball than they do about the life of a great noble like Nomru." Suddenly she jumped to her feet. "How can you stand it? How can we live among so many cowards?" she demanded, pacing the room, a tigress in cream silk. "To watch what they do to people—all kinds of people, not just the raka!—and say nothing, and simper, and take another stitch, and pretend the world's all lovely?"

"Because I have patience," Winnamine said quietly. "And because I like to sew."

"Patience?" cried Sarai. "The luarin nobles haven't done anything in centuries, and they're not going to. It makes me sick. In other countries, rulers can't just do as they like. Zaimid told me Emperor Kaddar set it up so that for *anyone* to be arrested in Carthak, their accusers must give evidence before a magistrate. The magistrate has to write out a warrant for the arrest, based on proof of wrongdoing. If Duke Nomru lived in Carthak, he'd be heard, not tossed into a cell."

"Emperor Kaddar got that idea from the Marenites," Winnamine pointed out.

Sarai shrugged. "As I say, other monarchs have to respect their people. You don't see Tortallans sneaking around, afraid to speak their minds. In fact, they're a little too zealous about that, especially when they visit us."

Aly raised her brows.

Sarai smiled and flapped a hand. "Not you, Aly. But some of your people have been painfully frank about what they think of the Kyprin way of life."

Aly, who knew someone who was painfully frank about more than that, looked at her needlework.

Winnamine leaned forward and caught Sarai's arm. "You're certain your men friends aren't going to try something? If need be, I'll send notes to their parents—"

Sarai shook her head. "That lot? They're gelded already. They'll do what the king stallion tells them to do. I wonder what it's like to live in a country where there are more stallions than geldings."

"I doubt they'd come running when you flutter your

lashes at them," Dove remarked, her voice very dry.

Sarai smiled. "Oh, a challenge! That would be new." She collapsed into a chair and looked at her stepmother. "Winna, Otaviyu Lelin and Rosamma Tomang have invited me to go riding tomorrow morning."

The duchess rested her needlework in her lap. "And their brothers?" she asked delicately. Dove smiled.

Sarai shot her sister a glare. "*And* their brothers, and the rest of our crowd, and Countess Tomang, and Otavi's mother. Boulaj will be with me, if she can keep up."

"I see no problems, then," Winnamine replied slowly. "Genore Tomang has a spotless reputation, and she is known for her skill as a chaperon." She grinned wickedly at Sarai, whose shoulders drooped.

Dove asked, "You haven't seen Boulaj ride, have you, Sarai? I mean, like you like to ride?"

Sarai glared at her. "No."

Dove chuckled. "She will be on you like a tick on a howler. Try slipping away with her on your tail!"

"You're being a brat, O wonderful, uncontroversial, educated sister of mine," Sarai retorted. She asked her stepmother, "So I may go?"

"You may go," replied Winnamine. "And if I hear of one escape attempt or of bad behavior, the only person you will be allowed out of this house with is Aunt Nuritin."

Sarai winced. "I'll be so good you'll hardly know I was there. Good night, dear Winna." She kissed her stepmother's cheek, and the top of her sister's head. "Good night, brat." She waved to Pembery and Aly, who murmured their own good nights, and left the room.

Once she was gone, Dove scowled at her stepmother. "Does she even *care* what becomes of this country? Of us?"

Winnamine leaned her head back. "Patience, Dove," she

said wearily. "I think she still hates herself for her father's death, just as she hates the houses that produced King Oron and Prince Bronau. I think she feels that people *meant* to stand up for us when we were exiled, until something distracted them. She thinks because things have always been this way, they will always *be* this way."

"Well, they won't," said Dove, getting to her feet. "And when they aren't, she had better live up to all those nice, shiny ideas about equal laws for everyone." She kissed Winnamine on the cheek and left the sitting room.

Aly followed her without a word.

10

ECLIPSE

Aly woke before dawn once more, although no tentacle tickled her nose.

"Are you sleeping late or something?" she asked Trick.

"Not sleeping," replied the darking. "Listening. Reportsreportsreports. All city mostly same report. Scared. Everyone scared. If people die just to look at her, what happens when she asks for throne? Most of the ones who want to know are raka or poor, or poor *and* raka. If duke in Kanodang, who next? some say. If Topabaw falls, who next? some ask. Most of those who ask are nobles or soldiers. If king die, if regents die, who rules? Most asking that one are nobles. More Stormwings come from north. Flame came home from Kanodang. All darkings in house back in Aly's room before warriors come to practice," Trick added mournfully. "They ask, when do they get to do real work? Boring, staying in house all day."

"Tonight," Aly whispered. "Most of you will go to the palace tonight, and those who go will stay there."

"But not me," said Trick.

Aly grimaced. She knew what it was like to be penned up all day, not allowed to go out and have what she thought of as fun. "Trick, if you can train someone to do for me what you do, you can stay at the palace," she whispered. "You deserve some fun."

"No!" squeaked Trick. "I was fooling!"

Aly considered that, grinning. "So where did you learn how to tease?" she asked.

"Like I say, you more fun than anybody," Trick replied, lightly tightening its beadlike self around Aly's neck in something that felt like a hug.

Aly leaned her cheek against the darking. "Nawat would like you," she murmured, missing her crow-man.

"Then I meet Nawat one day," replied Trick.

Aly got up. She practiced with the warriors, then took a complete bath. Once she had dressed Dove and sent her to breakfast, she threw open the shutters and looked outside. It will be perfect for an eclipse if the weather holds, she thought, watching Stormwings bait a lone crow in the cloudless sky. The crow flew lower and lower, until it nearly touched the treetops of Middle Town. An army of nearly one hundred crows exploded from the trees, going after the Stormwings.

The crows reminded her of a duty. Tilting back her head, she voiced a hoarse caw. Three crows, idly watching the Stormwings streak toward the palace, came to perch on the windowsill. Aly was asking them to gather their dropped feathers as they did those of Stormwings when one tried to grab Trick. The darking wriggled and turned itself into a cobra with its cowl fully extended, striking at the crow. The crow squawked and fell off the ledge.

"I teach *him,*" Trick said proudly, and turned itself back into a necklace. The other crows were too busy mocking their disgraced comrade to take offense. When they calmed down, they agreed to leave their feathers where Chenaol could find them. Then they spotted a five-man squad of the King's Watch marching in patrol on Joshain Street. They flew off saying, if Aly understood them correctly, that they would give the soldiers "wet face surprises."

Dove went out with Aly and her guard, visiting a maker of fine chessboards, a seller of Yamani goods, and a beggar on the steps of the small temple dedicated to Gunapi the Sunrose, the Kyprin goddess of war and flowing lava. Waiting for Dove and the beggar to finish an involved discussion about the rice crop, Aly kept her eyes on her surroundings. People were starting to add the open shackle to the embroideries on their clothes. She saw it on shop steps and the sides of wagons. If the people knew what it meant, the rebellion had more support in Rajmuat than she had thought.

When they returned to the house, Aly felt tension in the air, humming like a plucked bowstring. There was nothing she could do to ease it. After all, she wasn't supposed to know the details of the Kanodang escape, though thanks to the darking Lace she had everything but Nomru's boot size. By now she knew the raka conspiracy's true reach and numbers in Rajmuat, particularly in the city's jails, including Kanodang. She was impressed. They've been holding out on me, Aly thought. How sneaky of them!

She envied the spies of her pack. They were keyed up but able to joke as they passed on their day's gatherings of information. They, at least, would be having fun as Trick termed it.

Stop that, Aly told herself. You'll have a quiet bit of fun yourself tonight. It won't be as enjoyable as watching bad things burn, but life is imperfect that way.

By midafternoon the Balitang ladies were ready to leave.

The evening's festivities included a banquet before the eclipse party, with the regents and a chosen few dozen. Invitation to the feast as well as to the party was a gesture of condescension from the regents to the Balitangs, and they were all keenly aware of it.

"I think she's trying to be kind to us," Sarai muttered to Dove, reading over the letter of invitation one last time. "So people will say how charitable she is."

"What do you care?" asked Dove, snatching the letter from her. "All your puppy dogs will be there, panting after you—Ferdy, Druce, Zaimid . . ."

"Zaimid is hardly panting after me," Sarai told her younger sister. "And Ferdy is too conscious of his wealth to pant. Drool a bit, yes, but never pant."

For this trip to the palace, the dress boxes in the wagon held dinner gowns and party ones. Aly, Pembery, and Boulaj had gone over every stitch with exacting care, making sure their ladies would be perfectly dressed that night. In packing Dove's box, Aly also managed to slip in a garment of her own, a fresh suit from Ochobu that would cause anyone who saw Aly in it to forget they had done so. Aly hardly believed she would be so sloppy as to be seen, but there was no point in taking risks. Under the forgetting suit was a pouch full of very excited darkings. They squeaked with pleasure as Aly tucked them away, and assured her they would have no problem breathing in the box because they didn't breathe.

Once the boxes were stowed, the ladies' maids took their positions. Pembery and Lady Nuritin's maid, Dorilize, rode in the wagon. Boulaj walked beside Sarai, Aly beside Dove. Dove, cross at having to socialize at dinner as well as the eclipse party, read as she rode. If she noticed the people in the street or in upper-story windows who watched as their company passed, she gave no sign of it. At a nod from the duchess, the men-at-arms drew closer to their party. Aly checked the crowd often, noting her spies and their recruits mingling, spreading doubts about Topabaw and his standing with the regents.

The ladies changed for dinner in the Robing Pavilion. The duchess wore a dark maroon undergown and a sheer black silk overgown, her jewelry equally modest. Sarai gleamed in pale amber silk under creamy gauze, her jewelry simple as well. Dove had chosen dark amber under black gauze. All three wore sheer silk veils secured to their neatly done hair with jeweled pins. As they walked to the Rittevon Enclosure, Aly felt her heart swell with pride. They made the other nobles look overdressed.

Inside the wall they found the towering stone L that was called the Gray Palace. As they walked its halls, they saw countless goods the invaders had looted from their raka subjects on display. They included copper statues turned green with time, gaudy silk rugs and tapestries, figures carved of gemstone, and jewelry made of copper and gold, polished to a brilliant shine. It was all set up to present a message: to the rulers of the Isles, the raka would always be the conquered, not equals.

Royal servants separated the guests, escorting the men to one salon and the ladies to the next. Here maids gave their mistresses' appearances a last going-over. As Aly tugged a fold here and straightened a sleeve there, she placed a darking on top of one of Dove's shoes. The darking was to remain in the dining hall when Dove left there.

With their ladies gone, the maids settled to wait, in case their mistresses tore out a hem or stained their clothes during the meal. Later the servants could relax at the Robing Pavilion. For the time being they ate their suppers as they chattered with acquaintances. Aly nodded to Boulaj and opened Dove's dress box. Casually she drew out her forget-me suit and the pouch of darkings, tucking both into the large cloth bag that held a maid's necessities. When Aly had everything she needed, she went in search of the privy.

The nobles' servants not only had a separate privy at the Gray Palace, but one with stalls, for privacy. Aly entered one and bolted the door. She stripped off her clothes until she wore only her Trick necklace, a breast band, and a loincloth. She pulled the suit out of its bag and was nearly blinded as the spells on it, made by Ochobu, left spots on her magical Sight. She slid the garment on and secured it as her vision cleared. Then she donned the gloves and shoes, tucked the darkings' pouch into an opening in the suit, and pulled up and tightened the hood until only her eyes were visible.

Aly put her sarong and sash into the bag and closed it. She listened to make sure no one else had come in, then left the privy. Carrying the bag low, where few might notice it, she returned to the salon. Most of the servants were still at the food tables, loading their plates. Boulaj sat near their ladies' dress boxes, a full plate in her hands. Aly set her bag behind the boxes. Boulaj would not remember seeing her, but she knew what the bag meant. If anyone came looking for Aly, Boulaj would send them in all the wrong directions.

Thanks to the raka conspirators among the palace staff, Aly had memorized the map of the Gray Palace. Thanks to her magical Sight, she saw and avoided the alarm spells. The vision spells that littered the rooms and halls slid uselessly over her suit, not recognizing it as anything more than empty cloth. Moving silently, Aly placed two darkings in the small throne room of the inner palace. They chittered their glee and began to explore their new home.

Walking onto an outside terrace, Aly eyed the rough stone of the walls, then began to climb. It was simple enough.

The Gray Palace's builders had been in such a hurry to build a defensible stronghold that they had not smoothed the stones, and their approach to mortar had been haphazard. Cracks between the blocks gave a determined climber hand- and footholds. Once again she had her palace informers to thank. Masters here had no idea that their servants and slaves clambered up and down the walls to spy or to steal.

Moving as quickly as she dared, Aly released darkings in Imajane's and Rubinyan's rooms. She placed two darkings in the private audience chamber where the regents discussed delicate matters with favored subjects, one in the informal dining room used by the regents, and others in the clerk's office, Rubinyan's study, and a map room. One darking went to the office next to Rubinyan's study, where his personal spymaster, Sevmire, worked. She sent four in search of the kitchens and the servants' quarters. She even left a darking in the king's bedroom, just so she could say she had done it. She hardly expected anyone to discuss royal policy with Dunevon, but the regents might say something interesting to the King's Guard in a moment of irritation.

Feeling pleased with herself, she changed back into her normal clothes and returned to her fellow maids. The thinner pouch of darkings stayed with her as she left two more where the servants awaited their masters.

The banquet ended eventually. The nobles went back to the Robing Pavilion to change out of dinner clothes and into those considered appropriate for viewing an eclipse. The maids then completed the last touches on their ladies' hair and makeup. Vereyu presided over them all, taking in everything. She and Aly had exchanged nods when Aly had followed Dove into the ladies' side of the pavilion.

As the women worked and chattered, many part- or full-raka maids volunteered to do any service for Sarai or

Dove. Aly shared what duties she could, ignoring Dove's request for people to stop fussing. Boulaj stood back and let other maids tend Sarai if they could do so without their own mistresses' noticing. Observing that Nuritin watched this with a frown, Aly shifted her position to block the old woman's view. She wasn't sure how far to trust Nuritin or her secretary and maid yet, if she could trust them at all.

Sarai was oblivious to the quiet war for her attention. She smiled at everyone and gossiped with her friends. Aly let three darkings slip to the floor as she listened.

"It's not right," a young woman complained. "At least *five* men are jostling for your favors! You could share!"

Sarai giggled. "You could have most of them with my blessing. Really, some of these fellows must think we're no more intelligent than sheep. The only one who treats me like I've a brain in my head is the Carthaki."

"Does that mean Ferdy is out of contention?" one of Sarai's friends inquired, inspecting her lip color in a mirror. "I'll take him if you let him know you're not interested."

Sarai smiled at her. "And will you take that female Stormwing who gave birth to him?"

Isalena shuddered at the thought of living with Lady Genore Tomang. "Into every life some rain must fall. Besides, I don't want to *keep* him, just *use* him for a month or two." She sighed. "He has such lovely muscles!"

A footman wearing Obemaek livery appeared in the door to the outside and beckoned to one of the Obemaek maids. He had the air of a man with important news. All of the women fell silent and watched, while Aly's belly cramped. Had something gone wrong? Had the prison break been discovered before it had even begun?

The footman left. The maid turned and saw that all eyes were on her. "Oh, my," she whispered. Then she straightened.

"There is news. The raka on the Velochiru estates of Imahyn Isle have risen in revolt. They have burned the overseer's home and the Velochiru's family home there. The governor has sent to the regents for the army."

Oh, *that,* thought Aly with disdain. We knew about *that* last night.

Most of the women present made the star-shaped Sign against evil on their chests. Any slaves with raka blood retreated to the rear wall of the pavilion; raka and part-raka maids stepped back, wary eyes on their mistresses. All around the room noblewomen shifted, their hands and feet restless. Their eyes were unsure, their voices soft. They were frightened. Some had turned their eyes toward the raka. More were looking at the door to the Robing Pavilion.

Winnamine thanked Pembery and got to her feet. She looked at the other nobles and smiled. "It could simply be a rumor." She looked at Nuritin, who nodded. "I will inquire of Their Highnesses." She swept from the room before anyone could say a word against it.

"What has gotten into the raka?" asked a noblewoman, her voice quavering with anxiety. "This is the second rising this month. Do they forget what they owe to us?"

Those of raka blood in the room, all servants or slaves, looked carefully at the glossy boards of the floor, doing their best imitation of women who could not hear. Aly shook her head. People always believe what they want to believe, not what's true, she thought with disgust. They never use their eyes and see the world around them.

"These will be wild raka," said a woman in her sixties, one of Nuritin's friends. "Or slaves on some huge rice farm, ruled by a paid overseer. This is the ill that comes of not looking after your own lands. Those who farm for you can't feel a servant's affection for someone who is not there."

"Forgive me, Lady Ankoret," began Sarai politely, addressing Nuritin's friend, "but there are brutal owners as well as overseers. Some bitternesses come not from bad present usage. They come from seeing others profit from the lands where your ancestors are buried. Have you seen how the raka in the big rice farms and in the mines live? I don't understand how we can treat our people so."

"Saraiyu Balitang!" cried Nuritin. "Apologize at once and speak with respect for your elders!"

Sarai got to her feet. "Forgive me if I offended, Great-aunt, Lady Ankoret," she said proudly, her chin raised, "but I think also of the elders who work in the fields and the mines." She swept out of the room like a queen. Aly heard a worshipful sound, though it would be impossible to identify the ones who had made it.

Dove made a face. "Idiot," she murmured. "We need to put a muzzle on her."

Aly, kneeling beside Dove, raised an eyebrow.

"Don't look at me," protested Dove. "I'm going to marry Baron Engan and have my own personal observatory. Someone else can muzzle Sarai."

Aly couldn't help it. She giggled softly into her hands, then murmured, "Until the excitement of being married to you kills him, anyway."

She heard the whisper of silks and brocades in movement and rose instantly to her feet. The other maids and slaves, trained to notice such tiny clues, also stood as Princess Imajane swept in, Winnamine at her elbow. The maids and slaves bowed low and stayed that way. The noblewomen and young ladies rose and curtsied to the princess regent. Imajane was a sight to inspire awe and fear. She wore her hair braided and coiled on her head like a crown. Her large blue eyes, lined with kohl, blazed in a pale, tight-drawn face. Her mouth, red with color, was tight as well. Her hands clenched and unclenched in the folds of her ice blue silk gown and white silk overrobe.

"I see that news travels fast," she said, her voice cutting through the heavy spring air. "I assure you, ladies, the situation on Imahyn is trifling. We must not give it more attention than it deserves. The Goddess has blessed us with an unusual event tonight as she veils her face. We would not forego this for something of importance, let alone the unrest of a small rabble. Come. The Jade Pavilion awaits us. Baron Engan, His Majesty's own astronomer, has a new spyglass that I think is quite extraordinary. Lady Nuritin, Lady Ankoret, you would honor me if you gave me your arms."

With the two oldest ladies in the room, the princess left the pavilion. The other ladies trailed after her, Sarai at the center of a tiny knot of younger women, and Dove with her mother. Aly straightened from her bow along with the rest of the servants and slaves.

Whatever else you can say about the princess regent, she has the royal manner, Aly thought wryly. Once I'm rid of Topabaw—maybe even *before* I'm rid of him—I need to work out a way to drive a wedge between the regents.

Many of the servants settled in for their evening's wait. The male servants drifted over from the men's side of the Robing Pavilion to gossip or flirt. A few people had brought cards and dice. Some of the maids did embroidery or bobbin lace. Others went for a walk on the palace grounds as the day's heat faded. Aly, too, went out, stepping around a pair of crowned pigeons. She idled along the Golden Road until she entered the gardens at the southwest corner of the palace. Slowly she walked along, listening to other passersby as they speculated about the news from Imahyn, the rebellion on Tongkang, and the boy king's health. When she reached the path that followed the edge of the pond, Aly halted. Taybur Sibigat looked as if he'd been waiting for her. There was a broad smile on his boyish face. He stood casually in his black mail, one hand tucked into his breeches pocket.

"Do you know, I thought I might find you around here," he greeted her, his words pelting her in his usual rush to get them all said. "A wonderful evening for an eclipse, isn't it? How goes the contact-making process? Have you recruited anyone in the Gray Palace yet?"

Aly widened her eyes in fear, though inside she was delighted. She needed a playmate while Nawat was away. She could serve both the rebels and herself if Taybur held that position. "My lord—"

"Oh, please," he interrupted. "Spare me. Pretend that you've said the 'I don't know what you mean' speech and we may both continue our evening with more time for a proper talk. I've been dealing with dolts all day and I have a headache. And they're keeping His Majesty up past his bedtime, even though they know it makes him cranky." He held out the hand he'd kept in his pocket and opened his fist. It contained a darking: the one named Spot, because it was about half the size of its fellows. The one she had left in the king's bedroom.

Aly took a big step back.

"It's the most curious thing," Taybur said. "I briefly left the king in his room, and I return to find him bouncing on the bed with this little fellow. He's rather sweet, whatever he is. He even said hello. Dunevon said he caught him rolling around the walls. So I asked him what he is, and he said—"

"Darking," interrupted Spot, putting up its head so it could look over its blob shoulder at Taybur.

"Yes, that was it. So I asked his name, and he said—"

"Spot," the darking told him. "Dunevon like Spot. Spot like Dunevon."

Aly wanted to knock her head slowly and repeatedly against the nearest tree. Approached the right way, the darkings could be fatally friendly. Spot was younger than the rest, which was why she had used it in the king's bedroom. She honestly hadn't thought Spot would learn anything important, but the darking had been so depressed to see Aly collect most of its fellows that she couldn't bear it. This is what I get for being sentimental, she told herself.

"The thing talks," said Aly, playing the timid maid still. "It's not natural."

Taybur ignored this. "And then I asked Spot what he was doing in the king's bedroom. First he said . . ." With a nod, he indicated Spot could fill in.

"Nothing," the darking supplied.

"So I asked again, and this time he said . . ."

"Playing," Spot responded.

"And I asked him why, and he said . . ."

"Secret."

"Secret," agreed Taybur, smiling. "I've known the folk who poke their noses through the palace for years. Even the new ones are all alike. They use the same tools, corrupt people in the same positions, use the same codes. Then you arrive, Aly Homewood. You are *not* what I expect. And then I find another thing I do not expect, and I'm sure it's no accident that you're in the Gray Palace at the same time. I imagine you may have sowed these little creatures—"

"Darkings!" Spot insisted.

"These darkings in the hope they will gather information for you," Taybur said, closing his fist to hide Spot as several parties of nobles passed by on their way to the pavilions. Aly thought it over and mentally shrugged. If he'd meant harm to her, she would be in shackles. When the nobles were gone, she crossed the path to stand closer to Taybur.

As if he'd never gone silent, Taybur opened his fist and continued speaking. "I don't care if you've left darkings from the dungeons to the rooftops of the Gray Palace. If you've left one in my office, prepare for disappointment. I discuss nothing important in there. Topabaw has papered it in listening spells. Eavesdrop on palace gossip all you like, though if you can afford medicine for migraines, I'd invest in it. It's like eavesdropping on vipers. But this"—he patted Spot's head with a finger—"no. Dunevon is a little boy who deserves silence and consideration. And he is my charge. Please don't go into his bedroom again . . . though don't mistake me, I'd love to know just how you did it." He thrust the darking at her.

Aly knew she'd get nowhere if she argued. Instead, keeping an eye on Taybur, she reached out and took Spot. "It's warm," she said with surprise, as if she'd never seen one before. Holding Spot up to her face, she spoke to it as if she might a very small child as she asked, "Now, confess, little fellow. What were you doing in the king's bedroom?"

Spot looked at her, or at least, the position of its head-blob showed that it looked at her. It remembered this part of its instructions, that it was to act as if it had never seen or heard Aly before. "Secret," it told her.

She looked up at Taybur, still acting the part of an ordinary maid. "Can't His Majesty keep it? It seems harmless enough." She gave him a shy smile.

He grimaced. "Because I work very hard to keep those rooms like a proper child's home, and because he deserves a place where he can be himself with harm or advantage to no one *but* himself. Because I think someone should be able to cry himself to sleep in privacy."

Aly petted Spot with her finger, thinking about Taybur's approach with her. Many spies could be erratic. All her life she had dealt with her father's agents and with the agents of other countries, and she could testify that this was so. Some of them, however, knew the reality of the world. Her instincts told her that Taybur understood that spies were inevitable. If she did no harm to him, he would do no harm to her. She was under no illusions. If he'd been in Topabaw's place, guarding the kingdom, she would have been on the next ship to someplace nasty. But she couldn't see this man having a person killed just for doing their work unless it hurt someone. If he thought she meant harm to Dunevon, she would not be surprised to find herself dropping into a deep stream filled with meat-eating fish some night.

A child's furious "No!" cut through the summer air. Taybur shook his head. "If they let him eat soursop fruit again, I swear, I'll shackle the regents in the dungeon. It *always* makes him sick." He turned and hurried away. Aly sat on a bench tucked between hedges to think.

Point one, she thought as Spot climbed up her shoulder to be consoled by Trick. Dunevon has a devoted guardian. A devoted, clever, *attentive* guardian. One with very good instincts. Point two. What will the raka do with Taybur when they rebel? He won't let them murder his king without a fight. Three. How wide does Taybur cast his net? Does he know about Kanodang and Nomru?

That one was easily answered. If he had legions of spies at his beck and call, he would have set a few on Aly at Balitang House to understand her better. He was too relaxed for someone who knew the raka plans to open up Kanodang and steal its treasures. He probably kept most of his people inside the palace, where they could watch Dunevon and anyone close to him.

She nibbled her lip. She needed a plan to get Taybur out of the country without killing him, if possible. He was no fool, and he guarded a Rittevon king.

Even the rebels had an affection for the big man. Ulasim and Fesgao had mentioned that the new captain of the King's Guard treated raka as if they were luarin. The main problem would be getting him away from his charge.

That was the other problem: his charge. Aly had always thrust away the knowledge that Dunevon and Elsren would probably be killed for the crime of possessing Rittevon blood. She couldn't thrust it away now, not if she wanted to avoid killing Dunevon's diverting guardian, and not if she didn't want children's blood on her hands.

What if we let him *take* Dunevon? she asked herself. Ulasim and the others would kick at leaving the boy alive, but if Dunevon and Elsren both swear in blood they will never try to take back the Crown or the Isles, it might work.

It was a dream. Part of her knew that, the part that had been raised in the brutal schools of history and royal politics. She refused to listen to it.

Aly continued her amble toward the water. Crystal globe lamps shone on two of the water's three pavilions: the central one was dark. Shifting her Sight to see better over distance, she found Baron Engan's immense spyglass there, where the globe lights would not make it impossible to view the sky. Dove stood at his side, chatting, as did Winnamine and some other nobles. Aly hoped that Dove had stopped at the Jade Pavilion before she had joined the astronomer, so that the darking Aly had set on her mistress's shoe at the Robing Pavilion could eavesdrop. Not for the first time she thanked the gods the creatures were so light. Had Dove noticed it, she would have asked questions that Aly dared not answer.

From the Jade Pavilion Aly heard Sarai's infectious laugh. The regents were visible, seated in open-backed armchairs, surrounded by their cronies. A third empty chair with an extra cushion on the seat, obviously meant for the king, stood between Imajane and Rubinyan.

Taybur strode down the path that led from the Jade Pavilion with two guards at his back and a shrieking four-year-old in his arms. He nodded to Aly as he passed, then halted abruptly. Turning Dunevon to the side, he positioned his charge so he could vomit into a clump of bushes.

Aly had helped to care for Elsren for over a year. The minute she heard the king gurgle she stepped down to the water and quickly soaked the extra handkerchiefs any lady's maid carried for emergencies. She peeled off a wet linen square and offered it to Taybur.

"Soursop fruit?" she asked as he cleaned Dunevon's face. Another handkerchief went to cool the boy's forehead, a third the back of his neck. Gently Taybur smoothed damp black curls from the child's face.

"They don't know," he replied with soft savagery. "They weren't really watching him, since they knew the guards wouldn't let him off the pavilion and the walls on it are too high for him to climb. He could have eaten anything." He glanced at the vomit. "Oh, splendid—soursop fruit *and* curry. Excuse me." He strode down the path, the guards hurrying to catch up, the boy king sobbing quietly on his shoulder.

Aly frowned. She didn't enjoy liking those she was supposed to bring down, like Dunevon and his large protector. They stood between the raka and their freedom. Something had to be done, but the thought of killing either of them made her grind her teeth.

In soaking her handkerchiefs, she had spied a bench placed just by the water, one that gleamed with magical discouragements to insects and snakes. Though sheltered by a willow, the seat gave Aly a clear view of all three water pavilions. She settled there, hoping that no one chose this hidden place for a lovers' encounter, though it was clearly designed for that. The sounds of flutes, harps, and soft drums floated over the water through air like smooth balm.

Watching darkness fall, she considered the night's activities. Her own people would be taking positions on either side of the fortresses. Ulasim's had been seeping into Kanodang for the last day, locked up as prisoners until they could guide the freed captives to horses, boats, or hiding places.

"This is *taking too long.*" Kyprioth, dressed as a raka and tinkling with charms, appeared in front of Aly's nose.

Aly shrugged. She had been watching Rubinyan and two of his nobles discuss horse racing. She had already seen that no one on the Jade Pavilion dared to speak of the newest rebellion. "An eclipse party does have to wait for the eclipse to happen. You're blocking my view."

"I didn't mean the eclipse," snapped the god. "I can't distract my brother and sister forever, Aly."

She raised her brows. "We've done quite nicely for rebels who have only been back in town for a month. I would like to point out that this week will be quite eventful, thank you so much." She cocked her head and looked at him. "We need the luarin, Kyprioth. Unless enough of them come to our side, we'll fail. You need strength to battle the others? You say you get that from victories. We haven't won that many yet. Though it sounds peculiar, we short-lived creatures need time." She leaned back against the bench. "The country's coming to a boil. Once we convince those who are unconvinced that the regents are not good rulers but vicious ones, that this isn't just a matter of the raka bringing up old grievances, it will be war, and you'll have your victories."

Kyprioth tugged the emerald earring that glinted in the light from the pavilions. "Every day it takes to drive these people along, we are a day closer to my brother and sister's return. So it's vicious rulers you need? Maybe I can work at that." He vanished.

"If you use your power now, your brother and sister will know anyway," Aly told the empty air.

"There is power, and there is *power,* my dear," she heard him whisper. "My power can be vast, in the right places."

Aly shook her head. They moved forward as fast as they could, the conspirators in Rajmuat and the ones on the outlying Isles. Since she couldn't control any of them, she could only wait and do her own work. She remained on her bench, her Sight locked on the nobles on the Jade Pavilion. Most of them spoke of social matters. Officers of the royal navy complained to Lord Matfrid of strangely choppy seas and difficult voyages. Ferdy tried to tell the Carthaki Zaimid that nobles did not raise horses themselves. Sarai shoved him with one hand and told him he was stuffy.

Each time Aly tired of reading one conversation, she turned her gaze to Topabaw. He was always easy to find. His array of magical amulets and the glare of his magical Gift burned in her Sight.

Topabaw was restless. He fiddled with his charms, changed position, and rubbed the nape of his neck. For a while he paced around the edges of the pavilion, until Prince Rubinyan shot him a glare that made the spymaster halt.

The next time Aly could read Topabaw's lips, he was assuring a couple of nervous men that the winter had simply made the raka crazy, and it would wear off. Another time he refused to discuss Duke Nomru's arrest with Count and Countess Tomang. More than anyone else, he kept glancing at the regents, his jaw muscles clenched. Topabaw was nervous. And he was nervous about his masters.

Aly smiled.

The moon had begun to rise when she heard steps on the path. She stiffened, then relaxed: the steps were Taybur's. The big man walked straight down to the water's edge without hesitation. He pushed aside trailing willow limbs and entered her enclosure.

She looked up at him and raised an eyebrow as he sat beside her.

"Fear not, gentle maiden. I have no intentions on your virtue."

"You're no fun," Aly accused. If she'd thought for a moment he had such intentions, she would have made it plain she was uninterested. Once she would have worried more that he gave no sign that he thought her attractive, but these days she didn't care. She had changed from who she'd been in Tortall, but she refused to ask herself how.

Taybur leaned back and thrust his long legs out, crossing his ankles as he folded his hands on his chest. "Any other night and you'd have to fight for this spot, you know," he said blithely. "It's popular with lovers. But with the news from Imahyn, the servants not on duty are hiding, and the nobles want the regents to see their smiling, loyal faces." He sighed. "People don't know how to appreciate a spring night anymore. By the way, according to my agents, there is no family named Homewood in service at Fief Tameran in Tortall."

Only years of training kept Aly from betraying shock. Instead she yawned, keeping her eyes on the Jade Pavilion. Beyond it, on the dark Lapis Pavilion, Baron Engan adjusted his spyglass as Dove and a few young scholars looked on.

"If you're worried about Topabaw, don't," Taybur said lazily. "Look, there's the first firefly. Make a wish. Topabaw is so used to people being afraid of him that he's gotten lazy.

My people visited Tameran at a certain risk to themselves. I don't want to share their reports with a man who thinks torture gets honest answers. You *can* speak, can't you?"

Aly looked down. Her mouth quivered with amusement.

Spot emerged from its silent conversation with Trick, rolling along the back of Aly's neck to sit on the shoulder closest to Taybur. He offered his palm to the darking, who created four legs for itself and walked across his fingers.

"In case you're thinking I'm lazy, I did give my mages a chance at this little fellow before I returned him to you. Their magic just bounced off." He idly tossed Spot into the air.

"Whee!" cried the darking. It spread out two wings to slow its descent onto Taybur's palm.

"You are easily pleased," Taybur informed it. He passed Spot back to Aly and glanced up through a break in the leaves. "The Goddess begins to draw her veil. If you'll excuse me?" He stood, then seemed to think of something else. His face was shadowed as he looked down at Aly. "Things can't be easy for a full luarin in service in a household with so many raka. If you ever need a friend, come to me." He strode out of the willow's shelter, then turned back again, almost giving Aly a fit of the giggles. He was *very* good and had the timing of an actor. "Have you seen how edgy Topabaw's been lately? Wouldn't you love to know why?"

This time he continued on his way to the Jade Pavilion. Soon after his arrival the light globes winked out to allow the nobles a clear view of the darkening moon.

The eclipse was predicted to last nearly until dawn. Once the moon's face was covered, however, many nobles, including the Balitang ladies, said their good nights. Dove followed her mother and sister reluctantly, glancing up at the hidden moon.

Seeing them on the path, Aly trotted back to the Robing Pavilion, grateful that they would be home long before the alarm was raised at Kanodang. She had not liked the risk of being near the palace when the regents learned of the prison break.

"I was down by the Lily Water. Many of the lords are preparing to leave," she announced to her fellow servants. Immediately the men returned to their masters' side of the pavilion. Cards were put away, sewing packed up, boxes opened for a change to clothes better suited to riding or litters. Pembery sent a runner to alert the men-at-arms and the hostlers that it was time to go. When the ladies arrived, the maids helped them change clothes.

They were part of a large group of nobles riding into the city. Ferdy and Jevair Ibadun urged their horses to either side of Sarai, glaring at one another behind her back. Zaimid joined the Balitangs at the last minute, riding a spirited mare whose grace made Sarai's eyes shine. Instead of jostling with the other two men, he rode with the duchess and Nuritin, talking about the evening and politics in Carthak. Dove rode just behind them, listening.

Party by party, the nobles left the main group to finish the trip to their scattered homes. The Balitangs' companions, including Zaimid, turned away when they reached Joshain Street. They assured the ladies they were going straight to bed, but no one was fooled. There was plenty to interest lively young men in Dockmarket at that hour.

Once Aly was brushing out Dove's hair in the girl's bedroom, Dove glared at her in the looking glass. "*Now* will you tell me what's got you on pins and needles?" she whispered. She didn't want to rouse Junai, who'd gone to sleep the moment she lay down on her pallet. "You hide it well, but you've been too alert all day. It's the same with Ulasim, Fesgao, and

Ochobu these last two days. I asked Quedanga, but she says that the chiefs in different areas don't talk about special projects with anyone who isn't involved, just those who help them to pull things together."

Aly shook her head. "It's better for those of us who don't take active part to hear as things happen."

"So when anyone asks if we knew what was going on, we can say no, and it will read to a mage as the truth," Dove said, making sure that she had understood it correctly.

"If you're so clever, what do you need me for?" teased Aly, putting the brush aside.

Dove sniffed. "Two clevers are better than one." She turned on her stool to look at Aly. "But you know, don't you? Even though you aren't supposed to, you already know what's going on, because that's what you do. Ulasim told me once that he wouldn't be surprised if you'd found ways to listen to them when you aren't about. He thinks you probably know the shape of everything, the entire rebellion, throughout the Isles. I think so, too."

I could sometimes wish she were a bit less intelligent, thought Aly. No wonder most of her friends are adults.

"As long as I do no harm with what I've picked up, I don't see why anyone should even care," she assured her mistress. "Don't we each have enough on our plates, without adding more?"

"Except that it's your job to collect more for your plate," Dove pointed out, then yawned. She got to her feet and went to bed. "Good night, Aly."

Aly hesitated, watching Dove get comfortable. "I am sorry you missed the rest of the eclipse," she whispered.

"There will be a solar eclipse in August," Dove murmured sleepily. "Half the court says it's a grand omen, the other half claims it's troubles on the rise."

Aly said, her voice breathless and panicky, "But, lady, with these raka up to mischief, the gods are obviously trying to warn us. We could be murdered in our beds!"

"You will be if you aren't quiet," grumbled Junai.

Aly waited until both Dove and Junai fell asleep, then slipped out of the room.

11

A Few Changes

Aly found company in the kitchen. Ulasim, Fesgao, Quedanga, Chenaol, Ochobu, and Ysul all sat around the table in their nightclothes. Idly they played at dice, chess, or backgammon. Chenaol poured Aly a cup of arak and shoved a plate of fried dumplings at her. It was a mark of the cook's distraction, because everyone knew Aly hated arak. Aly set her basket of sewing on the table and watched the others' faces. She had wondered if Ulasim or Fesgao would choose to break their own rule and go on the Kanodang mission. The temptation must be overwhelming, after months of doing nothing but creating plans. She thought the better of them for staying out of it, but then, she had known they took their revolution seriously. If they made a mistake, it would not be any of the obvious ones.

"So *now* will you tell us what goes forward?" Chenaol demanded wearily. "Now that all the chicks are in their coops? Aly's little pack of wolves never so much as showed up for supper."

"No," Ulasim and Fesgao said at the same time.

After a moment Ulasim said, "You will know when it is done. It is not yet done."

"If I die of curiosity before it is done, I will wait in the Peaceful Realms and ensure that you do *not* find them peaceful," Chenaol warned. She looked at Aly. "All's well at the palace?"

Aly smiled. "They got word of the rising on Imahyn. They pretended it meant nothing. And Topabaw does not look at all well. Nor does Prince Rubinyan appear to regard him with any pleasure at all."

"I hear from a thousand sources that Topabaw plans to overturn the regents, or the regents plan to dismiss Topabaw," said Quedanga with a yawn. "They speak of it even at the palace, where such things are usually left in silence."

That was the extent of their conversation for some time. The watch was calling the fourth hour of the night when Ysul raised a hand for quiet. Everyone went still. Ysul had the best hearing in the household, but Aly already knew what he'd noticed. A moment later the others heard it, the tiniest ghost of an explosion down by the harbor. They ran through the servants' gate into the street, looking. A dull orange glow showed in the sky to the southeast. Aly knew as if she had seen it that her agents had set the kegs of blazebalm on fire in both fortresses. So much blazebalm, tightly packed in wax-coated kegs, would explode when it burned.

"Don't look at me," Fesgao said, holding up his hands when everyone turned to stare at him. "This isn't my doing."

Alarms sounded all around the harbor. Aly crossed her fingers and prayed that her people were safely away from the damage they had done. Servants from nearby houses emerged in their bedclothes, curious about the uproar. Word finally reached them via the other servants and householders who lived between there and the harbor that the Greater and

Lesser Fortresses were on fire, as well as the soldiers' barracks behind the Greater Fortress.

Aly finally complained of cold feet and went back inside. Her people would be careful to make their way home, using the web of tunnels to enter the grounds unseen. Just in case, she went to her workroom. There they were, everyone who had undertaken the night's diversion, using oil to clean off the soot that turned their faces to shadows. They were laughing and joking with relief. Only when Aly held a finger to her lips did they remember that most of the household was abed.

"Don't tell me you worried about us," one of the men said with a bold grin.

"It was the easiest thing." Guchol used a bit of cotton to remove a last streak on a friend's face. "We didn't lose a single recruit, and you can see we all came back in one piece."

"The silly clunches store all their blazebalm in one armory," Kioka said with a sniff.

Rasaj was combing out his long hair. "Both fortresses, they did it that way. We hardly needed to do anything more."

"But you did," suggested Aly.

"We stuck wedges under the barracks doors and the sally ports," Lokak told Aly with grim pleasure. "We disabled the drawbridges and the portcullises."

"It will take them all day to get out," said Jimarn quietly. "By then they'll have sampled their food and drink. They may not have enough alive in the Lesser Fortress to open the gates at all."

"They're not idiots," protested Olkey. "Once they realize all the places we hit, they'll have to check the food before they try it."

"*You* said nobody would be stupid enough to keep all their blazebalm in one spot," one of the women pointed out.

Aly caught the whiff of sewer that clung to her pack

even after they'd discarded the clothes they'd worn. "Baths," she ordered. "Get that smell off you." She went around the room and kissed each pack member's forehead. "You've done beautifully," she told them with approval and pride. "Let us pray all our adventures fare as well." She caught an especially strong whiff from Jimarn. "Bathed and dressed by dawn. And need I tell you—"

"No word to anyone, not *anyone,*" they chorused, having heard it from her often enough.

Aly grinned at them and returned to the kitchens to take up her mending again. She'd expected to feel sleepy once she was sure her pack was safe, but her nerves still hummed. Her thoughts passed over the Windward District, across the harbor, up along the tenements of Downwind and the pretenses of dwelling places in the Honeypot. Over the ridge and there it would be, gray stone Kanodang, with its thick walls and strong towers. What was happening there?

Soon enough the light turned the pearl gray that came before dawn. The household came down for the morning's exercises, Aly and the chief conspirators joining them after they'd changed into day clothes. As they practiced with and without weapons, the sun began to rise above the same long ridge of the Kitafin mountains that hid Kanodang from view. Ulasim and Fesgao both took bruises they normally would have avoided, because they kept looking northeast, toward the prison. After Ulasim took a staff hit that turned his left cheekbone purple, Aly dragged him aside.

"Were they going to burn it?" she demanded softly.

He glanced at her, startled. "Of course not," he replied. "Rapists and murderers, remember?"

"Then stop looking up there like you expect a column of smoke," she said. "We'll know if the warning bells—"

Ysul stopped in the middle of throwing a man-at-arms,

turning his face northeast. His victim struggled and protested, unable to break his captor's hold as Ysul listened. Then the others heard the toll of a bell from the far side of the harbor. Another bell took up the call, then others.

Above the booming of the bells came the thin, raucous screeches of Stormwings. More than a hundred of them flew overhead from the direction of the palace, sun dancing off their metal wings as they sped toward the source of the alarm gongs.

"Will you look at that," Aly said with a brilliant smile for Ulasim. "Whatever could have stirred them up so?"

He hugged her hard enough to make her squeak, then released her. To Ochobu he said, "You see, Mother? And you were all fretful."

Ochobu raised her eyebrows. "It is unseemly to gloat, boy," she told her forty-five-year-old son.

Aly sauntered back into the house. She did not delude herself. She would get the formal reports later, but she guessed they might have killed between two hundred and five hundred at the harbor fortresses, if some of the wedged doors had been those in the barracks. With Kanodang she could not be sure, since Ulasim had told her they had people who worked inside, but she could guess a death total of fifty to one hundred. She owed a debt to those ghosts. The Kanodang breakout had been her idea, as had the attack on the fortresses. This was what her parents had done all their lives, racked up lists of those who could thank them for their deaths.

No wonder Mother gets cranky when anyone asks how many people she's killed, Aly thought, washing her face before she went upstairs. I've lost count of every war and skirmish and raid she's fought in, not to mention the duels as Champion. That's why she never wants to talk about them.

She'll have to remember the lives she has taken.

There were people who had killed so often there was little humanity left in them. Aly had met plenty like that, helping her da with spy work. She knew a few of them among the household guards here, and in Topabaw she'd found someone who couldn't even remember what it was like to feel regret, or pity for the families of the dead. Her parents fought to hang on to their humanity, and Aly had never valued the struggle more.

I'll make it up to them when I go home, she promised herself as she trotted up the back stairs to Dove's room. *I'll be a better daughter.*

Dove was opening the shutters on her window: the night had turned chilly as they'd come home from the palace. The younger girl looked fresh and alert, not like someone who had reached home after midnight. "Alarm bells and gongs," she said as Aly changed into clean clothes. "And Stormwings," added Dove. "A *lot* of Stormwings." She turned to look at Aly. "Is there something I should know?"

"Oh, my lady, don't worry your head about these things," Aly said as she took out Dove's clothes for the day. "I'm sure some nice man will explain in terms you can grasp."

Dove raised her brows. "That big, is it?" she asked dryly.

Aly, her arms full of clothes, bobbed a curtsy. "It's not for me to say, my lady," she replied, her voice prim. It was wonderful, how she rarely had to explain things to Dove. "Will my lady be wishful of a bath this morning?"

The sounds had took up a particular rhythm: bong bong *bong*, bong *bong* bong, bong bong *bong*. The duchess, wearing a robe over her fine lawn nightdress, swept into the room and helped Aly open the rest of the shutters. "That's the alarm at Kanodang," she said grimly. "The prison. There's been an escape. Aly, get Fesgao. Have all the guards mustered and close the gates, *immediately*."

Aly ran to obey. For now all they had to do was lock the house down and wait for news. Since news could take time to reach the city, Aly thought she might get to catch up on the sleep she'd lost. That would have to wait, though. First she wanted to get to her office, to hear what her darkings could tell her. Sleep would come later, after they made all the motions of a house full of innocents.

She found Fesgao seated at the kitchen table, watching drowsily as Chenaol and the maids rushed to prepare breakfast. He blinked at Aly as she rested her elbows on the table beside him and leaned down so he could speak privately to her. "Seko's back," Fesgao murmured. "I thought it would please him, as a former bandit, to crack a prison. He says that they got more than a hundred and ten political prisoners out, including His Grace of Nomru. They are dispersed, by ship or horse, to the other islands."

Aly smiled. "Very good work," she said with appreciation.

Fesgao looked up at her. "Do you know, with any other girl of your age, if she spoke thus to me, I would give her latrine duty for a year. But from you?" He shook his head. "I am complimented beyond words."

Aly winked at him. "And that is as it should be," she told him. Before he could come up with a retort, she said, "Her Grace heard the alarms. She wants all the gates locked, with guards put on them right away."

Chenaol passed a chunk of cooked pork and two sago cakes to Fesgao. As he took them, he told Aly in a normal tone of voice, "Inform Her Grace it will be done immediately." He left the kitchen, as brisk and alert as if he had spent the night in his bed, sleeping well.

Ulasim leaned against the kitchen doorframe, grinning.

"The guards at Kanodang are worse than we thought," he said when Aly and Chenaol gave him questioning looks. "They didn't realize there had been an escape until the morning guards came for their duty. No one else checked on the place. It means those who got out had more time to get away than we could have hoped. Thank you, Bright One!" he added in tribute to Kyprioth.

"What about our people in the prison?" Chenaol inquired. "The ones who stayed?"

Ulasim shook his head. "They're safe. Our folk were disguised, and those who were to remain knew nothing of the plan. When Crown mages question them, our people will truthfully say they were captured and sent to sleep along with the other guards and prisoners." He straightened. "I'd best see Her Grace. She will have orders for me for today."

Not long after the family had finished their morning meal, servants from the nearby houses came to see if the Balitangs knew anything about the alarm. They were followed by hastily dressed masters and mistresses, who asked the same questions of the duchess. It wasn't long before someone realized that Elsren's escort of King's Guards had not arrived. He was left to kick his heels in the downstairs sitting room for a time, before the duchess decreed that he could change to more comfortable clothes and play with his sisters.

It was almost noon when they heard the tramp of feet outside the walls. The King's Watch had come in force. Their captain ordered everyone to return to their homes and remain there. When Winnamine's noble neighbors protested, he told them that they could walk back or be carried, again by order of the regents.

Their guests left. After lunch, the Balitang ladies dismissed their maids and retired for naps. Nearly everyone in the household did the same. Usually there was some activity during the afternoon rest time, but with no one permitted outside, most of the household except those on guard chose to relax.

Aly went to her office and closed the door, then closed the shutters on her windows and locked them in place, putting the spells in the wood up as a barrier to all eavesdropping. Only then did she allow her two-strand bead necklace, which currently sported anchoring beads on each shoulder, to reshape itself into Trick and Spot.

"You have a new name," she told Spot. "Secret."

"Secret," it agreed, and nodded. It plainly liked either the name or the idea, Aly wasn't sure. She looked at Trick. "What is happening in the palace?" she asked it. "What do our friends up there have to tell you? Wait." She found slates and chalk. "Go ahead."

What the darkings had to say fascinated Aly. Between the attacks on the fortresses and the escape from Kanodang, Imajane was furious. She was spending her day writing warrants for the arrest of the warden and his lieutenants in the case of Kanodang, and dictating instructions for the storage of blazebalm for the army and the navy, since the commanders and their staff at both fortresses were among the dead. Trick passed on the names on the warrants: none was a member of the raka conspiracy. Ulasim had issued orders years before that his people within the prison were not to be promoted beyond a certain level, because the Rittevons were notoriously fond of executing people in charge when things went wrong.

Rubinyan's darking told them that the prince had taken over the investigation beyond the grounds of Kanodang. He ordered the captain-general of the King's Watch to hunt down fugitives and question his informants about the jailbreak. He was also to lift the ban on people in the streets.

Both men knew it was risky to keep a population indoors for more than a day. The prince called for the commanding general of the Rittevon Lancers and gave orders for the horsemen to search for fugitives outside the city walls. He then tripled the Rittevon Guard's security at the palace. He was cool and crisp, giving each man he spoke to the impression that he was in control of the situation.

He then commanded the chief herald to put his scribes to two tasks. The more important job was a proclamation to be read at every crossroad, with copies sent to each person on a list of the noble houses and the city's wealthiest merchants. He decreed that there had been pirate attacks at the harbor's mouth during the eclipse, fought off with heavy losses to the Harbor Guard. There had also been the prison break from Kanodang. The people were asked to watch for twelve fugitives, five of them full-blood luarin. There would be a reward of two gold lans to anyone who gave information that would lead to the fugitives' arrest.

"That's sweet," Aly remarked cynically. "That way, if he gets any tip-offs, he can say someone else already reported them, so they got the reward."

"Cheating," Secret commented with disapproval.

The second proclamation was to go out through the Isles. It offered a hundred gold lans each for a list of ten men, one of them Vurquan Nomru, formerly a duke, whose lands and holdings were now Crown property.

Aly's hand cramped, she wrote so much as darking after darking passed her information the rebellion could use. It was Rubinyan's darking once again who provided Aly with the tastiest bit of information of all, as the late-afternoon light streamed through cracks in her shutters. When Aly heard it, she had to savor it, but she had the self-discipline to wait until she had given all of her darkings one last check.

She praised each of them through Trick and asked if they were having fun. All of them agreed they were most definitely having fun. They weren't sure what they liked best, the people whispering, throwing items, or jumping at noises, but all agreed these things were amusing. Aly suggested to them that they might try some of their own whispering, throwing, and noisemaking, and left them to it.

Then she sat back, crossed her hands on her stomach, propped her feet up on her desk, and savored. Back and forth she wavered: ought she to tell the conspirators or not? In the end, she decided to let them learn without hearing it from her. For one thing, Ulasim and Ochobu at least would like to know how she'd found it out, and she was not ready to tell them about the darkings. For another, she wanted to see the look on each face when they realized she had done what they had thought impossible.

She wished she could tell Nawat.

Realizing the time, she went in search of Dove, in case she had instructions for Aly. She found the ladies of the house in the nursery, Nuritin embroidering as Winnamine, Sarai, and Dove played with Petranne and Elsren. It was something they'd done all winter, but not as much since their return to Rajmuat. Aly left them alone. This might be the last time they could relax for weeks.

She spent the afternoon and the early evening reading reports from the palace. The chief armorer did not like the Rittevon Guard, who treated their weapons badly. The captain of the Rittevon Guard thought the armorer was a penny-pinching old fool. One of Imajane's ladies-in-waiting appeared to have an eye for Prince Rubinyan. Reading this in a report from Vereyu, Aly chuckled. *Now* she had a wedge to drive between the regents, if she could make the lady-in-waiting's interest obvious to Imajane.

There was more, from all over the city. Reading paper reports, Aly marked out who might be shifted to the rebels' side, given incentive, and made a list of rumors for her people to spread. The shakier the regents looked, the more eager people would be to do things they would not dare if the Crown appeared strong. There was the personal gossip—Rubinyan's possible involvement with one of his wife's own ladies-in-waiting—and the more ominous news about what had really happened at the fortresses. Rubinyan's personal spymaster, Sevmire, had told him, with Aly's darking to hear, that more than three hundred and twenty men had died at the fortresses, burned or poisoned. Rubinyan had ordered him to keep that number to himself. If Rubinyan heard that people knew the correct number of the dead, he might think Sevmire or his subordinates had been indiscreet. It could also be that by the time Rubinyan's spies heard the city gossip, the number of dead soldiers would be vast, amplified by gossip as it passed from one person to the next. She relaxed in her chair. It had been a very nice day for her.

Her pack sought her out shortly before supper, to see what orders she had. She handed over the list of rumors. They assured her that they would continue to pass on gossip about Topabaw and the regents. Aly only nodded.

Supper came and went. The ladies retired to their sitting room with their maids, sewing, reading, and talking softly, without once referring to the reason they had not gone out all day. At last Winnamine sent everyone to their rooms, though she and Nuritin remained where they were. Dove and Aly went downstairs to meet with the conspirators, where Dove and the others heard the details of what Ulasim, Fesgao, Ochobu, and Aly had pulled off among them to bring the city to a standstill.

"Gods bless me," whispered Dove when they were done, "we might just do this."

There were more plans to discuss, and then the conspirators broke up for the night. From the looks on Quedanga's and Ysul's faces, they had thought of some fresh ploy. Chenaol stayed with Ulasim to talk about a shipment of bows and spears that was scheduled to arrive soon, and where they would be stored.

Dove and Aly were halfway up the stairs to the family quarters when Dove turned and faced Aly. "They'll think the luarin did it," she whispered. Just because the house was spelled and watched for outsider spies was no proof that someone inside might not lose their nerve, or try to get a reward for what he or she knew. "They don't believe the raka have money, resources, mages, or the will to organize and fight. They'll think the luarin set Nomru free—and the others, to hide Nomru's trail. Topabaw will be watching the luarin more closely than ever, and with his usual touch. He'll turn more luarin nobles against him that way than if he'd just hanged their full-raka slaves."

"Don't mistake Topabaw for the regents," Aly advised. "Do you think they would act differently with another spymaster?" She took a step up, so that her mouth was on a level with Dove's ear, and she whispered, "We had to force that feeble luarin conspiracy of yours to *act.* So far, they're just an association that meets to complain about the government. You can't play with rebellion, Dove. You're either in it, or you're dead."

A small, strong hand fastened on Aly's arm. Dove towed Aly down the stairs, through the house, along the garden paths, and into the Pavilion of Secrets. "You don't understand the pressure they're under," she whispered fiercely.

Aly sank onto a bench. "I understand that this country's rulers have gotten away with things that are unthinkable in Tortall. They get away with it because their nobles haven't stood up for those in their care. I'm just a simple country girl. I rely on what people *do,* not how much they whisper."

"I can't tell the nobles about the raka," Dove said, slumping on the bench next to Aly. "I swore."

Aly stretched. "No. But you can tell them your market and merchant friends have whispered of other conspiracies in the outlying Isles, people who are prepared to do more than just talk. Let them chew on that for a time. And if you don't mind, I mean to retire for the night. I'm *exhausted.*"

"You're supposed to wait until *I* come up to bed and undress *me,*" Dove said as Aly got to her feet. They walked together into the house. "You're a terrible maid that way."

"You could always get rid of me," Aly replied, yawning so widely she half feared the joints in her jaws would give way. "But then you'd miss my charm and wit."

Aly was asleep the moment she lay down on her pallet.

Early the next morning, a herald came with the announcement that people could leave their homes. The family had just finished their breakfast when the news came. Rihani and Gian, Elsren's manservant—now a spy recruit—had to scurry to prepare Elsren for his daily visit to the palace. They were still dressing the boy when the squad of ten King's Guards arrived. As they waited, their sergeant was happy to talk to Quedanga. He'd noticed on earlier visits that the housekeeper was a handsome woman always willing to give a soldier a cup of tea and a bite to eat. He assured her that things were almost normal. There were more checkpoints on the streets, and folk wouldn't want to idle as they went about their day's business, but the regents had the city well in hand.

"He's not bad, for a luarin," Quedanga told Aly as the duchess and Dove waved goodbye to Elsren.

"Let him know," Aly said. "He might be useful." She trudged upstairs.

Despite permission to leave home, Nuritin advised the duchess not to allow Sarai or Dove to go out and about just yet. "The regents *have* to let people buy food and do business unless there is an army at our gates," Nuritin told both girls. "That does not mean we have no dangerous criminals running about. We should answer all those invitations that have collected on Winnamine's desk. It is more personal when one of the ladies of the house replies." Aly, Pembery, Boulaj, and Dorilize rolled their eyes at one another. For them, this meant a morning of needlework.

The morning was advanced when a sound made Aly look up. Wayan, a house message runner, peered at her around the doorframe with eyes as wide as saucers. As soon as Aly saw her, she fled. A few moments later, a footman did the same thing. Like Wayan, he stared only at Aly. A pair of kitchen maids followed him. Their whispers roused Nuritin from her concentration on the letter she wrote. She turned on her chair and scowled.

"Have you business here?" she demanded.

The maids shook their heads.

"Then get back to your work!" As the maids fled, Nuritin shook her head. "Silly young creatures, no more sense than finches. When *I* was a girl . . ."

This time Winnamine, as well as the other women, rolled her eyes.

It was almost time for lunch when Ulasim rapped on the doorframe. "Your Grace? My ladies?" he asked, his face locked in formal, senior-servant blankness. "I bring important news."

Winnamine beckoned him forward as everyone but Aly looked at him. Aly, sensing what news he bore, kept her attention on her needle.

Ulasim bowed. "Your Grace, my ladies, I . . ." He paused for a moment, so oddly for him that the ladies looked worried. Ulasim was the ideal manservant and never fumbled. "It's Topabaw," he said at last. "He's— They made an Example of him. By the harbor mouth."

Nuritin jerked, dumping a bottle of ink on her desk and herself. As the maids rushed to stop the ink's spread and to save the old woman's dress, the duchess stared at him.

"Ulasim, this is a very poor joke," she whispered.

He looked at her not as a servant looked at his mistress but as one human being looked at another. "Your Grace, I did not believe it, either. I have just come from the harbor. I have seen it with my own eyes. Topabaw is dead." He looked at Aly, his eyes holding a shade of the awe the maids had showed. "There is no proclamation of his crime, but the royal seal was placed on his chest. Burned into it, actually."

Nuritin stopped trying to clean up the ink and half-collapsed in her chair. "I know there was a time before Topabaw," she murmured, "for I lived and bore children in it."

"It must have been the prison escape," said the duchess, folding hands that quivered. "I've heard rumors that he was losing his grip, that the regents had come to think he was too old for the work. . . ."

"Who cares?" snapped Sarai, jumping to her feet. "They didn't kill him for all the people he's had murdered, did they? They killed him because he let Nomru escape! They only care about luarin lives around here. They always have and they always will!"

Winnamine's eyes flashed. "Do not forget you are half luarin, mistress, whether you like it or not."

"How can I forget?" demanded Sarai. "It's the only part of me people are interested in." She stalked out past Ulasim, skirts flaring around her.

Dove set down her pen and corked her ink bottle. "Things will be different," she observed quietly. "He kept all of the work of the intelligence gatherers in his own hands for years. He never replaced the assistant spymaster when the man was assassinated five years ago."

Nuritin frowned. "I'd forgotten. He never did, it's true."

"Whoever takes up his post won't know everything he did." Dove looked at her mother, then her great-aunt. "They won't know his files. They won't know his agents. And his agents won't be sure if they aren't next, or if the new man isn't there simply to hand out more blame. His networks will be all chaos for a while."

Suddenly Winnamine remembered the maids and Ulasim. "All of you, it's almost lunchtime. Go wash up. Ulasim . . ."

"Yes, Your Grace?"

"Tell our people, *Mind your tongues.* Say or do *nothing* that might look wrong to the regents," Winnamine insisted. "We don't know who will be taking notes for them."

Ulasim bowed to her again. "Your Grace is always wise."

12

Meddlers

There was no rest period that day. All of the servants watched Aly as if she were god-touched. Her own pack, when it met in her workroom, had that same look of awe mingled with fear. Aly was glad when callers descended on Balitang House. At least none of them stared.

For once the young nobles talked quietly about things other than themselves, though the young men were careful to tell Sarai she might count on them, just in case. They did not say in case of what. The only man of Sarai's circle not present was Zaimid. Sarai made the mistake of asking Ferdy where the Carthaki was.

"Caring for rioters over on Soursop Lane," the young count informed her with contempt. "The Watch had taken care of them as they should be cared for, and off goes our healer to tend the wounded. I'll be glad when we see the last of that sanctimonious face!"

"At least he helps," retorted Sarai. "At least he's doing something *for* people, instead of living off them and ignoring them when they need him."

"Lady Sarai, helping troublemakers only encourages them," Ferdy said gently. "Look at Topabaw. He got slack. Now we've had a prison break, attacks on the fortresses, and uprisings all over the Isles. It's time we had new blood to set the realm to rights."

Chenaol touched Aly as she watched the young nobles. "Vitorcine Townsend, Lady Isalena's maid, wants you," the cook whispered in Aly's ear. "She looks like she's in love. You'll find her in my rooms."

Aly raised an eyebrow and went in search of the housekeeper's private sitting room. Chenaol was right. Vitorcine looked as if she had shed years of her age or a great burden. Aly lowered herself into a chair. "You heard the news of Topabaw, then?" she asked Vitorcine.

The young woman nodded. "There's more. Grosbeak! Grosbeak is gone! I report to him as I run errands for my lady, and I was late, close to the noon bell. His shop is locked up, doors and shutters! I . . ." She looked down, blushing, then met Aly's gaze. "I picked the lock. The books, papers, all of it was gone. And everything was a mess, as if he'd packed in a hurry. So I took a chance and went to his home." In response to a question Aly hadn't asked, she rushed to say, "I tracked him there once, just . . . just in case."

Aly tapped her chin, fascinated. She hadn't thought Vitorcine had that kind of gumption. Perhaps she could find something better suited to her talents than simply reporting on the activities of the Obemaeks. Aly had decoded the information Vitorcine had brought, to discover correspondence about the things she already knew, that Lord and Lady Obemaek belonged to the luarin conspiracy.

"What did you find at Grosbeak's home?" she asked.

"Gone, him and his family," Vitorcine said eagerly, giddy at being free of Grosbeak and his master. "And they must have taken only what they could carry. The smith who lives next door said they went around dawn." She reached out and gripped Aly's hands. "Please, will you not free me of my vow? The Obemaeks are so good to me. I hate watching them!"

Aly looked at her meaningfully, as a mother might look at a daughter who had not thought a problem through. "If Topabaw kept records, his successor may yet come back to you," she reminded Vitorcine. When the maid's face fell, Aly patted her hands. "But there. Why borrow trouble? For the time being, do not fret over thoughts of spies."

That night, when the raka leaders met, all of them, even Ochobu and Dove, stared at Aly when she entered the room. She expected it. They had built Topabaw up into something more than human for years. Learning he was now an Example must have made them feel as if the earth had turned sideways. She helped herself to mango nectar. "I said it could be done. Remember, I'm an outsider. He'd been in power for so long that the people who live here forgot the man was human, and the regents more human still. Humans get jealous. That we can use, whether it is between Topabaw and the regents . . ." She paused and looked them over. "Or between Imajane and Rubinyan."

They were startled, as they'd been when Aly had suggested that Topabaw was vulnerable. This time, however, instead of denying that such a thing could be done, the conspirators appeared thoughtful. Aly let them turn it over in their minds, then asked Quedanga, "You'll make sure people know *we* created this, yes? That it is no coincidence that so soon after our return, the regents turned on their spymaster?"

Quedanga opened her mouth and drew in air, but nothing came out. She gulped from her cup and tried again. "Are you certain you are not an aspect of our Bright One? Because you begin to worry me in the same way."

"No, just a loyal servant," Aly reassured her, stroking her Trick-and-Secret beads. They hummed softly against her collarbone. "Things will be a mess in the spy service for now," she told the others. "Rubinyan put his private spymaster, a man named Sevmire Ambau, in charge. He was born on the Jimajen estates, got recruited as a spy at the university in Carthak, and came home to do intelligence for the army. That was when he came to Rubinyan's attention. He's worked for the prince for years, watching the king, Topabaw, even his brother. Sevmire's competent, but he was never a part of Topabaw's organization. He'll be scrambling to find and decode Topabaw's files. He'll try to grip Topabaw's spies, which will be like trying to get control of a runaway team of hurroks." Hurroks were the kudarung's less likeable, clawed and fanged kinfolk. "Some of you know people who worked for Topabaw. This is a good time to suggest to them that the new man is green. He's never had a network bigger than a few islands, or more than a hundred people, to run. He'll get into trouble fast. The more commotion we can stir up throughout the Isles before he can learn his job, the more overwhelmed he will be."

Ulasim stroked his small beard. "I can think of a few . . . possibilities."

Aly looked at him, then at their two mages. "Should something happen—should they fear the worst—Their Highnesses might well start calling in their best generals and mages. It would be nice if some, if not all, of them were unable to respond."

Ulasim chuckled. "We *were* at this before you came, Bright Eyes. Our plans in those areas already move forward."

Aly smiled back. "Then I won't worry, unless you tell me to."

The meeting went on as the raka discussed all they had learned that day. When they finished, Aly went to her work-room and shut the door. She lay on the cool wooden floor with relief. A muffled squeak made her sit up quickly as Trick and Secret dropped away from her neck. Only when they were free did she lie flat again. The two darkings trickled up her shoulders and onto her chest. If Aly tucked her hands behind her head, she could just manage to see them, ink against shadows in the dark.

"I take it you are not offering yourselves as a new, more fashionable breast band?" she asked softly.

"What is—" began Secret, and halted. Aly suspected that Trick had explained in that manner the darkings had, because Secret then said, "Oh. No."

"Bean get bored in eating room," Trick announced. "Bean explore in Gray Palace. Bean follow Sevmire to new workplace. Bean sitting under Sevmire desk now."

"Ah," Aly said. "Very good. What has Bean to say?"

The venturesome Bean confirmed what Aly had suspected: Sevmire could not find many of Topabaw's files. He knew his predecessor's code, but translations took time. Then Trick relayed something that made Aly pop up so fast the darkings tumbled into her lap. Sevmire was issuing writs for his people to kill Topabaw's principal agents throughout the Isles, and to take their places.

"Never blame an enemy for his stupidity," Da and Grandfather had often told her. Aly didn't blame Sevmire at all. She would have kissed him, if she kissed stupid men. Sevmire was doing to his agents what Rubinyan had done to him. He was placing them in jobs much too large for them.

The next afternoon the nobles came to call, more composed than they had been the day before. With Sarai's friends and their parents came Baron Engan and the priestess Imgehai Qeshi. They disappeared into the study with Nuritin, Winnamine, and Dove.

Once again Aly used her spyhole to watch the young nobility. Ferdy Tomang had thought to buy his way back into Sarai's good graces with an offering of an armful of blue-violet flowers. She simply thanked him and handed them off to a footman to put in a vase. It was only when he proposed a riding party the next day that she smiled at him. Then her smile faded. "Not if Winna and Aunt Nuritin have anything to say about it."

"Mother is talking to them," Ferdy assured her, unaware that his mother might go aside with Sarai's female relatives for more serious purposes. "She says the sooner we show people we're back to our daily lives, knowing the regents are in control, the sooner people will feel better. And maybe we'll even get Zaimid to come. If he doesn't have another emergency. I told him, you'd think we don't have healers in Rajmuat, but he only says this is the kind of healing he won't be able to do once he's the imperial physician."

"Ferdy, what do you mean?" demanded one of Sarai's female friends. "Zaimid left again today?"

"He got word of sickness over in the Honeypot and ditched us on our way here," complained Ferdy. "He said he'd come by and pay his compliments if he had time."

Sarai tossed her head. "Well, I'm not one to get worked up over a man who finds some Honeypot kennel more attractive than *me*."

Her friends laughed. Aly didn't. She knew that trick. Sarai was hurt that Zaimid had been absent two days in a row, and was going to show she didn't care. She flirted outrageously with all her young men, leaving even her female friends tapping their toes.

Feeling sorry for Sarai—Aly knew what it was like to miss one particular man—Aly turned away. She had a table full of reports to read, and the darkings' news to hear. Perhaps she could find some crows to talk with later.

The next day Winnamine reluctantly agreed to a riding party, but no farther away than the closest park, which had only simple horse trails and no room to gallop. At least Ferdy had been right about one thing, Aly thought as she and Dove watched the young nobles ride off. The prospect of riding—or the lack of emergencies—had even brought Zaimid back to Balitang House.

If the Carthaki's presence sweetened Sarai's mood, it was not evident when she came home. She slammed into the family sitting room. Dove and Nuritin were there, fanning themselves as they discussed preparations for Matfrid Fonfala's birthday party and for the king's birthday celebrations. Aly, passing in the hall with a load of Dove's gowns to be pressed, heard Sarai's outraged shout after the door slammed: "Five times! Five times they stopped us, and asked us—*us!*—our business, even after we *told* them who we were, and they poked in our saddlebags!" Aly leaned against the wall to eavesdrop as Sarai continued, "And then they did it to us again, on our way back! The same soldiers! 'Am I a Tomang or not?' Ferdy asked them, and they said it didn't matter who he was, it was the regents' orders!"

Nuritin's brittle voice cut the air. "Sarai! You forget yourself! Are you a lady or a shrieking Dockmarket trollop?"

"Neither, apparently, according to the regents!" Sarai replied, her voice a little quieter. "And it's sad when people who are related to the royal family aren't allowed to express opinions! In Tortall the monarchs *must* listen to the Councils of Lords and of Commoners. In Carthak the emperor has created an assembly of nobles. Landholders matter there, but not here. We are just going to rot from within."

The family was at supper when a Crown messenger arrived. Word spread through the house that Princess Imajane had requested Duchess Balitang's company the next morning when Elsren went to join the king. Winnamine accepted, puzzled. "Unless she wants to press her case to have you join her ladies-in-waiting," she remarked to Sarai as the ladies, children, and maids whiled the stormy evening away in their sitting room. Elsren squeaked each time lightning flashed and thunder boomed, and Petranne giggled.

"If she does," Winnamine continued, nudging Petranne and Elsren with a slippered toe, "I shall tell her I cannot allow you to join her at present, for the sake of the family's honor. You're not fit to serve in polite company anymore, Sarai."

"Because I'm not blind and complacent?" demanded Sarai bitterly. "Because I get angry when common people are treated badly and no one of our class tries to help? Or because I resent being pushed around by a bully in armor? A girl wanted to give me a flower on our way back, and a soldier shoved her away. He knocked her down! Zaimid cared for her—while Ferdy and the others looked on—but still, Winna, how can we stay in such a place? No one can live a decent life here anymore. Look what happened to Topabaw. He gave a lifetime of service, and they made an Example of him."

"*Definitely* not fit for polite society," Nuritin commented, her voice dry as she pushed a needle through silk.

The duchess, accompanied by Pembery and Yoyox, who looked most respectable in a footman's livery, joined Elsren and his escorts from the King's Guard on their morning ride to the palace. A squad of household men-at-arms fell in step behind the guards, the duchess's protection when she chose to return.

Dove waved goodbye until the house gate closed behind them, then turned to Ulasim. "I think I'll go visit Herbrand Edgecliff," she told Ulasim firmly. Looking at Aly, she added, "I had better request an escort of men-at-arms before it's forced on me."

Ulasim smiled at her as he might at a favorite niece. "If Lady Nuritin says you may," he replied. Dove scowled at him, for the moment an ordinary girl deprived of an amusement, then flounced into the library. She knew that Nuritin would not allow her out of the house with a hundred guards, not so soon after the prison break.

Aly watched her go. "You might want to put watchers on all the tunnels out of the grounds," she suggested.

"I shall," Ulasim answered, "but Lady Dove is too wise to try it. Lady Sarai I would have to shackle to a post. Lucky for us that it takes until noon for Lady Sarai to wake up all the way." He rested a hand on Aly's shoulder. "I received a communication this morning. It sits on your desk."

Aly, curious, went to see what had come. She found a grubby note, written by Nawat.

I am busy but I did good on Tongkang. Now I am at Imahyn. There is war smoke almost everywhere we fly over. Our cousins the raka are mobbing the soldiers everywhere. The sparkly is for you.

Aly looked. Beside the note was a small, many-colored piece of glittering rock. She held it in her hand as she reread the note, then kissed the paper and tucked it into her sash. She kept the stone in hand as she began to read her usual stack of reports.

The duchess returned at noon. She found Nuritin, her daughters, their maids, Petranne, and Rihani in the courtyard, mending clothes or reading. All but Nuritin rose as Winnamine hurried toward them. Her face was bone white.

"Aunt, Sarai, Dove, let's go to our sitting room. We will have lunch there, Boulaj, if you will tell Chenaol and the maids." Rihani was already taking Petranne inside, though she had to stop so the girl could give her mother a kiss. At a nod from Nuritin, Dorilize gathered all of her things and left. Boulaj, too, went to execute her orders. Only Aly remained.

"Are you still the god's messenger?" Winnamine asked.

Aly was worried. The duchess was trembling from top to toe. "I have always been, Your Grace," she replied, though she knew Winnamine thought she was Mithros's messenger, not Kyprioth's.

"Then come with me," said the duchess. She looked around the pool courtyard, distracted, then strode into the house, Aly trotting to keep up.

Once inside the ladies' sitting room, they spoke of Lord Matfrid's birthday. It was simply a way to pass time. The day was already so hot that the duchess closed and locked the shutters to provide shadowy coolness. No one touched their food, though they continued to talk as the maids left. The duchess locked the door behind them.

"Why does *she* remain?" demanded Nuritin, pointing a bony finger at Aly.

"It's a long story, Aunt," said Winnamine, taking a seat. She began to twist her handkerchief in her hands. "I haven't time to tell it at present. Just accept that I trust Aly as if she were family."

"Goddess bless, Winna, what did Imajane *say* to you?" demanded Sarai, resting a hand on her stepmother's arm. "You're shaking!"

The others waited, their eyes on the duchess.

"I met with the regents." Winnamine spoke slowly. "In their personal quarters . . ." She looked up at them and took a deep breath. "They have noticed—they've been told—how much attention you girls receive from people in the street," she said. "How they like to do things for you. They believe it is because you are half raka and yet close to the throne. They have made us a proposal. I said we need time to think. We have until the king's birthday." She turned to Sarai. "The regents propose a marriage between you and Dunevon," she explained. "The contracts are to be signed quickly, 'to give the people confidence in the Crown,' Rubinyan told me. I protested; I reminded them you were cousins. They reminded *me* you were second cousins, which is not as serious. There are precedents, in Carthaki, even in Kyprin history. The royal line of Siraj came from marriages between siblings or half siblings. They would ask you to move to the palace when the contract is signed, to convince the people of their sincerity. But they say it would bring peace and hope to the raka. And, when Dunevon comes of age, the Copper Isles would have a queen again."

Nuritin struggled with a lifetime of caution and lost. "Are they *mad*?"

"They are worried," said Winnamine, without taking her eyes from her stepdaughter. "The country must seem unstable, between the rebellions on the other islands and the escape from Kanodang. I think they want more support in case Nomru rebels. They know they will have serious problems if he does so, but if they can set your marriage against that, they might be able to preserve order."

"You *approve*?" Sarai asked, her voice tiny.

"I understand their reasons. I did not say I approve." Winnamine grasped Sarai's arm. "I can advise you, but the choice must be yours," she told Sarai earnestly. "Marriage to a child is no guarantee of stability. It does not comfort me that Imajane refers to him as 'the brat.' Rubinyan is an honorable man, and he loved your father. That does not mean he would hesitate to take the throne himself, if he thought the nation required a strong adult king."

"I cannot imagine that Imajane has ever forgotten that under the old laws of the country, *she* would have inherited when Hazarin died," Nuritin added. "She would have her own reasons to advise Rubinyan that the country would be stronger with them on the throne."

"Don't give them an answer yet," Dove advised. "Let them think you're considering it, but you can't decide. Find reasons to put them off until after the king's birthday—that's two weeks from now. They offer the Crown like a bauble—play with it, and with them."

"Buy time," Nuritin advised, nodding. "Dove is right. Promise nothing."

"Things change so fast," Dove went on. "Look at just this last week. And Sarai, once they get you in the Gray Palace, you won't ever be able to escape."

"But you all think I should do it," whispered Sarai.

"We didn't say that," Winnamine told her. "We present our ideas, and you consider them. You make the choice." She looked up at Aly, eyes pleading. "What do you say?"

Aly admired the regents' boldness. There were so many different ways this plan could be changed. It gave them a hundred options, some of which might even work. At the very least, if Sarai accepted, the people might well think it was a sign that a raka queen would reign again. Plenty of queens had seized power from much younger kings, and not just in the Isles or Carthak.

"I can say nothing, Your Grace," Aly remarked slowly. "I have no guidance in this."

"What?" demanded Nuritin with a frown.

"We'll explain later," Dove said hurriedly. "Sarai, *think*. We can *use* this. There are so many ways to manage it. All you have to do is pretend."

Sarai got to her feet. "I need time," she said quietly, not looking at them. "At least give me until after Grandfather's birthday to give *you* my decision. And ask them to wait until after the king's birthday for a reply, please." She looked at the duchess. "You must see that I can't possibly answer, not right away. Who would have imagined they'd make such an offer? I'll tell you by the end of the week."

Everyone nodded.

"After we come home from Grandfather's," Sarai told them. "I promise I won't discuss it with anyone but you." She left the room.

The raka conspirators were not happy when Aly and Dove told them of the regents' latest move. Even Ulasim lost his temper and shouted that the raka would fight in the streets before they allowed such a thing. It took Dove and Aly hours to calm them down. It was not official, the girls reminded the conspirators. It might never *be* official. All anyone could do until she reached her decision was to keep the rebellion going forward. They were due to leave for the three-day celebration of Matfrid's sixtieth birthday. Sarai wouldn't voice a decision until they returned.

"Things could change," Dove and Aly said over and over. "Things are changing already."

Two days later word came of a fresh uprising on Ikang Isle. The Crown sent a division of soldiers to crush it. Nawat wrote that he would go there with his crows and see what they might do. To Aly he sent a griffin feather. She kept it on her desk. She also reminded herself to tell the truth in her workroom, in case one feather had the same effect as an entire griffin, in whose vicinity no one could lie.

That night Aly was just going to sleep when a familiar, glowing shape knelt beside her pallet. Junai and Dove slept on, oblivious to Kyprioth's blaze in this form.

"I have an idea," he told Aly, "something to distract my brother and sister for a time. They really shouldn't have left their sun shield and moon shield in the Divine Realms, where some dishonest person might stumble across them."

"Perhaps they thought the Divine Realms wouldn't have that many dishonest people running about," Aly said with a yawn. It seemed Dove and Junai couldn't hear her, either. If they could, Junai would have been on her feet with weapons in her hands. "Except for you, of course."

"You wrong me," Kyprioth said in hurt tones, pressing a bright hand to the glowing area that was roughly the spot where a heart might be. "I am crushed. You think me no more than a low creature, and I a god. See what *you* get for your Midwinter's present from me! Besides, they would know I'd been there. I did, however, find myself a most enterprising young thief among the horse nomads east of Port Udayapur. He'll collect the shields if I guide him. There's an elemental who owes my beloved brother an ill turn or two. She will hide them well."

Aly yawned again. "Is this going to be a legend, or a hero tale, or something?"

"It's a diversion," said Kyprioth. "My brother and sister are about to return from the other side of the world. This will keep them busy for a time, though not forever. Tell Sarai that I have said she will never marry any Rittevon or Jimajen."

"If I get the chance," Aly said. "She's always with her friends, or her maids, or the family. And I think she ought to at least pretend she'll do it for the moment. . . ."

Kyprioth vanished.

"I've known mayflies better able to pay attention," Aly mumbled as her eyes closed.

The next morning the servants packed for the three-day celebration of Matfrid Fonfala's birthday, at his estates on the other side of the harbor's southern ridge. All of the Balitangs were going, which meant trunk after trunk went into the wagons.

Boulaj nearly went mad as Sarai dithered over what she would take. "She gets fussier every day," Boulaj confided, packing nearly everything Sarai owned. "And when she doesn't keep changing her mind about what to bring, she broods. I'm always relieved when her friends come—let *them* put up with her moods for an afternoon!"

Aly was preoccupied with a series of reports she had gotten about troop and ship numbers around the capital. She only nodded in response to Boulaj's complaint.

Dove shook her head. "It's this marriage thing," she told Boulaj. "She doesn't seem to realize that it's not real until the vows have been made. I keep telling her, there's no reason why she can't say yes and hold them off until something happens, but she's not listening to me." She smiled wryly. "Not a very good omen of my influence with her as a counselor when the time comes."

All three of them knew what "the time" was.

"She'll calm down," Aly murmured. "She's not a fool."

The afternoon was perfect for riding, the recent heat broken in a storm that had lasted all night. For once the air was warm and only slightly humid. The sole blot on the ride was the soldiers at various checkpoints who searched their wagons three times before they had left the city. Sarai was rude, despite warnings from Winnamine and Dove. It took a flat order from Fesgao to silence her.

Sarai remained quiet all the way to the Fonfala estate. There they caught up to another party, including Ferdy and Zaimid Hetnim, who charmed her out of her gloom. At supper, when the political situation came up, Zaimid found a way to distract Sarai from the conversation. He had her laughing by the time the second course was served.

"If he'll wait till I'm older, *I'll* marry him," Dove told Aly as she brushed her hair before bedtime. "We could use allies in Carthak, especially the emperor's personal physician."

Aly frowned. "Do you know, I think you're right," she said, considering it. "It won't do for Sarai—her husband should be from the Isles, and the queen can't live in another country. But I wouldn't sneeze at a Carthaki alliance."

The next day the celebration began at noon. Fonfala servants directed their guests to the areas of the estate they would most enjoy. For the younger family members, the Fonfalas had decorated the old nursery with enough toys to tempt the most fretful child. The doors at the side of the formal sitting room were open and tables were set on the veranda, perfect for the older adults. The library was available for the more studiously inclined. Dove settled in there with a chessboard and Baron Engan, though by midafternoon she had a score of other opponents, including her aunt Nuritin. Aly thought it funny that Dove had as many chess opponents as Sarai did dance partners.

Winnamine, her brothers and sisters from the family holdings on Malubesang, and Sarai and her companions went riding. They took their lunch together in a grassy clearing beside a small waterfall. Afterward they had an archery contest and a riding contest. Everyone changed clothes for supper, then again for the dancing. After she had set the last hairpin in Sarai's braided and curled hair, Boulaj came to Aly. She was sweating.

"Rihani, Dorilize, and Pembery are ill. So am I," she told Aly, sitting on Dove's bed. "I'm afraid the chicken sambal may have been off."

Aly had not had the popular dish at the servants' supper. She had tried sambal once and avoided the spicy dish on principle ever since. She had gotten accustomed to Kyprin spices, she liked to say, but never *that* accustomed. She told Boulaj, "I keep saying that stuff will kill you."

Boulaj gave her a tight smile. "No, but at least this time it makes it difficult to stray far from the privy. I should have listened to Lady Sarai—she said she thought it tasted odd. Can you look after Her Grace, Lady Nuritin, and Lady Sarai as well as Lady Dove? Our ladies are all dressed. We could manage that much, at least."

Aly smiled. "Go to bed. I think I can tend our ladies on my own for one night. It's not like they come rushing in to fix their clothes over and over." The Balitang ladies were the most self-sufficient noblewomen Aly had ever met.

"Gods bless you," said Boulaj gratefully. "Excuse me." She left.

Aly escorted the ladies to the ballroom. Dove headed for a chair next to Nuritin and Baron Engan and was welcomed into their conversation. Sarai and her female friends sat with the young men. Winnamine found a chair with the mothers.

Aly strolled into the gallery where the servants could observe their masters. Once she had explained the absence of Pembery, Dorilize, and Boulaj, she took up a position by the carved screen through which she could see the ballroom. For the first time in months she felt a pang of envy as she watched Sarai, glorious in a white lawn kirtle and doubled silk ivory gown, come down the lines of dancers with a different young man for every dance. Once that might have been Aly herself.

But the colors would have been different, she told herself firmly. Less . . . insipid.

She knew that was jealousy whispering in her ear. She couldn't help it, any more than she could help thinking how she and Nawat would look, properly dressed, going through the steps. Nawat danced beautifully, she had found out at Midwinter at Tanair.

A pang shot through her; her eyes burned slightly. First I start missing his kisses, then I miss him at a party where we wouldn't be allowed to dance anyway. What's wrong with me? she asked herself. She did not try to answer. Instead she tried to pick out who among the young noblemen might be a good partner, if she were allowed to dance. The only one she liked was Zaimid. He was handsome, graceful, clever, and he had a good heart. But he lacks something, Aly decided. Directness, perhaps. An odd sense of humor. He would never send a girl a shiny rock or a griffin feather as a token.

She was getting up to check her ladies again when brightness—the white-hot blaze of godhood—struck her eyes. She clapped her hands to them and retreated, then did complex things with her Sight, making herself better able to see through that fire. Had Kyprioth returned?

"Aly?" asked a Fonfala maid. "Are you all right?"

"Dust in my eye," Aly replied, blinking. "Yes, that's better." She looked up.

The source of the fire was just vanishing through the door to the hall outside. Aly slid between the other servants and stepped outside. An old brown-skinned woman in a black and orange headcloth and sarong hobbled away from Aly, a tray in her bony hands, godhood shimmering around her. Aly called, "Grandmother, wait."

The old woman glanced at her. She grinned, the essence of mischief in her expression. Then she turned the corner, moving more quickly than Aly would have expected of some-one of her age.

"Uh-oh," Trick whispered. "Gods not good. Gods sly."

"I know," Aly replied softly. "But we need to know what brings a god here." She followed, tracking the old goddess by her glowing footprints.

She had a very bad feeling about this. Might this be the Great Mother Goddess, who had returned to the Isles in her aspect as the Crone? Aly prayed it was not as she went on into the gardens. If the Goddess had come, she would uncover Kyprioth's plans. The war between the Great Gods would start with Kyprioth still unprepared.

Finally Aly saw her quarry on a bench near the estate's temple. Aly adjusted her Sight to allow for the dark as the woman shook off her headcloth. Only gray stubble covered her head. There was a scarred socket where one of her eyes had been. When she grinned, Aly saw gaps in her teeth.

"Bad. Wily. Careful." That was Secret, quavering from Aly's shoulder.

The goddess squinted at Aly. "Ah," she said in a cheer-ful voice. "You've little tattlers on your shoulders. How sweet. They will be silent for the time being." She pointed: white light swarmed over Aly. Trick and Secret immediately went still. Worried, Aly touched them. Their bodies in her neck-lace were warm, but she felt no heads.

"They're alive," the goddess assured her. "I just don't want them meddling."

And I don't need *you* meddling, Aly thought, though she said "Good evening" politely. From long acquaintance with her mother and her Aunt Daine, she knew it was wisest to be polite to strange gods. "I never thought the Fonfalas were so remarkable that they might draw a god to their house."

"But I like playing servant, dearie, just like you," the

goddess told her. "People think you're furniture. They hardly notice. You can have all kinds of fun without them realizing who's doing it, but you already know that. I love to see their little lives collapse in flames. It's even more amusing when they start blaming each other as things go wrong."

Goose bumps crept over Aly. There was something familiar about this goddess. "Are you a raka god?" she asked, still cautious.

"Gracious, no. Don't they have enough troubles with my cousin mucking about? Just be thankful his sister the Jaguar Goddess is locked up, and all the others are small gods," the goddess told Aly. She snatched at the air, grabbed a firefly, then popped it into her mouth. "Mmm, I like these. I wonder if I could get some at home."

Aly remembered where she'd heard of a goddess much like this one. Daine had told her about the Carthakis' quirky patron goddess. "You're the Graveyard Hag."

The goddess beamed at her, revealing all of seven teeth. "Aren't you the clever boots," she said with pleasure. "I'd heard that you were, but 'Count on it,' I told Gainel—that's the Dream King to you, dearie. 'Count on it,' I told him, 'they're always *said* to be quick, but it turns out to be all smoke.' No," she cautioned as Aly took a step back. "Don't run off. That wouldn't be polite, and I'm not done with you."

Aly could not move her foot—either foot, for that matter. Or her hips. Or her arms. She tried to open her mouth to scream and failed.

The goddess nodded. "Every bit as clever as my cousin says. Mind, I don't want to ruin Kyprioth's game. I just want to tweak it a little. Besides, I'm doing a favor for one of my own lads. Such a good one, he is. He built me a shrine—paid for it with his own money, too! One good turn deserves another, and he's in love."

Aly released the breath she'd meant to use to scream through her nose. Suddenly her mouth could move again. She could talk, but she also knew better than to try to call out. "May I ask questions?" she inquired. "Since I'm going to be here for a time?"

The Hag chuckled. "Oh, you are a treat. Well brought-up, even with a mother who's a violent bumpkin."

Aly ignored the insult. Her mother had been called worse things. "This worshipper must be very devoted, to bring you all the way here. Surely it would be easier to favor him at home. Unless you have other business?" She kept her voice light and sweet.

"It's more personal satisfaction than business," replied the Hag. "Normally I could give duckmole's dung about the Isles, but Kyprioth is annoying even for a god. He gloats. He's been saying we lesser tricksters couldn't fool Mithros and the Goddess . . . as if we don't know what we're doing. He deserves a lesson." She seized another firefly. "And I can do my worshipper a favor while I'm at it."

Aly raised an eyebrow.

The Hag grinned. "Besides, I owe Kyprioth. He's gotten the better of me twice. I mean to repay him."

Aly picked through the Hag's words. Aunt Daine *said* gods talk in riddles, she grumbled to herself.

The Hag replied aloud. "Naturally," she said with glee. "You mortals are so adorable with your faces all screwed up when you're trying to think."

Carthaki, Aly thought, shooting a glare at the Hag. A worshipper from there . . . "Zaimid Hetnim?" she asked.

The Hag chortled. "Bright girl." She stood, dusting off her hands. "By the time you can free yourself, my boy will have his heart's desire, Kyprioth will have his comeuppance, and *you* will have some work to do." Wriggling her fingers in a mockery of a wave, she vanished.

Aly didn't like it, but there was nothing she could do. The Graveyard Hag had sealed her lips. Her mind raced frantically. Stupid! she told herself over and over. Stupid, over-confident, *blind* . . . Why did I not see it coming with Sarai and Zaimid? Sarai's not good at hiding how she feels. I've been trained to spot intrigue in every form! But no, I was smug about Topabaw and creating more spies. And while I was being so festering clever, a girl in love cooked something up right under my nose!

She berated herself without mercy, remembering clues that should have been obvious, including Sarai's conviction that nothing in the Isles would ever change for the better. She remembered how quiet Sarai had been after Imajane's offer of marriage to the boy king. Despite everything her advisors told her, Sarai had appeared convinced that she would have to marry her royal cousin.

At last the spell that locked Aly into place began to thaw, like ice on a sunlit pond. It faded bit by bit, driving Aly half insane as she waited. Somewhere, she knew, the Graveyard Hag was enjoying her frustration. At last she was free.

"This bad?" asked Trick, once he and Secret were also able to move again. They settled back into their bead necklace shapes, with the two connecting medallions that were their heads on each of Aly's shoulders.

"It's not good," Aly told the darkings. "And I am an idiot." She didn't even bother with the servants' gallery, but ran into the ballroom itself. When she stumbled to a halt at the room's center, everyone turned to stare. Aly ignored them, scanning every face in the room. Sarai and Zaimid were not there.

She ran into the servants' gallery. Zaimid's attendant was gone. She told herself not to panic yet, then bolted outside. As the Fonfalas' daughter, the duchess had been given her own pavilion separate from the main house, where she and her stepdaughters slept with their attendants. Petranne and Elsren shared the nursery in the main house with the other children. Aly knew that Boulaj, Pembery, and Dorilize would be in the household infirmary, wherever that was.

She raced to the duchess's pavilion. Inside, a lamp was provided for the Balitang ladies' return. In the flickering light it cast, Aly could see that Sarai's trunk—the one into which the vexed Boulaj had simply thrown all her mistress's personal items as Sarai kept changing her mind—was gone. Moreover, there was a folded and sealed document on the duchess's bed. Aly went to look at it. The note was addressed, in Sarai's curling writing, to *Winna and Dove.*

Aly was sitting on the pavilion steps when the duchess arrived. "Aly, what's going on?" she asked, her sweet, deep voice concerned. "Papa said you burst into the ballroom looking as if the dead marched on your spine. . . ."

Aly held out the letter Sarai had left.

"Oh, no," said Winnamine. She hurried into the pavilion without taking the letter. Aly stayed where she was.

Soon more footsteps slapped the flagstone path. This time it was Dove. "Aly, have you seen Sarai? Ferdy Tomang is searching all through the main house, and he's saying he'll kill Zaimid or Druce or Vedec if they've sneaked away with her—" She cut herself off abruptly. "Aly?"

Winnamine walked onto the steps and sat next to Aly. "She left a letter for us," she told Dove, and broke the seal. Using the light from the torches that marked the pavilion's entrance, she read the letter to the girls in a leaden voice.

"Dearest Winna and Dove,

"I can only beg your forgiveness a thousand times for running away like this."

Dove sat in the walkway with a thump, ignoring the damage to her clothes.

"*I am so very sorry. By the time you read this Zaimid and I will be sailing for Carthak. There is a ship waiting for us at Moriji Cove.*"

The cove lay five miles downhill from the estate. It was a favored raka smuggling port because it was not readily visible.

The duchess continued.

"*I can no longer watch as good people are taxed into poverty, jailed, beaten, or killed. It makes me sick, the never-ending executions, the despair, and the fear. Neither will I marry a boy thirteen years younger than me, to be a puppet for the regents. I know you cannot fight them and win, and once they have won, I would not give a copper's chance in a volcano for Dunevon or for me to live to old age.*

"*Please tell Dorilize, Pembery, Boulaj, Rihani, and Junai that I am sorry I made them sick. The herbs will wear off by dawn. I knew they would stop me.*

"*I would have done none of this if I were not truly, deeply in love. Zaimid is kind and gentle. When people are hurt, he helps them. We can't bear to be parted. And neither of us can stand to see more people hurt where we can do so little. With him I can have the life I want, raising horses and our children, and helping him to build hospitals when he takes his post as the emperor's healer. Like me, he begs your forgiveness for our stealing away. I will write more when we are settled. Please try to understand, I did not do this on impulse. I have known I loved him for some weeks. The thought of marrying a child cousin was bad in itself, but it was so much worse when I compared it to marriage with Zaimid.*

"*I love both you so much, and Elsren and Petranne, too. I hope that you will wish me well. Zaimid has already said that our first boy will be named Mequen.*

"*Your devoted Sarai*"

13

A CHANGE OF PLANS

After hearing Sarai's letter no one had anything to say. They just sat in silent gloom on the steps.

Finally Nuritin came to see where they were. "What is it?" she asked sharply when she saw their faces. Mutely, Winnamine handed the letter to her.

While Nuritin read, Aly walked around the guesthouse to inspect it for listening spells. She found only a number of strong charms to keep any listening spell from taking hold there. There were similar protections all over the Fonfala buildings and grounds. The Fonfalas, she decided, loved their privacy. When she finished her search, she stopped herself from going to tell the ladies it was safe to speak here. She had been too overconfident for too long. Carefully Aly went over the place again. She even sent the darkings under the house to check there. When they returned to report they had found nothing, Aly then went back to find the ladies.

"There are no listening spells here that I could see," she told them numbly, sitting next to Dove. "And no spies."

Nuritin, rereading the letter, looked up with a frown.

"What makes you certain of that?" she demanded sharply.

"She knows, Aunt," Winnamine replied, weariness in her voice and face.

"Hmph," Nuritin said, still glaring at the seated Aly. Aly propped her chin on her hand and returned the old lady's look. She was tired and depressed. She was not about to stand because Nuritin thought her a servant. It was the older woman who looked away.

"Silly chit," Nuritin commented, giving the letter back to the duchess. "She obviously didn't believe that she could keep Imajane at bay on this marriage." Nuritin looked at Dove. "You will not make that mistake, though, will you?"

Dove blinked at her, startled. "Will the regents offer it to me? They're probably going to think Sarai as good as slapped their faces, doing this. I'm thinking maybe we should run for Tanair before they arrest us all."

"They dare not," Nuritin told her flatly. "You girls are too popular. Imajane admitted as much when she offered the marriage to Sarai in the first place. She needs to offer it to you, and you must do as we advised Sarai." Nuritin's abrupt smile was thin and frosty. "You're vexed that she didn't tell you," she added, glancing at Dove and Winnamine. "She did it to me, too, and I was as much her chaperon as anyone. She planned this under our very noses, the minx. She hid her interest in the Carthaki by including him with all her young men. She was good at slipping off for private assignations before you went to Tanair. Obviously she got better at it."

Aly, thinking of the raka and what this would do to them, shifted impatiently. It drew Nuritin's attention.

"And she gave *you* the slip, watchful as you are," Nuritin said, that smile razor sharp. "That must gall you." When Aly, Dove, and Winnamine all stared at her, Nuritin rolled her eyes. "Even apart from mysterious hints about this one being more than just a maid, I've noticed how very attentive she is. I don't know what she's up to, and I don't want to. When I must know, I'm sure one of you will tell me. For the time being, it's important that we deal with this, first here and then at home. The regents will have the news by the time we get there, if that new spymaster knows the least bit about what he does. It will still be important to let them know in person. They will be outraged for a day or two, and then they will make their offer to our Dove. Mope about here if you like, but I am going to bed, and I advise you to do the same. There is nothing more to be done tonight." She looked at Aly. "Since Sarai made certain that Dorilize would be in no condition to stop her, I require you to undress me." Standing, she shook out her skirts and marched inside.

Aly stared back at her with admiration. "I want to be *her* when I grow up," she murmured.

"Let's work on growing up first," Dove replied, her voice and face glum. "Then you can be anyone you like."

"Nuritin is right," said Winnamine, exhaustion in her voice. There were tears rolling down her cheeks. She appeared not to notice them. "It's too late to do anything but sleep."

Aly passed a handkerchief to her. When the duchess stared at it, not understanding, Dove touched her cheek. Winnamine angrily swiped her eyes. "I thought she trusted us," she whispered. "I thought she trusted *me.*"

"Except that you would have asked her to do her duty by her family and country," Dove said gently, her own eyes full. She did not cry, though. "You would have made her feel she was selfish to want her own freedom and happiness when others depend on her for so much. And you would be right. She knew that, too. So she ran away."

"Girl!" an imperious voice called from inside the house. Aly scrambled to her feet and went to assist Nuritin, thinking that Dove had the right of it. As she prepared all three ladies for bed, she berated herself. She had been overconfident for the last time, she hoped. She would pay for that. Only she and Dove knew that the raka and Kyprioth were not going to take Sarai's elopement well.

The duchess asked her to let the family know that Sarai, too, had felt unwell and had left the party early. Aly returned after delivering her message, but she did not sleep. Her mother had a rich vocabulary of curses, as did her father. Aly used all of those words first on herself, then on Sarai and Zaimid. Trick and Secret, understanding that she needed to think, kept quiet, though they hummed gently against her skin, offering comfort.

When she ran out of bad words, Aly decided that the joke was on her. Only a year before, she might have helped Sarai to marry her love rather than be trapped in a political life. At the very least, she would have loved Sarai's boldness. Aly's mother had done as Sarai had, chosen the life she wanted over the life that was expected of her. My, how I've changed, Aly thought ruefully. These days I *care* about duty to those who look to one to lead. These days I care less about fun and more about work. Though at least *my* work is fun.

Shaking her head, she began to prepare for the consequences of this night. Kyprioth had not appeared, which meant that he was still arranging for the theft of the sun and the moon shields. She would need all her arguments marshaled when the god returned, and when they brought the news to the raka conspirators. She wondered if the conspiracy wasn't to blame for not telling Sarai what they intended. Then Aly shook her head. If Sarai had known of their plans, she would have fled all the sooner.

The next morning Winnamine sent Aly for the ladies' maids. They had recovered, but they could tell that something wasn't right. "It's for Her Grace to tell you," Aly said, leading them to the duchess.

As they helped their mistresses dress for the day, Winnamine explained what Sarai had done. For a moment, hardy Boulaj looked as if she might faint.

"She dosed you," Dove said quickly. "She dosed all of you. She said so in her letter."

"She must have put it in the sambal," Aly put in. "Boulaj, remember? She tasted the sambal and said she thought it might be off, but she couldn't tell, and neither did you. That's when she added the herbs to make your bowels run. She knew she'd get most of you, because Chenaol makes dreadful sambal, and you all eat it at every house we visit."

"How did she escape Aly?" demanded Pembery, her voice sharp but her hands steady as she pinned up Winnamine's hair. "Aly was supposed to be looking after our ladies." Dorilize, doing up Nuritin's buttons, shook her head.

"Aly was lured away and locked up," Aly said absently, her mind churning with plans and questions. "If one of the Fonfalas' maids hadn't needed a nightshirt for a guest who forgot his, I might still be locked up." She wasn't about to mention the Graveyard Hag, not yet. She had already concocted a story for those who might not accept the truth. "One of Zaimid's servants brought a message saying you wanted to tell me something, Pembery. I knew you were sick, so I went running, and that's when they grabbed me." Even the hint that she might have been involved would stop Pembery from digging further into the mess they were in.

Winnamine shook her head. "We must put our best face on this," she told the maids. "To our men-at-arms and the rest of the staff. The thing is done. We all knew Sarai was more interested in her heart than politics." She got to her feet. "Let's show proud faces to the world, shall we? It will take some time to live down this shame. Give no one the satisfaction of seeing we are hurt. I must explain things to my parents, and let the rest of our people know we are leaving today rather than tomorrow."

As soon as she had left the house, Pembery and Boulaj pulled Aly out onto the porch. "How could you let this happen?" cried Pembery, tears running down her cheeks.

Boulaj, too, wept. "Can the god—?"

Aly put her finger to her lips. She motioned toward the house: Nuritin and Dorilize were within earshot.

Dove had followed them outside. "We can talk at home. Why don't you two start packing up, please?"

The women moved to obey as Dove turned to Aly. "Walk with me. I don't have that much to pack."

They strolled out into the misty air. It was cool. Howler monkeys proclaimed their territories; crows shrieked in reply. Aly walked at Dove's elbow without mentioning that her feet were soaked. Sandals were inadequate cover for early morning grass. They halted by one of the many streams that crossed the property. Aly looked around. There was no sign of magic anywhere.

"They act like it's the end of everything." Dove's soft voice sounded tentative.

"But it isn't," Aly replied. "It could be the beginning."

Dove looked at her, eyes ablaze in her small face. "How may I convince them?"

Aly thought about it. "Work," she said at last. "You're farming, that's all. The ground's been tilled and prepared and it's ready to take the seed. If one batch of seed gets moldy, we find another batch."

"One less vulnerable to mold," added Dove. "Will you help me?"

Aly held out her hand. Dove clasped her by the forearm.

After a moment's hesitation, Aly clasped Dove's forearm.

"I don't need a maid," Dove said. "I need a friend."

For a moment Aly found it hard to breathe. It had been hard to get passionate about Sarai as queen, as the raka had been. But Dove . . . Dove was no stranger to emotion, Aly knew, but it didn't govern her as it did Sarai. Dove understood duty to those who needed her. Dove could be trusted to keep a clear head. She was one of the most ferociously intelligent people Aly had ever known. Aly had seen it the night before: they must put Dove on the throne.

"I will be your friend until the end of time," she told the younger girl.

The ride home was silent. All along the way the raka who came to watch them pass saw that Sarai was not with them. Aly studied their faces, her mind busy. At the city's outskirts she saw members of her pack, as uneasy as the bystanders over Sarai's absence. To each query they made by way of hand-signal Aly replied: *When we meet at home.* She didn't want word getting to Balitang House ahead of them.

While Dove and Aly had settled the focus of the rebellion between them, Aly knew some raka conspirators would require persuasion. They were used to seeing Dove as Sarai's intelligent, bookish, quiet sister, a fine counselor, but not the kind of person who could rally the passions of her followers. Dove would have to show them they were mistaken.

When they reached Middle Town, Dove greeted many soldiers at the checkpoints by name. Vendors and shopkeepers waved and called to her; Dove waved back with a smile. Aly was instantly reassured. Dove *did* have charm. It was quieter and less flashy than Sarai's, but it was there. Aly also thought that once the people remembered they still had one twice-royal girl, their first concern would be to put her on a throne. Afterward they could fret about her ability to win the crowd.

As the riders clattered into the courtyard before the house, servants ran to take their horses. Ulasim trotted out the front door, bowed to the duchess, then pulled Aly down until she could hear his whisper: "Nawat and his crows got every one of the raka who rose on that Ikang estate off the island. Every one! He and his crows drove the army mad while our people made it to the escape ships. More than two hundred raka, safe thanks to him."

Aly's heart lifted at the sound of Nawat's name. She nodded her thanks and dismounted as Ulasim moved clear of her. Now that he'd unburdened himself, the big footman noticed there was something wrong with their company. He took the sleeping Petranne as Rihani handed the girl to him, but his eyes were busy reading their faces.

Suddenly they widened. Aly knew he'd realized who was missing.

"Ulasim," the duchess called. He went over to her, still holding Petranne in his arms. "Open the ballroom and summon the household," Winnamine ordered quietly. "Lock the gates and bring all the household in, even those who are off duty. We have news that everyone must hear."

It was not long before all but Rihani, Petranne, and Elsren, who had gone to the nursery, had assembled in the great ballroom. Aly stood just below the dais where Winnamine, Nuritin, and Dove sat, waiting. From the faces of the household she could tell they knew only that Sarai had not come home with the duchess. The maids and guards who had been at the Fonfalas' had told them nothing, leaving it in their mistress's hands.

Maybe, thought Aly, they were afraid of how people would react.

Everyone stared at the duchess, their eyes flicking from her to Dove to Nuritin and back.

"Good morning," Winnamine said. "Forgive me if I am blunt, but I know of no easy way to say this. Lady Saraiyu eloped from my father's party last night with Master Zaimid Hetnim, the Carthaki." She smiled grimly. "We shall be apologizing for what she has done for months, I think. Do not blame our maids for not looking after her. Sarai made arrangements to get them all out of the way. No one knew until Sarai was long gone."

The members of the conspiracy within the household stared at Aly with disbelief or outright suspicion. Aly made a note to herself to ask Ulasim to let them know about the Graveyard Hag. The conspirators had to learn Aly had not betrayed them, or she would find herself in very hot water.

Winnamine continued, "On Sarai's behalf I apologize to you. We must be happy for her. She wrote that she loves Master Zaimid. While we could have wished her to love closer to home, we had no choice in the matter. She was very sure to make it look as if Zaimid meant no more than her other suitors."

The duchess rubbed her temples. "We must write to people, explaining what has happened. Ulasim, I will require every message carrier you can spare, and a footman in livery to take a letter to the regents." She noticed that the servants were disturbed by this move and explained, "Lord Elsren is in the line of inheritance, and our girls are of royal blood. Their behavior is a matter of state." She smoothed her skirts with her hands. "Thank you all again. I am sorry to bring such tidings. Those of you on gate duty, see if any visitors will return another day. Only admit them if they insist."

Slowly, murmuring to one another, the household dispersed. Dove watched them go, then hugged Winnamine.

"I'll help you with those notes, Winna," she said.

"As will Jesi and I," Nuritin said.

Dove looked at Aly. "I believe we'll need tea in the ladies' study."

Chenaol grabbed Aly in the kitchen, but Aly shook her head. "Tonight," she said quietly. "Things will be a shambles today. We'll have company as soon as word gets out."

Chenaol gasped. "Gods, yes. Here." She stocked a tray with fruits, cheeses, flatbreads, and luarin-style sweet biscuits. "I'll need an assistant cook if all this entertaining keeps going on," she muttered. Thrusting the tray of food into Aly's hands, she said, "I'll send tea as soon as it's ready. Start heating oil," she ordered the kitchen maids. "Get out what bean curd we have. I'll need three of you to go to market, and if anyone so much as *breathes* word of what's happened, I'll filet her, understand?"

The footman returned from the palace around noon with a note granting the duchess a private audience the next morning, when Elsren went to attend Dunevon. In the afternoon the Balitang cousins came on the footman's heels, followed by Countess Tomang still dressed in riding clothes: she too had left the Fonfalas' early. She demanded a private conversation, but did not stay long. Aly, listening outside the Teak Sitting Room, heard Ferdy's mother shout that Sarai had made a monkey of her son, and that blood would tell. Winnamine did not answer. Aly knew the duchess probably agreed.

Nobody else came after the Countess and the Balitang relatives left. Apparently no one wished further contact at Balitang House until they knew how the regents would jump. Winnamine and Dove wandered through the rooms, talking to servants and slaves, showing themselves as steady and unshaken. Aly unpacked Dove's things, took her dirty clothes to the house laundry, and retired to her office to work. Two days of reports awaited her, as well as the darkings' news from the palace.

"Trick," she asked, "what do you hear from the regents?" Instantly her bead necklace turned into Trick and Secret, who stuck heads out of their blobby bodies to look at Aly.

"Yesterday morning regents in private audience chamber when head of shipwright guild ask for talk," Trick informed her. "He makes ships for king and navy. He is angry because man sail little ship to royal dock and show him a paper with Rubinyan order, saying put little ship there. He say little ship is for king's birthday. Guildmaster say guild and navy should make little ship for king. Rubinyan say he have man who build little ship for *his* birthday make one for king, so man feel useful. Rubinyan writes paper so navy shipwrights build six more ships right away and get three ready to sail. He says shipwrights here needed for serious work to send ships to kill rebels. Guildmaster go away.

"Then messenger come. Messenger say slaves on Rittevon estate, north Gempang, kill overseer, then kill Imajane's old nursemaid. Imajane very angry and say, kill all slaves on estates. Rubinyan sends order to army fort in north Gempang to kill slaves."

On and on the reports went. Aly realized that more estates throughout the Isles were experiencing violent upheavals. She set pins with red ribbons at every spot on the map where Trick reported trouble. They showed her a deliberate pattern. The rebellions began on the estates nearest the sea, closest to the lands and towns that would be the first on the island to get help by water. Army fortresses had also come under attack, even if the mischief was as subtle as the disappearance of patrols into the jungles, or the constant illness of the men.

Among the reports passed on by Trick were appeals for

help by landowners. The palace darkings had also heard Rubinyan and Imajane talk about how many remaining soldiers, cavalry, pikemen, fighting ships, and sailors they had. They had sent companies of soldiers and cavalry all over the Isles to back up troops already assigned there. Their reserves of men in the city were dwindling.

Aly saw it, as plain as day: *This* was Ulasim's grand plan. Bit by bit, the rebels were drawing protection away from Rajmuat. Ulasim had not lied when he'd said he had not ordered the first uprisings. But would I see a lie on him if I asked him about that now? Aly wondered. He knew his people. He may even have sent agents last year to whisper ideas to the raka who lived closest to the coast, where ships could unload men and supplies.

Rittevon Lanman had demoralized the raka three centuries ago. He had overrun the most powerful of the Isles, then captured Rajmuat, already torn by bloodshed in the royal family's never-ending feuds. He'd executed the queen and her remaining family. Then the still-feuding raka had come down from the inner lands to be fought, killed, or enslaved. Now the reverse was happening. The inland raka were drawing the Rittevon forces up onto their ground, taking them into the jungles. It was so devious that, unless Rubinyan and Imajane had grown up around maps of trouble spots, they might not realize how thinly they were spread. This was no accident. This was planned by Ulasim.

Aly was silent, awed. Years of preparations by Ulasim's predecessors had gone into the picture she saw here. They and he had built it up bit by bit, deciding who needed instruction, and who could be trusted to exercise their ancient hatreds of the invaders at just the right time.

She wanted to help. Someone should point out to Ulasim that more damage would result if the Crown's troops were weakened by hunger. An attack was a thing the enemy was prepared for. People driving wagons filled with supplies that arrived on schedule were another matter. It could be arranged for some of those supplies to be drugged, or for some of those wagons never to arrive at their destination.

What could she find for her own people to work on? The army was not the only group with storehouses. Wealthy merchants kept their goods in warehouses in Downwind and Market Town. After the attacks on the fortresses and on the slave docks, the waterfront and the royal and naval docks were under extra guard, but the storehouses were not.

It was late afternoon when the darking Bean reported the reaction of the court to news of Sarai's elopement. After Trick finished passing on Bean's report, the supper bell rang. Nuritin, Winnamine, and Dove went to the nursery to eat with Elsren and Petranne and try to explain what had happened. After the children were put to bed, Nuritin and Winnamine retired to their own rooms. Dove and Aly went nervously down to the conspiracy's meeting room.

Everyone was there: Ulasim, Fesgao, Ysul, Chenaol, Quedanga, Ochobu. As soon as Dove and Aly came in, Ochobu threw up the room's magical shields and glared at Aly. "How could you let this happen?" the old mage demanded. "You're the clever one, you're the spy—"

Aly shook her head. She was in no mood to be verbally whipped. "I was unable to stop it," she said. "You see, I had a bigger problem. The Graveyard Hag paid us a visit. She's the patron goddess of Carthak—of Zaimid. And while she's fun in a perverse way, she is no easier to cross than your Bright One. When was the last time *you* argued with a god?"

Ochobu scowled. "A likely story!"

Reproachfully Aly said, "You have forgotten I like to tell lies that will be believed."

Chenaol's mouth twitched in spite of her distress. "She's got you there," she told Ochobu.

Aly continued, "Kyprioth got the better of the Hag on a few occasions. She wished to pay him back. And yes, I made an immense mistake." She leaned against the wall, taking care not to smash her darking necklace. "I was so busy watching the world outside the house, I neglected to keep an eye on things inside. Can you possibly kick me harder than I'm kicking myself?"

"We have to get her back," said Chenaol. "Some of us will have to go after her. And at least one should be a mage, in case this Graveyard Hag is hanging around."

Ysul hand-signed, *You can't chase Sarai to Carthak. We don't have people or time.*

From her chair Dove said quietly, "Sarai isn't the only one with royal blood from both sides of the family."

Aly saw them all turn to look at Dove, and then her world went black. Aly was whipped through an immense, howling darkness. Trick and Secret keened in her ears. Everything around her roared, until she landed on her behind with a painful thump.

She sat in a pavilion house that looked bigger than the palace. She could have sworn there were clouds among the ceiling beams. Jewelry dangled along the walls in crazy ranks. Enormous pillows were strewn over piles of gaudy rugs. A number of large crows pecked through the contents of dishes on the floor.

Beyond them stood Kyprioth, his dark eyes blazing. "What have you done?" shrieked the god. Aly clapped her hands to her ears. He roared, "It's all ruined! Ruined! You bumbling, blind, oblivious *mortal*! How could you let her slip away? I leave to do one little thing and I return to find everything in ruins. *Ruins!*"

Thunder rolled in the ceiling clouds. Lightning bolts raced over the god's jewelry.

"I thought you'd be gone for a while," Aly remarked, as if this were another casual talk between them. "I thought you were preparing a trick of your own."

Kyprioth glared at her. An invisible force pressed Aly against the nearest marble column. "Give me one good reason why I shouldn't cook you where you stand," the god snarled. "You, the clever one, and you can't keep an eye on one lone, lovesick chit!"

"The way you're carrying on, I'd say you were in love with her yourself," Aly said lightly, her stomach in knots. "Isn't she a little young for you? Not to mention boring, but that could just be me."

"You mock me," he said, coming closer. He'd begun to blaze with light.

The crows suddenly rose in a thunder of wings. They glided through the air until they landed beside Aly.

"It's not like you're making it easy to have a proper conversation," Aly pointed out to Kyprioth as she shaded her eyes. What could she do but talk back? He was a great god and could do as he wished with her. If she was going to die, she wanted to die arguing. "Honestly, Kyprioth, how long would it have been before that lovesick girl lost the throne you schemed so to get her? How long before she got angry and insulted someone, or married the wrong noble and started the Haiming rebellions all over again?"

He pointed at her. "That's it. You die."

Aly forced a merry tone into her voice as she replied, "You'll lose your wager with the crows. You never said the bet didn't count if it was *you* who killed me, so you'd still have to pay them. And I know you hate to lose wagers."

"*This* is what I wagered," Kyprioth snapped.

A long necklace detached itself from a wall and flew at Aly to strike her full in the face. She yelped in pain and pulled it off. Blood dripped from a number of cuts on her skin. She had never seen anything uglier. It was made of gold and silver beads, gem beads in all colors, and gaudy glass beads. "You mean to tell me the crows were helping me for *this*?" she demanded, indignant.

One of the crows walked over and grabbed the dangling end in its beak. To Aly's surprise, little Secret rolled down her arm and wrapped around the end of the necklace that Aly still held, securing it to her hand. "Not yours," Secret told the crow. "You didn't win it. Help her."

The crow cocked its head, looking the darking over. Trick flowed down Aly to cover Secret and twine itself with a foot of the necklace beyond Aly's hold.

Dropping the necklace, the crow turned to look at Kyprioth. "How can she fail if she was tricked in turn?" the crow demanded sharply. Somehow it sounded male. "Ask the Graveyard Hag where she was that night the girl ran away."

"The—" Kyprioth said, his face dark with fury. There was a pop. Air rushed to fill the space he had occupied.

Aly knelt so she could be face to face with her defender. "Thank you."

Another crow walked over to take a lock of her hair in its beak. It gave a hard tug, making Aly wince, then let go. "Save your thanks," the crow advised in a voice that was the female version of the male crow's. "You're not back in the Mortal Realms yet."

Aly had guessed she was in the Divine Realms. She'd never heard of a human dwelling with clouds under the roof beams. "So you're the Dawn Crow and Sky, the crow goddess?" she asked. "But what are they?" She pointed to the others.

"The first flock," Sky explained. "I must say, I see why

our cousin Nawat feels so strongly about you."

"Oddly," said the Dawn Crow.

"Strongly," retorted Sky, fixing her mate with a beady stare. When he did not answer, she told Aly, "Not every mortal could talk back to Kyprioth when he's in one of his tempers. His nasty streak is *very* nasty."

"I've certainly enjoyed myself with what he's shown me so far," replied Aly.

"I do not approve of one of our kind changing his shape just for a mortal," the Dawn Crow remarked stiffly.

"You must ask Nawat if he cares," replied Sky. "He is free as all of us are free, to fly as he wishes and to steal as he may."

Aly smiled and ducked her head, suddenly shy. "I miss him," she found herself admitting to the goddess. "He—"

The air boomed with a sound that was hard to recognize at first: an old woman's laughter. It made the pavilion house shudder. It was followed by an immense shriek of rage. Both sounds grew fainter. Shivering, Aly gave the necklace a fresh inspection. "Kyprioth wagered my *life* on this thing," she said, aghast. "I've probably seen uglier, but the shock has driven them from my mind."

"Actually, he wagered one of them for each of us who helps you," Sky explained. "They are very sparkly and colorful. They are well worth our mortal cousins' efforts."

Aly looked at the necklace. "If you say so, goddess, then I must believe you," she said reluctantly. "It certainly is, um, sparkly."

Time passed. She itched to get back to the raka, but she was stuck in Kyprioth's home until he returned. The crows might have had the power to send her, but they told her it would be rude. She was Kyprioth's guest, which meant it was up to Kyprioth to send her back.

She talked with the crows a while, then took a sudden

nap as all the fright she'd felt in dealing with the god came home to her. When she woke, he was still nowhere to be seen. She explored the house, ignoring the part of herself that constantly reminded her time was passing. The crows brought her berries and a melon, and told her stories of all the other trickster gods in the Divine Realms.

Aly refused to think that she might not return home. If she didn't, then she didn't, but in the meantime, why waste so many uninterrupted hours with no one to call on her and no reports to read? Planning what she would set in motion for Dove, she dozed off again.

When she woke, Kyprioth sat next to her. "You were right," he told her, back to his cheerful self. "The old girl admitted to it readily enough. And I managed to remind her who is the boss Trickster around here. So. Do you really think Dove can win the people?"

"I think at the moment a howler monkey could win the people," Aly said. "They will rally to Dove because she is what they have. And they will be glad they did so, because she is everything Sarai is not, from cool head to cool heart. And she knows how to talk to different kinds of people so they feel she thinks of them as equals. Sarai's friends were all that young noble crowd. Dove is friends with beggars and street vendors, spice merchants, cobblers, booksellers, the royal astronomer, priests, priestesses. . . . Even that milky luarin conspiracy group that's been meeting with Winnamine and Nuritin listens to her ideas with respect."

Kyprioth's black eyes caught and held Aly's. "You've sworn to her already," he remarked, his crisp voice soft.

"Oh, stop that," Aly said crossly. "What's important is that Dove will do the thing right. She'll not only get your Isles back for you, but she'll *keep* them for you."

Kyprioth patted her cheek. "I would have been very

sorry to have killed you. You are the most amusing mortal I've dealt with in ages."

Aly gave him her sweetest smile. "All that flattery is going straight to my happy, unkilled head. May I go back? I've left Dove there all alone, convincing the raka she will be worth their support."

"Cheer up," he ordered. "She convinced them, without you. And you have convinced me. We shall continue. And it is time for you to . . ."

"I think she's waking up." That sounded like Boulaj. "Where's that pitcher of water? Wayan, go tell Lady Dove and Her Grace that Aly is coming around."

Aly heard bare, running feet, then the gurgle of water poured into a cup. She fought to open her eyes. "The god had me," she croaked.

Arms helped Aly to sit up: Chenaol's. "Drink," the cook ordered, putting the cup to Aly's lips.

Aly drank, thinking, The last time the god took me, it was Nawat who was there when I woke. She blinked rapidly to keep her eyes from watering.

"How long?" she asked.

"Three days, but they've been quiet ones," Chenaol said as Boulaj poured a second cup of water.

Aly looked at the older woman. There was a smug tone to her voice and a smug smile on her lips. "Quiet?" she asked.

"It was Atisa's idea," Boulaj explained. "She said if folk were going to be unhappy about Sarai's departure, they should be allowed to be unhappy. Quietly. Very quietly."

"Stop dancing," Aly said crossly, struggling to sit up. She was in Ochobu's infirmary, on one of the low beds. "What did Atisa suggest?"

"Shutdown," said Chenaol. "Except for the luarin

households, most luarin businesses, and the palace, the entire city has stopped work and has gone indoors. It took us a day to get the word out, and it started at dawn yesterday morning. It's a beautiful thing, and there are too many people in it for the regents to kill everyone."

Aly chewed a hangnail. "But what if the Crown holds reprisals? All they have to do is see what businesses and houses are open and which are not."

"That is a risk they must weigh." Ochobu stood in the open doorway. "But the regents must first consider where to exact vengeance first. The royal governors of Imahyn and Jerykun Isles are dead, shot near their homes with crow-fletched arrows."

Chenaol winked at Aly. "What do you call four dead governors?"

Aly blinked at her, her mind still trying to catch up. "I don't know."

Chenaol grinned a wolf's grin, all teeth and predatory intent. "A good start."

14

DOVE AMONG THE NOBLES

Aly woke in the dark, with a dark shape seated by her bed. She sat up with a gasp. She groped for knives—taken from her when she was put to bed in the infirmary—as she adjusted her Sight. The figure got up and opened the door to the torchlit hall, but Aly had already identified her visitor: Nuritin Balitang. Aly waited as the lady took a lamp from a niche in the hall. She placed it on the table at Aly's bedside and resumed her seat.

"You needn't rise," the old woman said. "I just wanted us to have a quiet chat. The family and the servants are at their supper."

It's not that late after all, Aly thought. It's just there are no windows in here, so no one can spy on Ochobu and Ysul. "I'm at your ladyship's service," she said cautiously.

"Winnamine says that your service is in fact the god's. Mithros's." Nuritin's eyes were sharp as she looked at Aly. "She has also said you know all our secrets. Is this true?"

Aly shook her head. Nuritin was every bit as sharp as the duchess, Dove, or Ulasim. "I'm only one person, my lady," she replied. "I couldn't possibly know *everyone's* secrets. It's a big household. I do know some."

"Don't toy with me, girl. I am out of patience with anything that crosses my path after Sarai's disgraceful behavior—which you *also* appear not to have known about."

Aly hung her head. "I'm not very happy with that myself, my lady. I would have stopped her, had I known." Would I? she wondered briefly. Really, would I?

Nuritin continued. "Do you know what is discussed in the Teak Sitting Room?"

Aly scratched her nose, considering. Let's see how far she wants to play this, she told herself. To Nuritin she said, "I do, my lady."

"And you have told . . . ?"

"No one," replied Aly. "Forgive my saying so, but it's not much of a conspiracy. It's more a complaint society."

Nuritin pursed her lips. "It is hard to get comfortable people to do anything when it might cost them their comfort. And only a fool takes on the Crown with a handful of allies."

Aly thought carefully. At last she remarked, "There might be allies, somewhere. It would help if your complaint society members showed they were earnest in some way."

Nuritin raised her brows with elegance. "And I suppose you have a suggestion?"

Aly shook her head. "Even chosen by the god, I am just a servant girl. But, do you know, with the city and the people so unsettled, your friends might consider bringing more men-at-arms, or even mages, to Rajmuat. Finding housing for them, and so on. If the men had extra weapons, they might even bring those. Just in case."

She waited, looking at the lady's face. Aly was taking a risk, but it was time to take a few. It was time for the luarin conspiracy to prove if it had what it took to be proper allies to the raka when the time came. There was a darking in Tomang House. Aly would ensure that darkings reached the other conspirators' houses. If she had guessed wrong about Nuritin or her friends, the darkings would warn her in time to stop the luarin from reporting to the regents.

It was an acceptable risk, Aly decided. Having listened as Feather passed on what was said by the luarin conspiracy, Aly knew they were frightened and angry. The regents should not have killed Topabaw without a trial. Duke Lohearn Mantawu had been a luarin noble before he was the spymaster Topabaw. Imajane and Rubinyan had killed yet another member of the class that would normally support them, without even a pretense at legality. That, the executions of the Ibaduns, and Nomru's arrest had told the luarin nobility that their bloodlines no longer made them safe. If the regents could be pushed to do something even more extreme, the luarin conspirators might throw their lot in with the raka. And Aly knew Dove would be able to talk the raka into joining hands with these uneasy nobles, if the raka accepted her in place of Sarai.

"You have given me food for thought," Nuritin said at last, getting to her feet. "I will broach the matter with my fellows, without mentioning you."

"Oh, please don't," Aly begged, glowing with false sincerity. "Thank you ever so, my lady. Such great persons would not care for ideas from the likes of me."

"You are an impertinent minx," Nuritin said drily. "Take care someone does not shorten that clever tongue."

"I do, all the time," Aly assured her earnestly.

Shaking her head, Nuritin left the infirmary, shutting the door behind her.

Someone had left fresh clothes on the bench at the foot

of Aly's bed. Her bead necklace lay on top of them. As soon as Nuritin had gone, Trick and Secret thrust heads up from their large connecting bead disguises. Aly set them gently on the bed, kissing each tiny head quickly.

"Thank you for helping me up there," she told the darkings softly as she put on a breast band and began to wrap her sarong around her body. She checked the seams. All of her thin, needle-like knives were in place.

"Had to help," Trick said. "Crow gods annoying."

"But fun," Secret pointed out.

"But fun," agreed Trick. "Kyprioth fun, too. Wailing and howling like Elsren and Petranne."

Aly grinned at them as she lifted her folded sash. It was heavier than it looked, because it held still more knives. Carefully she settled it around her waist, ensuring that the hilt to each blade was where it was supposed to be.

"What news from the palace?" she asked Trick.

"Regents say bad things about Sarai," the darking replied instantly.

Aly waved the comment away. "Sarai opened us to that," she replied grimly. "What else?"

"Imajane want to arrest people in every third house that is closed," said Trick. "Imajane shake all the time now. Too many noises in the night, she complains. Too many people talking but she cannot tell what they say. She tells maid she will feel better if people who make her nervous die. Rubinyan say killing many people make others angry. Imajane throw a vase at him. They not share bedchamber last night." It stopped talking for a moment, then told Aly, "She shouts at him about it now. She say with mages saying two more governors are dead, Examples must be made. She say death only thing raka understand. She say, burn rebel villages and hang headman or headwoman of every town near rebel villages."

For a moment Trick stopped, tiny mouth agape in wonder.

"Tell," urged Secret. "Tell, tell."

Trick raised its head as if meeting Aly's eyes with its own invisible ones. "Rubinyan say *they dare not.* Rubinyan say, soldiers spread too thin." Trick rose up to look Aly more closely in the face. "This good, yes?"

Aly smiled. "Let us but stretch them a wee bit more," she told the darkings, not aware that she sounded much like her father. "Just to be thorough."

"Thorough good," said Trick, nodding.

"Thorough fun?" Secret asked.

Aly put on her sandals. "We shall have to see."

Aly went to her workroom, braced for the heap of reports from her pack and their recruits that she would find there. To her surprise, the heap was smaller than she had expected after three days' absence: the more people her spies recruited, the more reports had come. Then she saw the thick notebook next to a stack of reports. Opening it, she found notes in Dove's precise handwriting. They were in the proper code and condensed the reports into vital information including the informant, date, and anything that might be of use. Dove had even adopted Aly's way of sorting which of the conspiracy's leaders could most benefit from a particular bit of intelligence. Being a cautious Dove, she had left the reports in a wooden box to the side of Aly's desk, each with a number that matched its location in the book. Aly read through both the notebook and the reports rapidly, and realized that Dove had done as good a job as she could have herself.

With a lighter heart—it was always nice to have help—Aly reviewed the newest pack reports, condensing them and writing information onto sheets for each leader at the nightly meeting. The light outside her office faded. At last she heard the raka conspirators come down the hall to their meeting room. Aly gathered up the information to be passed on and went to join them.

Ulasim smiled at her. "I take it the god was displeased." He looked as if he lazed his days away, rather than conducted a small series of battle campaigns in secret.

Aly returned the smile, glad to see him. "And *I* take it you all agreed a nice, three-day work stop throughout Rajmuat was just what the healer ordered."

Fesgao chuckled. "It gave our people something to do. Hotheads in the Honeypot were all for burning the city down around our ears over losing Sarai. Then one of their old grannies got up and said, 'You act as if Sarai is the *only* one who is twice royal.' They still required persuasion, but after my lads dented a head or two, the idiots decided to see how Dove manages."

"In case I fall flat on my face," remarked Dove with a yawn. "How's the god?" She patted a seat next to her.

"Feeling better since he's had a chat with the Graveyard Hag," Aly said, taking the offered seat. "I confess, I was a bit worried that he might go off in a pout. Not enough to give me wrinkles, but a bit. I talked him into giving you a try." She looked around. "And from the looks of things, I take it you have convinced our friends."

"It's not like we have a choice," said Chenaol as Ochobu sniffed.

"Well, it would be a waste of all this planning, and all these dead governors," Aly replied, falsely helpful. She looked at Dove. "Her Grace formally told the regents?"

"They knew already, of course, but she still had to tell them in person," Dove said. "They made remarks that weren't very nice, along the lines that blood will tell. Winna came home and broke those two big vases in the front hall."

"Those vases were ugly anyway," Aly commented, thinking the regents must have said *very* bad things for the duchess to lose her temper. She began to pass out the reports to those who could best use the information in them as their usual meeting began.

They were nearly done when Dove announced, "The day after tomorrow I'll start my walks again. People are worried. They wanted Sarai, and she's gone. They'll be happier if I remind them I'm still here."

"Absolutely not," snapped Fesgao.

"It doesn't look right, you being the heir's sister," added Chenaol.

Dove looked at Aly, who shrugged. "She needs to show the people that being the hope of the raka hasn't gone to her head, and she needs to show the Crown's spies that she hasn't changed her routine. You'll need more guards," Aly said. "I'll see who my pack recommends for mingling with the crowd. Fesgao, maybe another ten fighters not in livery?"

"It's mad," Ochobu announced. "She is all we have."

"There are still hotheads in the Honeypot," replied Dove, leaning forward to make her point. "They need a real candidate to look at. I'm not beautiful, I'm not elegant on a horse, but I talk to people. And there are others I should speak to, people who could be of use to us. The only way I can do that is to continue visiting the marketplaces."

"Ysul wants to say something," Aly noted.

In hand-signs the mage said, *I will go with Lady Dove, too.*

"Yes," said Ulasim. He saw Dove's frown and said, "No complaints, and no tricks."

Dove thought it over, then nodded.

As the meeting broke up, Aly asked Fesgao and Ulasim to stay a moment. When the others had left, she told these two, in charge of the combat troops, about Rubinyan, the coming arrests, and the regents not daring to expend more soldiers to punish the raka. Ulasim and Fesgao looked at one another and smiled, their eyes alight. They could use this information to direct their fighters to the Crown's softest spots and to halt arrests.

When Aly turned to go, Ulasim said, "Wait."

She looked at him, raising an eyebrow.

"How can you be so sure of what you've just told us?" the footman asked. "You speak as if it's fact, not rumor, and you've been unconscious for three days."

"Because it is fact," Aly assured him. "Ulasim, didn't your mother ever tell you to leave a girl some secrets? I was picked by the god, and this particular information is real. If Rubinyan thinks they dare not punish the villages and estates that have already rebelled, what will he do if more rise up? He'll have to send someone, and at the moment, all he has are the reserves in Galodon. Wouldn't it be dreadful if he were having problems with the reserves? With food, say, or good water?"

She left the men to their planning, fluttering her fingers at them as she walked out and closed the door. Before it shut, she heard Fesgao tell Ulasim, "Old Lokeij used to say she'd never say a thing straight out if she could come at it from the side. He never mentioned the headaches you'd get listening to her."

Aly found Dove in her workroom, calmly going over reports. "Just the person I wanted to see," Aly remarked, locking the door. "Thank you for sorting those out while I was . . . away. You did wonderful work."

Dove put down her quill. "Honestly? I don't know how you keep up. I thought I might go blind." She nudged at the quill with a finger, her face shadowed. Finally she asked, "Aly, what if it goes to pieces because I'm not Sarai? Because it really should have been her?"

"It won't go to pieces," Aly told her. "The last piece is finally where it's supposed to be—that's you. The raka have planned this for generations, and planned it well. The only change is Sarai. Now we have you instead. Sarai may have gotten all passionate about the people and how they're being trampled, but you're the one who *knows* the people. Go to bed, my lady. We have one more day of the halt to work here in Rajmuat, one more day of peace for us to settle our plans. If you don't go get some rest right away, I'll come up to prepare you for bed. Maybe put lotion on your face for you to wear as you sleep. Oh, and I'll brush out your hair a hundred strokes. . . ."

"Stop it!" cried Dove. "I'm going, I'm going! Don't follow me! I can undress myself!"

Aly watched her go, thinking, a little sadly, And when you are queen, you will have proper ladies-in-waiting who will do all of those things for you. You will not be able to dismiss them for fear of offending their powerful families. So enjoy dismissing me while you can.

She locked the door behind Dove and returned to her work. There was more news from the palace darkings as well as more reports to read. Near midnight a darking posted in Rubinyan's chamber gave Trick a message that made Aly grin. She found Ulasim and Fesgao still in the conspirators' meeting room. She told them what she had learned and invited them to her workroom to talk.

She then gathered her pack's most determined members: Fegoro, Yoyox, Eyun, and Jimarn. They joined Ulasim and Fesgao. It's good to be home, Aly thought.

In the morning a palace messenger arrived with an invitation to a lily-viewing party the next day. Nuritin, Winnamine, and Dove were included in the invitation, which was not a request but a demand. Winnamine sent a note of acceptance. The house was quiet as everyone caught up on chores. It was during the noon resting time that the King's Watch swarmed into the city to arrest a third of those who had taken part in the three-day stop of work. By then Ulasim and Fesgao, forewarned by Aly, had hidden any important rebels from the searches. Those unfortunates caught by the Watch were sent to the slave market's pens, to be sold in Carthak as soon as vessels were ready to take them. The Watch expected to ship them out in two days. Aly prayed that Jimarn, Yoyox, Eyun, and Fegoro would concoct a suitably firm surprise for the slave markets before then.

Word of the arrests reached Balitang House in the early evening. Dove, furious, came flying into the workroom as Aly met with her pack. Aly smiled at her young mistress as sweetly as she knew how.

They understood each other. Dove did not need to ask if Aly had known about the arrests. Aly did not need to tell her that she had the matter in hand. The girl turned and walked out again.

"Where were we?" Aly asked her pack as she viewed her notes once more.

The ride to the palace the next afternoon was quiet, though not as quiet as it might have been. Rajmuat was simmering over the arrests. The regents had obviously expected this response. Rittevon's Lance was heavily guarded, with soldiers at each major crossroads and square and guards in pairs on every block.

As always, the men-at-arms left them at the gate. The ladies were to meet the regents in their private audience chamber. Aly assumed they would offer Dove the marriage they had Sarai. As she waited, Aly spent her time in the Robing Pavilion investigating something the darkings had relayed. According to them, the regents distrusted their mages. Aly had to confirm this, not because she didn't trust the darkings, but because she could hardly believe it. Someone had once complained that in the Tortallan palace it was hard to turn without stepping on a mage. Except for Topabaw and his staff, the monarchs here preferred to send their mages to support soldiers outside the capital, and to man the harbor fortresses. The servants Aly asked about it waved off the question with a reply that boiled down to, "Everybody knows that!"

How have they stayed in power this long? Aly wondered as she flirted with servants on the men's side of the pavilion. Were they smarter at first, and the intelligence got bred out of them, or were they simply lucky at the beginning?

At last the Balitang ladies came to the Robing Pavilion to change. As Aly helped Dove to remove her overrobe, Dove hand-signed to her, *They offered me the marriage.*

Aly slid a lightweight sleeveless silk robe over Dove's shoulders, then signed, *And?*

"I dithered," Dove murmured. She didn't care if this part of the conversation was overheard. "It was so sudden, and such an honor after Sarai. . . ." She shrugged. Aly smoothed her young mistress's hair and shared a smile with Dove in the looking glass.

Aly kept an eye on Nuritin and Winnamine. At last they rose, ready for the party. "Dovasary?" called Nuritin.

As Dove stood, Aly bent close, fussing with the line of her overgown, then followed them out. She had already talked this out with Dove. Pembery and Dorilize would remain in the Robing Pavilion; they always did. Aly would go with her young mistress and fan her. The Lapis Pavilion would be warm, and other maids would be there performing the same duty. Winnamine and Nuritin had looked askance when Dove had told them what Aly would be doing, but they had not argued, though they believed in fanning themselves. They both understood Aly was not there just to show how spoiled Dove was.

Down the Golden Road they walked, nodding and bowing to nobles they passed, until they reached the trails around the Lily Water. If they heard the whispers about Sarai that began before they were out of earshot, they did not speak, though crimson flags burned on both Winnamine's and Nuritin's cheekbones. Dove showed a calmly smiling face, even after the nobles could no longer see her.

"You do that very well," Aly said with approval after they had bidden farewell to an especially annoying dowager.

"They only talk about it because they're thinking, 'There but for the blessings of the gods I go,'" Dove said thoughtfully. "Lady Merani"—one of the women they had just left—"has a sixteen-year-old daughter who's a handful. And her husband drinks."

"It's no excuse," Nuritin said in a low voice that shook with fury. "They should have sympathy, and keep their mouths shut."

"This is why my lord and I always hated this place," added Winnamine softly. "Because everyone is encouraged to bite and pinch and cut at one another with words, until the words are so real the courtiers end by trusting no one. It's a poisonous life. Frankly, I'm envious of Sarai."

The two older ladies moved ahead as the path narrowed. Aly waited until they could not hear, then asked Dove, "Tell me, do you know *everything* about everybody here?"

"No, but it's easy enough to get information. The merchants keep track of the nobility because they affect their lives." Dove's mouth curved in a tiny, impish smile. "You know a lot of my friends are merchants."

"I had noticed," Aly said, trying not to smile herself.

Dove clucked to a marmoset, offering the tiny creature a grape she had tucked into her belt-purse. Gingerly the animal, who had a magnificent white mane, leaned down to accept the grape. Once it snatched the fruit, it fled back into its tree. Dove continued, "Besides, I like gossip." She smiled shyly. "I like knowing what people are doing and why. It's just so interesting."

"I always thought so, too," Aly said. They left the shelter of the garden and emerged onto the open ground. Nuritin and Winnamine had already climbed the steps of the Lapis Pavilion and walked over to curtsy to the regents. The pavilion was a roofed stone square set in the water and approached by a short stone bridge. Around it floated water lilies, lotuses, and swans.

Inside the pavilion, the group of ladies seated closest to the bridge was commanded by Princess Imajane. She looked ethereal in white, almost transparent silk with gold embroidery. Aly wasn't sure if it was decent, but then, she still felt half dressed in a sarong with her shoulders bare. And the day was impossibly hot. Maybe Her Highness is the wisest of us all, Aly thought as sweat trickled down her spine.

Nuritin and Winnamine, having saluted the princess and received a nod from her, drifted over to the prince and his companions. Aly saw why as she and Dove curtsied to Imajane: Countess Tomang sat next to the princess. Ferdy's mother looked as if she sucked on a lemon.

"Lady Dovasary, welcome," said Imajane lazily. "I am honored. With your brother attendant upon His Majesty, all the Balitangs but little Petranne are here." She indicated the group of boys at the far corner of the pavilion. Dunevon and his small court stood on the steps that led down to the water, each boy with a wooden sailboat in hand. "As you can see, His Majesty minds the sun less than we fragile adults," she drawled, causing the ladies seated with her to chuckle. "Though we had to supply a mage so the children might have a breeze."

Sure enough, a young man whose hands sparkled with his magical Gift crouched on the lowest step to the water. Tiny puffs of power pushed at the sail of each little boat to the boys' gleeful yells. Aly wondered if the mage heard Imajane, and if he had studied magic so his Gift could be spent on the amusement of children. Admittedly, her experience of mages was extraordinary, but even such confident mages as her mother, Aunt Daine, and Uncle Numair did not appreciate being slighted.

Imajane flicked her fingers at the woman who sat on her left. She obediently got to her feet and curtsied to the princess. As she left the company, Aly looked for Nuritin and Winnamine. They were still talking easily with Rubinyan and his friends.

Dove curtsied to the princess again, then moved to the vacant seat. She sat gracefully, apparently unaware of the glare that Countess Tomang leveled at her. Aly wondered if the princess knew that the last meeting between the countess and the Balitangs had not gone well. From the creamy, self-satisfied smile on Imajane's mouth, Aly would happily bet that she did.

Dove snapped her fingers. "You may fan me," she ordered Aly, nearly as haughty as the princess. Aly installed herself behind Dove. She took the woven palm-leaf fan a maid passed to her and began to wave it gently.

Imajane placed a graceful, well-cared-for hand on Dove's arm. "We had no chance to talk about your sister's elopement earlier," she said archly. "Your mother says you did not know, but I fancy I may know a little more about young girls. Tell me honestly, Dovasary, did you not have some *tiny* hint of what Lady Saraiyu intended?"

Dove lowered her head, shamefaced. "Your Highness, I would never be so foolish as to tell you a falsehood," she said quietly. "Besides, Sarai is five years older than I. Girls with suitors have little interest in talking to sisters who are bored by them." She picked at her skirt. "And she knew I'd tell Winna—Her Grace," she amended herself artfully, "she knew I'd tell, to keep her from disgracing our name."

Aly wanted to hug her. Thirteen, and already aware enough to maneuver around a question about the duchess's watch over her stepdaughters. In the games played at palaces, the whisper that Winnamine could not keep her family under control might cause Elsren to be dismissed from court. By that game's rules, Elsren's position in the king's group of playmates was the kind of thing families used to gain advantages. Even Aly wanted Elsren to be one of the king's companions. It meant the Balitangs were invited to more palace events than most nobles, so there could be more trades of information with palace rebels. The darkings couldn't be everywhere.

"These young girls," one of the ladies across from Dove remarked with a sigh. "No patience. I'm certain Lord Zaimid's family would have accepted Lady Saraiyu if they had gotten married in the proper way. Carthakis are so . . . cosmopolitan about their marriages."

Aly felt the breath desert her lungs at the implication that brown-skinned Carthakis didn't care if they married half-raka girls. Her gentle waving of the fan did not falter. And why do you care what's said of Sarai? Aly asked herself. You're the one who thinks her running off with Zaimid was for the best, even if it *was* a black eye for your ability to watch members of the household.

She was relieved to see that Winnamine and Nuritin were wrapped up in their conversation with the prince. How many such darts had the two women taken since Sarai eloped?

"Oh?" Dove asked politely, as if she discussed a change in fish prices. "Cosmopolitan. How wonderful that sounds! Have you been to Carthak, Lady Uniunu?"

The lady smiled at her. "Actually, I have not."

Dove raised her dark brows. "Have you visited Tyra, then?" she inquired.

The lady shook her head.

Dove pressed. "Tortall? Scanra?"

With each shake of her head, the lady looked less and less pleased.

"Oh," Dove murmured, tracing a design in the embroidery on her sleeve. "But travel is what *makes* us cosmopolitan, or so I was taught." She looked up and smiled girlishly at Lady Uniunu. "But perhaps our own cities count? Have you been to Fajurat on Malubesang? I hear the water is so clean there you can view coral reefs from a ship's deck. Or Ambririp? Or Yimosuat on Gempang?"

The lady had stopped bothering even to shake her head. Her hands, tucked into her lap, were white-knuckled as she clenched them into fists. "Our lands are here, on Kypriang," she said, her voice trembling. "I have learned all I know of what is cosmopolitan right here, Lady Dovasary."

Back off, Aly thought to Dove. She's gotten your point. Drop it, before she becomes your enemy.

As if she heard Aly, Dove gasped and put her hand to her lips. "I hope you didn't mean I thought . . . ," she said, her face dismayed. "Please believe me, I meant only that I am eager to learn of other places." She hung her head. "I have spent my entire life here in Rajmuat, or at Tanair, on Lombyn." Glancing up, she made a face. "Tanair was not in the least cosmopolitan, I'm afraid. We were all living in the keep last winter, because a keep was all the holdings Tanair has. Well, that and outbuildings."

The woman, who had started to fluff like an irate pigeon, slowly resettled. "You are young, and no doubt unschooled as to the proper form of conversation among grown women," she said graciously. Dove hung her head even lower.

"Tell me," began another lady, "do you know why those people were always staring at your sister?"

Dove's lower lip protruded slightly. She looked the spirit of the pouting thirteen-year-old. "I suppose because she's so beautiful, your ladyship," she said, clearly unhappy. "Aunt Nuritin said my looks will improve, but it seems to be taking a long time."

This produced polite laughter from the ladies. The talk moved on to other things, such as the boy king's approaching fifth birthday. "I have an invitation on its way to your home," Imajane told Dove. "There is a separate invitation for Lord Elsren," she explained, leaning closer to the girl. "You see, my dear, His Majesty has been asking for a true ship of his own. On His Majesty's birthday, he and his little friends will board his very own ship, the *Rittevon*."

Dove bowed her head. "We're all honored by His Majesty's invitation to Elsren," she said with just the right amount of awe in her voice. Inclusion in such a party would tell everyone that Imajane and Rubinyan meant to keep Elsren in Dunevon's household, making him a veritable brother to the king.

Aly continued to fan, listening and reading lips. A group of ladies and nobles talked about the hottest part of the summer, when everyone would move to their country estates for a month. Some of the young men in Rubinyan's group urged him to let them go fight the rebels. Winnamine pretended to be interested in the conversation. Nuritin did not.

Aly sensed him behind her before Taybur Sibigat leaned down to speak into her ear. "Do you rest easier since Topabaw has been replaced by a complete nincompoop?"

Aly turned slightly, never allowing her fan to stop its movement, to whisper, "Which nincompoop would that be, my lord captain?"

"Tease," he said, amusement in his eyes. "Sevmire. His Highness took him from a fish pond and tossed him into the ocean. I'll wager you he doesn't last till September."

"I never wager, my lord," Aly murmured flirtatiously. "Particularly not with the nobility. It's so hard to collect."

"What a charming little creature you are," he said with frank admiration. "Really, you're wasted among the Balitangs. You'd have more scope here in the palace."

Aly coughed to hide the giggle that almost escaped her. "I have scope enough, sir," she replied demurely. Behind her laughing face lay a bleak thought: This man might die in the storm to come, and I like him.

And that's your first mistake, lass, said the part of her that sounded like her da. You can't afford to like one of the enemy in this game, and he *is* the enemy.

Raucous shrieks cut through the humid air like knives. Along with the rest of the people on the Lapis Pavilion, Aly turned to find the source. Over the Lily Water, Stormwings and crows battled for possession of the sky. At last one female Stormwing escaped the battle to land on the waist-high balustrade around the pavilion. She was a handsome female, despite the claw marks on her flesh. If her broad, steel-toothed grin was any indication, they didn't bother her.

"More fun for you mortals," she announced in a musical voice. "Remember the Imahyn revolt? Five estates along the Susashain River are burning. Over two hundred dead, or so my nest-kin tell me. Each human smells different to us, you know. All that lovely fear." She ran her tongue over her teeth. "Keep serving them up, Your Highnesses! We accept all contributions of terror and rage, we're not picky!"

"Konutai, you're being a bore," Taybur drawled, wandering over to her. "And you'll make His Majesty throw up in the Lily Water."

Dunevon did look rather pale. He was certainly downwind of the Stormwing.

"Be a good girl and gloat elsewhere," Taybur continued. "I'm sure we'll get proper reports in due time."

The Stormwing cackled wildly and took to the air, heading for the battle between Stormwings and crows over the water. This time it ended with the crows in retreat. Aly crossed her fingers in the hope the crows would go unhurt.

"Don't believe them, Highness," Countess Tomang said to Imajane. "You know how the ugly beasts like to start trouble."

Imajane looked at Taybur, her eyes blue ice. "Which is it, Sibigat? They like to start it? Or they like to live off it?"

The big man bowed to Imajane. "Far be it from me to instruct Your Highness in the behavior of Stormwings," he said quietly. "I am certain that you were as well schooled in that as you are in other things pertaining to the Crown."

Imajane showed a razor's edge of smile. "Your nimble tongue has led you out of a potential situation yet again, Captain Sibigat. I fear you are too clever for me."

As the other ladies protested that no one could be more intelligent than the princess, and Dove chimed in a beat behind them, knowing what was expected of her, Aly met Taybur's gaze. For a moment she thought she saw fear. Then it was gone, replaced by Sibigat's boyish smile.

The talk resumed once more on a false, light note. No

one wanted to admit that they had believed the Stormwing. Imajane herself seemed determined to carry on as if everything were normal. Slowly the ladies began to relax, though the young knights were begging Rubinyan once more to let them sail north and fight. Rubinyan calmed them, insisting the army had matters well in hand. Aly's admiration for his ability to lie soared. She knew that this man had only recently told his wife they dare not send more soldiers.

He must tap his reserve forces in Galodon, Aly thought. And then he'll have next to no one to defend Rajmuat. He may even have next to no one to send, if Ulasim and Fesgao mess with their stores soon.

Why does he send his young knights? she wondered. That's what the hotheads are for, Grandfather always said. Then she saw it. He fears they will get beaten, she told herself, and their parents will turn on him. Either that or he fears they might be good enough to come back and get rid of him.

A shift of silver and gold at the corner of her eye made her look at Imajane. The princess regent had turned slightly to look at her husband. Her crimson mouth was tight. She had seen Rubinyan smile at Duchess Winnamine.

If I don't get overconfident again, if I don't make any more mistakes, we might well do this thing, Aly thought. We might bring these people down. There are so many ways they can be led astray that I'll be hard-put to choose.

At last the Balitang ladies begged the princess's indulgence so they could go home. Not only did Imajane grant it, but she gave them leave to take Elsren with them. Taybur was already talking to the boys about going inside to dress for supper. The ladies and Aly collected Elsren and left the Lapis Pavilion.

On the way home they found the streets were clearing.

Above them faces in the windows stared at Dove, looking for a sign that she was kin to Sarai and their hope for freedom was not misplaced.

"My lady," Aly murmured as they put three blocks between their group and the palace checkpoint, "please look at the folk in the windows. Smile, at least, and nod. Don't wave. We don't want these soldiers taking news back to Sevmire that you are encouraging the raka's fascination with you. But a smile never hurts."

A flush rose in Dove's bronze cheeks. "I forgot," she admitted. Hesitantly she smiled up into some second- and third-story windows, then looked at the people nearest her. A woman stood with a cluster of children. Dove slowed her mount and bent down to look at them. Finally she smiled at the woman. "Not all yours, I hope?" she asked.

The woman hesitated, unsure of Dove's intent, then saw the smile. She grinned. "Gods, no, lady," she said with as much of a curtsy as she could manage with the attached children. "I watch them all while their mothers work in the shops."

Winnamine rode over, Elsren seated before her. "Dove, we must go home," she murmured, with a cheerful nod to the woman. After a moment she thrust her hand into her beltpurse and fished out some coins. "I'll wager you wouldn't mind a treat," she told the children with a smile. She offered the coins to the woman. "Because I have little ones of my own," she explained.

The woman turned crimson and curtsied again. "And you love them, I can see that," she replied, beaming at Elsren, who was half asleep. "Goddess bless you, ladies."

As they rode on, Dove said, "Winna, you didn't have to do that."

The duchess kissed the top of Elsren's head. "I wanted

to have something good to remember about today," she replied quietly. "Something that wasn't petty and mean. Sometimes you have to provide such moments yourself."

As they passed through Rittevon Square, Aly wished that lightning would strike the first king's immense bronze statue, rising above the flat dish of water that surrounded it. She was about to look somewhere else when a detail caught her attention. An anonymous carver had made an addition to the statue's belt line. A deep-cut open shackle shone brightly around the weathered bronze of the statue's waist, above the dip of the sword belt.

Aly grinned, and followed her mistress to the next checkpoint.

15

REBEL PREPARATION

The ladies and their maids retreated to their rooms to change after the hot ride home. Aly was about to help Dove with her buttons when a knock sounded on the door. One of the house's runners stuck her head into the room. "Excuse me, lady," she said, bobbing a curtsy to Dove, "but Chenaol says Jimarn and her folk need to talk to you in the meeting room."

Aly looked from the runner to her mistress. She ought to help Dove to change clothes, but Jimarn, Fegoro, Eyun, and Yoyox were operating on a time limit. The Crown would start shipping the captives in the slave pens the next morning. She sighed, trying to make up her mind.

"Let me help?" asked Boulaj. "I liked being a lady's maid. It's very soothing," she told Junai defensively. "There's no reason why I can't do her hair and clothes and protect her at the same time."

"Go on," Dove ordered Aly. "We'll sort it out. I *do* know how to remove my own clothes," she protested yet again.

Aly followed the messenger to the servants' stair. It occurred to her that she had less and less time to attend Dove as the rebellion began to pick up its pace. She didn't mind being Dove's maid, but she was needed to deal with the material from her spies. Is it always like this? she wondered as she trotted downstairs behind Wayan. The more successful your work, the more it shoves other things to the side?

She wondered what her mother had given up when she had become the King's Champion. Da had given up being an outlaw as he'd made the transition from thief-king to spymaster, but what had Mother surrendered?

I'm going to have to let Boulaj take over, she realized. I'm more use to the rebellion getting information out to people as quickly as I can. But I'll miss talking to Dove.

When Aly reached the conspirators' meeting room, Jimarn let her in. Aly nodded to the others who sat in the room. She recognized five from households nearby, but six she did not know at all. Eyun, Yoyox, and Fegoro waited behind them, frowns of worry on their faces.

Aly went to an available chair and sat. "What is it, my dears?" she asked. "Surely you have not come to tell your old Duani they have shipped the captives already."

"The slave pens are a harder knot than we expected," Yoyox admitted ruefully. "We can whittle that stick down a day or two, but they're moving both faster and slower than we expected."

"They have about five hundred people to ship," explained Eyun. "And the head clerk told me the regents have ordered them to get as many out of the Isles as they can, as soon as they can." She smiled slightly. "The clerk has taken a liking to me. He says the regents want to free up the soldiers who guard the slave pens, because they're needed elsewhere. They expect an attack from the kinfolk of those they arrested, so they won't be reassigned until there's less danger."

"Getting to their kitchen is tricky," admitted Fegoro. "I

won't have a shot at it tonight, not if they're loading slaves." He pointed to a chunky young luarin. "Tell her," he ordered.

"Three ships leave for Carthak tonight from Fifth Dock," the young man explained. "They'll load at midnight and sail at dawn. All of the other ships have cargo in the hold, or are off-loading cargo and taking new cargo on. We won't be able to save those who get shipped tonight."

Aly shook her head. "Children, children," she told them in a sorrowful voice. "The solution is right under your noses, if you would but look. Yes, they have three ships scheduled to sail, only three ships, all due to sail at dawn. There is no law that says they must be *able* to sail."

The conspirators looked at her, mouths agape. Then Yoyox struck his head with his palm. "We focused on the pens and the guards. We didn't think to look at the ships."

"Such vulnerable things," Aly remarked. "All that wood and tar—it's a fire hazard. I tremble to think what would happen if, oh, a ship lost its rudder or its masts." She looked at them from beneath raised eyebrows. "Need I go on?"

They shook their heads, suddenly eager to get back to mischief.

The heavy luarin chuckled.

"Share the joke, Callyn," ordered Yoyox.

"I work at the harbormaster's," the bearded man explained. "We're still wading through bills submitted to the Crown for payment for the ships that burned when the slave docks did. That's one of the reasons they could only find three ships right away—their masters are nervous about cargo from the slave markets. If something happens to these three, I bet they won't be able to find *anyone* at anchor here who will take on slave cargo. In fact, they might decide they've taken on enough goods and sail anywhere, as long as it's not Rajmuat harbor."

Jimarn smiled. "Thank you, Duani," she said.

"Shall you require a mage?" Aly wanted to know.

The bearded man shook his head. "No, see, Duani, the last seven or eight months we've had these twin hedgewitches hiding out in the Honeypot. They have this spell that cuts clean through a piece of wood. In October Her Highness went to inspect a new royal navy ship named for her, and she leaned on the rail, and she'd've gone straight into the harbor if the prince hadn't grabbed her. If the girls can do a rail, they can do masts just fine."

Aly nodded. She would have liked to see that.

"We could use some bows and arrows," one of them remarked. "But not for the slave market. For Downwind. So the folk there can have them."

Aly looked at Jimarn, who nodded. "Then speak to the armorer," she said. "Get crossbows—they're easier for inexperienced archers. Is that everything?" she asked. When they said nothing, she went on, "Very well. Go forth, with my blessing." When they were gone, she ran her fingers over Trick and Secret.

"Stupid?" asked Secret.

"No," Aly replied. "My children are not stupid. But sometimes you can stand too close to a thing to see it. It takes a fresh set of eyes to tell you where to find the cracks." She went to her workroom and assembled paper, ink, and a quill. "What happens in the palace?" she asked.

That night, the raka conspirators had plenty of news to report, particularly Ochobu. Aly had not known that the mages of the Chain had been laboring to eliminate any mages who had worked magic on the Crown's behalf. So far they had killed seven of the most powerful.

Chenaol would call this count of the dead another "good

start," Aly thought grimly. This crude business of counting up lives taken struck her as a bad idea. It took the horror from death. When Ochobu named four mages on Lombyn who had been killed in the streets of their towns, it was about numbers, not lives.

Maybe this is how you become a Rittevon, she thought. You get used to the dead being described as numbers, not fathers or daughters or grandparents.

She turned to Dove when Ochobu finished. "Don't ever be like this," she urged. "Don't think that it doesn't matter if you only hear of murder as a number. If you keep it at a distance."

"They serve the Rittevon Crown," growled Ochobu. "They have killed in their numbers, too. We must even the odds between us and the Crown, and the mages matter. It was the mages who destroyed us when Rittevon invaded."

"They and our own feuds," Dove said quietly. "That's why we have to make peace with the luarin who agree. So we aren't so torn that we are easy pickings for some of the Carthaki malcontents."

Everyone winced. While it had been eleven years since Emperor Kaddar had taken power, he continued to struggle with his western nobles, all of whom thought they would make better emperors that he. It was all too easy to imagine them turning their attentions to easier pickings in the Isles.

As the meeting broke up, Aly drifted over to Ulasim. "How go things at Galodon?" she asked, curious, though if he refused to answer, she would ask Trick to query Ace, the darking who hid under the chair Ulasim normally used.

Fesgao stood and stretched. "All we did today was ensure that the army's provisions for the next five weeks were delivered and neatly stored. We'd hate for them to run short."

Aly grinned and left them. She worked for a while before she went to bed. As she slept, she dreamed of the whispers of the darkings, and the endless black scrawls of reports.

It was nearly dawn when she was roused by the clang of alarm bells sounding down by the waterfront. Aly smiled as she sat up on her pallet. "I could get very fond of that sound," she commented as Boulaj and Junai sat up as well.

"Aly?" Dove asked warningly. "What have you done?"

"I, my lady?" Aly said, holding her hand to her breast as if she were unsure of Dove's meaning. "I have done nothing whatsoever. I was here all night, and I was at the palace with you yesterday, if you recall."

Junai listened at the window. "It's coming from Dockmarket or the wharves," she said after a moment. "Forgive me for saying so, my lady, but if it is, you won't be having your walk again today."

Dove scowled and rang for her wash water to be brought up. It took some time, enough that Dove, who normally did not press the servants when she knew they would also be busy with the others, rang a second time. Soon after, a pair of kitchen maids practically tumbled into the room, hot-water jugs in their hands.

"Forgive us, my lady," said one as she filled a basin, "but Fesgao was telling us the news. He likes to drill the men before dawn, you see, and when they heard the alarm—"

"Does he know the cause?" Dove interrupted.

"Oh, my lady, such a shocking thing!" said the other girl, who filled the servants' basin. "Three ships destroyed, right at the wharves! One sank, one burned, and one had the rudder and the masts and the anchor chain and the mooring ropes just cut, Fesgao said!"

"They meant to ship out some of the folk they arrested because they stopped working," the first maid said, shadows in her eyes. "They meant to ship them to Carthak. But now they can't, and there are no more ships."

To say there were no more ships was an understatement. From Jimarn's recruit Callyn and the palace darkings, Aly learned of furious arguments as Rubinyan and Imajane tried to order other captains in port to put off their loads and ferry the newly enslaved to Carthak. Some claimed they needed hull work done before they could sail. Others showed their master's papers, each with a clause that they not transport slaves. Some captains sailed before the harbormaster could order the harbor mouth barred. Then there were the officials who complained the harbormaster had been suspiciously slow to close the entrance.

Aly was taking darking reports midafternoon when the second blow came to Rubinyan. A thousand of his reserve soldiers, and more than half of the sailors, were confined to their beds with violent dysentery. The darking present when the prince regent heard this news was so impressed with Rubinyan's language that it copied him, earning the name Foul.

The news arrived just before word came that a company of soldiers had been lured into the mountains of northern Kypriang and massacred by renegade raka. Imajane demanded the deaths of everyone in the village closest to the fight. Rubinyan was forced to tell his wife that the soldiers were too ill to move.

That night, when it came Aly's turn to report to the raka conspirators, she asked, "What happens if the army and navy have food shortages? If, say, they have to replace poisoned stores? Who handles the emergency supply, at least until more food can be brought from outlying islands or even overseas?"

The conspirators looked at one another. It was Dove who said, "Local merchants are invited to share warehoused provisions with the Crown, who pays them . . . something. Not full value. Full value when there's a shortage is higher than full value in good times. The merchants who are asked to share with the Crown will see their other friends make money hand over fist while they're forced to practically give food away. But that hasn't happened in ages."

Aly twiddled her thumbs. "But it *could* happen?"

"They would approach the merchants and remind them of their obligations," replied Dove. "And they're already pressed, the merchants. It's been a dreadful year, and the harvest doesn't look good. Nobody's that far away from debt bondage, Aly. The regents might as well ask them to empty their pockets. They . . ." She stopped, her eyes wide.

She sees it, Aly thought.

"No, we can't trust these regents to be careful, can we?" Ulasim asked softly. "They might annoy the merchants. They might turn the merchants into—"

"Enemies," said Fesgao, his eyes bright. He looked at Aly. "You'd thought of that when you suggested it would put a dent in Rubinyan's reserve troops to poison their food."

"You flatter me," Aly said shyly.

"Here I just thought you would deal with information," Ochobu remarked slowly, her eyes on Aly. "But you understand a thing or two about war, don't you?"

"As much as any girl reared under the sign of the Trickster would," Aly replied smoothly.

Ulasim smoothed his beard. "You are a gift and a marvel to me," he said. "What are you doing at the slave pens?"

"Me?" inquired Aly. "Nothing. I sit here and interpret reports. My bottom is going flat from all the sitting I do."

Ulasim shook his head. "Very well. Keep it to yourself. If you require assistance, only ask. Now. Through the Chain we hear that the raka of southern Lombyn have risen up against their masters. And the governor of Lombyn is dead, as is his chief mage, as is the general in command of the army posts on Lombyn, all shot with crow-fletched arrows. Nawat and his people are helping the Lombyn rebels retreat into the highlands, where the new general may hunt for them until he encounters a ribbon snake. Or a hundred."

The next morning Dove finally persuaded Ulasim and Winnamine to let her take a walk to the Dockmarket.

"I'm going mad in here all day," she informed them. "And Fesgao has got layers of protection on me that an onion might envy. I swear, the moment anything untoward happens, I'll trot right home. But seriously, Winna, Ulasim, I'm going to rend the next person who speaks to me if I can't go out for a time."

Pressed, the duchess and the head footman gave way. Aly, too, was grateful for the chance to go out, though she thought she ought to deal with reports. Information was pouring in at a rate she was hard-put to manage. A walk will do me good, she told herself firmly.

At the Dockmarket people went about their business, but they kept one eye on the soldiers present. The ship that had lost its masts had drifted to the center of the harbor. Men were out in rowboats, securing lines to bring it in. The ship that had burned had also drifted when the fire devoured its hawsers. No doubt it would be sunk: it was only a charcoal shell. There was no sign of the third ship, which had sunk.

She could see Dove taking note of the changes, though she said nothing. No one could miss the increased guard around the royal dock where the king's birthday present rode at anchor, its colorful sails furled. There were even men on its decks, watching no doubt for whoever could navigate the harbor waters well enough to burn the slave docks and destroy three merchant ships, in case they turned their attention to the king's ship.

As Aly looked around, Dove crouched to talk with the old raka who sold good-luck charms. She had known the woman since she was small, she had told Aly, and the charm seller always knew the best gossip. As they talked, a part-raka woman who carried a basket of seaweed approached the girl. Aly hand-signaled the men-at-arms to keep to their places. The woman lingered until Dove kissed the old charm seller on the cheek and stood. When Dove looked at her inquiringly, the woman blurted out "Good morning" and fled.

As Dove walked on, a sailor came close enough to tell her that she looked well that day. He was followed by a gaggle of well-wishers, all of whom were happy simply to say hello or to venture an opinion about the weather.

Aly led Dove's group in another direction when they neared the part of Dockmarket where soldiers in the armor of the Rittevon Guard and the King's Watch protected the slave pens. Several of those guards did not look at all well. Jimarn and her cohorts finally got into the slave market kitchens, Aly thought.

A little girl ran up to Dove to show her a dirty rag doll, obviously much loved, then ran away.

"I don't understand," Dove murmured to Aly as they finally left Dockmarket. It was almost noon. Normally Dove would have visited friends at some of the nearby shops, but that was before it had taken her the entire morning to go from one end of the markets principal to the other. "They don't queue up to say hello to anyone else."

"But you let them," Aly pointed out. "You're walking down here with street muck on your sandals, asking what the squid is like today and how business is doing. They'll have heard from your friends that you're not the kind of girl who rides by with a smile and a wave. You understand business. You don't want a fuss. You just want to learn. And they need to see for themselves if your friends have spoken truly." She looked back at the market. A number of the people there were staring in Dove's direction. When they saw Aly turn, they hurriedly went back to work.

"But I'm no warmhearted people lover!" Dove protested softly. "I like to know how business is doing. I'm interested in things like who's importing and who's exporting, who buys and who sells. I like to try and figure out trade, that's all."

Aly shrugged. "Even if they did know that, it would probably only make you more of a real person to them. Don't forget, their fortunes rise and fall with the tiniest drop of the squid-fishing industry. A blight among sheep, and prosperous merchants are selling their old clothes to make some money." She leaned in so that only Dove would hear. "They will look at you, as you ask them questions about how they manage to earn a living, and they'll compare you to people who tax them without asking if they can pay."

Dove's eyes were startled as she stared at Aly. At last she said, "Care to wager on how many days it takes before the regents hire someone to kill me?"

Boulaj and Junai heard, and moved closer. "Just let them try, my lady," Junai assured her. "We'll send whoever takes the job back to the Gray Palace in pieces."

That night Jimarn and her crew killed the brokers' guards who were still healthy enough to fight. The former slave and her companions raced through the slave pens with keys to open the locks, and baskets of weapons. Every captive who could lift one took it—sword, axe, knife. Most raced through the shadows to the Honeypot and up over the ridge, vanishing into the forest that lay on its northern side.

Others were given places to hide in the city.

Many returned to their old homes in Downwind. Once they had reached their district, they scrambled to lay wagons, tables, benches, even stable doors on their sides to block streets. As they did so, Yoyox, Fegoro, Eyun, and their cohorts scattered, to bring out crossbows and quivers of bolts they had hidden away. Jimarn remained, helping people as they blocked the streets, reinforcing the wood barriers with cobblestones and pavement flags. When word got out, soldiers would comb the area. They would quickly learn that for every person who had fled, five had stayed to fight.

Too anxious to sleep, Aly waited until the house had been quiet for a couple of hours, then climbed to the second-story room where the family placed winter things and ancient keepsakes. The door was locked with a hasp and padlock. As a professional, Aly was offended that someone of her skill was taken so lightly. As she chose her lock picks, she felt Trick and Secret put up heads to watch.

"What that?" whispered Secret, always curious.

"It's a lock, and I'm opening it," Aly whispered back. The lock sprang open easily.

"That not a key." Secret understood keys. Quedanga wore a bunch of them on her sash.

"No, it's a lock pick. Actually, both are lock picks. You need different kinds."

Aly stepped into the storeroom. It was huge, but everything from Tanair was near the door. She spotted the trunk she needed immediately. It too was locked. At least this was more of a challenge. She went after it with her picks. It resisted her a little longer than the padlock had.

Opening the trunk, she found Duke Mequen's correspondence going back three decades. Here were bundles of letters from Winnamine, tied up in scarlet ribbon, and letters from Sarugani, his first duchess, in gold. He had letters from family members and friends. Then Aly found what she needed, a bundle of letters in bold, slashing handwriting, with a distinctive signature: Rubinyan.

Carefully she replaced everything but Rubinyan's letters and did up the lock. She dusted the floor to hide the marks left by her knees, then dusted off her knees. After making sure all was in order, she left as quietly as she had come, doing up the padlock. Then she carried the letters downstairs so she could practice the prince regent's handwriting.

She found Kyprioth at her desk, sandaled feet on top of a stack of reports, hands locked behind his head as he leaned back in her chair. Aly squinted at him. Had he grown larger?

"What a wonderful night this is," he told her, his black eyes dancing. "How such small mortals like you and Ulasim cause so much damage . . . I tell you, it fills me with a sense of wonder. It truly does."

"And if it were just us, you'd be right to wonder," Aly said. "We have good people and we trust them to trust their training. I take it you've been down by the slave pens."

"A work of art," the god replied. "I'm beside myself." For a moment there were two of him.

Aly cringed. "Please stop that," she begged. "The thought of two of you makes my head ache."

"I understand. It would be too much glory for your poor mortal body to withstand. When do you rise? When does the rebellion begin?" he wanted to know.

"When the regents give us an excuse," Aly said, taking a chair. "You know, you're getting marks on my papers."

"I'll take them off. I *am* a god, you know."

"So you keep telling me," replied Aly. "Why ask when we rise? Are your brother and sister on their way?"

"Not yet," said Kyprioth, polishing an emerald bracelet

on his wrapped jacket. "Why wait for them to push you forward? The regents?"

"Because we're supposed to be the heroes, rescuing the Isles from oppressors," Aly explained. "It never looks good to other governments if we rise up against a lawful monarch."

Kyprioth smiled. "I thought that might be it. Perfectly sensible, of course. I'm sure it will all work out in the end. Get ready, Aly."

"Are you bigger?" she started to ask, but he was gone.

Aly waited up for her pack to return. They were tired but content, and complained only from habit when she insisted that they scrub every trace of blood from their persons before they went to bed. Only when they were tucked in did she go to her pallet. She was certain she had just nodded off when the alarm bells sounded, rousing the entire household. Someone had found the ruins of the slave pens. It would not be long before they also discovered that when they went to search for fugitives in the city, they would get a far warmer welcome in Downwind than they expected.

Aly followed her morning routine, then cleaned up Dove's room. Boulaj went over the girl's dresses. The day before, an invitation had come for the three Balitang ladies, asking them to a riding party in the palace parks. Aly suspected that Imajane meant to press Dove on taking her place among the regent's ladies-in-waiting, where she could persuade Dove to accept Dunevon as her betrothed.

Aly hoped they would not have to cancel their outing due to those alarm bells. She wanted to pass some incriminating bits of paper to Vereyu to be placed where Imajane, or someone stupid enough to inform her, would find them.

Their plans went unchanged. Two squads of the Rittevon Guard came to escort the ladies and their maids to the palace. Their group had just reached Rittevon Square when they saw that people stared and pointed at the northeastern part of the city. Columns of smoke rose from Downwind; the Honeypot itself was blanketed with it. The King's Watch had discovered the barricades, and fighting had broken out.

Imajane greeted her guests as if there were no fighting on the streets of Rajmuat and led them away to ride with her. Aly sat outside the Robing Pavilion, watching the sky. The crows reigned supreme over the palace. The Stormwings had gone. They've plenty to feed on today, Aly thought.

Suddenly she drew in her breath. Above the crows soared a golden kudarung, great wings outspread. It was the most beautiful thing she had ever seen.

She was dozing off when Vereyu poked her. "Late night?" she asked, sitting next to Aly.

"Only because I worry too much," Aly replied. "Here." From the front of her sarong she drew some battered, dirty scraps of paper with bold black handwriting on them. One read simply *meet tonight,* another *must not know.* A third mentioned *your blushing lips,* a fourth *cannot live with this secret for much longer.*

Vereyu looked them over with a frown. "That's the prince's handwriting."

Aly smiled. "Certainly that's what we want the princess to think. Over the next week can you leave these in places where he might drop them? His dressing room, for instance, or the hall outside Her Highness's door, or their private dining room."

"She may not even see them," Vereyu told her.

Aly wrapped her arms around her legs and leaned her chin on her knees. "You've known Her Highness far longer than I," she murmured. "Do you honestly think she never slips into his rooms when he's not around?"

"But who is this foolish woman, if that's what you mean

Her Highness to think?" asked Vereyu. "Who would be mad enough to get involved with His Highness?"

"If you can get samples of her handwriting for me, Lady Edunata Mayano," Aly replied.

She watched Vereyu's face as a flinty light filled the raka's eyes. Lady Edunata was infamous for having taken a raka lover and then claiming he'd raped her.

"It will be our pleasure," said Vereyu. "I think I can lay hands on some of the lady's writing right now. Wait here."

Ah, revenge, Aly thought drowsily as she listened to peacocks cry. People never lose interest in it.

She stood, stretched, and returned to gossip with the other servants at the pavilion. Only when she saw Vereyu at the servants' door did she leave off flirting with a boastful manservant to talk to her. With the ease of long practice Vereyu slid papers into Aly's hands. Aly in turn rolled them casually and tucked them into her sash.

Imajane seemed determined to incorporate the Balitang women into court life. They rode to the palace nearly every other day over the next week and a half. The regents did their best to pretend the fighting in Downwind was minor, but Aly knew of their real worry from the darkings. The rebellion was spreading like wildfire: for each rising that was put down, two more broke out elsewhere.

"Rubinyan say they maybe need mercenaries," Trick told Aly two nights before the king's birthday. "Princess say can they afford? Prince say they can't *not* afford."

Aly smiled. Mercenaries were always such a problem. If they weren't paid on time, they got unhappy and did damage. If they were without work, they often looked for trouble out of boredom, burning villages and robbing travelers for their amusement. People feared them as much as they respected the need to hire them. The luarin nobility would also see mercenaries as Rubinyan's attempt to build an army that would answer to him alone.

While the princess entertained the ladies, Aly supplied Vereyu with incriminating scraps in Edunata's handwriting. These were hidden in Rubinyan's chambers and study. One of the prince's earrings also found its way into the sweet dreams bag that Edunata, like many luarin women, hung over her bed.

Sooner or later Imajane would find something to make her uneasy, in her husband's or in Edunata's rooms. When she did, Aly was willing to bet that the roof would come off the Gray Palace.

16

DUNEVON'S BIRTHDAY

The day before King Dunevon's birthday, the regents sent an announcement throughout the city. The "unpleasantness" was over. The criminals who had barricaded themselves in the Downwind district had been captured and killed.

Aly wondered if the proclamation fooled anyone. The truth was that the rebels had set fire to the Honeypot, then melted away, into the city via sewers and tunnels or up and over the ridge, into the mountains. The Watch had killed some, but the victory was not as great as the regents claimed it was. That same afternoon the bodies of the King's Watch night commander and its captain were placed at the harbor mouth. Aly chuckled grimly when she heard of it. Once again the regents did her work for her by putting men unaccustomed to the job into positions of authority.

The king's birthday dawned bright and hot. The Balitangs were already awake and dressed, as were their servants, ready for the first ceremony of the day. Elsren was sleepy and irritable in blue silk and white lawn. Winnamine held him in front of her as the family rode out of the house; Dove had

Petranne, who was tired of being left behind. Servants and masters wore their best clothes. They joined party after party of nobles, all on the way to the broad green lands around the palace walls.

They did not have long to wait before the royal party rode out to meet them there. For the occasion the regents had assembled all the pomp that should attend a king, from the Rittevon Lancers to the King's Guard. King Dunevon was not allowed to doze against a friendly breast like his cousin Elsren. Dressed in scarlet, half asleep in the saddle, he rode his pony between the regents. Taybur Sibigat led the pony, one hand behind the little king's back. As the royal group passed, Dunevon's attendants and their families rode into place behind them.

Behind them came the other luarin and raka nobles, all in their finest day clothes. Down the broad avenue lined with soldiers they rode. People waved from their windows and cried birthday greetings to Dunevon. It was impossible to hate the little boy, even if he was a Rittevon. Banners and garlands hung everywhere, their colors as bright as the parrots that flew overhead. Even the Stormwings could be seen as decorative, the sun glinting from their steel feathers as they idly circled in the air.

Through the city they rode, and down to the royal docks, where the *Rittevon* was moored. Taybur excused himself as he turned Dunevon's reins over to Rubinyan. The ten men of the King's Guard dismounted as one and followed their captain aboard the pretty boat, spreading out to inspect it for the third time in two days. Everyone waited, getting warmer and sweatier. Only when Taybur reappeared at the top of the gangplank and nodded did Rubinyan look down at his charge.

"Your Majesty," said Rubinyan, his voice carried on the

breeze, "from Her Highness and me, to you, with love, we give your first sailing vessel. For the king of an island kingdom must have his flagship, do you not agree?"

Dunevon bounced in the saddle, applauding. Everyone around him relaxed, taking honest pleasure in his happiness. He dismounted and strode up the gangplank, chest thrust out with pride. Taybur, his men, the captain, and the sailors lined along the rail bowed deeply to him.

Imajane rode over to the four boys waiting with their families and smiled at them. "Lord Elsren, Master Huldean, Master Gazlon, Master Acharn," she said teasingly, "I do believe that if you do not hurry to board, His Majesty will order the ship to sail without you."

The boys bowed to the regents in their best courtly fashion, then to their families. Well-coached, they did not run to board, though they did walk very quickly.

Funny, Aly thought, Elsren's the only real lord of Dunevon's little court. The rest are younger sons.

The gangplank was drawn up, the boarding gate secured. Aly grinned to see the captain at the wheel behind his king, clearly allowing Dunevon to steer as tender boats guided the craft out into the harbor. Sailors raced to unfurl canvas as the *Rittevon* was turned to catch the breeze. The sails filled. Off the boat sped, all other shipping kept back as the king took his maiden voyage.

Imajane yawned politely behind one hand. "Anyone of a mind to go back to bed?" she asked the nobles around her. They even laughed.

Imajane and Rubinyan left the dock for the ride up to the palace. The mothers of Dunevon's companions waved until the boys leaning over the stern rail, also waving frantically, could not see them. Then they said their farewells for the day, promising to meet that evening for what one of them described as "the mariners' triumphant return." With her own bodyguards, Winnamine returned home.

To no one's surprise, Dove set out along the dock, Ysul, Boulaj, and Junai around her, with an outer guard of household men-at-arms. Other guards and Aly's spies, dressed in everyday clothes, spread through the crowd as her invisible protectors. Aly followed as Dove greeted her friends and asked how they did. She did not linger in Dockmarket. Except for the food sellers, shops had closed in honor of the king's birthday. Instead the shop workers decorated their windows and doors, while day laborers prepared the flowers and garlands for that night's grand celebration.

Dove eventually drew her mare to a halt and dismounted. She sat on a silversmith's doorstep and asked the shopgirls there if she could help. Nearby workers stopped to look at her.

Aly crouched beside her as Dove tried to braid vines. "If you joke about your lack of skill, they'll like you better," she whispered. "I know it's hard to admit you're not perfect—ouch!" she cried as a thin elbow caught her in the side. Aly rose, wincing. "I was only telling you what folk might say, my lady!"

Dove took the braided garland she'd just finished and placed it on her head. It promptly fell to pieces, startling a laugh from those who watched. Just as instantly they stopped laughing and drew back.

She pelted them with vines. "And *that* for making fun of a poor, fumble-fingered country girl!" she told them with a smile. Laughter went through the onlookers. A couple of them ventured to give Dove hints on how her work might be done better. Dove looked at Aly from the middle of a cluster of advisors.

Aly gave her a pleased thumbs-up.

It was nearly time for Dove to return home when a sudden cold burst of air slapped Aly's face. Startled, she looked at the sky. The clouds that boiled there were blacker and lower than those that usually wet down the city in the afternoon. They moved quickly, a yellowish green glow collecting in the air below them. Flickers of brilliance caught Aly's vision. She stood in the street, staring, trying to get a better look. Was it lightning?

Dove stood. "I suppose the farmers are right. You only make a fool of yourself trying to predict weather," she remarked as the shopgirls hurriedly gathered their materials. "It's a good thing the king has an experienced captain."

Thunder rolled; lightning flashed. The wind flattened everyone's clothes around their bodies, chilling them. Aly frowned. "We're going home," she told Dove, "if you please, my lady." Aly wouldn't put it past the regents to arrange for Dove to be struck by lightning. The darkings couldn't be everywhere and hear everything. Aly's job was not to work only with those things she was sure of. She also had to consider the things she did not know, as Sarai had taught her.

Dove said quick farewells to the shopgirls. A gesture from Aly brought the men-at-arms in close, forming a ring around Dove. The wind whistled around shutters and signs, making them flap. One sign was yanked from its moorings. It missed Ysul by an inch as it cartwheeled down the street. Off the group of them went, dodging people who raced to the harbor to secure their ships. Tree branches flew through the air, ripped from their trunks. The wind yanked at shutters, dragging some from their mountings. Dove and her companions were only halfway home when the skies opened. Within a breath all of them were soaked.

At last they entered the grounds of Balitang House by way of the servants' gate. Maids descended on them with umbrellas and blankets. Inside, Quedanga ushered Dove upstairs to a waiting hot bath. Aly changed into fresh clothes, patted her darking necklace dry with a cloth, and went in search the mages. Ysul sat in Chenaol's kitchen, wearing dry clothes, a bowl of water in front of him. It shone with silvery magic in Aly's Sight.

He turned as she reached out to touch him. "This isn't your doing, is it?" she asked him in words and in sign language. "To sink the king's ship?"

Ysul emphatically signed back, *And kill other people at sea? No!*

"Very well," Aly said, not even bothering to apologize. "Where is Ochobu?"

Workroom, signed Ysul, as two kitchen maids and Chenaol said, "The mages' workroom."

"What are you so excited about?" Chenaol demanded. "It's just rain."

"With cold gusts that rip up trees and signs?" demanded Aly. "On a day when the court mages said the weather would be as usual?" She turned and ran to the mages' workroom—no Ochobu. She found the raka woman in the infirmary, grinding aromatic herbs in a mortar.

Aly stopped just inside the door. "Tell me you had nothing to do with this storm," she told the old mage.

Ochobu turned, her brown eyes suspicious. "What?"

Aly pointed to the window. Though the shutters were secured against the outside of the building with hooks, they clacked as the wind tugged them from their moorings. Overhead, thunder boomed.

Ochobu dropped her pestle and went to the window, where she stared at the storm-swept kitchen garden. The plants had been flattened by the hard rain. "This is not right," Ochobu muttered. "There is magic in it."

Aly rolled her eyes behind Ochobu's back. I don't need a mage to tell me that, when it's the wrong weather for Rajmuat! she thought, impatient. This is like a *winter* storm!

"We are taught to leave weather alone." Ochobu was talking more to herself than to Aly. "It is ungovernable. It is likely to turn on the spell caster or to exceed its limits." She glared at Aly. "And I never would have done it this way, either. Five of our people that I know of are on that ship. And there are raka and part-raka out in their boats, fishing. Do you think they will go untouched? A storm this strong will scour the harbor and the coastline for miles. Once a weather spell is begun, there is no way to stop it." From beneath her wraparound jacket she drew a leather cord. On it dangled a circle of obsidian, set in silver. She murmured something, passed her palm over the circle, then gazed into it.

Aly Saw the flare of magic as Ochobu tried to scry for what happened at sea. Waiting, Aly realized that Trick and Secret were shivering. Gently she ran her hands over their living beads. Sweat began to roll down the raka mage's face.

Aly bit her lip. One of the first lessons she had learned was *Never interrupt the mage.* She was about to try it anyway when the old woman straightened and jammed the disk back under her jacket.

"I see nothing," Ochobu snapped. "*Nothing.* My vision of the sea is blocked, and by the magic of luarin mages."

"How can you know that?" demanded Aly. "Magic is magic. It's not luarin or Carthaki or anything."

"In the Isles it is," Ochobu replied wearily as she sat. "Luarin magic hurt us the most during the Conquest. Raka mages began to devise ways to hide our work. You often say our magics look odd—so they should. We shape them to be done in plain sight, without detection from the luarin. What I scryed is pure *luarin* magic. That is to say, *Crown* magic, because any other mage with sense learns how *we* work. Why do you think Zaimid Hetnim came here? It wasn't to be called 'brown dog' behind his back by the regents."

Aly grimaced. "Very well," she replied. Distant thunder got her attention. "Will you be all right? Will you ask other members of the Chain if they can see anything?"

Leaning on the window ledge, Ochobu nodded.

On her way to see Dove, Aly heard a commotion at the front door. Ulasim stood there, arms spread wide to block the way out. Before him stood the duchess, tension in every line of her body. She was wrapped in an oiled cloth cape against the rain. Nuritin, Dove, Pembery, Dorilize, Boulaj, and Junai stood behind her, also in rain gear.

"Ulasim Dodeka," Winnamine was telling him in a voice that shook, "you have been a friend to me, and I know you think you are being my friend now, but as the gods are my witnesses, you will either stay behind or carry my umbrella, but you *will* let me through that door. I want to be on the royal dock when they come home. You know—" Her voice cracked. She swallowed, then went on, "You know that Elsren does not care for lightning. He will be frightened. He will want his mother."

Aly signed Ulasim that she would get men-at-arms. He nodded, then told the duchess, "At least wait until your guards are here, Your Grace. And then I will be happy to hold your umbrella."

Fesgao led the men-at-arms himself. Aly also called for Ysul and three of her spy pack still in the house as she found her own waterproof cape and broad-brimmed hat. She fell back with her spies as Ysul joined Dove and Winnamine.

"Get to the marketplaces, wherever you find people," Aly murmured to them. "Say this is an uncanny storm, and too convenient with His Majesty at sea. Go." They went, as

Aly followed the Balitang ladies, biting the inside of her cheek. She knew what had happened, but she could not say it, not to these people. They would want to put off hearing the truth as long as they could.

Aly caught up with Dove. No one spoke as they walked. Winnamine didn't seem to care that her feet were soaked, any more than Nuritin or Dove cared. The duchess and Nuritin held hands, like children.

When they reached Dockmarket Way, Winnamine looked at them. "It's the wrong time of year," she said, indicating the street and the harbor. "The wrong time for such damage. And this is the snuggest harbor in all the Isles. What did it do outside in the open sea?"

Aly saw what she meant. There were tiles, ribbons and flowers that had been torn from decorations, a few signs, and the collapsed remains of stalls all along the waterfront. The ships were tangles of torn sail and spars. Small boats had been driven against the pier and smashed.

When they reached the royal docks, the guards at the wrought-iron gates let them in. Winnamine led them to the berth where the *Rittevon* was supposed to drop anchor. Sailors rigged a canvas awning to shelter them from the downpour and pulled up a bench. Nuritin sat, looking older than she had at dawn. Winnamine and Dove stood, looking toward the mouth of the harbor, veiled by rain. The duchess's lips moved in silent prayer. Dove began to pray and stopped. Aly wondered if her mistress had been about to call on Kyprioth and had stopped herself, either because she didn't want her stepmother to hear her address a raka god, or because she wouldn't like what he might say.

Aly had no such compunction. She wanted information; she wanted it immediately. *Kyprioth!* she shrieked silently. Show yourself! Is this *your* doing?

The god remained silent.

Aly stepped back to question the palace darkings. They reported that Imajane was supervising the arrangements for Dunevon's party that night. Rubinyan met with officials and officers of the army and navy about the newest revolt on Malubesang. Aly's ears pricked when Trick whispered the holder of the lands in rebellion: Duke Nomru. Trick added that Rubinyan had snarled at his absent wife for arresting the duke in the first place. Aly nodded. All was not well with the regents. As she had observed in the case of her parents, it was hard for a man to silence a too-frank wife when she spoke in front of company. Da was usually amused, but then, the pricklier her mother, the happier her father. Aly had never understood it. She did understand that Rubinyan had to keep the peace with Imajane. She was the source of his power.

Let's see what he does when the source of his power goes bad, Aly thought, returning to her ladies. Let's see how he feels when she turns that Rittevon gaze on *him*.

The mothers of the other three boys in Dunevon's court came to the docks as the rain eased, to join Winnamine's vigil. The sailors found more benches. By late afternoon, the rain and the cold had moved on. A normal summer's heat dropped on the city like a wet coverlet. Their wet clothes began to steam. The king's ship was supposed to return by sunset. People were drifting out to line the harbor walkway and the docks around those reserved for the Crown, keeping a mostly silent watch.

The Balitangs should have gone home to change—the other mothers wore their court costumes under their oiled capes in case all was well—but the duchess refused to move. Both Dove and Nuritin had to persuade Winnamine to drink a cup of tea. More tea was fetched for the other ladies. When they had finished it, Nuritin and Dove sat on either side of

Winnamine, Nuritin holding Winnamine's hand, Dove keeping an arm around her stepmother's shoulders. The other mothers did not talk with each other or the Balitangs. All of them were fixed on the harbor's mouth.

"They really should dress and meet the regents for the procession down Rittevon's Lance," Ulasim murmured to Aly. "Her Highness may not be pleased to find our ladies here, not attired for the festivities. At least the others are properly clothed."

Aly looked up at him. She stifled an urge to swear at the regents and instead replied, "Do you mean to drag her?"

Ulasim shrugged. His face was impassive as he stared out at the harbor. Aly was not fooled. She knew that he had been in the Balitang household since before Elsren was born.

"He is half Rittevon," she said. She knew him well enough to be sure that he, too, believed the boys were dead.

"I know that. Don't you think I know that?" Ulasim's voice was a harsh whisper. "But we could have worked something out, for him at least. . . ."

Aly didn't have to say that he fooled no one. She felt only a small, hard knot beneath her breastbone tighten as she looked at Winnamine, Dove, and the other boys' mothers, or when she looked at the harbor mouth. Someone was going to pay for this, she promised herself. She meant to present the bill herself.

The city's shadows spread across the harbor, which grew dark while the heights still lay in the sun. Along Dockmarket Way people cleaned up debris and brought lanterns to light the watchers and the dock workers. When sailors tried to light the royal docks, the duchess asked them to wait. Light would make it hard to see the harbor mouth.

The regents arrived in gala dress, surrounded by their households. Rather than dismount, they rode halfway onto the dock. Their noble companions dismounted from their horses and walked out in their wake, dressed in their finest and followed by the rest of the court. Two of the other mothers who waited instantly rose to greet the regents. The third was urged by her servants to go to them. No one dared say a word to the duchess.

Rubinyan was the first to notice the small group of Balitangs waiting by the *Rittevon*'s mooring-place. After a whispered conference with Imajane, he sent one of her ladies-in-waiting to approach the duchess.

"Your Grace, my ladies, what is this?" the lady asked, smiling. "You are not prepared for the evening, you did not meet Their Highnesses with the rest of us. . . . Her Highness is concerned."

"As are we," Nuritin said, her voice a croak after long, tense silence. "You *do* remember that storm today, do you not? It was quite severe." The lady nodded, still apparently puzzled. "We fear—Her Grace, Lady Dovasary, and I—we fear that something has happened to that ship. Our family has had more than its share of trouble of late. Should the *Rittevon* dock at the appointed hour, we will submit ourselves for the regents' forgiveness and make haste to dress and come to the palace. But we shall remain here until we are certain His Majesty and Lord Elsren are safe."

The lady favored them with a stately nod and returned to the princess. When she whispered her report, both regents nodded in understanding. Prince Rubinyan dismounted and came to see the ladies. "Winna, surely you are overreacting," he said when he was close enough, his elegant voice warm. "It was a storm. Our best seamen crewed the *Rittevon*. And our weather mages predicted fine weather for this first sailing. Violent storms in the spring rarely have much reach." He took Winnamine's free hand in his and chafed it. "So cold!

My dear, you shouldn't do this to yourself."

Aly glanced at the princess. Had Imajane's face gone pale? She spoke to one of her guards, who helped her to dismount. As graceful as a swan she came to join them.

"My dear," Rubinyan said, turning to show Imajane Winnamine's white hand. "She feels like ice!"

Dove got to her feet so that the princess regent might sit. Imajane inspected the bench, then settled into place next to Winnamine, taking the hand Rubinyan had held. "While I am not a birth mother, I think I know your feelings," she said graciously. "The chance that anything may have happened to our dear little boys . . . My own blood runs cold at the thought."

After that, she kept silent. Aly was grateful. She wasn't certain that Winnamine had even heard either regent, her eyes straining toward the shadowed entrance to the harbor, but Aly had seen sparks in Nuritin's eyes. If Imajane had continued to talk, Aly wasn't at all sure that the older woman wouldn't have slapped the princess regent.

By the time the city watch cried the candle hour past sunset, people all along the docks shifted nervously. The king should have returned. When the watch cried the second candle hour past sunset, they were restless. Rubinyan walked away from the group of women and servants, beckoning to the guard captain assigned to the royal docks. Once the man trotted to his side, Rubinyan began to speak. They kept their heads close together. Between that and the flickering light it was impossible for Aly to read their lips, but it didn't matter. There was only one way for the regents to proceed if they did not want to appear guilty.

Soon horsemen galloped down both sides of the harbor. Galley drums began to pound. Sailors in the uniform of the royal navy raced to their ships. Aly was impressed by how quickly they were able to board the vessels and cast off.

At the half-candle hour, the twin beacons at the Greater and Lesser Fortresses went from gentle gleam to blazing light: they had been the destinations of the horsemen. As the mages who worked the beacons brought them to full power, Aly closed her eyes. She gave her Sight the twist that would keep her from being blinded by either the beacons or the magic in them.

When she looked again, she saw a small, two-masted ship slowly moving through the harbor's entrance. It was not the *Rittevon.* When Aly sharpened her Sight, she saw that this craft had taken a battering. One mast was broken in half; the sails were tattered. A handful of men slumped on the deck. Others worked slowly and painfully around them.

A small hand clasped her gently by the elbow. "Is it the king's ship?" Dove asked as Ulasim, Fesgao, and Junai looked at them.

Aly shook her head.

Two naval galleys moved in to bracket the mauled vessel. They were too far away for those on land to hear what was shouted between them and the newcomer, but they could see when the galleys' oars were shipped and gangplanks were swung across the distance between the vessels. Men, carrying weapons, trotted across the gangplanks to inspect the vessel. Aly nodded. That was sensible: something nasty might lurk in the hold. The navy would not allow the ship farther into the harbor until the galley captains were sure that everything was as it seemed.

At last the sailors roped the newcomer to their own vessels and returned to them. The galleys towed the ship straight to the place where the *Rittevon* was supposed to dock. Aly heard footsteps and turned. Here came the court, looking properly worried. The mothers of the other three boys gathered around Winnamine, helping her to stand or drawing strength from her, it was hard to say. Princess Imajane and Prince Rubinyan stepped up to be the first to meet the little ship. They, too, looked prepared to face bad news. Beyond the dock, on the street, the crowds waited in utter silence. The only sound in the soft night air was the mild slap of harbor waves against the land.

Finally the battered ship was tied up. The first man to come down the gangplank, bearing a small, motionless form in red satin, was Taybur Sibigat. His eyes were red and swollen. His mail was gone, his clothing ripped. There was a long gash over his left temple, and the entire right side of his face was one purple-black bruise. He limped as he carried Dunevon's corpse to the regents.

People in the crowd moaned. Someone shouted, "He's just a boy!" and was silenced.

Behind Taybur came a raka sailor. In his arms he carried one of Dunevon's court, Acharn Uniunu, very much battered but alive. He wept as he strained to reach his noble parents. They ran to him, his father seizing him while his mother wept and kissed him. Aly recognized three other men who came down from the vessel that must have rescued them, two of the *Rittevon*'s sailors and one man of the King's Guard, helped off by two raka seamen. He'd lost half of one leg. One of the royal sailors had a bandaged head; the other had an arm in a sling. The rescue ship's sailors were in no better condition.

Taybur turned away from the regents and came over to the families of the other three king's attendants who had not returned. He didn't seem to realize that he still held the dead king. Looking at them, his eyes overflowed. "I'm sorry," he whispered.

"What happened?" asked Lord Lelin as his lady and daughter began to weep.

"The storm came out of nowhere," replied Taybur. "Gale-force winds, waterspouts . . . It was a ship killer. We weren't the only ones caught out there." His voice broke. "Forgive me. My boys and I tried to save them all, but . . ." He looked at the boy in his arms, then at the mothers of the other three lads. "We couldn't even find their bodies."

"I, too, am sorry, Captain," said one of the noblewomen who had lost a son, her voice cracking. Her husband put an arm around her and led her away.

"We must go home." Winnamine stood very straight, her brown eyes wide in a face that had gone dead white. "We must . . . tell our people. . . ." She reached out with hands that shook. Dove took one, Nuritin the other.

Without saying farewell to the regents, the Balitangs left the pier, the servants and guards in a tight cluster around their ladies. Aly brought up the rear. When she glanced back, she saw something that looked like contempt on Imajane's face, and heartbreak on Taybur's. Rubinyan's face showed nothing at all.

Somehow they broke the news to the household and fumbled their way through changing clothes, trying to eat, and getting the ladies to their beds. Finally Aly could slip away into the flattened and littered gardens. The moment they were out of the house, Trick and Secret spread themselves out blanket-like over her shoulders and tightened. "Is this a darking hug?" Aly asked with a sad smile.

"Is a friend hug," Trick said. The pair had left only their heads out of the embrace, leaning them against Aly's cheek. "No crying, but sad, Aly."

"It was a decision I didn't want to make. You'd think I'd

be happier that it was made for me, but I'm not." She found a bench by a lily pond and sat down. As she did, miniature winged horses crowded around, nuzzling her.

"I'm sorry," Aly told them softly, petting one after another. "If Nawat were here, he could tell you what's wrong. I just don't speak kudarung."

A small winged mare braced her front hooves on Aly's leg and fluttered her wings. That much kudarung Aly knew, at least. She bent down to pick up the mare, cuddling her in her arms.

Secret shifted, pulling together to flow down to the bench next to Aly. There the small darking rolled and moved, shaping itself as a miniature kudarung. When the shape settled, Secret jumped down among the other miniature winged horses and went muzzle to muzzle with the stallion who governed them, to tell them what had happened to the Balitangs.

Aly looked up at the sky, blurred slightly through the spells that covered the house and grounds.

"Kyprioth," she said, running her hand over the mane of the winged horse in her lap, "I want you, my dear. And not in a happy, let-me-kiss-your-grizzled-cheek way, either."

"My grizzled cheek may wither of neglect." The god was there, seated on the rim of the lily pond, dabbling his toes in the water. "You've been very noisy in your calls for me, I would like to point out. If I got headaches, you would have given me one."

"If you knew I was calling, why didn't you come?" she demanded.

"Because I knew you would scold, and scoldings bore me," he replied. "As if they do any good after the fact."

"Was this your work?" she asked softly, gently, that hard place under her breastbone scorching the inside of her skin. "Did you murder those little boys?"

"I? Please. I'm busy preparing for battle, mustering my fellow tricksters. I refuse to worry over what mortals are up to," he said carelessly. "And I won't do everything for you. It's bad for your character."

Aly shifted until she had a clear view of that clever face. "What did you do? It's not like you to be evasive about your tricks. Bragging's more your style."

Kyprioth looked at her. Aly felt his power as he tried to overwhelm her. She closed her eyes and fought. "Stop it," she told him stubbornly. "You've already tried this with me, and it ages *very* fast." The force of his godhood slacked off enough that she could breathe.

"I told you, my brother and sister are near to their return to the Isles," he said, as if she were not very bright. "You and my raka have given me some of my old vigor, but it won't be enough. The only way I will be strong enough to fight my brother and sister is if you stop tiptoeing around the king and take this country back. Since you could not seem to reach that point, I made a few suggestions here and there." He eased up on his power completely.

Aly took a breath and ignored the sweat that trickled down her face. The little kudarung in her lap whickered and licked up the salt. "What kind of suggestions?" Aly wanted to know.

Kyprioth inspected his rings. "I mentioned to the regents that it's a shame they must bow to the whims of a four-year-old, when they have more experience and intelligence than any Rittevon boy king. Ludas Jimajen—Rubinyan's ancestor—"

"I know," murmured Aly.

Kyprioth grinned at her, white teeth flashing in the dark. "*He* was supposed to have been the next king, or his son." He began to juggle balls of gold light. "That was the agreement he made with Rittevon, so that both of them could claim the throne. But Jimajen was killed supposedly by a raka assassin after Rittevon's second wife gave birth to twin boys. Amazing how these things work, isn't it?"

Rubinyan Jimajen had no children by his marriage to Imajane, but he did have sons from his first marriage. He even had grandsons. Had Imajane ever wondered if he didn't want to take the throne and make the next monarch a Jimajen king?

"I love to watch you think," Kyprioth said. "Your face gets so agreeable."

"Was the storm yours?" she asked.

He shook his head, as if disappointed. "Why should *I* need to brew one?" he inquired patiently. "They had mages who can do it. Mages who care only that they keep their untrusting master and mistress happy."

"Is that all you did with the regents themselves, then? A suggestion?" she wanted to know, eyebrows raised in casual interest.

"Well, I reinforced it with repetition," the god admitted. "Whenever he had a tantrum, whenever he shouted that he hated them, as children so agreeably do when they are crossed. Aly, you aren't usually so dense. Dunevon was in the way, as was Elsren. They had to go. If I waited for you tenderhearts, my brother and sister would return and wrap me in chains, then kick me off the edge of the universe. I didn't care to wait."

Aly looked at him, a mantle of cold settling over her skin. Twice she had erred very badly. The first time was when she had been too cocky to think Sarai might surprise her. The second time was at present. She had forgotten that Kyprioth was not a wildly eccentric, magically powerful human. She looked into his face and saw that those lives meant nothing to him. He was a god. He might care for a few chosen humans. He might even enjoy their company. But in the end, he could no more feel as humans did than could Stormwings.

She got to her feet. "I'm sorry you can't grieve for those people," she said quietly. "You don't know what you miss." She set her dozing miniature kudarung down and returned to the house. Once she reached her workroom, she put her head on her table. "Tell me about the dragons," she whispered to the darkings. As they talked of burning sands and fields of stars, she tried to imagine them and nothing else, particularly nothing to do with the sea.

She woke in the morning slumped across her worktable. Her head felt as if it were stuffed with cotton. Somehow she cleaned herself up and made herself eat, a ghost in a household full of ghosts. Conversations were quiet and kept to the basics. The ladies retreated to the nursery to tell Petranne and to mourn for the second time in less than a year. Finding herself unneeded, Aly retreated to her workroom. Automatically she busied herself with information, starting with the darkings.

She expected the news they gave her: The regents had summoned the chief Mithran priest to crown them, with their luarin cronies as witnesses. The official coronation, with all its pomp, would be held the day after the coming eclipse of the sun, in celebration of Mithros's victory over the dark, Trick said.

Aly turned a silver coin over in her fingers, walking it across their tops, then under them. "They have to put it that way," she said quietly. "It's that or admit their god is vulnerable for a day."

She assembled more reports, taking in information and writing it up for the raka leaders. Even if they had been able to meet that day, she couldn't have borne it. She had told Elsren stories, changed his clothes, taught him to somersault. She did not want to think of him cold and alone in Kyprioth's uncaring waters. Instead she lit a stick of incense to the Wave-Walker, the merciful sea goddess, in the hope that she would see Elsren properly to the Peaceful Realms. Aly did not know how she would attend the memorial service held when there was no body to bury, but she knew that she must.

It was almost noon when the clamor of crows drew Aly out into the garden. A cloud of them flew overhead, calling to each other, telling the native crows that they were allies, come from the north. Aly watched them, numb. Tomorrow I must get to work, she told herself. There are opportunities now, with the Crown unsettled. I must not sit here like a lump, or allow my people to do so.

At least she had custom on her side. With the announcement of the emergency coronation had come the proclamation of a week of mourning for the Isles, a week when all but the most necessary work was to be set aside. Aly did not mean to idle that entire week away, but she needed at least one day to collect herself. From the shock on all the other faces of the Balitang household, she could see that everyone felt the same, even Ulasim. Even Ochobu.

She returned to her workroom and to processing information. Someone had left a stack of reports for her while she'd been roaming. Most of her pack and their recruits had been out and about, listening to what people had to say. Except for Boulaj and Junai, they'd had little or nothing to do with Elsren. His death had less of an impact on them, and in Dunevon's death they saw an opportunity. Aly had expected them to: she had trained them for that, as she herself had been trained. It was just very hard to get excited over the opportunity when that knot of fire under her breastbone had turned to ice.

Someone opened her door without knocking. Aly looked up from her work, scowling, and froze. It was Nawat, sun-bronzed, bearing a scar on one cheekbone, wearing a loose cotton shirt and breeches, and tired boots. He set a bow and a quiver of crow-fletched arrows by Aly's door and came toward her, an odd look on his face.

It was a look she would have known on any other man's face as he greeted the love of his life. She had seen it blaze in her father's eyes, King Jonathan's eyes, and Uncle Numy's eyes, but never in Nawat's. It was there now.

Aly jumped to her feet and threw herself into his arms. It was no crow-turned-man who caught her up, but a man, confident in who he was and what he wanted. Aly had time to emit one squeak before he covered her mouth with his. She clung to him and lost herself in warmth and a melting in her belly and legs that went beyond desire. Nawat drew back, took a breath, and kissed her again, his lips sweet and moist, his arms hard with muscle as he lifted her off the floor. Aly's hands explored the muscles of his back and the softness of his black hair, but her mind could escape his mouth for only a second before it came back to his kisses. Nawat carried her to her worktable and sat her on piles of reports so their faces were at the same level.

Trick and Squeak dropped from her neck, where they were being mashed. Aly didn't see them watch with interest as Nawat kissed her forehead, her cheeks, and her palms. Finally she tugged away and rested her forehead on the V of brown flesh that showed in the collar of his shirt.

"We were fifty miles away when we got word of the nestlings," Nawat whispered. "I had to come ahead faster. I knew you would need me."

Aly looked up into his eyes. She felt her chin quiver. All she could do was hide her face against his shirt again as the tears came in a rush. Nawat held her close and preened her hair with his fingers as Aly cried herself out. She didn't even try to apologize as her head slowly cleared. She knew he understood.

"They were a problem," she whispered at last. "But I never wanted it solved like this."

"Good," Nawat replied over her head. "I would not wish you to drown our nestlings."

She laughed and sobbed at the same time, then pulled herself away. Taking a handkerchief from her sarong, she mopped her face. "I got your shirt wet," she pointed out. Then she looked at him. "If you came the fastest way, did you steal those clothes?"

Nawat's smile made her heart do funny things. "I hid some of mine away in case I should have to come home this way," he explained. "My clothes fit better than stolen ones. There are little creatures on your table."

Aly half turned and saw the darkings. "They're darkings," she explained. "And my friends. That one's Trick, and that one's Secret."

"Is this lovemaking?" Secret inquired.

"No. It is kissing. Lovemaking comes after kissing," Trick replied.

"That is true," Nawat said. There was a look in his eyes that made gooseflesh ripple over Aly's body. "Please go away, little friends of Aly."

The darkings plopped to the floor and rolled out of the room. Nawat went over and locked the door. Aly watched him with a mixture of nervousness and anticipation.

"I don't think this is the best time to do what I think you want to do," she pointed out.

"There will never be a good time until Dove is queen." Nawat walked over to put his arms around her again. "We might be dead by then." He kissed her temple, then his lips drifted until they found hers again. This kiss was long, slow, and sweet, the kiss of lovers who had all of time.

At the end of it, Nawat held Aly's face in his hands. "I am no longer a crow who turned into a man, Aly Bright Eyes," he told her soberly. "I am a man who can be a crow at need, but I am still a man, and I love you. I have seen so many people die since I left you. I do not want to wait for priests to say words or for you to want chicks. If I go to the Peaceful Realms tomorrow, or the day after, I want to go with the taste of you on my lips."

He kissed her again, slowly, folding her into an embrace that left her breathless. Aly had time to gasp when he pressed his mouth against the tender skin on her neck and collarbone. Dizzy, she suddenly realized that he'd undone her sash.

"Um, wait," she said, her voice wobbling.

"No," he replied, gently placing the sash, and its cache of knives, out of their way. "No more waiting, Aly."

"I didn't mean that kind of waiting, exactly," Aly told him, holding him at arm's length. Nawat lifted the arm, kissing the inside of her wrist, then the inside of her elbow. I had no notion those areas were so sensitive, she thought giddily. "Nawat, stop. There's, um, a thing, for us females. . . ." He was kissing her palm. It was very distracting. "Nawat, we can't bring chicks into the world, I'm not ready, we're not, and well, there's a thing women wear, only I haven't got one." Babbling again, observed that cool corner of her brain. "Until we have a safe nest, I can't—not without that charm."

Nawat smiled and pulled something from his pocket. It shone gold and shimmered silver with its touch of magic. "My fighters told me," he explained as he draped the antipregnancy charm around her neck. "It is a thing women put on, until they want chicks," he said, laughter in his dark eyes.

"Oh," Aly said weakly. "That, well, that changes some things, definitely—"

Nawat kissed her again. This time his free hand worked at the tie of her sarong. Aly couldn't help him. She was too busy undoing his belt.

"I want to always have the taste of you on my lips," Nawat whispered as they sank onto the floor.

Aly slept, the first deep sleep she'd had in a long time. She woke to find Nawat setting a pallet on the floor beside her. He'd brought a lamp and a blanket as well. Eyeing the lamp, she murmured, "It's night?"

"Nearly midnight. Ulasim said to let you rest." Nawat knelt beside her and cupped her cheek with his hand. "I did not think it would hurt you. Lovemaking."

She smiled at him. "It often hurts the first time, when you're a girl. So I've been told."

"Only the first time?" Nawat asked.

She kissed his palm. "I think so."

"Then perhaps we should try again," Nawat said gravely, bending down to kiss Aly.

She nodded vigorously until their lips met.

17

MOURNING

Aly opened her eyes. She was curled inside the curve of Nawat's body, his arm over her waist. On the floor next to their pallet was an audience: a few miniature kudarung and five crows, all watching with fascination. Warm lips met the back of her neck, raising goose bumps on her body.

"What time is it?" Aly inquired drowsily.

A crow made the sound for "before the sun rises."

"If the sun is not awake, *I* am not awake," Aly said. She turned under the blanket to burrow her face into Nawat's shoulder.

"Go away," he told the others.

It only then occurred to Aly that the crows and the kudarung could not have entered through closed shutters or a closed door. She sat up quickly. The door was open, but the frame was not empty. A number of weary yet fascinated faces—Ulasim's, Junai's, Yoyox's, Boulaj's, and Kioka's—looked down at them. Aly was grateful that Nawat had left her in the blanket as he proceeded to dress.

She raised an eyebrow at their audience. "Enjoying the view?" she inquired.

Yoyox grinned. "Actually, yes."

"I enjoyed the other view," said Kioka, watching Nawat pull on his shirt.

Aly glared at her. "I know a hundred different ways to make you disappear," she warned the young woman.

"This is all as beautiful as the flowers of spring," observed Ulasim. "Nawat, where are your warriors?"

Nawat kissed Aly gently, then straightened. "Thirty miles north, sir," he replied, a soldier in answer to his general. "I brought two hundred and fifty, as many as could be spared. They should be on the outskirts of the city by tonight."

"Come give me what news you have," Ulasim ordered, beckoning. "You may settle romantic matters later. The regents have decided they no longer need a Rittevon male to rule." He shooed the others away from the door and led Nawat across the hall. Nawat closed the door. Aly scowled at it, remembering it should have been locked. "This is the problem with training people to open locks," she complained as she dressed. "They can turn what you taught them against you." As she picked up her darking necklace, Trick and Secret poked out their heads. "Human lovemaking looks silly," Secret told Aly.

"Darking way more sensible," added Trick.

Aly settled them around her neck. "Our way is more fun," she replied absently, her mind on the rebellion. Getting up to wrap her sarong, she stared at the map that marked the path of the war. As soon as her sash was arranged, she set a pin for Nawat's warriors, on their way to Rajmuat.

What had possessed the regents to kill those boys? she wondered. Now, when they are stretched so thin? They will lie and say it was the storm, but who will believe them? Do they think people will accept them on the throne? They'll have to fight, and they haven't got the soldiers.

The numbness of the day before was gone. Her heart still ached for Elsren and the others, but she could wall it off to consider her next move. Sitting at her desk, she began to pore over the reports she had not yet reviewed, looking for signs of weakness and for ideas. It took the breakfast gong to break through her concentration. She was ravenous.

She could not have forgotten their loss even if she had wanted to. In the servants' mess hall she saw black armbands everywhere, and eyes still red and swollen from weeping. Talk was kept quiet. Chenaol had retreated inside herself, dishing out food as if she didn't even care what it was. Aly simply accepted her bowl and did not try to distract the cook. When Nawat came to eat beside her, they slid together until their legs touched and ate in silence.

Once the meal was done Aly went upstairs to get clean clothes. "She slept on a trundle bed in Her Grace's room," Boulaj said when Aly asked for Dove. She was shaking out black clothing for Dove to wear. "So did Lady Nuritin. I'm glad Nawat came back."

Aly, caught as she wrapped a clean sarong around her, blinked. "I know *I* am, but why are you?" she asked, startled.

"You seemed a little lost after he left," Boulaj explained. "Not lost as a spy, but lost as a woman. As if he'd taken a piece of you away that you needed. He has changed."

Aly tucked her fresh sarong, remembering that man's look, and those very male kisses. "I, um, hadn't noticed. Much." She began to wrap her sash. "How is Her Grace?"

"Her Grace is livid," Winnamine said coldly from the door. Aly turned to face her. Dove and Nuritin stood behind Winnamine, watching her. "Her Grace wants to know why the god sent you to this house, Aly."

Aly swallowed. You should have expected this, she told herself.

Winnamine continued, "Where is our great destiny that was promised by the god? Can it be the god *meant* my husband and son to die? That my little boy had to drown so the regents would take power and the throne would be strong? Was *that* it?" Her eyes were overbright, but no tears fell. Aly was certain that the duchess had no tears left.

Gently Aly said, "No, Your Grace." The sight of her pain made her stomach knot. "There is no greatness in what happened to Elsren, or to the duke. I'm afraid the gods don't care what makes their servants happy. They see only what they desire. We are tools to their ends."

"You speak knowledgeably about gods," the duchess said bitterly. "You know a great many, do you?"

"I have seen the god-touched in Tortall, Your Grace," Aly replied, thinking of her parents and Aunt Daine. "They did not look entirely happy. They looked—driven, at times. As the god drives me."

Winnamine turned, nearly colliding with Nuritin and Dove. They moved out of her way just in time and followed her back to her rooms.

"That's the problem with luarin," Boulaj observed softly. "They think gods have rules and follow them. They should dedicate their lives to the Trickster, as we do. They would not be comfortable, but they would not have this illusion that life is supposed to make sense, either."

"Thinking of trying for the priesthood?" Aly wanted to know. She blinked rapidly. She would not cry, not for the duchess, or the Balitang family, or herself. The time for tears was over.

"To be a raka under the luarin is to be a priest of the Trickster," replied Boulaj. "Will you help me fold this sheet?"

Aly and Boulaj straightened Dove's chambers, then Aly went back downstairs. She met Quedanga in the hall that led to her workroom. "I left the night's gleanings on your table, and I rolled up your pallet," the housekeeper said. "The city is quiet—there is little to pass on. I think we are all in shock."

"Thanks, Quedanga," Aly said. "It won't last, you know."

"I know." Quedanga's grin showed a wolfish number of teeth. "And then the raka's time will come."

And then the raka's time *may* come, Aly replied silently. Imajane and Rubinyan have opened the door for it, but it is not yet set in stone.

She went to her table and began to make her way through the heap of news Quedanga had collected from her own network within the city. Aly wasn't sure how long she worked before the runner Wayan rapped on the frame of the door. When Aly nodded, she came over to lean against Aly affectionately. She opened her hand to show a folded piece of paper, sealed with a blank circle of wax.

"A man at the servants' gate gave me this for you," she said. "He said it was from his master."

"Is he waiting for a reply?" Aly inquired. She inspected the note to see if the wax had been tampered with. She had taught her people ways to remove wax seals, but she also knew how to tell if somebody had been playing with one. This note had not been opened.

Wayan shook her head. "He gave me a silver gigit and left."

Aly kissed the girl's cheek. "Then you don't need a tip from me. Scamper."

Giggling, Wayan left. Aly got to her feet and locked her door before she heated a thin knife and slid the hot metal under the seal. The note popped open.

That boat came apart in the first big wave. They didn't need a storm that sank a number of other ships, too. Whatever it is that you intend to do, I am your man.—T.S.

Only one T.S. that she knew of would send her such a message: Taybur Sibigat. The regents—now the monarchs—had made a stupid mistake in killing the boy king he had loved. Aly was certain that Sibigat had been meant to drown, and just as sure that he had noticed that.

Aly ran her fingers over her darking necklace as she tucked the message back into her sash. She would keep this to herself for the present. The time would come soon when she would ask Taybur to make good on his promise. At this point, they both needed him to remain where he was and do his job. History was rife with palace revolts spearheaded by the very fighters who were there to protect the rulers.

They never should have killed his king, thought Aly as she returned to her work.

Two quick raps and an open slap on her door told Aly she was wanted in the meeting room. She locked her workroom and went in. Her pack, from Boulaj to Yoyox, waited there for her. They all watched her with bright attention, that look of hounds who had at last caught the scent.

Aly closed and locked the door, then settled in a chair. "We're in mourning," she stated.

"We would like our own way to mourn," said Jimarn. "Guide us, Duani."

"You've been doing this for a while," Aly pointed out. "Surely you don't need me."

Atisa rolled her eyes. "You're being aggravating."

"Sometimes aggravation is the irritant that forces a result," Aly replied quickly, then sighed. "My goodness. You young people are so impatient."

"We know *you,*" Olkey explained patiently as he popped a snow pea into his mouth. "Knowing you, we decided you probably have a list of things to tidy up in that clever head of yours. Lazy children that we are, we'd rather you did the thinking, and we handled the details."

Aly twiddled her thumbs, staring at the ceiling. This was what she had been working for since the fall before: the time when their minds and hers would work to reach the same place at the same time. I've done well with them, she told herself. It's time for them to see what they can do.

"I don't know how this can be, but the naval shipyards are a mess," she remarked at last. "All that wood and tar, all those ships being repaired. What if company comes to call?"

"That's a big one," said Guchol. "That will take work." Aly raised an eyebrow. Guchol responded to her unspoken question. "We can *do* it," she said hurriedly. "There are some knots to untie, though."

"Come to me if you need help," Aly said.

"I don't want to burn ships," Junai snapped. Like Boulaj, she had been closer to the family than the others, which meant that she had known Elsren. "I want them scared."

"People are very scared by bad things that seem to have come out of nowhere," Aly observed, her gaze back on the ceiling. "Things like a basket of rats in a closed bedroom. Or a dead rat." She looked at Junai and Boulaj. "A dead rat appears on the streets of the Windward District, where folk think they are so safe . . . it frightens them."

Boulaj and Junai exchanged bright-eyed glances. "We can do that," Boulaj said. "At night, once the house is abed."

"What about the regents?" demanded Lokak, dark eyes hard. "When do we strike *them*?"

"Giant-killing is tricky," Aly replied, knowing Lokak had spoken for the pack. "If you go for his eyes, he kills you by stepping on you. Instead you cut his legs from under him. With a weak army and navy, the new monarchs will struggle to protect themselves. Duke Nomru's estates have risen on his behalf against the Crown. His New Majesty needs more troops, but he doesn't have enough for Malubesang *and* the other rebellions. He'll have to scramble. As he does, he and his queen will be vulnerable. Our general can see that day come. He'll let us know when it is time. For now, we help him by doing what we have trained to do."

Most of them gathered around Guchol. As they whispered, Aly returned to her workroom. It would be foolish to suggest anything to them, when she didn't know the shipyard and they did. She *would* leave the list of Sevmire's spies in the Windward District out where Junai or Boulaj could find it. If they could pick her lock to see who had kept her in her workroom all night, they could pick it to find the list, too.

Back at her worktable, Aly set her darking necklace on its surface. "What happened while I was—occupied?" she asked them.

"Royal tax collector for all of Lombyn is dead," Trick announced. "Royal governor of Malubesang is missing."

Aly nodded. "Very good. Is that it?"

"For yesterday, with Rubinyan and Imajane," said Trick.

"What of my friend Sevmire?" Aly wanted to know.

"Bean say he draws up list of possible enemies," piped Secret. "Balitangs on it. Also Fonfalas. Also Engan."

"Also Obemaek," Trick added. "Sevmire asleep now."

"He drink too much wine," Secret explained. "He drools on desk."

"Bean ask, can he take list away from Sevmire?" Trick relayed.

Aly stretched. "Sevmire will just make another one."

"But he will wake up with dry quill and open ink bottle and no list," explained Secret. "Bean say, he will search everywhere, and then he will think someone took it."

"Bean say, Sevmire will twitch and drink and suspect his people," added Trick. "He will think they try to take his place with Rubinyan. Bean say—says," it corrected itself, to Aly's surprise, "that Sevmire worries all the time about everything. Bean says, if he worries more, he trusts people less."

So not only have I taught them to be spies, but it seems they're also learning to speak more like human beings, Aly mused. I wonder if this is a good thing or a bad one? "Tell Bean that by all means it should take the list if it can," she said. "And if Bean can think of more things to do to Sevmire *without* getting caught, it shouldn't worry about asking, just go ahead." I do it for my pack, she told herself. I can surely let the darkings off the leash as well.

After a moment Trick said, "Bean is very happy. He takes list into Sevmire's dung room."

"He will drop it in the dung pit," explained Secret.

Aly nodded. She loved their term for a privy. And a dung pit is where Sevmire himself belongs, she thought. Where they all belong.

She worked on papers until her belly reminded her that she had missed lunch. Out she went, in search of cold meat, bread, and some fruit. Once she had her meal in her hands, she went out into the garden to the Pavilion of Secrets. She wanted some time alone, to think in privacy of the wonderful things that had happened the night before. She knew moments like that were stolen from time, and she did not want to forget any of it. Leaning into a corner of the pavilion, she closed her eyes to remember, and dozed. When the food tumbled from her hands to the ground, the miniature kudarung swooped in for the feast.

She woke to their whickering and a shadow that loomed over her. Her senses identified a large body between her and escape. Aly was on her feet with two knives in her hands before she realized it was Ulasim.

He crouched to pet the clamoring kudarung around his legs and looked at Aly with appreciation. "That was very quick for someone who just woke up," he remarked. "It is as I always suspected—you sleep with one eyelid cracked."

"Only sometimes," Aly replied with a sheepish grin. She put her knives away. "If I slept that way all the time, I'd be predictable, wouldn't I?"

"Very true," Ulasim said, the corners of his eyes crinkling in his secret smile. "Nawat went out to see to his people. He said he would return for supper. Have you new information for me?"

Aly nodded and told him the news from Lombyn and Malubesang. "Nomru's people rising against the monarchs, that's bad."

Ulasim nodded. "Nomru is the chief landholder on Malubesang."

Aly bit her lip. She wanted him to look beyond the raka. "Call it a hunch, but I bet the Fonfala estates won't be far behind," she suggested, watching his face for his reaction. "They were friends, before the duke's escape. They're neighbors on Malubesang. The lands are held by Her Grace's brother. It stands to reason."

Ulasim's thin smile hooked to one side. "And the Nomrus and Fonfalas both belong to that pathetic luarin sewing circle," he added. "Why should I deal with them now, when they have been good for nothing before?"

"Because Dove is one of them," Aly informed him. "And—I think they are ripe to actually do something."

"I shall consider it," replied Ulasim. He hesitated, then grinned. "It is good to see you are not *completely* distracted by . . . other things."

Aly made a face at him. The sight of the black armband

he wore punctured her good mood. "I wish I could stay distracted. I need to get one of those."

"Don't feel guilty because you are alive," he counseled, wrapping an arm around her shoulders as they walked back to the house. "I feel guilty enough for twelve people."

"Because the choice of what to do about the Rittevon heirs was taken from your hands?" she asked.

The arm around her shoulders tightened, then relaxed. "That," he admitted.

"We can and will all feel guilty about that," Aly consoled him. "And we can share our feelings with our new rulers."

Nawat returned, as promised, in the late afternoon. Aly heard the bawling of amused crows and translated that they were laughing at him for changing shape and putting on uncomfortable clothes. When he emerged from the stable loft where he had changed, she was waiting for him. They kissed, and then she asked, "Would you talk to your friends for me?"

"So we are back to that," he commented, shaking his head. "My only value to you is as a crow."

"Nawat!" she cried, grabbing his shirt. "That's not true, I . . ." She saw the glitter in his deep-set eyes and gaped at him. "You're *teasing* me?"

He kissed her. Even when their lips parted, he kept his arm around her waist. "You look beautiful when you are shocked. It is sweet," he said, a man's grin on his face. "This is more fun than dragging Ochobu's clothes in the mud."

Aly pushed him away lightly, not hard enough to make him let go. "I swear she still expects you to do that," she said. "And I have some fun for your kindred, if you would like to explain it to them."

He tipped his head back and called in something far better than Aly's clumsy crow-speech. Immediately three of the birds came flapping down to land in the branches of a nearby tree.

"I was thinking," Aly began, "that winged messengers come and go from the palace all the time. It would be nice if your people could force them to lose their messages or even drive them to the ground."

One of the crows admitted, in caws and clicks, that this *could* be interesting.

It would require more skill than tormenting Stormwings, Nawat replied in the same language.

The crows flicked their wingtips and took off, already calling the news to the other crows within earshot.

"So they'll do it?" Aly wanted to know. "Or will they just talk about it?"

Nawat held her close. "It amuses them. They'll do it," he said with a grin.

That night the rebel leaders gathered in the meeting room to hear the news from all over the city and the realm. This time Nawat joined them to report what he'd been doing as a warrior and what news he had gathered from the crows. Once more Aly was awed by the change in him, from ill-at-ease bird in a human's body to confident young man. Ulasim was thanking him when suddenly their world went a bright, roaring white. The air boomed as if they sat inside a monstrous kettle drum. That vast roaring sound filled Aly's ears until she would have screamed to drown it out, except that she feared she was already screaming.

The roar stopped abruptly. Outside, thunder crashed directly overhead.

Kyprioth appeared next to Aly's chair. "This is where I leave you all," he told them as he looked apprehensively at the ceiling. "My brother and sister have returned." He kissed

Aly's cheek. "Good luck. Victories, remember!" He vanished.

They didn't even wait to discuss what they were doing: all of the leaders raced outside to look skyward. Pale white flames spread from the moon, which shone full at a time when it was only supposed to be a quarter full. Bright orange waves of light spread across the sky in sheer curtains. Lightning flashed everywhere and faded.

"And so the fun begins," murmured Ulasim. He clapped his hands together and rubbed them. "Come, my friends. Let's see how much trouble we can cause."

Aly and Nawat spent the night on a pallet in the Pavilion of Secrets, talking through much of it. When dawn came, they went outside to join the fighters for morning drill. Everyone watched for dawn when they weren't actually facing off against one another. When it came, they could see the gods were still locked in battle. The sun shed light and heat as it always did, but its rays were far longer than normal, dark orange pennants around the gold disk. White, fiery veils that had to represent the Goddess drifted in the morning sky, while everywhere the sparks that showed Kyprioth and the lesser tricksters winked in and out, points of color that never stayed the same hue for more than a moment.

Aly shivered and concentrated on her staff work. It was unnerving to see a sky so different from normal. She didn't like it at all, and she was nearly certain that the others felt the same. It was a relief to go into the laundry with Nawat and take a long bath together. Afterward he left on errands for Ulasim, while Aly went upstairs to see if Dove needed anything. Once again she found Boulaj gathering up Dove's washing. The bed was freshly made, the room aired out, the water basin dumped and cleansed. "What's this?" Aly demanded with a frown. Dove's night table had been straightened. So had the stack of books next to her bed.

Boulaj faced her, determination on her long face. "Aly, you're needed for other things," she said. "I trained to be a maid as well as bodyguard for Lady Sarai, and I like it."

"She's right." Dove emerged from the dressing room she had once shared with Sarai. "Things will heat up now that Imajane and Rubinyan rule us. You're needed to do what you do best. Boulaj and I manage nicely as mistress and maid."

Aly was a little hurt that they had come to an understanding without her. The moment she recognized the emotion, she thrust it away as meaningless. Dove and Boulaj were right, and that was that. What mattered was her own ability to pass information quickly to the rebel leaders. She needed to concentrate on that and on the kind of mischief that would drive their new rulers into a rage.

Boulaj yawned. Aly looked at her and raised an eyebrow. "Late night?" she asked wickedly.

"We got *some* sleep," Boulaj replied. "And the work itself was satisfying." She caught Dove's curious glance and said, "Spy stuff."

Aly held up a finger and went to the window. Something, some sound, made the shutters quiver under her palms. She opened them. In the distance she heard a roar of noise from the direction of the market districts and Downwind. She glanced above the nearby trees and saw smoke in the distance. Without a word to the other two she raced downstairs.

Outside the front door stood Nuritin, Fesgao, and a sweat-bathed Olkey. His eyes registered Aly's arrival as he told the other two, "It was the gods fighting that set them off, my lady, sir. Over in Downwind, folk were weeping in the street over the little boys' deaths. They've got three songs written about it already, and one of them calls it *murder*. And then there was last night, and they all waited for the dawn, and saw all the lights and colors. . . . They went mad. They're rioting in Downwind and the Honeypot, and the folks in Dockmarket are closing up. It's just a matter of time before they call for a lockdown of the city."

"Secure the gates," ordered Nuritin. "Put more guards on them."

Fesgao saluted her. "Very good, my lady," he said.

Here in the open Aly heard the distant calls of horns and the clang of alarm gongs. She went back inside to see what her people knew.

The regents kept the city under martial law for three days, not caring if people had enough food to eat. Those foolish enough to challenge the King's Watch found themselves hustled off to local jails. If the Watchmen got very annoyed, they sent the offender to Kanodang. The fires were put out; a number of rioters were hanged. There was nothing anyone in Balitang House could do but wait it out. People crept in and out using the tunnel system, but they had to be careful. Aly nearly lost Atisa and Ukali of her pack to the Watch, until the pair's recruits spotted them and swarmed their captors to help them to escape.

The flow of information into the house continued, courtesy of the darkings, the crows, and the mages of the Chain. Through them the household learned of riots all over the cities and towns of the Isles. It was too much for the people to take, coming all at once: word of the little king's drowning, the informal coronation of two new monarchs, and the gods' battle overhead. Most riots were put down savagely. Others burned themselves out by the end of the week.

Seven days after the boy king had drowned, memorial services for him and his three dead companions were held in the Black God's temples. The people of Rajmuat came to pay their respects in numb silence, mourning not just the children but the hundred-odd others who had drowned with them, their boats capsized or their homes crushed by falling trees. After the prayers to the god ended, the faithful carried flowers down to the harbor and tossed them into the brown, soupy water. In silence still, everyone returned to their homes.

At noon that day, the regents lifted martial law, though soldiers were everywhere. Roaming the city streets, Aly took note of the damage, most of it in the poor districts of the town. Trudging back to Balitang House, she wished the people would turn that wrath on the sources of their pain rather than on their own homes. We need more rumors about the monarchs and their plans for the kingdom, she told herself. The poor need to hate the monarchs as much as they fear the gods. This time it was the gods who drove them to riot, I think. Next time it must be Imajane and Rubinyan.

During that hot afternoon's rest time, a number of people visited the house. Aly joined those who had come to see her in the meeting room. There she found members of her pack who were not out in the city and a number of trusted recruits who had been approved by Ochobu or Ysul. Vitorcine Townsend was present as well. Aly had decided she would make a good addition to her spies.

Nearly everyone had written reports for Aly, information that had piled up while it had been so difficult for their contacts to get to them. They placed the reports in Aly's hands. A representative of the rebel spies in the palace was present, this being his normal free day. He too gave a sheaf of reports to Aly. She glimpsed at the topmost one. The first line read: *I. went into a rage over a scrap of paper.*

Aly nodded and yawned. That plan seemed to be unfolding nicely. Folding her hands on her belly, she looked at the packed room. "Has anyone anything special for me?"

The man from the palace raised a hand. "Lord Sevmire dismissed three of his secretaries this morning. He says he refuses to work with those he cannot trust. And there is an armed guard at the mages' house. Stormwings roost on the roof peak. No one is allowed to leave."

Aly whistled silently. "An interesting development."

Bacar, the footman from across the street, raised his hand. "The housekeeper at Murtebo House was found with her throat cut. There was a paper pinned to her clothes that read *Spy*."

A ragamuffin wearing only a loincloth spoke. "Up on Junoh Street, they found two like that, a footman and a maid. Dead the same way, both wearing *Spy* signs. That's what the folk who found them said."

"Any more?" Aly inquired. They all shook their heads. She nodded. "Very well. You already know the rumor that the storm that sank the boys' ship was not a natural one. And here's another thing—a source I trust says the boat went to pieces suspiciously fast. Add also that the mages who serve the Crown appear to be under house arrest. Those are interesting bits of news, aren't they?"

Her listeners nodded.

One of the Obeliten maids asked, "Duani, everyone knows the Crown mages have been known to meddle with weather before, though they know they can't control it." There was a chorus of yesses and calls of "She's right." Emboldened, the maid continued, "And isn't it strange how the one child saved belonged to a family known to be great friends of the regents?"

Aly thought that was more luck than attention to that particular boy's life. At the same time, she had not forgotten that the only heir to a family title on the *Rittevon* had been Elsren. Dunevon's other three companions had been younger sons unlikely to inherit the title. Their families could afford to lose them, a fact of which the new rulers had been aware.

Aly nodded. "Those also are good points to make with those you talk to," she told her people. "Ask your particular friends on the streets if Mithros and the Goddess are not angry because they are represented by monarchs with the blood of children on their hands. Especially the Goddess, as children are her care." She noticed their startled glances: they had not thought of this. "One more thing. The royal fortress at Galodon has lost at least half of its soldiers and sailors to bad food. The strongest fighting force in Rajmuat is now only the Rittevon Guard." She waved them out. "Be watchful, and take no unnecessary chances," she warned as they prepared to go. "We are going to make our new monarchs very unhappy, and for that I need you all."

A number of them touched the arm of Aly's chair on their way out. "Gunapi the Sunrose guard you, Duani," some whispered. Others remarked, "The luck turns our way."

Aly waved them off, not sure of what was going on, uncomfortable with the awe of her in their faces.

18

CONSPIRACIES

Supper was quiet. Aly ate at her worktable, reading over reports and making notes. She was sweating as she burned the reports she had condensed when Fesgao knocked on her door and looked in. "We're gathering," he told her.

Aly nodded and collected her papers that the other leaders might use. In the meeting room, she saw that everyone was present but Dove.

"Perhaps we should begin?" she asked Ulasim. "I think at the moment Dove wants to be with the duchess."

"No doubt you are right," Ulasim agreed. Quedanga closed the door as Ysul woke their security spells.

Aly had just finished passing out the reports when a knock sounded on the door.

"She came after all," Quedanga murmured, surprised, as she opened it.

In walked Dove, followed by Winnamine and Nuritin. The conspirators started to their feet, all but Ulasim, who measured the two haggard women with his eyes. In this room he was the raka general, who stood at attention for no one.

"I thought it was time," Dove told him, a mulish set to her mouth. "*Past* time."

"The rebellion—if that's what you are about, I want to be part of it," said Winnamine, her voice quavering. "I've known—my lord and I knew—there was something going on, but we let it go. We did not much care for our laws and hoped that a good fright would lead to better government. You were all so careful that we could not see how anyone might discover you. And . . . I want to help."

"As do I," said Nuritin, folding her arms over her chest. "There are others, just as appalled by this child murder as we are. Others who can bring arms and finances and fighters to this cause. In fact, one of them is at my house in town."

Ulasim looked from Dove to the two older women. "You see me in a delicate position."

"You're going to have to trust my judgment at some point," Dove reminded him. "I think that now would be a good time. I won't be a puppet, Ulasim. If I rule, I *rule*."

Ochobu poked Nawat with a finger. "Give the Lady Nuritin your chair," she ordered. To Nuritin she said, "Who is this guest?"

"I have sent Jesi for him. She knows to be careful," replied Nuritin, lowering herself into her chair.

Ulasim gestured for the duchess to take Aly's seat as Dove assumed her usual place.

"We just let them in?" demanded Quedanga. "And when members of their families die, what is to keep them from running to the monarchs with all they know?"

"Members of this family *have* died," snapped Nuritin. Quedanga looked down.

"If we were going to go to the Crown, we would have done it long before this," said Winnamine, her voice tired. "While we still could walk away from you with our own skins intact. No one will believe we were ignorant of your activities all this time."

"We'd like to avoid a bloodbath," Aly told Quedanga. "So unsightly, and it will give entirely the wrong impression to any greedy foreigners who are watching us. That means coming to terms with some luarin."

"You think the great lords will give up their lands and titles to the raka?" asked Nuritin.

"They will have to give up *some* of their lands," replied Fesgao. "But let us face it, many of the raka families who held those titles originally are long dead. Unless a luarin has been cruel to his or her people, or has supported the Rittevons and all they did, we must be ready to negotiate."

"How can we trust *your* allies?" demanded Quedanga. "Those luarin you plot with? Any of them could be an agent of the Crown simply waiting for you to pose a real threat before he reports you—or she reports you."

Aly cleared her throat. "With regard to the main members of their group, *I* can vouch for their loyalty," she said modestly. "I've had them watched." With normal spies she would have waited for them to observe their quarry for months before she could say with near-certainty that they were loyal to their fellow conspirators. With the darkings able to follow those who met in the Teak Sitting Room, she was certain that none of them was in communication with the Crown. Not only had her small allies watched the heads of those families, but they had inspected their desks, their wardrobes, and even their diaries.

"They could have hidden something from you," argued Quedanga.

Aly shook her head. "You must trust me."

"What good might you do us?" Ulasim asked the duchess and Lady Nuritin. "You are formidable allies in your own persons, but we need fighters, and weapons, and horses. We need ships, and crews. We need money."

"All of which we have," said the duchess.

"What if your warriors choose not to obey your wishes?" Chenaol asked, curious rather than hostile. "What if they report you to our new rulers?"

"Remind them of Topabaw's fate, and that of two commanders of the King's Watch," said Dove. "Remind them that Imajane and Rubinyan are less than loyal to those who serve them."

"You might also want to mention those dead persons who have appeared with the word *spy* on their clothing recently," Aly murmured. "And those who will be found tomorrow, and the day after. I think we'll have the Windward District fairly well cleared by then." She gazed at them under her lashes. Everyone had turned to look at her. She added, "After that, we'll start on the rest of Rajmuat. District by district, that's the best way to handle these things."

"And only think, she is on *our* side," Fesgao said at last.

Nuritin smiled frostily at Aly. "Or we need simply to remind such would-be traitors that the Crown will not believe they were innocent while their fellows conspired."

Aly grinned. "That will work, too."

Someone rapped on the door in the rebels' signal. Aly went to open it, to find Guchol outside. "Lady Nuritin's secretary, Jesi, is here with two priests of the Black God."

Aly looked back at Nuritin, who nodded regally. "Bring them," she ordered.

"Here?" asked Guchol, startled. "But . . ." One look at Aly's raised eyebrow changed her mind. "Right away, Duani." Guchol trotted off down the hall.

"Duani?" Aly heard Nuritin ask. Aly remained in the doorway, listening to the talk as she watched the hall.

"She is our spymaster," Ulasim explained. "Her people call her that."

"And how did a maid from Tortall become a spymaster?" demanded Nuritin, outraged.

Aly flapped her hand for silence as people came down the hall, Jesi in the lead. She nodded when she saw Aly, and stood aside to let the priests go ahead. When they walked into the room, Imgehai Qeshi put back her hood, revealing her pale luarin face lit by amber eyes. With a nod to Winnamine and Nuritin, she leaned against the wall as Aly locked the door. The other priest looked around the room from the shadow of his hood, then pushed it back. Aly recognized the eagle nose and short-cropped gray hair of Duke Nomru. Some of the raka murmured in surprise.

You sly thing! Aly thought, beaming at Nuritin with approval. All the realm's soldiers and spies are hunting for him, and you've had him tucked away in your vacant town house! She bowed to Nuritin to show her appreciation.

Winnamine and Dove stood to kiss the renegade duke on the cheek. Nomru's eyes swept the room, lingering on some faces, then settling on Ulasim. The raka met the duke's gaze with one of equal strength. Ulasim would make sure these people, normally luarin masters, would learn right away who was in charge here.

After a moment the duke asked Ulasim, "May I join you?" Ulasim nodded.

Secret stretched a long neck up from its place in Aly's bead necklace to whisper to her.

"Excuse me," Aly said. She went into her workroom for privacy, locking her door behind her. Taking off her necklace, she held it in her hands as it reshaped itself into her two darkings. "Say that again?"

They conferred. Finally Trick said, "Servants took food

to house of mages inside Gray Palace walls, took food to guards on watch. A man of Rittevon Lancers comes to say fresh guards come soon, but guards eat now because mess is closed. Guards eat. Dark come. Guards start to fall. They try to breathe, but breath not come. Their faces swell. They lay down, no breath coming. They stop trying to breathe."

"How do you know?" asked Aly, her mind ticking away. "All the guards? They're all dead?"

"Peony go to mage house, after Grosbeak run away," explained Trick. "Peony not want to go with Grosbeak, and we think darking should watch mage house. Darkings know mages. They stir things up. Peony stays at mage house."

"Oh, dear," Aly said ruefully. "I didn't even try to find Peony."

Trick and Secret shook their heads. "Darkings here to work. Aly can't do everything," Trick said. "We think of some."

"No, I do not remember everything. And I should have taken you more seriously," she admitted.

"Darkings learn," Trick said with pride. "Peony check all guards outside mage house. All dead. Peony go inside mage house. Five mages there and families. All dead."

Aly felt her bowels tighten. Were the new rulers *mad*? "What else?" she asked.

"Wagons coming to mage house," Secret continued. "Men packing up dead mages, dead guards. Rubinyan send them. He say, give the dead to meat-eating fish. He wants no one but trusted guards to know what happened to them."

Aly shuddered. It was a fate she would not wish on anyone. "What are the king and queen doing now?" Aly wanted to know. "Are they, I don't know, slumbering the sleep of those without cares?"

Both darkings shook their heads.

"Imajane screaming and throwing things at Rubinyan," replied Secret. "Bottles, brushes, mirrors. She says Rubinyan . . ." It cocked its head as if listening. "She says he is tumbling a lady?"

"Ah," Aly replied. "It means he is making love with a lady. If Imajane is throwing things, she believes he is in love with some other woman. Is she still throwing things?"

"She has nothing to throw unless she picks up chair," said Trick. "Uh-oh."

"She picked up chair," Secret explained.

Shaking her head, Aly returned to the meeting room, interrupting an intense discussion of numbers of household men-at-arms. She waited for a lull in the conversation, then announced, "I have some interesting news." She looked at Ulasim, who nodded for her to speak. "Someone—I suspect Imajane—has poisoned the court mages. Either a natural poison was used, one no one would notice in food, or they didn't look at their supper properly."

They stared at her. Nomru was the first to speak. "My dear young woman, not even Imajane is so mad. For that matter, how can you possibly know this?"

"She has means that we do not," Chenaol told him.

Aly knew Chenaol probably thought the god had told her. That was good enough for the time being.

"Imajane would certainly be that mad if she were getting rid of evidence," said Nuritin. "Everyone knows the storm that sank the *Rittevon* was no accident. The Rittevons have been wary of mages since that cabal that worked for Carthak was uncovered fifty years ago and since Oron's mage killed his father. And the Crown does have a reputation for doing away with their tools, once used."

"Rubinyan is no Rittevon," Imgehai Qeshi remarked.

"Rubinyan didn't know," Aly told her. "She ordered their

deaths without consulting him. He is quite upset."

"And so he should be!" Nomru said. "Letting a woman decide a matter of state . . ."

He looked down at the strong brown hand that gripped one of his arms, then up into Fesgao's eyes. "Perhaps we have not made ourselves entirely clear," Fesgao told him mildly. "We are not in this to put another luarin man on the throne. We are here to reclaim our homeland and set a proper queen of our own blood to rule."

Nomru took a breath, as if to argue, then halted, and released it. "I confess, we have done poorly with our charge," he admitted reluctantly. He looked at Dove. "Of course. The one who is twice royal." He fell silent, then nodded. "I am an old dog, but I believe I am still able to learn. Dovasary might do very well for us all."

The next day callers returned to visit the duchess. That night Duke Nomru moved secretly into Balitang House. One or two or three at a time the luarin conspirators, starting with the Fonfalas, learned they had new allies, people who were not prepared to allow them to take over. It took little to persuade most, particularly because Aly urged the duchess, Nuritin, and Dove to let them know what had happened to the court mages, their families, and the men set to guard them. The luarin conspirators could work it out for themselves that Imajane had done all this to cover up some dreadful act like regicide.

Two days after Matfrid Fonfala visited his grieving daughter, Trick told Aly that the Fonfala estates on Malubesang, next to the Nomru lands, had risen against the Crown. They were led not by servant and slave rebels, but by Winnamine's brothers. That same day word came from Malubesang of the discovery of the royal governor's body, hanging from the cliffs that overlooked Fajurat Bay.

When a twentieth Crown spy turned up dead, courtesy of Boulaj and Junai working from Aly's lists, Rubinyan and Imajane instituted a twilight curfew throughout Rajmuat. Even with the curfew, neither spies nor the night patrolmen themselves were safe from the rebels. From her sources Aly cheerfully reported growing unease in the warehouses commandeered for use as barracks and in the barracks proper for the army. The men complained that death in battle was expected; simply disappearing from the street was not.

Two nights after the curfew began, the chief conspirators, including Duke Nomru, the priestess Imgehai Qeshi, Winnamine, and Nuritin, met outside at Aly and Nawat's suggestion. Certainly it was stifling indoors; the garden was cooler by far. Urged by Nawat, the miniature kudarung came out to meet the four luarin, who were charmed and awed. No kudarung had come voluntarily to Rajmuat in over two centuries. Aly thought better of the stern Nomru when she saw how gently he handled a small piebald foal that tried to eat the trim on his tunic.

The curfew gongs were ringing when the southeast horizon flared orange. Aly pointed it out to her companions as a big explosion thudded in their ears. Nomru started to his feet, the ladies and then the raka beside him. Over the southeastern wall of the house the orange glow expanded. Where the white light-veils and the multicolored sparks shifted over the sky, the orange glow kept its place on the horizon. Soon they heard the now-familiar clang of the city's alarm bells.

Nomru frowned. "That looks like it comes from the naval shipyards," he said.

Aly sighed happily. "It does. My little ones do such wonderful work."

"Their Majesties will start executing people over deeds like this," Nomru warned.

"They would do it sooner or later in any case," replied Ulasim. "They must, to show they have control. They will find it is not so easy to kill rebels here. And while they search for people to execute, they will force those who did not want to choose between them and the rebels to pick a side."

Aly pointed upward. The multicolored points of light scattered across the sky blazed more strongly than ever. "So nice to know our work is appreciated," she remarked.

The next morning, when she went to her workroom, her pack was already there, freshly washed and wearing clothes that did not smell of blazebalm.

"Very good work last night, my lambs," she told them as she flung herself into her chair and laced her fingers on her stomach. "Very inspiring. What is left?"

Jimarn unfurled a small, deadly smile. "Very little. No wonder it's a death sentence for a raka to possess blazebalm. It's very useful stuff."

"What next, Duani?" Olkey wanted to know. "We have ideas for our recruits, of course, but do you have anything special in mind?"

Aly tugged an earlobe. She would have loved to get to work inside the palace, but the raka there were too easily trapped. For the time being she named four people in the city as targets. All were the prince's cronies, placed in high offices when he became regent. It was even more galling that the lone raka among them was in charge of the Crown prisons on Gempang and Kypriang, where the prisoners were also mostly raka. If he felt anything for them, he had yet to show it.

"You might advise these four that it's a mistake to

support the current government," she said. "They should be allowed to live. But they should remember they cannot hide from us. Indulge your imaginations. Be mindful of their children. Many times children grow up to make different choices than did their parents. Jimarn, you might want to visit the Crown warehouses on Josefa Street. They are packed with grain. Wouldn't it be nice to hide it someplace so we can share it with those in need this winter? Do as you like with the empty warehouses."

"Duani, remind me to stay on your good side," Hiraos commented, shaking his head. "You really know how to hold a grudge."

"*And* she makes it painful," Guchol remarked soberly.

Aly waved goodbye and watched them go. Their tasks would keep them occupied for a few days. By then she ought to have some ideas for the palace in general, and the Gray Palace in particular. The darkings had already mentioned that their noisemaking and item-throwing had increased the tension of all who lived there.

As soon as the pack was gone, Trick told Aly that Imajane was sending Lady Edunata home to her family covered in bruises. The morning after Edunata left, Imajane woke to find that two more ladies-in-waiting had left her service in the night. They did not want to risk Imajane's jealousy.

That same day Rubinyan brought Varwick Jimajen, his oldest son by his first marriage, to court from his home estates. Aly passed on to the conspirators that Rubinyan confided to Varwick his fear that he could not control his queen. It worried him that she had ordered the deaths of the mages without consulting him. He rightly asked himself what other orders she might give.

Nawat expanded the work of the crows. They had already put a stop to the Crown's attempts to communicate with the outer Isles by winged messenger. The only reliable ways to get news or give instructions were through messengers on the ground or by mage. Since the queen trusted what her new mages told her no more than she had the old mages, the newcomers were a jumpy crew. Nawat then made sure that it was not safe for a noble or soldier on the open palace grounds. When Imajane tried to do a day's hunting just outside the walls, Nawat and his friends mobbed the falcons, driving the royal party back to the Gray Palace.

Seventeen days after Dunevon's death, Kioka raced into Aly's workroom. "I just came from the docks!" she announced, panting. "You won't believe it! They posted it on the docks while their messengers delivered the letters to the palace. They're calling their ambassadors home!"

Aly drummed her fingers until Kioka caught her breath. "I would share your joy more quickly if I understood what to be joyful about," she said gently.

"I'm sorry, Duani. It's the Tortallans, and the Carthakis. They say their mages discovered the storm that sank King Dunevon's ship was magical, and they traced the magic back to the Gray Palace. They say they will not trade with king-slayers! Every Tortallan and Carthaki ship in port is weighing anchor, even if they don't have cargo. Even if they're half unloaded! Olkey says the Tyrans are debating cutting their trade with the Isles, though he isn't sure they'll do it. Tyrans are less choosy about where they get money."

Aly stopped drumming her fingers. She hadn't expected this. Tortall and Carthak had just put the Isles under a trading ban until the king's murderers were caught. With a bad harvest and national unrest draining the royal treasury, this was a heavy blow. How would the monarchs cope? They would have to find someone to take the blame. A pity that Imajane had been so quick to kill the mages, but Aly supposed the princess had decided she couldn't be certain that the mages would keep quiet about who had issued their orders.

Would the Crown try to hold the Tortallan and Carthaki ambassadors here in Rajmuat? Aly hoped so, but surely Rubinyan and Imajane wouldn't be that stupid. If they did try, they could expect the Tortallan and Carthaki navies within the week.

"It's good, right?" Kioka asked, brushing her hair back from her eyes.

Aly sighed. "Think how distressed Their Majesties must be," she said. "And shouldn't the people know our two richest, most powerful neighbors have stopped trading with us?"

"Got it," said Kioka. She raced from the room, squeezing past Nawat.

Aly raised her eyebrows. "You left me to sleep the rest of the night alone," she said.

Nawat grinned. "I was helping to steal soldiers who couldn't keep up."

"What do you do with them?" she asked, curious. "I haven't heard of bodies being found."

"Nor will you," Nawat informed her, sitting on a corner of the worktable. "They were still alive when we gave them to my warriors at the edge of the jungle." He picked up Aly's hand and laced his fingers with hers. "My warriors will be able to say *they* last saw the missing soldiers alive, when the troops went on a visit to the jungle."

Aly walked her free fingers over their entwined hands. "But why would Crown soldiers visit the jungle?"

"They didn't think they would at first," Nawat admitted. "So my warriors show them the beauties of the deep jungle. They take away all the things the soldiers have of the civilized world, such as clothes and weapons and armor, so the soldiers will appreciate the jungle with their entire bodies.

But my warriors have seen jungle before, so they get bored and leave. The soldiers stay longer."

"Like the tax collectors," Aly whispered, awed by the beauty of what he described. "Take away all they have and leave them to survive the jungle. If you're questioned under truthspell, you can say they were alive when you left them. And the only way they could survive naked out there . . ." Nawat was shaking his head. Aly nodded. "I take it you don't leave them near any trails."

"They are there to appreciate the jungle that has been untouched by humans," Nawat told her, a teacher to a student who did not quite understand.

Aly sighed. "I am limp with envy," she told him. "Simply limp."

Nawat raised the hand still entwined with his and kissed it. "I knew you would be." He got to his feet.

"You're leaving?" Aly asked, dismayed.

Nawat bent down and kissed her thoroughly enough to make her limp again. "I am bored with nobles and soldiers who hide," he explained. "The flock that watches the palace will keep them busy. I thought the city flock and I could play for a time. But I will come back." He cupped her cheek in one hand. "I promised myself that I would not let any day go here when I did not see you once, and not just for kisses." He tweaked her earlobe and left her there among her reports.

She propped her chin on her hands. There was a great deal to be said for having a former crow as a lover, she decided. They kissed as if they meant it to last. They kissed as if you were the only one they had ever kissed or would ever want to kiss. And this one . . . there were no two ways about it. He was a man.

"I won't be able to push him around anymore," she observed aloud.

"You have work," Trick reminded her. "Do not let kissing distract you."

"I don't, not for more than a moment or two," Aly replied. She glanced at the darkings. "You know, my mother always told me you had to seize the bright moments, because you never know when they will come again." She smiled dreamily. "The older I get, the smarter she seems."

"Rubinyan visits Sevmire," Trick told her. "Sevmire is drunk."

Aly glanced out her window. "It's barely noon."

"Rubinyan is very unhappy," Trick added. "Rubinyan knocked Sevmire down."

"Well, the man's drunk when he's supposed to be on duty," Aly remarked. She looked at them, sitting up a little straighter. "I suppose you could say the same of me."

"You are happy," Secret told her. "That is nice. You don't have many nice times."

Aly smiled. "I believe that is changing. Is Rubinyan going to get rid of Sevmire?" She wasn't sure she wanted that, not now, when Sevmire was doing such a terrible job.

"Sevmire promise not to drink," Trick told her. It straightened, then quivered. In a flash it joined with Secret to become a two-stranded necklace again. Aly was putting them on when Boulaj poked her head into the workroom.

"Our ladies have received an invitation," she told Aly. "The new queen invites us to a late breakfast tomorrow morning. She wishes to consult with 'certain valued friends' about the coronation ceremonies."

"Oh, splendid," replied Aly, reaching for reports. "Has she said how they will pay for those ceremonies?"

"Not in the invitation," Boulaj said with a shrug. "Is the treasury really so low?"

Aly nodded. "They have to keep the armies and navy

happy, which is to say, paid. There's not much left over. They're discussing an invitation to the merchants and the nobles to contribute to the ceremonies as a proof of loyalty. I'm sure everyone will be delighted to hear they must beggar themselves to confirm the new king and queen."

"No doubt," Boulaj replied. "Anyway, Lady Dove asks if you will come with us."

"I wouldn't miss it for the world," Aly assured Boulaj.

The conspirators, particularly the luarin ones, were not as eager as Aly. That afternoon, they protested when the duchess told them about the invitation.

"I don't like it," Lehart Obemaek declared. "Bringing so many of our ladies together at the palace—what if they mean to hold them, to ensure the lords' obedience? Because it's not just you and Nuritin and Dovasary, Winna. My wife and daughter have been invited."

"As have Rosamma and I," said Countess Tomang.

"Lehart, I have never thought you overburdened with sense." Baron Engan looked dry and frail, but he did not sound it. "But even you must perceive that they dare not offend us—and there *are* far more of us in the outlying estates, who won't be meeting with Imajane. They need us if they mean to survive."

"If you please, my lord Obemaek," Aly said politely. "My palace sources say that His Majesty—"

"Faugh!" interrupted Nuritin.

Aly bowed to her. "His Majesty keeps Her Majesty under constant watch. *She* is the uncertain element. He has told his people they must bring her orders to him. He also understands that his power base is shaky. For the present he grips the reins. My sources tell me nothing sinister is planned for tomorrow morning."

"I find it hard to have faith in intelligence garnered by

a young woman, and a foreigner at that," Genore Tomang announced with a sniff. Matters between her and the Balitangs were stiff, Sarai's insult still raw, but the Tomangs were still willing members of the conspiracy. They had been heavily taxed for the third year in a row as one of the wealthiest families in the Isles.

"I could make myself up as a raka man, if that will appease you, my lady," Aly offered. "I think it would be a waste of my time, but I live to serve in any small way that I can."

Even Duke Nomru's mouth twitched at that. "Stop it, Genore," he told the countess. "Have you forgotten this young foreigner brought about the fall of Topabaw?"

"So we are told," said the countess.

"So we *know,*" Ulasim said flatly.

"So *I* know," Dove added, soft-voiced.

Her comment brought silence. Many of the luarin conspirators still were not quite sure what to do about their future queen, though Nomru, Engan, and Qeshi addressed her as an equal, as did Winnamine and Nuritin.

Aly sat back as Quedanga began to pass on what her people had gathered. Aly did not want to tell the luarin conspirators that Imajane and Rubinyan had taken to walking in the gardens at night, out of earshot of her darkings and well away from any of the raka spies. It could be something as basic as Rubinyan wanting to calm his excitable wife and to reinforce their affection after the problem of Lady Edunata. They could also be deliberately discussing plans someplace where it would be hard for a spy to hide, and where it would mean death for the mage who put a listening spell there. Aly could not be sure.

In any case, Aly wanted their party to be ready for everything. The breakfast with Imajane was to be held in the Jade Pavilion. Breaking out of the main palace enclosure in an emergency would be easy enough. Some of Fesgao's people would enter the grounds in the morning, driving wagons of foodstuffs through the Gate of Carts. Dorilize and Pembery would remain at home, allowing warriors Jimarn and Junai to play at being ladies' maids. They had the crows to interfere if the rulers planned treachery. And Fesgao would come, disguised as a footman, bearing a small gift for the new queen from the Balitangs. He knew where the Haiming Tunnel was, the secret exit from the palace that had allowed Dove's forebears to escape with their lives. The rebels hoped those precautions would be enough to keep Dove safe.

The luarin conspirators left at last. Aly looked for signs of the darkings she had placed with them but found none. She didn't expect to. Some days they journeyed with their people to Balitang House, but they also spent much of the time exploring their new homes and reporting to Trick. They had understood when Aly told them to watch for spies in the conspirators' household as well as traitors among the nobles.

Dove waited in Aly's workroom, glancing at her maps. "I feel so useless," Dove complained. "It seems like all anyone will let me do is look promising. All this important work is being done, and you won't even let me visit Dockmarket anymore."

"I know, and I am sorry, but the risk is too great," Aly told her. "It's a bad idea to remind Their New Majesties how popular you are, particularly since they can no longer use a marriage to Dunevon as a leash on you. Though if anything happens to Imajane, Rubinyan might come to your door with a gift of flowers."

Dove grimaced. "I'd as soon sleep with a ribbon snake," she told Aly. "Not that I think I'll be offered the marriage. We're nearly ready to move, aren't we?"

"Nearly, yes. As ready as anyone can be in a fix like this,"

Aly said. "The night before the day of the solar eclipse. They might expect something the day of the eclipse, and certainly they expect trouble on their coronation day."

"And while everyone else does something real, *I* get to be protected," said Dove bitterly.

Aly put an arm around Dove's shoulders. "If all goes well, you'll have the hardest task," she said quietly. "Bringing a country together. Making sure your reign isn't marked by bloodletting, which should be an agreeable change around here. It's a scary task, but you have good people to advise you—Her Grace, Lady Nuritin, Ulasim, Fesgao, Ochobu—"

Dove looked up at her. "Will I have you?"

Aly blinked at her. You should have expected this, her brain clamored, seeking a quick answer. You should have had your story all prepared. Lie, idiot, lie! Tell her you'll be there! You've lied millions of times, so do it now!

Dove pulled away from Aly's arm. "That's what I thought," she said, and left the room.

Aly started to follow, and stopped. Catching up to Dove would only work if she were ready to lie, and she wasn't. She couldn't. Not about this. If she survived, and she wasn't entirely certain that she would, she had to go home. The daughter of Tortall's spymaster had no business so close to the Kyprin throne.

By late afternoon people were bringing news of the crows' latest rampage through the skies over Rajmuat. Aly listened to the reports with admiration and envy. Nawat and his friends had sprinkled Crown officials and soldiers with urine and dung. They attacked soldiers at the checkpoints as the men inspected carts and saddlebags, using their claws and beaks and, as a last insult, more dung. Any shop that carried the emblem of supplier to the Crown—something that was no longer a guarantee of more business—soon had a doorstep piled with crow dung, and no customers. The crows drove them away.

At supper she was picking at her food, thinking about information, when a very warm presence thumped onto the bench next to her. A man's hard thigh pressed hers. She looked up into Nawat's eyes.

"You forgot about me," he told her, shaking his head. "My heart is broken forevermore."

Startled, Aly pulled back, then recognized the twinkle in his deep-set eyes. "You're *teasing* me again," she said, outraged. "And I could hardly forget you, with all the ruckus you stirred up today."

"You are no longer the one who does all the tormenting," Nawat informed her, reaching across her for a bowl of rice. She forgot what she was about to say in the brush of his arm against her breasts. Warmth flooded her veins. Nawat looked into her face and smiled as he slowly brought the rice bowl over to his plate. "I have learned to torment, too."

You have indeed, she thought, tearing a piece of bread in half.

Others came to sit with them, applauding the latest behavior of the crows. Aly listened with a smile, shaking her head, without forgetting Nawat's warmth against her side.

She excused herself, her meal half-eaten, and clambered out from between Nawat and Junai. Nawat smiled up at her and continued his conversation with Chenaol.

Aly met with some of her spies and their recruits after supper, taking in the day's reports. The wider they spread their net, the more information she had to sift for nuggets of real worth. These nuggets were what she wrote out and handed to the other rebels in the house. Once the humans were gone, Trick and Secret passed on their most recent gleanings from the palace and the homes of the luarin conspirators.

This is why Da spends his days at a desk, Aly told herself as she worked. *It's why he jumps at the chance to meet with an agent. Because sooner or later all you can do is review information and pass it on to those who will use it.*

At least when I'm done for the day, I have Nawat, she thought. Suddenly the night ahead looked much brighter.

19

RITTEVON SQUARE

When they rose before dawn to train with the warriors, Nawat made sure to kiss Aly thoroughly once more before they left the Pavilion of Secrets. They had both agreed not to show too much affection for one another before their fellow conspirators. Neither wished to be accused of not paying attention, Nawat because he had discovered he enjoyed command over his human warriors as much as that over the crows, and Aly because so much depended on the rebels seeing her as reliable. "Another day," Nawat said, looking up at the pearl gray sky. The moon was veiled by the colorlessness of the sky. Only the Trickster sparks continued to show, winking on and off, never the same color or in the same position twice. Kyprioth continued to hold his own.

"My kin will be in the air to watch over you today," Nawat said as they walked toward the stable yard where everyone practiced. "And my warriors and I will be near, at the edge of the jungle."

Aly smiled up at him. "I love you," she replied. "If you get yourself killed, I will be very unhappy with you."

Nawat grinned. "I have loved you since I became a man, or even before that," he reminded her. "You must try to stay out of trouble, too."

Between breakfast and the summons to court, the house was bustling. Aly put on fresh clothes in the dressing room off Dove's chambers. Boulaj added the finishing touches on Dove's appearance as Aly emerged with her hair combed and tucked under a sober headcloth. Boulaj winked at her over Dove's head.

"Why do you always wear that same old bead necklace?" Dove wanted to know. "I have dozens that are prettier that I never wear."

Aly heard a muffled squeak from the double bead on her right shoulder. She stroked the darkings quiet with a smile. "They have sentimental value for me, my lady," she explained. "If you'll excuse me . . ."

She trotted downstairs, ignoring the outraged squeaks from her necklace.

Outside she reviewed the guard chosen to escort the ladies. Fesgao had assembled twenty men-at-arms in livery. Half were armed with spears and short swords, half with swords and the shield-stick called a tonfa, a good weapon for trapping an enemy's blade by edge or point. Some members of Aly's pack and their recruits lounged near the gate. They would range out along the streets, watching for potential trouble as the Balitang ladies rode. The soldiers of the King's Watch would be vexed at so heavy a guard for an ordinary palace ride, but there had been unrest in the city, and the Balitangs were not about to tell them that they distrusted Crown troops more than Downwind rioters.

As their party moved out, Aly walked on the side of Dove's horse closer to the double ring of guards. Boulaj walked on the inside. Fesgao, in a footman's livery, walked just ahead of Nuritin's and Winnamine's mounts, the small wooden box that held their gift for Imajane under one arm. He stood just behind the corporal who was supposedly in command of the men-at-arms. When he gave the signal, their company moved out, the wagon with the ladies' court dresses bringing up the rear.

It was still early enough for traffic to be light. They soon joined other ladies on their way to the palace. Aly watched the crowds. It made her uneasy to see this many people outside, all paying attention to the noblewomen as they negotiated their way past the soldiers' checkpoints along Rittevon's Lance. They were everywhere, in the windows and on the roofs that gave them a view of the ladies. Of Dove.

Go away! Aly thought. Go home, go to work! Stop drawing attention to us!

Shrieks sounded overhead. The crows had come to play with the Stormwings. They arrived in hordes, scattering the immortals as they darted among them. The Stormwings shot toward the relative safety of the distant palace, the crows in pursuit.

When they reached the green belt outside the palace, Aly gave an internal sigh of relief. She'd never thought she'd be so happy to see those streams full of meat-eating fish. Crossing a bridge, she looked off to the side, but the water was too murky to allow her a view of them. Was it possible they were still full from the feast of dead mages, families, and guards? Or had the poison that killed the humans also killed the fish? She didn't have time to see for certain as their party moved on.

As before, their men-at-arms parted from them inside the Gate of Victory while the ladies and their maids rode to the Robing Pavilion to change. When Aly bent to place the wooden box with their riding dresses against a wall, her darking necklace dropped from her neck onto its lid. Trick and Secret nodded to Aly, then dripped into the shadow. They were off to make contact with the other palace darkings.

Once the ladies set forth for the Jade Pavilion, Aly followed at a distance like any disinterested servant on a stroll, careful to step off the garden paths when other noblewomen passed. Aly turned at the edge of the Lily Water and wandered into the shelter of a familiar-looking willow. As she had suspected, Taybur Sibigat sat on the hidden bench. He put his finger to his lips for silence, then rose and walked off down a lesser path, back into the gardens. Aly waited for a party of ladies to go by, then followed him.

He led her to a semicircle of hedges that framed another bench, affording a view of the water and some black swans as they glided by. There were spells here, but not for listening. They would damp the sounds made around the bench, luarin version of the spells that guarded Balitang House from eavesdroppers.

"It's safe to speak here," he told her, digging his hands into his breeches pockets as his mail jingled. "Not that I've much to say. I have to swear my allegiance in blood on the day they are officially crowned, you know. All of the Guard must. Those who wish to stay."

Aly looked up at him. "You're certain the ship was tampered with?"

He nodded. "Plenty of good ships went down in that storm, but only after the winds and waves knocked them about for a while. The crew didn't even have time to furl all the sails before the *Rittevon* crumpled like rice paper."

"I'm sorry," Aly told him. Her eyes stung as she remembered Elsren's glee as he had marched aboard that vessel. "I truly am."

"Thanks," Taybur said. "Have a care for your young

lady—her popularity is noticed." He hesitated, then added, "I suppose the next time I see you, we'll be at the gate to the Gray Palace." With a nod, he strode off down the path.

He'd given Aly a new concern. If Imajane and Rubinyan had decided to do something about Dove's popularity, they would be idiots to try it inside the palace, where no one would believe they were blameless. After the jailbreak at Kanodang, they would be reluctant to imprison another popular luarin. Aly would lay odds their attack would come on the street.

Taybur had also let Aly know the part he was ready to play once things came to a fight. I'll keep him to myself, just in case he changes his mind, she decided. No one *needs* to know what he'll do, if he chooses to.

She returned to the Robing Pavilion to sit with Vereyu. They "talked" about hidden stores of drugs and weapons by writing on a slate and passing it to each other. There was no corner safe from eavesdroppers in the Robing Pavilion. When their conversation was over and they were picking through a plate of dumplings, Fesgao—still dressed as a footman—wandered into the ladies' side of the pavilion. "Pretty Aly, will you walk with me?" he asked, offering his arm.

"You want to watch this one," Vereyu warned Aly. "He's got a wife who's a trapper on Imahyn."

Aly fluttered her lashes at Fesgao, the image of an empty-headed flirt. To Vereyu she said, "It's only a *walk*. What could happen on a walk?"

Fesgao leered and led her down the Golden Road to the Pavilion of Delightful Pleasures. "This was the old Haiming palace," he murmured, for all intents looking like a man who whispered secrets in his sweetheart's ear. Aly giggled as she clung to his arm. "They tore down the New Palace to build their gray stone monster," Fesgao continued, "but the old one was still used for celebrations and guests. And the old escape tunnel is still here, kept up by generations of raka." Slowly they wandered around the side of the Pavilion of Delightful Pleasures, Aly stopping to smell a flower as a squad of the Rittevon Guard marched by on the Golden Road. Once the soldiers had passed, Fesgao led her around the pavilion's side, between the bubbling stream and its veranda. Marmosets cheeped to each other in warning from overhead, while brightly colored finches peered at them from the trees. Aly looked up to see a dart of light from a Stormwing's feathers, then the shifting white veil in the sky that marked the Great Goddess's war with Kyprioth.

When they could see the pond that lay behind the pavilion, Fesgao drew Aly across a bridge over the stream, to a small building set behind a screen of trees. Aly flinched and put up a hand to shield her eyes. Raka magic might be hidden to luarin mages, but not to anyone with the Sight. The building and the ground at its rear wall blazed with it. "You people are lucky no one with the Sight came near this place," she informed Fesgao, blinking to twist her vision so she would See the magic, yet not be blinded.

"Raka prefer not to trust in luck," the man replied. "This place is watched, and not by mages. Had you crossed that bridge with anyone but me, or walked down the other side of the building, you would soon find polite gardeners to turn you back. If you are stubborn, they can be less polite." He knelt and ran his hands through the grass behind the building. He stopped at what looked like a trailing vine and yanked hard. The grass and its bed, several inches of earth, lifted as if it were hung on oiled hinges. Fesgao raised it only a foot, to show Aly a wooden door below. At its center was a ring of steel to use as a grip.

"Now you know," Fesgao said. "That makes five of us:

you, me, Ochobu, Ulasim, and Chenaol."

"I don't know where it opens out," Aly reminded him. "Beyond both walls, I assume, but not where. Why haven't the raka used this way to attack the luarin from inside?"

Fesgao raised his brows at her as he lowered the grass mat again. "Because we were told to wait for the one who is twice royal," he told her. "Because there were too many luarin, and we were too beaten. And because the kings before Oron liked mages and kept them around. Then Oron talked a mage into killing old King Hanoren so Oron might take the throne. No one of the royal family has trusted mages since. Besides, we needed the god."

"All right," Aly said, holding up her hands in surrender. "You had plenty of reasons." I still would have tried it, she thought as they walked back toward the Golden Road, once again arm in arm.

"You will be shown how to enter soon," Fesgao murmured. "When it is time."

Aly spent the rest of the morning with the maids, waiting for her ladies to return. The main thing she learned from the servants was that they were too frightened to talk of anything important. As they spoke of the coming eclipse and coronation, their voices sounded false to Aly, as if they forced themselves to sound eager for the holiday. They chatted of weather, dress, and hairstyles, and of places where they found the best bargains.

I'll be happy when Dove's on the throne and I can go home, she thought as a maid came to say the ladies were returning. I'm tired of living with fear and fearful people. Of course, first we have to get Dove *on* the throne. Opening the box of riding dresses, she found her darking necklace waiting for her. Carefully she slid it over her head.

"Enjoy yourselves?" she murmured.

"Rubinyan says he must take soldiers from Imahyn and Ikang and some from Gempang to fight rebels on Malubesang," Trick whispered by her ear. "He says they must retake Imahyn later. He says he may have to use soldiers from Lombyn to defend north Kypriang. Imajane not know Rittevon estates on north Kypriang all in revolt."

Aly whistled softly as Jimarn, Boulaj, and Junai took the riding dresses from the box. Having lived among warriors, Aly knew it was a sign of weakness to give an enemy one position in order to hold another. Rubinyan might as well have shouted that his armies were spread too thin.

She shared that news with Fesgao as the Balitang ladies dressed. She also passed on to him, Boulaj, Junai, and Jimarn the word that Dove's popularity no longer sat well with the Crown, though she didn't name her source. Fesgao went to tell their men-at-arms they were leaving, and to pass on the order to watch for trouble on the way home. The wagon would follow outside the ring of men-at-arms this time, so that they made a tighter double circle around the women.

Down Rittevon's Lance they went, the servants on foot beside their mistresses. Boulaj kept her hands tucked into her sash: she wore cestuses, leather gloves with iron plates sewn across the knuckles. She was adept with the cestuses and could even deflect sword blows with them. Junai carried her spear, a weapon that, when the grip was twisted, presented a blade at each end. Jimarn and Aly had their knives within quick reach.

Though their ladies must have noticed the warlike preparations—Fesgao had produced his own longsword from the wagon—they said nothing. Instead they let their maids walk between their mounts and the two rings of guards, and drew their horses closer together. They could not ride three abreast on Rittevon's Lance, so Nuritin changed places with

Dove, allowing her to ride beside her mother, closer to more men-at-arms.

As they left the green belt for the city, Aly noticed immediately that there were more civilians outside. There were also more soldiers, placed in lines along the pavement as well as at the checkpoints. The streets were packed, as were the buildings on either side of their route.

Something red fluttered in the air above them. Aly flinched, but it was a flower, tossed from someone's window. Another flower dropped on them, followed by more. Soon they were passing through a rain of blossoms.

Aly ground her teeth. Civilians. If the new monarchs had wanted proof that someone in the Balitang family drew the crowds, they had it. They could, if they chose, lock up the entire household on suspicion of rebellion with nothing more than this.

They neared the intersection and checkpoint at Rittevon Square. The great bronze statue of the first Rittevon king was now covered with open shackle insignia, each showing gold through his weathered bronze skin and clothes. As they entered the square, the Balitangs moved out of the range of the flower throwers. It was then that Aly, her head swiveling, saw a crossbow poke through a third-floor window into the open, crowded square.

"Down!" she yelled, shoving Dove toward Winnamine, out of range. The bolt struck a man-at-arms in the shoulder. His knees buckled; another man kept him on his feet.

Winnamine stood in her stirrups. Dove was already off her horse, standing on the ground, shielded by the two mounts. "Soldiers of the Crown," the duchess cried in a voice any field general might envy, "protect us!"

The men of the King's Watch did not move from their positions. Fesgao dragged Winnamine from the saddle and beckoned for Nuritin to dismount. On foot, they were less visible targets.

Aly put a foot in the stirrup of Dove's horse, gripped the saddlehorn, and pulled herself up, balancing for a look over the men-at-arms' heads. The line of soldiers parted in two places, one on either side of their group. Men in rough laborers' clothing armed with knives or short swords darted through. Aly yelled, "There! And there!"

The men-at-arms faced the invaders, weapons up. Aly glanced at the squad of the King's Watch at the checkpoint. They lazed at the barricades, no expression on their faces. They already knew they were not to interfere.

Aly didn't see the first rock fly. She did see it strike a soldier's helmet, just as she glimpsed the dent it left before the soldier went down.

"They're killing her!" someone screamed. "They're killing our hope!"

Suddenly the men of the Watch were the targets of a rain of flowerpots, pans, stones, and chamberpots both empty and full. People held back by the soldiers shrieked and surged forward, clawing at their old oppressors. The soldiers fought for their lives. They killed and killed, but they could not kill everyone. Thrusting his sword into one civilian, a soldier would be swarmed by five more armed with belt knives, stones, or fingernails. The crowd boiled through the gaps in the lines as soldiers began to fall.

The assassins pushed past the men-at-arms, where they collided with Junai, Jimarn, and Boulaj. Jimarn leaped onto an assassin's back and clawed at his eyes. Boulaj killed one man as Junai accounted for a second. The horses fidgeted, eyes rolling, wanting to panic. The three Balitang ladies hung on to their reins for their lives. In these crowded quarters, the horses might kill the very people they served.

A crack opened in the doubled ring of household fighters in front. Aly saw the assassin pair slip through, one engaging Fesgao as another came at Dove. Aly pushed off the saddlehorn, swinging her legs over the restless horse's rump, smashing into the killer with both feet. She was down on him with a knife in each hand, taking his life before he even understood where he was. Trick and Secret screeched their disgust as blood struck them.

"Sorry," Aly told them, panting. She mounted Dove's horse properly so she wouldn't need to use a time-wasting jump like that a second time. Everywhere she looked she saw chaos. People streamed in to fill the square, many carrying weapons. Others fought to escape it. Some failed and were trampled. The square filled with a roar of sound: screams, furious yells, battle-voiced commands. Above that animal sound was a high, warbling trill. The Stormwings had come to feast on the pain and fear.

A little girl, shrieking, tried to climb the statue to escape the mob. A boy who might have been an older brother pushed her from behind, trying to get her to the top, the only safe place he could see. A handful of other children splashed through the fountain. One of them was pushed into the water, toward that bit of safety, by a woman who fell then beneath a man's club.

Light blazed from steel. Down came two Stormwings, deflecting the rare arrow with a sweep of deadly wing. The first seized the girl in her claws; the second grabbed her brother. Others came for the remaining children, carrying them up to the balconies that overlooked the square.

Aunt Daine wasn't joking, thought Aly in awe. They *do* like children.

A rotting melon struck the back of her head, jolting her. A moment later a rock flew past her nose. Aly dismounted in a hurry, remembering her grandfather Miles's adage: "A spy is not a target. A spy *points out* the targets." Moments after she touched the ground, an arrow caught her mount in the withers. Dove's horse screamed in pain and reared. The men-at-arms tried to get out of the maddened animal's way as it yanked its reins free. A flying hoof caught one man's shoulder with the crack of breaking bone as the horse plunged into the crowd.

Their remaining men-at-arms instantly closed the gap. Once more they placed themselves as a living fence between the mob and Dove.

"Soldiers come," Trick shrieked in Aly's ear. She looked around, hearing nothing but the crowd and the Stormwings. Then, in a break in the overall noise, she heard the tread of heavy boots. At the far end of the square a stallion neighed. From Middle Way came a company of the King's Watch, half wielding clubs, half with short swords. From Shield Way on the southwest side of the square Aly heard the clatter of hooves. She adjusted her Sight and strained for a look. It was a company of Rittevon Lancers, armed with swords and spears. They cut a route through the mob.

Suddenly the Lancers' disciplined line of riders bent outward, then split. Organized columns of raka and part-raka in leather tunics stitched with metal rings plowed into the horsemen. Ulasim's secret troops carried small round shields and longswords, and they hammered at the cavalry. Once the lancers' lines were broken and the mounted soldiers were fighting in groups of twos and threes, the raka warriors, men and women alike, surrounded them, striving to cut away their saddles and bring them to the ground.

The men of the King's Watch on Middle Way slammed into the mob, which turned on them. Those civilians who had been fighting each other now had a better target, one that wore a uniform. They swamped the new arrivals, grabbing weapons that fallen guards had dropped, wielding them with enthusiasm if not expertise.

Slowly the group that guarded Dove moved out into the open square, trying to make it to a side street. Instead the battle forced them forward, though they fought to hold their ground. They would be crushed against the fountain.

A gap opened before Aly. A soldier had grabbed a club. He was about to bring it down on the skull of a toddler who clutched his knees, screaming. Aly lunged out, knifing the soldier in the back as she yanked the child away with her free hand. Another soldier descended on her with a roar of fury. She slung the toddler toward the Balitang group and blinded the soldier before she cut his throat.

"I know it's nasty," she told the darkings, panting as she wiped her blades, "but this is the not-very-fun part."

Trick and Secret didn't answer. Both of them leaped from Aly's neck to cover the faces of two soldiers who were headed for Dove. As the men fought to breathe, a raka woman with muscles like rocks bashed one with a piece of stone. A luarin woman thrust a short sword home through the other soldier. Trick and Secret leaped to Aly as the two unknown women continued to fight soldiers, shoulder to shoulder, falling back until they filled the gaps in the line around Dove. Aly stayed behind them, in case this was a ruse to let assassins get close to her mistress. The ladies paid attention to nothing but the people who smashed into them.

Aly looked around in despair, wondering how they were going to escape. The riot was growing. It would help no one if Dove got crushed.

Crows and miniature kudarung rained down, shrieking and gouging, biting and blinding, driving everyone from a space in front of the fountain. In their wake came a much larger shadow, one so big that even those who battled around Aly's companions looked up. Everywhere else the insanity raged. Here there was a moment of quiet as a bright chestnut kudarung stallion spiraled down to land in the open space. As regal as any king, he walked over to the Balitang defenders, who moved aside. At last he stood before Dove.

Slowly, gracefully, the great creature furled his batlike wings and knelt on his forelegs, a plain salute to the girl.

Aly was the first to recover. "Don't just stand there, climb on!" she cried, yanking Dove's arm so she would advance. "Fesgao, your sash!"

"But . . . a saddle," Dove murmured, stroking the chestnut's muzzle. "Where do I, um, mount?"

Aly envisioned the messenger who had come to Tanair the year before on a captive kudarung. "Behind his wings," she said. Fesgao thrust his sash into her reaching hand. "Excuse me," Aly told the great creature. "It's demeaning, but necessary." She tied the sash around that powerful neck, and passed its ends to Dove. She hesitated, then slung the toddler she had rescued up in front of Dove. "If you don't mind?" she asked the kudarung.

He straightened his forelegs. Then he nodded.

"Balitang House?" she asked.

Again the kudarung nodded. His hindquarters bunched, and he jumped, massive wings opening with a snap. Up he soared, scooping at the air until he was above the houses. Then he flew into the distance, toward Balitang House.

The afternoon was half over when the rest of them came home. Footmen and maids waited for them beside the guard at the locked gate. They took charge of the worst hurt, carrying or helping them to the infirmary. All were bruised, scraped, and bloody. Petranne shrieked to see her mother and her great-aunt disheveled and carrying the red-bladed spears they had grabbed to help in the fight. The duchess passed her spear to Nuritin and scooped up her daughter, hugging her until Petranne yelped. Nuritin placed one spear on the front hall bench and, taking out her handkerchief, began to clean the blade of the one she held.

Chenaol had followed them from the gate. She grinned at Nuritin and collected the other spear. "If you want me to take that, my lady, I'll clean it properly," she said, nodding toward the weapon Nuritin still held.

Nuritin looked at the spear, then at Chenaol. The old woman trembled from top to toe, but her voice was firm and clear as she replied, "I thank you, but I will clean it myself. I suspect I may need it again. My father said a good blade should always be seen to by the one who uses it."

Chenaol scratched her head for a moment, then offered, "Would my lady like to see our armaments, and choose something more to her taste?"

"I would," Nuritin replied stoutly. "This is a bit heavier than I can manage easily." As the two women walked to the back of the house, carrying spears, Nuritin added, "And since we are to be comrades in battle, we had best do away with this 'my lady' nonsense."

Dove was seated at the foot of the stairs, her arms wrapped around her knees. When Aly looked at her, Dove said, "Next time, I want a saddle."

Fesgao and the rest of their group, who had been catching their breath until now, knelt as one and bowed their heads to her. Aly followed suit.

"Mama, why did they do that?" asked Petranne. "They're only supposed to bow like that to the king."

Winnamine turned, Petranne still in her arms, and saw their escorts and Dove. She set Petranne down. "Because

Dove is to be the next king," she replied, and curtsied deeply.

Petranne did the same, as well as her six-year-old coordination would allow her. Despite that, she said, "But Dove can't be king. She's a girl."

Dove rose and walked over to them. She said, her voice shaking, "And this girl isn't going to be that kind of king. Get up, all of you, please. I never want to see any of you on your knees again, for anyone. Winna, please, don't. You're my mother, Petranne's my sister." Her chin wobbled. "Please don't close me out." She looked at Aly. "That applies to you as well."

Winnamine rose and hugged her stepdaughter. Kissing the top of Dove's head, she said in a mother's croon, "It's all right. We're all home and safe."

Safe for the moment, thought Aly. The riot in Rittevon Square had not diminished once Dove had gone. If anything, it had intensified, spreading north and east through Middle Town. The household had lost three men-at-arms, killed in the fight. Five more were seriously hurt. Boulaj had dislocated her shoulder.

"If you will excuse me, I need more information," Aly told the others, and headed for her workroom. Passing a door that opened out to the pool courtyard, she saw the great chestnut kudarung there, drinking sedately. Three full-sized mares and a handful of miniature kudarung cropped the grass that grew outside the tiled court.

So much for secrecy, Aly thought tiredly, and walked on. She ducked into her workroom to collect herself. Nawat was there, to her surprise, caught in the act of placing a lotus on her worktable. He swept her up for a hard kiss and embrace. "My kin told me you were well and fighting your way home," he said, "or I would have come for you. Were you pleased when they came to help Dove? I didn't even ask them to, or the little kudarung. They did it because they wanted to."

Aly pressed a hand to his mouth. "I'm *very* grateful," she said. "Is anyone in the meeting room?"

"Many of your spies, and Ulasim, and Fesgao, and Quedanga," replied Nawat. "They have information for you, as have I, from my kinfolk."

"Information is good," said Aly as they crossed the hall. They could barely fit in, so many sat in the chairs and on the floor. She managed to wriggle her way through to a counter along the wall. Sitting there, she had a view of everyone's face. Nawat remained by the now-closed door, leaning against the wall. Guchol took a few slates from her lap and handed them over; Atisa provided a lump of chalk.

Aly murmured her thanks, nodded to Ulasim and the other senior conspirators, then looked at her pack and their recruits. Placing a clean slate on her knees, she said, "Very well, my children. Since we all have much to say, let us be organized about it. Who has word from Downwind and the Honeypot?"

She released them to go learn more once they had emptied their budgets of news. She noted that Fesgao and Quedanga came and went, pursuing their own duties. Dove arrived at some point, followed by Nuritin and Nomru. The last three stayed, as did Ulasim, while still more messengers arrived. Dove even took over the note-taking briefly so that Aly could ease her writing hand and eat something.

Aly took a short walk to unwind and visit the privy, then stepped out into the garden and looked up. Was it her imagination, or were the multicolored sparks that represented the Trickster now brighter?

When she returned, she reviewed the notes for what she had missed, then began to take things down again. Finally Ulasim called for lamps. Aly hadn't even noticed it was growing dark; she had simply shifted her Sight so she could work without interruption as the light grew dim. Knocked from her concentration, she looked up and around. Winnamine had come, as had Baron Engan, Ferdy Tomang, and Lord Obemaek. Nawat returned soon after lamps were lit. As Aly stretched her neck to ease a cramp, Imgehai Qeshi arrived, her black priestess's robes disordered, her hood shoved back.

"The fighting has reached the middle of Market Town," she told them, panting. That was where her temple was located.

Aly looked at Ulasim. "There's been no dwindling of the riot since we got home," she told him wearily. "It's spread. And don't ask me how I know this bit, but Rubinyan has sent two hundred of the Rittevon Guard and four decades of Rittevon Lancers out. Their orders are to beat the fighting back to the lower edges of Middle Town, but they're stalled at Rittevon Square. The Honeypot is burning again. Who knew they had anything left? The King's Watch is trying to contain another riot in Downwind. With a little help from people who know what they're doing, their lines can be broken there, if you are in the mood. That riot's spreading to Dockmarket and up to Flowergarden. That is the state of affairs in Rajmuat at this time." She massaged her neck. "What are your orders?"

Ulasim sat, his eyes going from one conspirator's face to another's, ending on Dove's. For a very long, still moment the big raka said and did nothing. At last he made a face. "I think it is plain to all of us that the war has begun ahead of schedule," he said drily. "Any child knows it is better to swim with the tide than against it. We attack in force at dawn."

20

BATTLE JOINED

Messengers left the house with orders for the fighter groups hidden all over the city. Members of the luarin conspiracy sent their loved ones, with some guards from their own households, to the Balitang home. Lord Obemaek told Fesgao that if worse came to worst, the families could flee Rajmuat from the house closest to the docks. Aly thought it sweet, though unrealistic. If Crown troops showed up in the Windward District at all, it would be because the rebels had been beaten, and no ship would be able to sail.

Ochobu made certain that everyone who entered Balitang House first had to submit to truthspells wielded by Ochobu, Ysul, or the handful of Chain mages who had entered the city, or to questions under Aly's Sight as she looked to see if they lied. Those who failed the test of loyalty were locked up rather than executed. It was time to start changing their old policies, Ulasim had told the conspirators. If people who were not on their side were spared when possible, it might create goodwill after the fighting was done.

As everyone bustled about in the hours after midnight,

Aly sought a private moment with Ulasim. "You'll see Nawat later," he said before she could open her mouth. "He and his fighters will meet you and Chenaol." When Aly did not leave, he sighed. "That's not it? Well, can the rest wait?" he asked, trying to tie back his hair and write at once.

"It cannot," Aly said, taking control of his hair. "Believe me, I'm not here to waste your time." She did an efficient braid and tied it off.

Ulasim finished his document and handed it to a waiting messenger. "Close the door," he ordered her. As the door thunked shut behind her, Ulasim looked up at Aly. "What is it?" he demanded.

Aly crouched and held out a hand. "Lace," she called. "It's time."

The darking had been hiding under Ulasim's chair. Now it rolled forward onto Aly's palm. Aly picked it up and showed it to Ulasim.

"This is Lace," she told her general, whose eyes had gone wide at the sight of the odd creature. "I cannot tell you how I came to know it, or where it comes from. You would *really* dislike the answer. Lace is a darking. Say hello to Ulasim," she instructed.

Lace stuck up a neck and head. "Hello. What one of us knows, we all know. We can even show sometimes, if you are not in a hurry."

Aly offered the darking to Ulasim. "I mean to give one to Fesgao, Ochobu, Chenaol, Nomru, Her Grace, and Dove." Gingerly Ulasim accepted Lace. "They're all I have left," Aly continued as he rolled the darking on his palm. "The others, but for my personal darking, are at the palace. You keep yours by you, as I always keep mine by me. Say hello, Trick."

Trick put its head up from its necklace shape. "Hello," it said. "It is a fine thing to say hello to you people at last."

"How long have they— No," Ulasim corrected himself as Aly raised a finger. "No questions. But can we trust them, whatever they are?"

"We have kept your trust for weeks," Lace informed him. "We have heard everything, and we have told only Aly."

Ulasim started to speak, then stopped. He looked at their surroundings, the conspirators' meeting room, then at Lace. "For weeks," he repeated, his voice very dry. "And you reported only to Aly."

"We do not *lie,*" Trick said in reproof. "Not much."

"Lies are boring," added Lace.

"A good thing we never planned to betray *you,*" Ulasim told Aly.

Aly smiled at him. "Now you're being silly," she replied. "The best place to wear one is around your neck. That way they can speak in your ear."

Lace rolled up Ulasim's arm, raising goose bumps on the man's skin. It shaped itself like a band around his neck. "I tell you what is happening around other darkings," Lace explained.

Ulasim hitched his shoulders. "It is the strangest feeling," he remarked. "Bright Eyes, it is always something new with you. Fesgao, Mother, Nomru, Chenaol, Her Grace, and Lady Dove?" Aly nodded. Ulasim smoothed his bearded chin. "And you. Very good. The Crown's mages can interfere with the communications of our mages. Will that affect these creatures?"

"No," said Trick, authority in its tiny voice. "We are not shaped from the Gift of mortals, but by Stormwing blood and magic in the Divine Realms."

Ulasim looked startled.

"It will go better if you treat them as people," Aly said gently. "With their own minds and thoughts. Treat them as you would any message runner. The only differences are, these never leave you, and they get news from widely scattered forces more quickly than any runner." She raised her eyebrows. "Have I permission to give one to the others?"

"I would be a fool to stop you," said Ulasim. "Though if your sources are limited, I would keep one back for Nawat. He will be meeting Chenaol's party."

"Quartz," suggested Secret. "Quartz came with Countess Tomang. Quartz doesn't want to stay while we hunt."

"Good idea," Aly told it.

Ulasim gazed at Lace with a frown. "These . . . darkings . . . are in the palace?"

"We hear things and we tell Aly," explained Lace. "Fun."

With his free hand Ulasim rubbed his eyes. "I bless the day the god sent you to us, Aly." When Lace squeaked in indignation, he added, "And you darkings. I hope the god has no more surprises left. I have had all the surprises I can wrap my mind around." He flapped a hand in dismissal.

Aly had similar conversations with Fesgao, Ochobu, Duke Nomru, Chenaol, and Winnamine as she introduced them to their darkings. She made sure to talk to each of them alone. It would be a bother to explain her small friends to even more members of the conspiracies. As it was, Ochobu threatened her with blisters for keeping them to herself.

The last person she sought was Dove. The girl sat on the edge of the courtyard pool, little kudarung tucked and slumbering all around her, the big stallion and his mares dozing nearby on the grass. Though there were no torches lit in the garden, Aly could see Dove's face plainly. It was the face of mutiny.

"If you've come to say I serve best by waiting here . . . ," she warned as Aly approached. "'Stay safe,' they tell me, while people are dying in my name. What kind of queen sits around eating guava while her people are in danger?"

"A creative one," Aly told her, kneeling beside Dove. "I have someone I want you to meet, my lady. Secret."

There was a squeak from her left shoulder. While Trick, on her right, had spoken up with its own firm opinions as Aly introduced the others to their darkings, Secret had shriveled against Aly's skin, making itself smaller and smaller. Secret had believed it would have to stay with Aly.

"I have to meet someone secret?" asked Dove, confused.

"No, someone *named* Secret," Aly said, holding out her left arm and open hand. Secret rolled down her arm and into her palm, producing its head the moment it came to a stop. "I kept you back for Dove," Aly explained to the darking, which shivered with excitement. "I wasn't going to leave you out." She made her introductions and explanations and transferred Secret to its new friend. It gave her a pang to part with the little darking, but she could tell from the way Secret wrapped itself around Dove's slender neck that it had badly wanted work of its own.

Aly got to her feet, her heart pounding. She kept her voice even as she said, "It's important that you stay safe. Without you, we have nothing to secure any kind of victory with. But there's safe and there's *safe,* if you take my meaning." Dove stared at her, then frowned. Aly continued, "True, it would do the fighters good to *see* you, but not if it will bring you within arrow-shot." She bowed to Dove. "My pack and I go hunting at dawn," she said. "If I don't see you again, I just want you to know, I would have worked for you gladly even without the god's involvement."

Aly left the garden, thinking, If she takes the hint, Ulasim will kill me. She grinned. Though he'll have to dethrone Imajane and Rubinyan first. I can live with that.

Her pack and their recruits assembled in her workroom

while Aly changed into a specially made sarong that included hidden sheaths for her thin, flat knives. The sash also had a few surprises in its folds. Breifly she envied her mother, able to tuck herself into armor with a number of weapons at hand. Aly felt virtually naked. There was nothing more she could do apart from settling a length of chain in her sash. Her work was different from Mother's, that was all.

"We've been taking orders from a girl who's younger than *any* of us?" cried a recruit who had never met her.

Boulaj and Junai fixed him with stony eyes. "She is the god's gift," Boulaj said in a voice like ice.

"I have a *daughter* her age," protested a woman who loaded grain at the Dockmarket as she gathered information for Eyun.

"I am ancient in treachery," Aly said with an agreeable smile. "If you're going to whine, you may stay and tend the real children here."

Someone whispered, "She brought down Topabaw. She said she would do it, and she did."

"He still rots out by the harbor," added Vitorcine, Aly's first double agent. "I haven't had to betray my masters since he got dead. I'll follow her wherever she likes."

After that, there was no more discussion. They all checked weapons and each other's clothing. Chenaol arrived as they were doing a final count. The cook was also dressed to fight, a cutlass belted at her waist. In one hand she carried a heavy ax. Light slid along its curved, sharp edge.

"Let's go, my dears," she told them. "We have to cross the city by dawn."

Getting to Flowergarden, the district west of Downwind, took them triple the time it would have taken if conditions had been normal. Royal patrols that numbered twenty and thirty grim-faced men roamed the streets. They did not submit to the rain of garbage and stones that fell from the buildings, but killed anyone foolish enough to be caught outside. Any fighter who shot at people who threw things went down the next moment with an arrow in his throat.

After her people's fifth plea to help those attacked by the soldiers, Aly asked Chenaol for a quick halt and gathered them close. "We *cannot* stop and fight every fight along the way," she told them softly, firmly, keeping anger and nerves out of her voice and face. They had to see her calm and in control, these people who had only ever known the pack member who had recruited them. "If you want to drop out and die foolishly, do it without argument. The rest of us have a mission, a vital one. We can't afford distractions, however many old ladies douse the King's Watch in night soil. Either leave or be silent."

After that, they kept silent. Aly wasn't sure if it was her words or the glares of those who had recruited them. Either way, no one left their group. They moved on through the night, through tunnels, alleys, and sometimes up stairs and over rooftops, any course that would keep them clear of the patrols and the pockets of fighting scattered throughout the city. North and across Dockmarket, Market Town, then Middle Town they followed Chenaol, who seemed to know exactly when to hide and when to advance. As they crossed the city, Trick whispered in Aly's ear. Ulasim and his fighters had met Crown troops on southern side of town. These soldiers came from the Greater Fortress. They were hesitant and inclined to run. As the survivors of the deadly raids and fires at the fortress, they lacked the spirit of other men who had come to battle on the Crown's behalf. Ulasim told his darking that he thought these soldiers felt that they'd had enough raka fighting the night the two fortresses had burned.

They would be remembering that there should have been more of them, and that many of them should have been whole and strong, not marked with burns.

Fesgao's soldiers collided with nearly one hundred men-at-arms in service to loyal luarin families on the northeastern edge of the Swan District, where it met Market Town. The luarin troops were outnumbered but fighting well, his darking reported. Fesgao was far short of his destination, but Ochobu, hearing of his delay, sent two Chain mages to his aid. Three more mages joined Ulasim, while Ochobu herself led a small group of mages, hooded and cloaked like the Black God's priests, up Rittevon's Lance, straight into the fighting on the square. They started to blast their way through the soldiers of the hated King's Watch.

Nomru and his fighters cut across the city at an angle to Rittevon's Lance, driving across Middle Town and into the Swan District, attacking guards at the checkpoints and any household troops foolish enough to get in his way. He gave the same rough treatment to anyone on the edges of the riot if they did not move when he ordered.

Everyone had plenty of light. The Honeypot was ablaze again, its fires spreading into Downwind. Isolated fires burned in Dockmarket, Market Town, and Middle Town. Aly and her group heard the roar of the riot and the shrieks of the injured. Over it all rose the eerie trill of feeding Stormwings. Lit from below, they looked like monsters from the realms of Chaos.

Once Chenaol's group reached the border between Market Town and Flowergarden, they followed the ground as it began to slope upward. There were fewer soldiers to interfere as they cut across the house and temple gardens that gave the district its name. Aly frequently glimpsed a steady flow of warriors that came from the ridge where Flowergarden met the jungles at the city's back. These people stayed clear of Chenaol and her companions. Their faces—male and female, raka and luarin—were grim and eager in Aly's Sight as they flooded into the city to do battle.

Higher Chenaol's group climbed, through a maze of cottage gardens where people grew vegetables for the city's markets. At last they crested the ridge, halting where a dirt road ended in a small shrine to the Jaguar Goddess. As they stopped to drink from their water bottles, each member of their company tossed a small token—a button, a flower, an arrowhead—down the deep well at the heart of the shrine. Even Aly contributed a flower. It was her philosophy that it never hurt to be polite to strange gods.

She heard the rustle of branches, and a crow fledgling's unmistakable call for more food, followed by the call for "friend." Chenaol responded with a soft howler monkey call.

"You do that well," Aly whispered as warrior shadows approached from the shelter of the trees. The sky in the east shone with a pale gray light that just touched the edges of plants and weapons.

"A misspent girlhood in the jungles of Gempang," the cook explained.

Nawat reached them, flanked by a hard-faced raka woman and a thin, whipcord-lean man who looked as if he might be related to Nawat. He had the same nose and floppy black hair, and he sported a knot of crow feathers at the crown of his head. Also like Nawat, he carried an unstrung bow and a fat quiver of crow-fletched arrows. Without making a sound their companions drew up around Aly's group. There were nearly two hundred of them, all wearing clothes that showed signs of hard use, under mismatched and battered armor. All carried bows and quivers of black-feathered arrows, just as all carried swords, from the sailor's heavy cutlass to longswords in nicked sheaths. Like the other groups of raka fighters Aly had seen, this one was composed of both men and women.

Mother would love it here, Aly thought, then shook the notion out of her head. When preparing for combat, it was a good idea to concentrate on that and nothing else.

As the new arrivals crouched to wait with Aly's pack and their recruits, Aly beckoned Nawat aside. From her pouch she took the last darking, Quartz, and introduced it to him. Once they had reached an understanding and Quartz had settled around Nawat's neck, Aly looked at the eastern horizon. The sun was coming. Already the extra-long rays that indicated the god was locked in battle thrust into the sky over the horizon.

Positioning himself so that no one could see him do it, Nawat kissed her fingers. Aly smiled into his eyes. They said or did nothing else, but for them, that was enough.

"We go in first," Chenaol told Nawat's assistants, her voice soft. "Then you. We'll be out doing our work for a time before we call you in—Aly will signal Nawat. Then you must come through and attack anything in a uniform."

"Try not to kill any more than you can help," Aly reminded them. "Particularly among the servants. It's time to start trying to live together. Tie them up or lock them in somewhere, if you get the chance."

"What about the Gray Palace?" asked Lokak. "There are no tunnels there. How will we take the place?"

"Leave the Gray Palace to your old Duani," Aly told him. "We haven't come so far for nothing." Nibbling her lip, she looked at them all. She wanted to tell them to capture Imajane and Rubinyan, not to kill them. It would be nice if the new queen could show neighboring countries that the deposed monarchs had gotten a fair trial. Inspecting their faces, she realized it would be better to hold her tongue. She'd often heard her mother and other warriors say, "Never give an order if you are not sure it will be obeyed." She wasn't sure that her position as Duani gave her the authority to issue orders at all, let alone that one, just as she knew from the grim faces around her that she would not be obeyed if she gave it. She settled for "Don't take trophies from those you slay. They never look as good as you think they will."

A wave of soft chuckles passed through the group.

"The sun comes," Nawat said, raising his face to its rays. "Mithros is angry."

They all turned to look. The sun was the sun, shedding light and heat as it always did. Its rays streamed like dark orange pennants around the disk, whipping and rippling as if a hard wind blew them. The white veils of fire that had marked the Goddess in the daytime lengthened to cover the parts of the sky left to it by the sun, rippling like the sun's rays. Everywhere overhead the sparks that showed the Trickster's fortunes had expanded to the size of greater stars.

On the slopes below their position, the rebels could view the city. The Rittevon Square riot still went on. Pillars of smoke from burning buildings rose all over town.

"Let us vex the sun god some more," said Jimarn. "Or do we wait until we die of old age?"

"No one wants to live forever," added Yoyox.

Aly had already seen the suspiciously sturdy vine that twined around one of the shrine's pillars. Chenaol beckoned for one of the bigger fighters to help her. They hauled together on the ropy vine, teeth clenched, sweat soon gleaming on their faces. Two of Aly's pack went to help. Slowly the square of a doorway became visible in the ground. A handful of Nawat's people circled it, using blades to cut away the bush and grass roots that had woven themselves into the door's cover in the years since this exit had been used. With a last, long rip, the grassy hood pulled free. Those hauling on it dragged it back to rest against the shrine, then tied ropes around the ring in the door below. It too had settled into the ground and was reluctant to leave its bed. Growling, the warriors pulled it up.

"The one at the palace didn't give so much trouble," Aly murmured, watching.

"We make sure of that. We've had to use the palace entry as a hiding spot. There used to be other exits," said Chenaol, panting. "But this one is so isolated, it's hard to get at. And there's no way to keep people from coming on you here without warning."

The door was up. Someone struck a flint to light the torches they had brought. Aly looked at the steps that led into the ground. "It's going to be nasty down there," she whispered.

Nawat looked at her and gave his bird shrug, as if to say, Nasty is as nasty does.

"Trick, what news?" Aly wanted to know. Warriors went into the tunnel with torches and swords, clearing away cobwebs and roots. Aly, Chenaol, and Nawat followed them, ignoring the muttered comments from their people about the accommodations.

"Nomru at Rittevon Square," the darking said as the rebels passed along the tunnel, "catching soldiers between him and Ulasim. Fesgao's fight done. They are near the edge of Flowergarden. Fesgao says Fonfalas wait for signal to attack the Grain Gate." Aly nodded. The Grain Gate and the Gate of Carts were the side entrances to the palace, where supply wagons brought in ordinary goods for those who lived there. Ulasim and Nomru meant to attack the Gate of Victory once they combined forces.

It seemed like hours until they reached the tunnel's end at the stair that opened next to the Pavilion of Delightful Pleasures. The rebels hesitated there. If Vereyu hadn't got the message Ulasim had sent to her during the night, they might come up among Crown soldiers, who would be able to hack at them at will. Nawat beckoned one of his people forward, a small, perky young luarin with a headful of red curls, bright blue eyes, and a whip-weal that divided her face in half. As she climbed the stairs toward the closed door, the silvery fire of her magical Gift streamed upward to wriggle through cracks in the wood.

She was nodding to Nawat—friends waited outside—when Trick whispered into Aly's ear, "Dove *flies*."

Aly grinned. She wished she could see it: Dove astride the big chestnut kudarung as its great wings caught the air, carrying her over the battles in the streets. It was a risk. A well-placed arrow might ruin everything. But Aly's heart lifted at the thought of Dove in the sky, running risks so that her people might see her. If Aly were out there, fighting for the freedom of her native land, that sight would inspire her like nothing else.

Trick added mournfully, "Secret flies too. Not me."

Aly moved aside so that some of the fighters could get under the tunnel door to push. "I'll make it up to you," she whispered as the warriors thrust at the wooden barrier. Hearing the noise, those outside helped to raise it. Climbing the stairs, Aly looked up into Vereyu's face. "Lovely day, don't you agree?" she asked, stepping into the open air. "Perhaps we'll have lunch on the water pavilions later."

Vereyu's face was grim and set. "Only you would make jokes at a time like this," she told Aly.

"If not now, when?" Aly wanted to know as she brushed off her sarong, trying not to look at its bright colors. It only reminded her that she couldn't wait for the fight to be over, so that she could wear luarin quiet colors again. Eyun of Aly's pack, Vitorcine, and several of the full- or nearly full-luarin recruits wore similar clothes, the kind meant to attract attention. Two of the women who waited with Vereyu were dressed the same way. All of them had been chosen for their looks and their pale skin.

Vereyu and her companions had set a number of shallow open baskets on the ground. Most were loaded with fruit, bread, and rolls filled with slices of meat. Two baskets were full of water flasks, and had handles on either side so that they could be carried by two people.

"We did our best with breakfast in the mess halls," Vereyu told Aly. "Plenty of the men on duty have already run to the privy. I took your advice—I didn't drug everything, so they may not suspect you. Get off the wall if they realize their problem lies in the food." She looked down into the tunnel, where Nawat and his warriors waited. "How will we know when to turn these folk loose?"

Aly smiled at Nawat, who stroked the band around his neck that was the darking Quartz. He'd discovered the darkings' relaxing purr. "They'll know," she said. "I hear Her Majesty has company." The Gray Palace darkings had been announcing the arrival of loyal, panicked nobles since early the night before.

"All the rotten eggs together," Vereyu said, and spat on the ground.

I suppose it would take an extraordinary degree of hate to serve here, day in and day out, in the hope that sometime you would be able to tell your masters what you really think of them, Aly thought. Her respect for Vereyu, already high, doubled. She would tell Dove's spymaster to make good use of Vereyu. Bringing peace to the outlying Isles would be a long, hard job once the capital was won. Vereyu would be good for the distance.

"Any parting words of cheer?" Aly inquired.

Vereyu grinned. "Get stuffed. And send anyone who needs care to the Pavilion of Delightful Pleasures."

Aly nodded and looked at those who were playing royal servants, come to help the soldiers on the Luarin Wall as they stood guard in the hot sun. The soldiers would welcome their burdens of food and water, not realizing the annoying or, in enough quantities, deadly secret in many of the fruits, rolls, and flasks. "Ladies, shall we?" she invited.

They strolled down the Golden Road, past the servants' mess hall, and out through the Gate of Carts. That gate was nearly closed, those who kept watch on it fidgeting nervously. The Grain Gate, one hundred yards from the Gate of Carts, was shut and barred. Wagons had been rolled in front of it as an extra barrier.

Aly and her girls reached the stair to the watch posts on the Luarin Wall and began to climb. They braced their baskets on one hip, a position that ensured the bearer's gait would have a little extra sway. Once they reached the top of the wall, Aly fluttered her lashes at the tough-looking sergeant who waited for them beside the steps. "Something to wet your throat, Captain?" she asked, thrusting her basket of fruit at him with one hip. Men always liked it when a girl promoted them. The sergeant grinned and took his time selecting a star fruit. Aly's companions passed food and water to the men who watched the green belt through the crenels at the top of the wall.

"Tell me, Captain, should we be afraid for our lives?" Aly inquired, her eyes lingering on the man's face. "I've heard these wild raka are no better than animals." He swelled with pride and self-importance, never asking why a girl like this appeared so interested in a blue-chinned fellow whose arms and legs were covered with tattoos.

"Just rabble, girlie," he told her. "Rioting, burning up their own homes. Half crazy with snake fever, if you ask me. And make no mistake. His Majesty will come down hard on them. They'll never get the city fixed up in time for the coronation." He tried to snag Aly around the waist.

Nimbly she stepped just out of reach, glancing at him sidelong from under her lashes. "I've work to do, sir!" she said, and put her nose in the air. Apparently relenting, she smiled and added, "Perhaps when I come round again."

He guffawed as she ambled down the walkway. You keep laughing, she thought amiably. Things will be different when you see me next.

Slowly they worked their way around the broad stretch of wall, distributing their offerings, until they reached the Gate of Victory. Here they found a surprise. Aly did a fast count. One hundred and fifty Lancers waited on the ground by the gate, men and horses alike in battle armor. If they rode out, that would leave only fifty Lancers to help defend the palace. Behind them stood three companies, or three hundred men, of the Rittevon Guard, drooping with heat and boredom. They too were dressed for battle and stood in combat formation. The captain of the Guard and the commanding general of the Lancers conferred with each other and with messengers in the shadow of the gate. Obviously they were waiting for orders.

Aly asked Trick to pass the information to Ochobu, Ulasim, and Nomru, who were supposed to meet where Rittevon's Lance entered the open green lands around the palace. They would have to deal with these fighters. Once Trick finished, Aly crossed over the gate on a walkway, her girls behind her. There were whistles and called remarks of appreciation from the bored men below, until their officers silenced them. The young women giggled or laughed, and offered their drugged goods to the rest of the men on the wall.

Vereyu's people met them with fresh supplies by the Gate of the Sun, the closest gate to the Gray Palace. This Gate had been closed and blocked with stone, hastily laid but solid. No one could enter and leave the palace there. Aly and her women continued around the wall, joking with bored sentries whose posts overlooked little but cliffs or jungle behind the palace as they passed them food and water. The women had almost reached the Grain Gate when Trick said, "They come. Fesgao, Nomru, Ulasim, they come all together. They are on the grass."

Aly looked at the Crown's men around the Gate of Carts. Faces were already missing, the guard smaller by a third. "Tell Nawat to come," she whispered to Trick. To the women who followed her she hand-signaled, *Retreat. Get off the wall.*

On she walked with her empty basket, coming up beside the sergeant who had been so complimentary earlier. He had gotten none of the drugged food, she guessed, since he still looked hearty enough, though he sweated in the day's remorseless heat. Aly handed him a flask of water. He took it absently, scanning the merchants' road with a spyglass. "I feel like there's more to all this than a riot, even if it's just a riot close to us," he murmured. "It's more than a herd of ragged beggars crazy with the summer sun."

She sharpened her Sight. The Fonfala men-at-arms emerged from the jungle in the distance. With them were armored raka warriors, bearing a crest on their breastplates: a chest topped with a copper key. She had seen that emblem on things that Sarugani had left Sarai and Dove. It was the coat of arms of the Temaida family, the shadowy relatives who lived on other islands and waited for their last hope to become real.

The sergeant put down his spyglass and surveyed the men around him. "Where's Hessken? Mayce? Rufert?"

"Privy, sir," called another man. "Something off with breakfast, I think. I'm not so well myself."

"Breakfast, or . . ." The sergeant turned to look at Aly, the picture of innocence with her empty basket. The sweat on his face was heavier, the drops rolling off his cheeks.

"Let me help you, Sergeant," she said, hooking his feet from under him with one of hers. He collided with the wall and slid down until he sat, his eyes fluttering as the sleep drug took him. When he gave her a last glance, she said kindly, "I'll look after things up here."

"Help me!" she cried to the closest men. "His eyes just rolled up and he fell." She went down on her knees as if to help. Two soldiers turned to come to her, only to sprout black-feathered arrows. They toppled from the wall to the ground outside the wall.

Aly ran for another stair to the ground rather than get in the way of Nawat's people as they scrambled to the wall. A few more arrows whizzed past her. She wove from side to side to throw off the Crown's archers who could still aim. Once on the ground, she raced for the cover of the trees as a storm of crows descended on the wall's defenders. In the distance Aly heard men roar as the rebels swarmed onto the green belt. She saw them in her mind's eye, carrying gates they had removed from buldings on the way here to use as bridges over the streams and their deadly occupants.

"Gate of Victory opens," Trick informed her as she trotted down the path to Sevmire's headquarters. "Rubinyan comes with soldiers. He leads Guards and Lancers out to fight Ulasim, Fesgao, Nomru."

"I love it when warriors get noble," Aly said as she yanked open the door to the spymaster's building. "They get themselves killed with hardly any help from us. It's the best time-saver." Here was the corridor where the spymasters hanged the victims of recent tortures to frighten people like Aly Homewood. Sadly, each pair of shackles held a captive. In one bloodied, broken-armed wreck Aly recognized a cook whose dumplings were one of Dockmarket's main attractions.

Running to Sevmire's office for the keys, Aly halted when Vitorcine emerged from it. She held a bloody knife in one hand. Behind her something cast flickering orange light through the door. She had set the place on fire.

Aly brought out her lock picks. "I don't suppose you thought to get his keys when you lit him up?" she called, running back to the captives. Starting with the one closest to the hall where the fire burned, she got to work on the padlock on his chains. A moment later a grimy hand thrust a ring of keys under her nose.

"Why do you think I went in there?" asked Vitorcine.

Aly looked the keys over and singled out the one that opened the shackles. "Catch them as we take them down," she told Vitorcine as she began to undo locks. "You know, Sevmire wasn't worth killing."

Vitorcine gently helped the cook to stand. "He wasn't worth leaving alive, either, Duani."

Aly shrugged. "You have a point." She glanced at the end of the hall. The fire was brighter. "Let's get them outside," she suggested. "I'm sure they'd be happy for sunlight, and we don't want them getting all crispy in here."

Vitorcine nodded and began to escort people out of the building. Aly freed the last prisoners as flames began to crackle beyond Sevmire's office. Some of the captives could walk. They and Vitorcine helped the rest outside.

Aly followed them into the open air. "See if you can get them to the Pavilion of Delightful Pleasures," she told Vitorcine. "And nice work." Moving off toward the Golden Road she asked, "Trick?"

"Nawat's friends put wedges under barracks doors to trap soldiers who sleep," Trick replied obediently. "Ulasim attacks Rubinyan from the left, Fesgao and Nomru from the right. Ochobu, Ysul, and Chain mages come up Rittevon's Lance with their spells hiding in the air and in the ground. Luarin mages not looking at air or ground, only at Ochobu and Chain. Ground is eating luarin mages and their horses. Air is pushing other mages under soldiers' horses. The crows attack soldiers on the wall. Dove says more royal soldiers come to protect Gate of Carts from Fonfalas and Temaidas."

Aly looked up. Overhead circled the chestnut stallion with Dove in a saddle on his back. Outside the walls, she heard a deep-throated roar as men and women cheered the girl's appearance. With Dove looking on, they plowed ahead without letup, battling their way toward the Gate of Victory.

21

WORK

"Uh-oh," said Trick.

Aly, her eyes on Dove, said, "What oh?"

"Soldiers on horses ride up from city," Trick replied. "Secret sees them. Soldiers and archers. And archers climb to walls near the Gate of the Sun."

Aly cursed. The nobles who had taken refuge with Imajane in the Gray Palace must have left men in the guest barracks. If they were so healthy, they couldn't have eaten the food Vereyu's people had poisoned. Perhaps they'd brought their own rations? She'd find out later, if there was a later.

"Tell Nawat of the archers on the walls," she ordered Trick. "Tell Fesgao that an attack comes up behind Ulasim. Nobody else, understand? Just those two."

A squad of soldiers wearing the crest of a luarin noble house came toward her at the trot. As they swerved around Aly, she reached into her sash for a small packet of sleep dust. Suddenly a soldier screamed and went down, a crow-fletched arrow in his eye. Other arrows flew from a clump of trees, followed by the archers: Nawat's people, bows set aside and swords taken up.

"Stop!" Aly yelled. Everyone, the soldiers and Nawat's warriors, turned to stare at her. "Wouldn't it be nice to be able to trust the person on the throne?" she asked their enemies. "To not have to live wondering each day as you wake if your family is safe, or if your master is rotting by the harbor?"

Nawat's people waited.

"Do you really want to die for the Rittevons?" Aly asked more quietly.

Three soldiers raised weapons and fell, shot by Nawat's suspicious archers. The rest hesitated. Then one of them, a sergeant by the bright red bands on his breastplate, set down his sword and dagger. When he straightened, one of his own men tried to attack him. Two other luarin soldiers grabbed the attacker and wrestled him to the ground. He lay there, killed quietly by one of his fellows. They in turn dropped their weapons. Others followed suit.

A woman with crow feathers in her hair shrugged and took a coil of thin rope from her belt. "Our brother said if they surrendered, bind them and move on," she said. She looked at the surrendering soldiers and grinned, teeth flashing in her lean face. "If I meet you again in battle, I won't be so nice," she warned them.

Aly moved on. "Trick?"

"Crows drive archers from the wall and knock some off," Trick replied. "Some crows are shot dead. Fesgao fights soldiers who attack Ulasim from behind. Nomru leads his people forward against Rubinyan's. Mages fight each other. Ochobu is saying many bad words to them."

On and on it came, a flood of information. Aly finally had to stop helping her people, Nawat's, and Vereyu's clean out pockets of resistance in the greater palace. She hid in a corner of the Robing Pavilion and sorted out who needed to know what piece of information. Trick pooled in her lap, allowing images to form inside it. Now Aly could see what the darkings saw when she asked Trick to focus on each of them.

Dove and Secret gave Aly a view of the entire battle that raged all around the Luarin Wall. They pointed out breaks in the lines of enemy soldiers where Nomru, Fesgao, Ochobu, and Ulasim could swamp them, and when an attack came at them from the sides or the rear.

Dove told Aly that fifty of Nawat's people had cleared and opened the Gate of Carts and the Grain Gate, allowing the Fonfala and Temaida fighters to stream into the palace. Secret showed her Nawat and another band of his people, picking more defenders from the walls of the Gray Palace with arrows. Quartz, riding around Nawat's throat, showed Aly the front of the Gray Palace. The gates were shut and barred. It was finally serving the purpose for which it was built, a last stronghold for the luarin Crown.

Ochobu's darking reported that the old woman was ill, tottering as she pulled up all the strength she had in one last spell. Her heart burst as she flung it out, taking five luarin mages to the Peaceful Realms with her. Aly cringed as Ochobu's darking fell to the ground with her, seeing it all as the darking did. Keening its grief, the creature moved promptly to Ysul, who took command of the Chain. There was little he *could* command, as Trick and Aly could see. His cohorts were locked in their own battles. Ysul used his power briefly to direct them to new targets as they each finished wrestling one enemy mage to powerlessness or death. When the mages were occupied again, Ysul looked for a project of his own. Trick and Aly looked with him.

Behind Rubinyan and his troops loomed the Gate of Victory, shut tight, locked with heavy timbers, written over with spells of protection. Ysul's darking told Aly that he was "up to something." While it could feel magic course through the raka mage, that was a sensation it couldn't pass along to Trick or Aly. Instead the two looked around, prepared to warn Ysul if someone was about to attack him. No one was. As if they sensed the power Ysul summoned, the people who battled near him left him alone at the center of a rare open space. Once Ysul sent his magic out into the ground, hidden like most raka magic, Aly could See it course through the earth. It passed under the fighting men of both sides. The luarin mages didn't even notice it, hidden as Ysul's spell was. His magic streamed up into the Gate of Victory. Aly held her breath. Suddenly the dense, bespelled wood of the gate burst into white devouring flames.

Lace broke in, showing its views of the battle. Ulasim, wielding a longsword, had cut his way through the last of Rubinyan's protectors. Aly and Trick watched as Rubinyan closed with Ulasim, hacking at him from horseback. Lace dropped from Ulasim's neck to batten onto the cinch strap on Rubinyan's saddle. For some moments all Aly could see were Ulasim's straining legs. Then the saddle slid. Down tumbled Rubinyan, twisting to fall on his back. In lunged Ulasim, his blade passing through an opening in Rubinyan's armor to cut deep. Rubinyan, grimacing, rolled and thrust his sword through Ulasim. For a moment the two men stared at one another.

Then Ulasim looked up. Dove swooped in on her kudarung, venturing close to the enemy's archers in her need to save him.

"Look!" Ulasim bellowed, pointing up to her. His voice rang over the clash of weapons and the shrieks of warriors and Stormwings. "Look at her! There! See our future? See how we can be great?"

He swayed and fell as his darking keened. Beneath him lay Rubinyan, already dead.

Aly didn't realize tears streamed down her face as she told Fesgao's darking what had befallen their general. Fesgao didn't hesitate. He plowed through the warriors, crying for them to follow him, in the queen's name. As the raka, howling, surged forward, the Gate of Victory collapsed, burned to cinders by Ysul. Behind it, the Raka Gate, too, burned.

Ysul dropped to his knees. When the Raka Gate fell to ashes, he lay down. Two rebels ran to pick him up. His darking told Aly that Ysul was alive, but worn out. The creature went to the next mage to take command of the Chain.

From Dove's position Aly saw that the fighting had slowed in many places close to where Ulasim now lay. Seeing that Rubinyan was dead, a dozen or more luarin warriors raised their hands in surrender. The other Crown troops, mauled by the attacking Fesgao and his fighters, had borne enough. They turned and ran through the destroyed gates. Nawat's warriors and the Fonfala and Temaida troops met them there. Caught between Fesgao's rebels and the forces that had taken the palace grounds, the luarin soldiers fought or surrendered, as they preferred. The more soldiers farther back who saw them put up their hands, the more surrendered.

Aly wiped her eyes, gathered up Trick, and began the weary trudge from the pavilion to Rittevon's Lance. They weren't finished yet. Chenaol caught up to her. The cook and her weapons were smeared with blood. Silently they joined the rest of their people, watching as the last of the Crown's forces inside the walls gave up. Soon Nawat, sweat-soaked and disheveled, came to stand with them. The Fonfala and Temaida warriors stripped the weapons from those soldiers who had surrendered and herded them against the wall to be held under guard.

At last Fesgao strode through the gate, Nomru behind

him. They joined Aly, Chenaol, and Nawat, looking with dull eyes at the ruin that surrounded them. None of them was unmarked. Even Aly had picked up a handful of cuts, though she couldn't remember when. Fesgao looked them over and nodded, as if they'd just met in the marketplace. As soon as those mages of the Chain still able to work caught up, he turned and led the way to the wall that surrounded the Gray Palace. Nomru, Aly, Chenaol, Nawat, and the rebel warriors followed him, weapons in their hands.

High above Stormwings shrieked in ecstasy. Seeing the bulk of the soldiers were surrendering, they began to swoop down, to plunder the dead. Nawat raised his voice in a raucous crow bawl, a sound that told other crows a hawk had come to steal from them. Cawing in one thunderous voice, hundreds of crows rose into the sky above the palace and turned, heading for the Stormwings.

Aly looked at Nawat. "I could not bear for Stormwings to touch the old woman," Nawat admitted, his eyes bright with unshed tears. "Or Ulasim."

Aly touched his cheek, her own lips quivering. "If she thought you cried over her, Ochobu would just throw magic at you again."

"That is why I waited until the death god had her to do it," replied Nawat.

At last they stood before the granite walls of the Gray Palace. Aly looked at their heights and blinked. There was no guard in view. For a moment Fesgao waited, unsure of what happened now.

"Trick?" Aly asked. "What do the palace darkings say?"

"Surprise," Trick replied. Extending a tentacle, it pointed to the top of the wall.

"We need to make a ram," Fesgao said wearily. Nomru nodded. Aly stepped up to them and put a hand on each man's arm. When they looked at her, their eyes reddened from the dust, she pointed to the wall. Taybur Sibigat stood there at parade rest, hands clasped behind his back. He looked down at them and nodded, his face expressionless.

Slowly the gate to the Gray Palace swung open. Soldiers in the black clothes and mail of the King's Guard, all of whom looked the worse for heavy fighting, lined the flagstone road that led to the residence with dead men all around them. It was four of the Guard who had opened the gate.

"Those troops still loyal to the Rittevons are locked up. So too are those noble families and servants who remained loyal," Taybur called, his voice and face as emotionless as if he read a marketing list. "I surrender the Gray Palace to your war chief. Queen Imajane is being held."

"Does he lie?" Fesgao asked Aly without taking his eyes from Taybur.

"No, sir," Aly replied. "He tells the truth."

A long shadow fell over them. Everyone looked up, then backed away to clear a space as Dove's mount slowly descended. At last the kudarung stallion stood on solid ground, its sides streaked with sweat. Fesgao strode over to help Dove from the saddle.

At the corner of her eye Aly registered a wave of motion. She looked around. First those of raka blood went to their knees. Slowly the luarin troops, even stubborn Duke Nomru, followed suit. Aly knelt slowly. At last only Nawat and those who looked as if they had recently been crows stayed on their feet.

Dove saw them and grinned, her small face lighting up. "Cousins," she said with a nod.

The rattle of chain mail drew Aly's gaze to the men of the King's Guard on the flagstone road. They, too, knelt and bowed their heads. Taybur, who had descended from the walkway overhead, knelt at the center of the open gate.

Dove looked at him. "Imajane?" she asked, her voice steady.

"In her rooms," Taybur replied. "Your Majesty."

Aly glimpsed a flutter of pink high on the side of the residence, on a balcony that overlooked its small garden. "There's a balcony outside her chambers," she said, refusing to look at that spot with her close-in Sight, amazed her voice did not quaver at what the deposed queen was about to do.

"I know," replied Taybur as the bit of pink plummeted from the balcony rail.

"At least we don't have to pay to house and try her," Jimarn murmured from somewhere behind Aly.

Fesgao pointed at the sky. The white veil that showed the Goddess's battles with Kyprioth and his allies was shrinking. The long, swordlike rays that framed the sun, Mithros's sign, were shrinking, too. The brilliant sparkles that had shown the Trickster's growing power flew together to form a single multicolored globe, with a handful of brilliant stars scattered around it: the lesser tricksters, Aly thought. The Goddess's veil and Mithros's rays did not vanish.

There's still work to do, Aly thought. We haven't won, not completely.

In the weeks that followed, Aly learned the truth of something both her parents said: cleaning up always seemed to take much longer than the fighting. She would have told them it only seemed that way because everyone was tired, except that she was too weary to write a letter home.

The Islanders buried their dead quietly, with services held for a week in the temples of the Black God. Dove insisted that Ulasim have a grave beside the steps to the Throne Hall, covered over in malachite and bronze, with a white marble marker stating his name, dates of birth and death, and the simple epitaph THE STRONG ONE. Ochobu was buried on the far side of the steps from her son, her grave covered in lapis and bronze. Her epitaph read THE WISE ONE. In time, Fesgao would join them as the warrior of the old prophecy. Aly knew where she fit in, but she wasn't sure that she wanted a marker on her grave that read THE CUNNING ONE. It seemed to her most fitting that no one know where she was buried at all.

Ulasim and Ochobu were not their only losses. Vereyu was alive but would limp all her days; Imajane had slashed the tendons behind her knee when Vereyu went to take her prisoner, and the healers had not reached her in time to completely mend the damage. Of Aly's pack, seven had been killed in the fighting: Lokak, Hiraos, and Ukali among the men, and Guchol, Eyun, Kioka, and Junai among the women. Aly mourned them bitterly where no one could see her. Junai had watched her back all that summer at Tanair. The others had been her pack. Only Nawat understood how cruel it was to lose them, just as she understood his grief for sixteen of his flock-mates, as he called the humans and transformed crows he had led.

The priestess Imgehai Qeshi had perished in her burning temple, Lord Obemaek in the fighting. Countess Genore Tomang was dead, killed helping to defend Balitang House. Her son Ferdy lost an eye in the battle before the palace gates. Aunt Nuritin had kept looters from breaking through the servants' gate at the house before a stroke felled her. She was working now to speak again, but the healers said her left hand would never regain its strength.

Once the fires were put out and the palace secure, Dove met with the captive luarin nobles. Chenaol, the duchess, Quedanga, Ysul, and Duke Nomru were present to advise her. From those who surrendered and acknowledged her as queen, she required a blood oath on the spot. She did not ask for one from Taybur.

"They murdered his king," she explained to her council of advisors. "As far as he was concerned, their authority over him ended there. I will trust him."

Her elders argued. They told Dove that, having betrayed one set of monarchs, Taybur could never again be trusted, but Dove would not be swayed. Aly said nothing in front of the others. She had already convinced Dove that Taybur deserved a chance.

Dove also sent out messages to the commanders of the Rittevon forces in the outlying Isles, and to the rebel raka. She received replies in trickles, promises of surrender or vows of resistance. A number of noble luarin hurried to court, anxious to convince their unofficial new queen that they deserved to keep their wealth and lands. Dove told them, every time the subject came up, that property would be redistributed. The luarin could be content with less wealth than they had possessed before, or they could leave the Isles. Most chose to stay, particularly as the Nomrus, Balitangs, Fonfalas, Obemaeks, and Tomangs began to divide their own lands with those who had a legal claim.

For the challenges to her rule, Dove sent out troops led by Fesgao, Nomru, and others. Nawat, who wore a multicolored, incredibly gaudy necklace these days, as did every crow Aly saw, also went out to persuade the fighters to stop. As summer deepened and began to wane, crops were far more important than battle. By the end of August most of the Isles had decided to see how they'd manage with a half-raka queen. Only Ikang and parts of Malubesang and Lombyn continued to resist.

Aly worked even harder than she had before the fighting. Rubinyan's old study, with its well-executed maps and many useful books, became her office. Soon she had to clear rooms on either side to make space for her deputies, Vitorcine, Yoyox, Olkey, and Atisa. They took in the information that arrived each day and rendered it in a form that could be presented to Dove and her counselors. When she could leave things in their hands, Aly ventured out into the Isles, turning the spies of the raka conspiracy into her agents. She chose people from every walk of life. By the start of September she had broken the Kingdom into districts and appointed an agent to take charge of each.

One September morning she woke up—she had fallen asleep on her desktop again—to find Trick squeaking in her ear and Dove settled in a chair in front of her desk. Aly, her brain muddled, struggled to push herself to her feet.

"Stop that," Dove said crossly. "When was the last time you slept in a bed, not at your desk?"

Aly yawned. "Recently, Your Majesty."

"When was the last time you saw Nawat?"

Aly grinned. "Very recently, Your Majesty." She touched the antipregnancy charm he'd given to her. She wore it on a chain long enough that she could tuck it into her breast band under her sarong.

"Better. When are you getting married?"

"Before I lay eggs," Aly said, awake at last. "Why is Your Majesty asking me these questions?"

"Do you plan to nest here or at home?" Dove wanted to know. "Because of all those I have worked with, you are the only one who hasn't sworn to me. Are you going back to Tortall?"

Aly bit her lip. Why couldn't Dove have started this after Aly had spent a night sleeping in a bed? At last she replied, "I wouldn't sell your secrets to other realms, Your Majesty."

"That isn't why I'm asking," Dove snapped. Secret squeaked from its position around her throat. She and the small darking had been inseparable since their first meeting, just like Aly and Trick. "I'm sorry, Secret. But really, Aly, one moment you're braiding my hair and the next you're at least a table length away, giving reports. It's not the same." She looked down at her bronze silk lap. "I thought you were my friend," she added quietly. "I still need a friend."

Aly sighed. It was time to make choices about her future. "Taybur would do very well as your new spymaster," she said, shuffling papers. "He's got the right shifty turn of mind."

"Until the Isles are at peace, I need Taybur with the Queen's Guard," retorted Dove. "He's thorough. If I'm to visit some of the Isles next week, I want him preparing the way. I want *you* for spymaster."

Aly looked at her sadly. "There are things about me you don't know," she told Dove, her belly clenched with tension. "Things that make it impossible for me to be your spymaster. Things that as your permanent spymaster I *must* tell you."

"Oh, stop bouncing and say it." Kyprioth appeared in a window seat, dressed in a jacket and sarong like woven copper, jangling with jewelry. "You know you want to."

Aly scowled at him. "I thought you were going to be really large if you won."

"I am large," retorted the god. "This is only the part you see. I imbue this palace with my essence, every stone and every drop. My visit will do wonders for the flowers."

Aly propped her chin on her hand. "So does manure," she observed.

Kyprioth chuckled. "Whyever would you want to leave me, my dear? We're *made* for each other, in a god-to-servant way." He looked at Dove. "I see you're removing those statues of my sister and brother outside." His face lit with anticipation. "Will you have them melted down?"

"Perhaps *you* can afford to offend them," Dove replied. "I can't. They're going to the temples of Mithros and the Goddess in Rajmuat, as is proper. Do you want me to put up a statue to you? Our custom says it's very unlucky."

"Put a statue up of me? Nonsense," scoffed the god. "I am multitudes. You see but one of my faces. I am—"

"Vast," Aly interrupted. "Yes, you've mentioned it."

"So when's the big day?" Kyprioth asked Dove, unmoved by Aly's sarcasm. "When is my queen to be crowned?"

"The day after Midwinter," Dove replied, a smile tweaking her mouth. "So my official reign begins with the rebirth of the year."

"With the rebirth of the sun," the god corrected her. "Not that I begrudge him, poor fellow. He still hasn't gotten his shield back. That thief I got is truly talented." He raised an eyebrow. "Ah. A summons." He looked at Aly, black eyes dancing. "If she's crowned at Midwinter, the foreign delegations will have to come by the end of October and stay the season," he pointed out. "Your monarchs are sending their very favorite people. You had better hurry up and tell her." He vanished, leaving a thin layer of copper sparkles where he'd sat.

"What did he mean by that?" Dove wanted to know.

Aly had a very bad feeling. "I'd like to tell Winna at the same time, if I may," she said wearily. "I think you both should hear it from me. Trick?"

Trick sat up on her shoulder. "She comes," it said. Like the other darkings given to specific people, Winnamine's had chosen to remain with her as the duchess took over the running of the domestic side of the palace. She had long since ordered Aly to call her by her nickname.

Waiting for her, Aly and Dove talked over plans for Dove's visit to the nearby Isles. The chief problem lay in finding ways for her attendants to keep up, since she would be riding the winged stallion she had named Kypry. "I just won't land until I know the place is safe," she was telling Aly as Winnamine swept in.

The duchess had set a new fashion, wearing her darking as a glossy band twined throughout her hair. Other ladies of Dove's new court were trying the same style, without success, since a darking could grip better than a satin ribbon. "Midget says you two want to discuss something with me," she said as she settled into a chair. "It's not bad news from the outer Isles, is it?"

"You should wait," said Trick. "Fesgao and Chenaöl come, too. We told them."

"Why?" Aly wanted to know.

"The darkings are right," said Dove. "They were with us at the beginning. They should hear whatever it is, too."

Aly changed position, hiding the fact that she was making sure the knives in her sash and under the top of her desk were ready to hand. Sheer self-preservation had made her flinch from telling members of the old raka conspiracy. Of all the people Aly had dealt with since her arrival in the Isles, she felt they had the most right to be vexed when they learned the truth about her.

"While we're waiting," the duchess said, pulling a folded parchment from a pocket. Dove and Aly recognized the bold writing right away.

"Sarai!" cried Dove, and grabbed the letter.

As Dove read greedily, Winna told Aly, "They married when they reached Carthak. Sarai is expecting a child next spring." She smiled, her lips trembling. "If it is a boy, they do mean to name him Mequen. They won't be here for the coronation, but they promise to visit as soon as it's safe."

Chenaol arrived from the kitchens, her arms covered to the elbows in flour. Dove had pressed her to accept a more important position, but the raka had refused flatly. Her place was in the kitchen, she'd told Dove. If people wanted to talk weapons, they would find her there.

Fesgao was not far behind the cook. As commander of the queen's armies, he kept an office at the headquarters building near the Rittevon enclosure. He had settled into his work, spending his days like Aly, sorting through papers to decide what mattered and what did not. He'd told Aly that he looked forward to Dove's trip as a break from documents.

When the door was closed behind them, Aly took a deep breath. "Your Majesty, friends," she said quietly, her hands resting on her sash, "I cannot be your spymaster. I am the daughter and granddaughter of Tortall's spymasters, and the daughter of Tortall's King's Champion. The god did not teach me most of what I know—I learned it at my father's knee. I am *not* working on Tortall's behalf. Kyprioth claimed me after I'd foolishly left my home, and set me to work with you. That is the truth of it." She looked down, listening for the slightest hint of movement. The knives in her sash were the quickest to reach, but if it was Fesgao who came for her, she'd need the sword secured under the desktop.

For a very long moment, much too long for Aly's taste, no one spoke or moved. Then Chenaol hoisted herself to her feet. "If that's all, I've got two wagonloads of flour coming from Digger Brothers' mill. I want them to explain how I found gravel stitched into the bottoms of the bags last time. Then I need to decide how much I'll take out of them in blood."

Aly stared at her. "That's it?" she demanded, shocked. "Or will I find you waiting for me in some dark night with one of those thousand and three new carving knives you bought for the kitchens?"

Chenaol rolled her eyes. "Half for the kitchen, half for the armory," she explained. "Why *should* I care? The god picked you. How many times do you have to prove whose side you're on? Oh, I remember—you've already done that." She stomped out.

Fesgao called after her, "Wait." To Aly he said, "She's right, you know. The god wouldn't saddle us with someone who worked for a rival country. I wonder what happens now. Will your father spank you for playing with the neighbors?" He followed Chenaol. "I thought I asked for a *thousand* knives for the armory," he told her.

"Five hundred is what you get with the treasury in the mess it is," they heard her reply. "Talk to Quedanga, if you want to hear her moan about all the money spent on food supplies for those whose crops didn't make it."

Aly blinked, then looked at Winna and Dove. "Maybe the god's recommendation is good enough for you, Your Majesty," she said to the queen. To the duchess she respected she added, "But, Your Grace . . ."

Winnamine smiled and rose to her feet. "Chenaol is right. You have more than proved who has your allegiance, Aly." She came over and leaned down, in a puff of lily-of-the-valley scent, to kiss Aly's cheek. "I would hate to force you to choose between your family and us, but it goes without saying that we need you more." She smiled at Dove and left them, gently closing the door behind her.

Aly looked at Dove.

"Are you going to be my spymaster or not?" demanded the younger girl. "Winna's right. We need you more. We met your father, didn't we? Last year, at Tanair. Only he said he was a merchant."

"Your Majesty, he lies," Aly said, shaking her head with regret. "He lies all the time. I think sometimes he lies just to stay in practice."

Dove smiled and stood. "And to protect his daughter, alone in the enemy's country," she pointed out. "Will you be my spymaster, please? I still do need a friend."

Aly got up and walked over to her, then knelt, took Dove's hand, and pressed her forehead against the younger girl's fingers. "I will serve you all my days, Your Majesty," she told Dove softly, meaning it with her whole heart. Then she looked up. "You're wearing five rings. You promised you'd never wear more than three."

Dove giggled. "Boulaj says they look nice." The young woman had decided that she liked the post of bodyguard-maid and kept it.

"She's Kyprin," Aly scolded. "They think twelve necklaces on one neck is nice."

Dove pulled a ring off, a gold band with a piece of basalt set in it. Embedded in the smooth, matte black stone was a small copper kudarung. "Then here," she said, holding the ring worn by her personal household to Aly. "You wear this one."

For once Aly had nothing to say. She could only nod, and slide the ring onto her index finger.

Someone pounded on the door. "Your Majesty!" called Nuritin, pronouncing each word with care. "You have an audience in the Throne Hall this morning. Will you be late to your own audience?"

Dove grimaced and walked out to meet her obligations.

Aly looked at her jumbled desk. "Well," she said wearily, "if I'm staying, I'd better recruit some more help."

The day after the end of Midwinter, the Throne Hall of the royal palace blazed with the light cast by a thousand lamps and candles. It glittered on gold and silver jewelry, hoards of gemstones, silks and satins, and in the hundreds of pairs of eyes that were fixed on the dais. Incense rose to form clouds against the high ceilings, scenting the air. Chimes tinkled as breezes moved through the hall.

Taybur Sibigat, captain of the Queen's Guard, knelt on the second-highest step of the dais, holding a cushion above his head. On it shone gold shaped as a crowned headdress at the front, with a spray of copper sprigs at the back, each dangling gold drops. Copper drops hung from a forehead plate. Dovasary Haiming Temaida Balitang, dressed all in silver satin patterned in black, reached for the Crown, made from old descriptions to look like the original Crown of the Isles. With hands that trembled, she raised it for her audience to see, then carefully lowered it to rest on her own head. It was how the Kyprin queens had always been crowned, since no one wanted to offend their peculiar god by claiming his priesthood.

The onlookers, noble and common born, sent up a thunder of applause and cheers that startled the small winged horses from the beams overhead. They swooped around the new queen, who stood there patiently, waiting for quiet.

To the side, tucked into the shadow of a pillar, her spymaster leaned against Nawat Crow with a happy sigh.

EPILOGUE

At the Kudarung Inn
Rajmuat in the Copper Isles
April 2, 464 H.E.

In the morning the Tortallan delegation would sail home, with reports for their monarchs on the new queen and her government. For this occasion some of its members had taken a private room for a very private dinner. Their two local guests came separately, one as a crow who changed into human form once he reached his father-in-law's chambers. Aly came disguised as a Carthaki lady, complete with veils.

She and Nawat sat at the table with her family, everyone full of good food and busy with lively talk. Aly, whose morning sickness extended sometimes to evenings, had contented herself with a mild broth and fruit juices. She looked frequently at the slight swell of her belly, mystified by the thought that another human being was taking shape beneath her navel.

She sat between her father, George Cooper, baron of Pirate's Swoop, and her mother, Alanna the Lioness, lady knight and King's Champion of Tortall. From that position she could look at her brothers. Alan wore a squire's gear. His knight-master had allowed him to carry word to his parents that it was time to come home, and to attend his twin's wedding before he returned with them. Thom was bouncing Sarralyn Salmalín on his knee, explaining to the two-year-old the difference between a star and a moon, while Sarra beamed up at him. Next to him Veralidaine Salmalín, known as Daine the Wildmage, gently rocked baby Rikash and talked softly with the crowd of darkings assembled on the table before her. Her husband, the mage Numair, was deep in conversation with Aly's grandfather, Tortall's official spymaster, Myles of Olau. Eleni, lady of Olau, discussed bird lice cures with Nawat.

"Well, I never thought you would do it," Alanna remarked as she sat back in her chair.

Aly gave an inward sigh, certain she was about to get a speech in how she ought to behave. "Do what, Mother?" she asked, keeping the impatience from her voice. It's the last time I'll see her, she scolded herself. I can take a little lecture from her, surely.

"Find a cause that caught you up and gripped you in your very veins," Alanna replied quietly, her eyes on the raka tapestries on the walls. "Find some passion that would consume you. Make you a fool with the rest of us fools."

"I'm *hardly* consumed," Aly began to say. Then she looked at her mother, at the lines at the corners of her mother's famed violet eyes, at the blue pearl drops hanging from her ears, Aly's Midwinter gift, at the callused and scarred hands that Alanna had folded on the table. Slowly Aly's sense of reality overcame her. Her mouth twitched. Her mother was right. Aly *had* found something to consume her, even if she didn't show it as her mother did. "Have I ever mentioned that I hate it when you're right?" she asked instead.

Alanna shook her head. "No, I don't believe you have. As far as I could tell, you never thought I was right."

Another bubble of vexation fizzed up out of Aly's belly and popped. She could see a smile tugging her mother's lips. "Since you mention it, no. Except now, Mother." She offered her hand.

Alanna took it and kissed Aly on the cheek. "Goddess bless you each and every day," she whispered. "The Great Mother is surely too wise to hold a grudge simply because you helped her brother."

Finally Aly and Nawat had to go, or fall asleep on the table. Aly took leave of her family, hugging everyone hard, fixing their faces in her mind. She saved her father for last. Standing on tiptoe, she whispered, "Da, I'd like all of your agents out of the Isles by the end of the month. Elsewise I'll arrest them and ship them home."

George looked down at his daughter, his eyes lighting up with amusement. He raised an eyebrow at her.

Aly knew what he meant by it. He would simply recruit new people in the Isles, because that was his job. Smiling wickedly, she raised one eyebrow of her own.

Back in their palace quarters, Nawat watched as Aly walked onto the veranda. The late-night air blew around her, molding her light nightgown to her body. "You will find ways to see them, and they to see you," he called to her. "They are not lost to you, or you to them. They will always be your flock."

"I know," Aly called, looking up at the sky. The sliver of the moon and the dots of the stars were as they had been in the months before the gods had waged their battle in the Divine Realms. Kyprioth had reclaimed his true throne in full, and Mithros and the Goddess were still searching for their shields. "I know. There's no reason we can't see each other, if we're discreet. Though we're going to be frightfully busy."

"There is much for us to do," Nawat agreed. "But there must be time for fun as well. Fun, and sparklies, and nestlings, and all the other things that make life interesting. For example, you could make my life interesting right now, if you chose."

Aly laughed. "And where would you be if I didn't choose?" she asked, walking inside once more.

Nawat smiled at her, the smile of a man who loved a woman. "Right here," he said confidently. "I would wear you down."

Aly was drifting off to sleep when a familiar, crisp voice whispered in her ear, *There's a girl. You get some rest. The Isles will give you all the interesting things you can stand.* Kyprioth added, *And so will I.*

CAST OF CHARACTERS

Acharn Uniunu	boy noble, member of Dunevon's court
Adona	luarin noble house
Alan of Pirate's Swoop	Alianne's seventeen-year-old twin brother
Alanna of Pirate's Swoop and Olau	the Tortallan King's Champion, lady knight
Alianne of Pirate's Swoop	daughter of Alanna and George of Pirate's Swoop, former slave
Ankoret Obeliten	noblewoman at regents' court
Atisa Libo	pretty, plump, Guchol's sister, one of Aly's spy pack
Bacar	footman for a Balitang neighbor
Bean	darking placed in the palace
Boulaj	raka warrior, maid to Sarai, one of Aly's spy pack
Bronau Jimajen	Rubinyan's deceased brother, murderer of Mequen Balitang

Callyn	spy recruit, works for the harbormaster
Chenaol	free raka head cook for the Balitangs, armorer for rebels
Dorilize	Nuritin's maid, member of raka conspiracy
Dovasary (Dove) Balitang	Mequen's half-raka daughter from first marriage
Druce Adona	nobleman, one of Sarai's suitors
Dunevon Rittevon	boy king of Copper Isles
Edunata Mayano	luarin noblewoman, one of Imajane's ladies-in-waiting
Eleni of Olau	Myles's wife, Aly's grandmother
Elsren Balitang	Dunevon's heir, luarin son of Mequen and Winnamine
Eyun	part-raka warrior, determined, member of Aly's spy pack
Faithful	supernatural cat, Alanna's former companion

Feather	darking placed in Teak Sitting Room, Balitang House
Fegoro	hard raka warrior, member of Aly's spy pack
Ferdolin Tomang (Ferdy)	one of Sarai's suitors, count, wealthy luarin
Fesgao Yibenu	raka sergeant of Balitang men-at-arms, rebel war leader
Flame	darking placed to spy on Duke Nomru
Gazlon Lelin	boy noble, member of Dunevon's court
Genore Tomang	dowager countess, Ferdolin's mother, member of luarin conspiracy
George of Pirate's Swoop	Alanna's husband, Aly's father, baron and second in command of his realm's spies
Gian	Elsren's manservant, spy recruit
Graveyard Hag	trickster, primary goddess of Carthak, Kyprioth's kinswoman

Grosbeak	Topabaw's spy, collector of information
Guchol Libo	plump, good-humored, Atisa's sister, one of Aly's spy pack
Haiming	former raka ruling house
Hazarin	deceased former king
Herbrand Edgecliff	luarin bookseller, member of raka conspiracy
Hessken	soldier, Rittevon Guard
Hiraos	handsome raka, member of Aly's spy pack
Huldean Obeliten	boy noble, member of Dunevon's court
Hunod Ibadun	noble executed by the regents
Imajane Jimajen	born Rittevon, King Oron's half sister, princess regent
Imgehai Qeshi	priestess of Black God of death, member of luarin conspiracy
Inayica	female ship captain
Isalena Obemaek	luarin, one of Sarai's friends

Jesi	Nuritin's secretary
Jevąir Ibadun	noble, one of Sarai's suitors
Jimarn	former slave, deadly member of Aly's spy pack
Jonathan of Conté	king of Tortall, Aly's godfather
Junai Dodeka	Ulasim's daughter, Dove's bodyguard, one of Aly's spy pack
Kaddar Iliniat	emperor of Carthak, patron and cousin of Zaimid Hetnim
Kadyet	noble house, Balitang neighbor
Kioka	pert raka, one of Aly's spy pack
Konutai	female Stormwing, Taybur's friend
Kyprioth	trickster god
Lace	darking placed in raka meeting room, Balitang House
Lehart Obemaek	luarin lord, member of luarin conspiracy
Lelin	luarin noble house

Lohearn Mantawu	Topabaw, duke, Crown spymaster
Lokeij	raka hostler for the Balitangs, deceased
Ludas Jimajen	second in command of the luarin invasion of the Copper Isles
Lutestring	Topabaw's agent and information gatherer
Matfrid Fonfala	Winnamine's father, lord, member of luarin conspiracy
Mayce	soldier, Rittevon Guard
Meipun Kloulechat	raka baron
Mequen Balitang	deceased duke, father to Balitang children
Merani	luarin noblewoman
Murtebo	Balitang neighbor
Myles of Olau	head Tortallan spymaster, Aly's grandfather, Alanna's adoptive father
Nawat Crow	crow who turned himself into a man

Numair Salmalín	powerful mage, Daine's husband
Nuritin Balitang	great-aunt to Balitang children, unofficial head of extended Balitang family
Obeliten	luarin noble house
Ochobu Dodeka	mother of Ulasim, leader of mages of the Chain
Olkey	chubby, thoughtful, one of Aly's spy pack
Oron Rittevon	deceased king of the Copper Isles
Otaviyu Lelin	one of Sarai's friends, parents are members of luarin conspiracy
Pembery	part-raka, Winnamine's maid, belongs to rebellion
Peony	darking placed to spy on agent Grosbeak
Petranne Balitang	Mequen's first child with Winnamine
Qovold Engan	baron, royal astronomer, member of luarin conspiracy

Quartz	darking placed with Countess Tomang
Quedanga	Balitang housekeeper, head of communications, member of rebel leadership
Raoul of Goldenlake and Malorie's Peak	lord, knight-commander of the King's Own, Alan's knight-master
Rasaj	handsome raka, member of Aly's spy pack
Rihani	raka healer, nursemaid to Petranne and Elsren
Rikash Salmalín	Daine and Numair's infant son
Rittevon Lanman	leader of luarin conquest of Copper Isles
Roald of Conté	prince, heir to Tortallan throne
Roger of Conté	King Jonathan's deceased uncle, rebel
Rosamma Tomang	one of Sarai's friends, Genore's daughter
Rubinyan Jimajen	luarin, husband of Princess Imajane, prince regent

Rufert	soldier, Rittevon guard
Saraiyu (Sarai) Balitang	Mequen's oldest daughter, half raka, from his first marriage
Sarralyn Salmalín	Daine and Numair's daughter
Sarugani Temaida	Mequen's first wife, raka, mother of Dove and Sarai, deceased
Sevmire Ambau	Rubinyan's personal spymaster, luarin
Shinkokami	princess, wife of Prince Roald, heir to Tortallan throne
*Spot (*now *Secret)*	darking first placed in king's bedroom, then with Aly
Sulion	royal governor of Tongkang
Taybur Sibigat	captain of King's Guard
Temaida	raka noble house, keepers of the Haiming bloodlines, Sarugani's family
Thayet of Conté	Queen of Tortall, co-ruler with her husband, King Jonathan
Thom of Pirate's Swoop	Aly's older brother, a student mage

Tkaa	basilisk, immortal and friend of Aly's family
Topabaw	people's name for Duke Lohearn Mantawu, Crown spymaster
Trick	darking who stays with Aly
Ukali	wicked, dangerous, one of Aly's spy pack
Ulasim Dodeka	head footman to Balitangs, general of rebellion, raka, Ochobu's son, Junai's father
Uniunu	luarin noble house
Vedec Golzai	young luarin noble
Veralidaine (Daine) Sarrasri Salmalín	half goddess, called the Wildmage for her skills with animals, Aly's adoptive aunt
Vereyu	raka servant, head of raka conspiracy at palace
Vitorcine Townsend	double agent, maid to Obemaek family
Vurquan Nomru	duke, luarin, popular, member of luarin conspiracy

Wayan	raka child, message runner at Balitang House
Wesedi	luarin noble house, friends of Winnamine's
Winnamine Fonfala Balitang	duchess, mother of Petranne and Elsren, member of luarin conspiracy
Yoyox	cheerful, bold raka, member of Aly's spy pack
Ysul	mage of the Chain, mute, member of raka conspiracy
Zaimid Hetnim	handsome Carthaki healer, friend of the Carthaki emperor

GLOSSARY

Ambririp: harbor on northern tip of Imahyn Island.

arak: distilled palm-sap liquor.

Azure Sea: body of water between Imahyn, Jerykun, Ikang, and Lombyn islands, known for its calm, bright blue waters.

basilisk: immortal (cannot be killed by old age or disease), lizard-like creature, can be seven to nine feet tall, walks erect, is skilled with languages, possesses a shriek that can turn its targets to stone.

Bazhir: collective name for the nomadic tribes of Tortall's Great Southern Desert.

Birafu: estates on Tongkang belonging to Jimajen family, in rebellion.

Black God, the: hooded and robed god of death, recognized as such throughout the Eastern and Southern Lands.

blazebalm: sticky, paste-like substance that clings to everything it touches and burns very hot.

Carthak: slaveholding empire that includes all of the Southern Lands, ancient and powerful, a storehouse of learning, sophistication, and culture. Its university was at one time without rival for teaching.

Chain, the: network of rebel mages, mostly full and part-raka, spread throughout the Copper Isles, with members on every isle, including one posted especially close to the isle's royal governor. It has been in existence over one hundred years. Its present commanding mage is Ochobu Dodeka.

Copper Isles: originally named the Kyprin Isles, once ruled by queens of the Haiming noble house, presently ruled by the Rittevon dynasty. The Isles form a slaveholding nation south and west of Tortall. The lowlands are hot, wet jungles; the highlands cold and rocky. Traditionally their ties are to Carthak rather than Tortall. Kyprin pirates often raid along the Tortallan coast. There is a strain of insanity in the Rittevon line. The Rittevons hold a grudge against Tortall (one of their princesses was killed there the day that Jonathan was crowned).

Corus: capital city of Tortall, on the banks of the River Olorun. Corus is the home of the new royal university as well as the royal palace.

darking: creature made in the Divine Realms that has evolved into an independent being; small, blob-like, able to manipulate shape, reproduce by splitting, capable of thought and learning; some reside in Dragonlands in Divine Realms, others have returned to Mortal Realms.

Dawn Crow: male god of the crows.

Dimari: eastern harbor town on the island of Lombyn.

Divine Realms: home to the gods and to many immortals.

Dockmarket: section of town defined by Dockmarket Street along wharves; open-air markets for food, spices, various products; includes warehouses, slave market.

Downwind: poorer section of Rajmuat.

duan: raka word for old man, boss.

duani: raka word for old lady, boss.

Eastern Lands: name used to refer to those lands north of the Great Inland Sea and east of the Emerald Ocean: Scanra, Tortall, Tyra, Tusaine, Galla, Maren, Sarain. Original home of the luarin nobility and kings of the Copper Isles.

Ekallatum: one of the most ancient kingdoms in the history of the Southern Lands, now part of the Carthaki Empire.

Emerald Ocean: body of water west of the Eastern and Southern Lands, containing the Yamani Islands and the Copper Isles, among others.

Examples: Kyprin term for nobles and wealthy people who are executed by the Crown and displayed on posts as a warning to others.

Fief Tameran: neighboring fiefdom to Pirate's Swoop.

Flowergarden: district north and west of Downwind, contains lower-class residences, also district of brokers of domestic animals, fullers, tanners, blacksmiths.

Gainel: god of dreams, with one foot in the Mortal

Realms and one foot in the realms of Chaos.

Galla: country to the north and east of Tortall, famous for its mountains and forests, with an ancient royal line. Daine was born there.

Galodon: housing town for military and royal navy fortress and reserves.

Gempang: island in the Copper Isles, across the Long Strait from Kypriang.

Gift, the: human, academic magic, the use of which must be taught.

Gigit: smallest coin of the Copper Isles: 10 copper gigits equal 1 silver gigit; 50 copper gigits (5 silver gigits) equal 1 copper lan; 1 copper gigit will buy a cup of tea, a bun, or an orange.

Gray Palace: Eastern Lands–style castle built inside a separate wall on the palace grounds, to house the Rittevon family.

Great Mother Goddess: chief goddess in the pantheon of the Eastern Lands, protector of women. Her symbol is the moon.

Greater Fortress: citadel that guards the southeastern approach to Rajmuat harbor.

griffin: feathered immortal with a cat-like body, wings, and a beak. Males grow to a height of six and a half to seven feet at the shoulder; females are slightly bigger. No one can tell lies in a griffin's vicinity (a range of about a hundred feet). Their young have bright orange feathers to make them more visible. If adult griffin parents sense that a human has handled their infant griffin, they will try to kill that human.

Gunapi the Sunrose: raka warrior goddess of volcanoes, war, and molten rock.

Haiming: name of the former ruling line of raka queens, supposedly wiped out during the Luarin Conquest, with members who survived in secret until the present.

healer: health-care professional with varying degrees of education, magic, and skill.

his realm's spies: network of a kingdom's agents, charged with gathering intelligence at home and abroad; spies in service to a particular country.

Honeypot, the: worst of the Downwind slums.

hostler: person who cares for horses: their feed, medicine, grooming, cleanliness, saddling.

Human Era (H.E.): time period that begins 463 years prior to the present book, marking the exile of the immortals from the Mortal Realms.

hurrok: immortal shaped like a horse with leathery bat wings, claws, and fangs.

Ikang: island to the southwest of Lombyn (the northernmost island).

Imahyn: island just northwest of the Long Strait and Gempang.

Immortal: creatures from the Divine Realms who cannot get sick or grow old. They can be killed, but otherwise they live forever.

Immortals War: short, vicious war fought in 452 H.E., named for the number of immortal creatures that fought, but also waged by Carthakis (rebels against the new emperor Kaddar), Copper Islanders, and Scanran raiders. These forces were defeated by the residents of the Eastern Lands, particularly Tortall, but recovery is slow.

Jaguar Goddess: feral and bloody goddess native to the Isles, overthrown by Mithros and the Great Mother Goddess during the Luarin Conquest and chained below the earth until she should be freed. Sister and sometime consort of Kyprioth, who also prefers that she stay chained.

Jerykun Isle: smallest of the Isles, situated between Imahyn in the south and Ikang in the north. Virtually all of Jerykun is held between the Tomangs, who have grown rich from the trade in sunset butterflies (a source of precious blue dyes and magical ingredients), with smaller estates held by, among others, Sibigat House.

Kanodang: prison to the northeast of the Downwind slums, over the ridge of the Kitafin mountains that runs between Rajmuat and the coast.

King's Council: Tortallan monarch's private council, made up of those advisors he trusts the most.

King's Guard: small contingent of soldiers/bodyguards responsible for the safety of the ruling monarch of the Copper Isles, presently led by Taybur Sibigat. Their armor is chain mail painted black.

King's Watch: patrol group that polices the city, wears armor painted red.

K'mir: brown-skinned nomadic horse tribes of Saraine, expert at guerrilla fighting against the Saren ruling class of lowland whites. Queen Thayet of Tortall is half K'mir on her mother's side and has been responsible for a migration of K'miri, who now work for the Tortallan Crown.

kudarung: Kyprish (raka) term for winged horses.

Kypriang: main island of the Copper Isles, holding the capital, Rajmuat, and its harbor. Location of the Plain of Sorrows, site of the last great defeat of the raka by the luarin.

Kyprioth: Trickster, greatest of the trickster gods, former patron god of the Copper Isles, overthrown by his brother Mithros and his sister the Great Mother Goddess, now relegated in the Isles to rulership over the seas that surround them. Cousin to the Carthaki goddess the Graveyard Hag.

lan: largest money coin in the Isles: 1 gold lan equals 10 silver lans; 1 silver lan equals 5 copper lans; 1 copper lan equals 5 silver gigits, or 50 copper gigits.

Lesser Fortress: citadel that guards the eastern arm of Rajmuat harbor.

Lombyn: northernmost island of the Copper Isles, home to the Tanair estates of Lady Saraiyu and Lady Dove Balitang, the legacy of their mother Sarugani. The location of the Turnshe Mountains, Kellaura Pass, Dimari town and harbor, and the villages of Tanair, Inti, and Pohon.

Long Strait: narrow, tricky body of water between Kypriang and Gempang islands.

luarin: raka term for the white-skinned invaders from the Eastern Lands, now used in the Isles to indicate anyone with white skin.

mage: wizard, male or female.

Malubesang: largest and most southern of the Copper Isles, notorious for streams that are home to meat-eating fish. Home to the most prosperous estates of the Isles, particularly those of Nomru House. The extended Fonfala family also has lands bordering the Nomru ones.

Maren: large, powerful country east of Tusaine and Tyra; the grain basket of the Eastern Lands, with plenty of farms and trade.

Market Town: pricier market district west of Dockmarket.

Middle Town: district that is part residential for middle class, part shopping area, includes Rittevon Square.

Midwinter Festival: seven-day holiday, centers around the longest night of the year and the sun's rebirth afterward. The beginning of the new year. Gifts are exchanged and feasts held.

Mithros: chief god of the Tortallan pantheon, god of war and the law. His symbol is the sun.

Moriji Cove: cove on the southern coast of Kypriang near Fonfala estates.

network: group of spies or other persons who exchange information among themselves.

pavilion: an outdoor structure that can be open on its sides, walled halfway up its sides, or fully walled in.

Port Udayapur: port city-state on the northeast corner of the Great Inland Sea, entry gate to the mountains called the Roof of the World.

Rajmuat: capital of the Copper Isles under both the raka and the luarin.

raka: copper/brown-skinned natives of the Copper Isles, under the lordship of the luarin arrivals from the Eastern Lands for nearly three hundred years.

Rittevon Guard: guard that covers the palace grounds and walls; combined sun and moon engraved on breastplates.

Rittevon Lancers: light cavalry military force. They generally carry lances and swords as weapons.

Rittevon's Lance: major street of Rajmuat and the palace, running through the center of Rajmuat and up through the Gate of Victory to the center of the palace enclosure. Ends in the palace street called the Golden Road.

sarong: for women, a dress-like wrap-around garment that extends from under the arms to the calves. For men, a skirt-like wrap-around garment that can be kilted in the middle to make rough breeches.

Scanra: country to the north of Tortall; wild, rocky, and cold, with very little land that can be farmed. Scanra's war with Tortall began in 460 H.E. (the events are covered in *Lady Knight*) and has moved into its third year, though Scanra is visibly weakening.

scry: to look into the past, present, or future using magic and, sometimes, a bowl of water, a mirror, fire, or some other peering device.

shape-shifter: someone who can take the shape of an animal or another human.

Sight, the: aspect of the magical Gift that gives its holders certain advantages in matters of vision. It can be erratic, showing holders only lies, illness, magic, or future importance. In its fullest form, it can allow the holder to see clearly over distance, to see tiny things in sharp detail, and to detect illness, lies, godhood, magic, death, and other aspects of life.

Sky: the crow goddess, consort of the Dawn Crow.

slave broker: one who buys and sells slaves.

Southern Lands: another name for the Carthaki Empire, which has conquered all of the independent nations that once were part of the continent south of the Great Inland Sea.

Stormwing: immortal with a human head and chest and bird legs and wings, with steel feathers and claws. Stormwings have very sharp teeth, but use them only to add to the terror of their presence by tearing apart bodies. They live on human fear and have their own magic; their special province is the desecration of battlefield dead.

Swan District: residential neighborhood for the newly rich, north and west of Dockmarket, Market Town, and Middle Town.

Tanair: Lombyn Isle estates that form part of the inheritance of Lady Saraiyu and Lady Dove Balitang, granted to them by their mother, Sarugani Temaida. Estates include Tanair Castle and village and the villages of Inti and Pohon.

Tongkang: island to the south of Gempang, between Gempang and Malubesang isles.

Tortall: chief kingdom in which the Alanna, Daine, and Keladry books take place, between the Great Inland Sea and Scanra. Home to Alianne of Pirate's Swoop and her family.

Tusaine: small country tucked between Tortall and Maren.

Tyra: merchant republic on the Great Inland Sea between Tortall and Maren. Tyra is mostly swamp, and its people rely on trade and banking for income. Numair Salmalín was born there.

Vassa River: river that forms a large part of the northeastern border between Scanra and Tortall.

wild magic: magic that is part of the natural world. Unlike the human Gift, it cannot be drained or done away with; it is always present.

wildmage: mage who deals in wild magic, the kind of magic that is part of nature. Daine Sarrasri is often called the Wildmage for her ability to communicate with animals, heal them, and shape-shift.

Wind: Kyprioth's cousin, a god.

Yamani Islands: island nation to the north and west of Tortall and the west of Scanra, ruled by an ancient line of emperors, whose claim to the throne comes from the goddess Yama.

Yimosuat: capital of Gempang Island, known for its many temples.

Notes and Acknowledgments

Aly's story is a pair of books instead of a quartet thanks to J. K. Rowling (I haven't met her!), who taught adults that American kids will read thicker books, which means I don't need four books to tell a complete story.

My thanks, I think, also go to my beloved editrix, Mallory Loehr, who suggested both that I write about a spy and that I write a character who is laid-back and easygoing, not driven. One day I will find the proper manner in which to express my appreciation of an exercise that made a Moebius strip of me for the last three years. Sarai's fate is her idea as well. My gratitude also goes to my Australian editrix, Margrete Lamond, for her very provocative pointers on pomp and on the behavior of gods.

Thanks as ever to the home team, those who gave me help with so many of the problems that cropped up in the *Trickster* books: my excellent Spouse-Creature, Tim Liebe, who gives me so many plot ideas and twists, and also supplies necessary photographs; my best friend Raquel Starace, fashion consultant on flattering colors for everyone who is not a fair-skinned redhead like me, and the progenetrix (through her discussions of making an inanimate object animate and her analysis of the differences between human and computer animation) of the darkings; my wonderful assistant, Sara Alan, for her proofreading and for her reassurances with regard to my feminist credentials as well as for her tolerance of major author flake-outs; my agent, Craig Tenney, he of the watchful eye and the sound advice; Peter Glassman at Books of Wonder for shoring up my faltering courage; and the excellent Christina Schulman and the National Aviary for crowned pigeons and tropical woods mood enhancement.

I bow also to the *Law & Order* franchise, World Wrestling Entertainment, *National Geographic*'s photographs of people around the world, and photographer Joyce Tenneson's *Wise Women* collection in thanks for their inspiration for a number of characters; to the novels of John Le Carré, particularly *Tinker, Tailor, Soldier, Spy* and *Smiley's People* for insights into effective spycraft, as well as to the innumerable books by innumerable experts I have read on the art of guerrilla warfare.

For musical inspiration I have turned to sources that may appear odd and unrelated, but aren't: Alan Lomax and the singers of his collection *Negro Songs and Work Calls*, performed by Southern blacks in the 1930s and 1940s; pianist Glenn Gould and his classic recordings of Bach's "Goldberg Variations"; composer Ottorino Respighi and his incredible "Pines of Rome," of which I have at least three recorded versions with three different orchestras and conductors; and "Two Cries of Freedom: Gypsy Flamenco from the Prisons of Spain," sung by José Serrano and Antonio "El Agujetas," Reachout International Records, Inc.

Those interested in the historical sources of some of my ideas and conflicts may want to examine Alexander the Great's conquest of Egypt and his placement of the Greek Ptolemies over the native Egyptians; William the Conqueror's arrival in England and its centuries of consequences; American slavery; the history of Tudor England during the childhood of Edward VI and the beginning of the reign of Queen Elizabeth I; and the history of any power that invades a country that is not its own and attempts to keep it. As the Rittevons and Jimajens learn, it's hard to completely pacify a country when the bulk of the people who live there are opposed to being pacified.

TAMORA PIERCE captured the imagination of readers more than twenty years ago with *Alanna: The First Adventure.* As of 2008, she has written more than two dozen books. The quartets the Song of the Lioness, the Immortals, and Protector of the Small; the two Trickster books; and *Terrier,* the first book in the Beka Cooper trilogy, are set in the fantasy realm of Tortall. She has also written the Circle of Magic and The Circle Opens quartets, as well as the stand-alone Circle title *The Will of the Empress,* and she cowrote *White Tiger* for Marvel Comics. Her books have been translated into many languages, and a number of them are available on audio from Listening Library and Full Cast Audio.

Tamora Pierce's fast-paced, suspenseful writing and strong, believable heroines have won her much praise: *Emperor Mage* was an ALA-YALSA Best Book for Young Adults, *The Realms of the Gods* was listed as an "outstanding fantasy novel" by *Voice of Youth Advocates, Squire* (Protector of the Small #3) was an ALA-YALSA Best Book for Young Adults, and *Lady Knight* (Protector of the Small #4) debuted at #1 on the *New York Times* bestseller list. *Trickster's Choice* spent a month on the *New York Times* bestseller list and was an ALA-YALSA Best Book for Young Adults. *Trickster's Queen* debuted at #1 on the *New York Times* bestseller list and was named a Bank Street College of Education Best Children's Book.

An avid reader herself, Ms. Pierce graduated from the University of Pennsylvania. She has worked at a variety of jobs and has written everything from novels to radio plays. Along with writer Meg Cabot (The Princess Diaries series), she cofounded SheroesCentral, an online discussion board about female heroes; remarkable women in fact, fiction, and history; books; current events; and teen issues. Though she no longer sponsors Sheroes Central and SheroesFans, as she did for five years, she is still a devoted member of the sites.

Tamora Pierce lives in Syracuse, New York, with her husband, Tim, a writer, Web page designer, and Web administrator, and their five cats, two birds, and various rescued wildlife.

For more information, visit www.tamorapierce.com.

Don't miss the first installment
of an all-new Tortall trilogy!

BEKA COOPER
TERRIER

Beka Cooper begins her training with the law-enforcing Provost's Dogs, and she's assigned the toughest beat there is. In the constant battle for the Lower City's streets, Beka will have to use her smarts and her own eerie brand of magic if she hopes to survive.

Excerpt from Terrier copyright © 2006 by Tamora Pierce.
Published by Random House Children's Books,
a division of Random House, Inc., New York.

Prologue

From the journal of
Eleni Cooper,
resident, with her six-year-old son,
George Cooper,
of Spindle Lane, the Lower City,
Corus, the Realm of Tortall

March 18, 406 [H.E.: the Human Era]

In all those lessons for which I was made to memorize chants and prayers I never used, couldn't our temple priestesses have taught one—just one!—lesson on what to do with a boy who is too smart for his own good?

I am at my wit's end! My George was taken up for stealing and I had to go to the Jane Street Guard station.

I thought I might die of the shame. I know it is this place and the friends he makes here. Even the families who do not teach their children the secrets of theft look the other way because it puts food on the table. And I am too newly come. I cannot tell them, "Keep your children away from my son. Do not let them teach him to steal."

I want him to rise in the world. We are poor now, but I pray we will not always be so. And I cannot afford a better place to live. My family will not have me back, not after our last meeting. So I am left here, trying to raise a lad who sees and hears and thinks too much, in the city's worst slum.

At the station there my scapegrace was, seated on a bench with the Guard who'd caught him. "It was but a handful of coins left on a counter, Mistress Cooper," the Guard said. "And I recovered them all. It's his first time, and I owe you for makin' my wife's labor so easy." He looked at George. "Next time it's the cages for you, and maybe a work farm," he warned. "Don't go makin' your good mother weep."

I grabbed George's arm and towed him out of there. We'd no sooner passed through the gate into the street when he tells me, "Up till a hundred year ago they was called Dogs, Ma." He was talking broad Lower City slang, knowing it made me furious. "Ye know why they changed it? They thought folk mightn't respect 'em if they went about callin' them after curs like they done for three hundred–"

I boxed his ear. "I'll have no history lessons from you, Master Scamp!" I cried, tried beyond my sense of dignity. "You'll keep your tongue between your teeth!" Everyone we passed was smirking at us. They knew our tale, knew I'd been dismissed from the temple. They believed I thought myself better than they were, because I kept my home and my child as clean as may be and taught him his letters. Let them think it. We will not always live in the Cesspool. My George is meant for better things.

Thieving is not among them, I swear it.

When I got him to our rooms, I let him go. He stared at me with his hazel eyes, so like mine. The beaky nose and square chin were his father's, a temple worshiper I saw but for one night. George would be the kind of man women would think was so homely he was handsome, if he lived. I had to make certain he would live.

"The shame of it!" I told him. "George Cooper, how am I to face folk? Stealing! *My* son, stealing!"

He looked me boldly in the face. "We're gettin' no

richer from your healin' and magickin', Ma. I hate bein' hungry all the time."

That cut me. I knew he was hungry. Did I not divide my share so he had more, and it still wasn't enough? So he would not see me in tears, and because he needed it, I sat on our chair and turned my rascal over my knee. I gave him the spanking of his young life.

I stood him on his feet again. His chin trembled, but he refused to cry. The problem is, my lad and I are too much alike.

"There's more important things than wealth," I said, trying to make him *listen*. "There's our family name. Us above all, George, we don't take to thieving." I had thought to wait until he was old enough to understand to tell him about Rebakah Cooper, but I believe the Goddess's voice in me was saying it was time. He *needed* to hear this. I took down the shrine from the wardrobe top, where I kept it safe from small boys. I opened the front to show him the tiny figures of the ancestors.

"See how many of your great-grandfathers wore the uniform of the Provost's Guard? What would our famous ancestress say if she knew one of her descendants was a common thief?"

"We've got a famous ancestress?" George asked, rubbing his behind.

I picked up Rebakah's small, worn statue. I took it out often when I was a girl, because *she* was a woman, of all the ancestors who wore the black tunic and breeches of the Guard. There was the cat at her feet, the purple dots of paint that were its eyes worn away just as the pale blue paint for her eyes was worn away. The shrine was old, given to me by my great-aunt when I was dedicated to Temple Service.

I showed him the figure. "Rebakah Cooper," I said. "Your six-times-great-grandmother. Famed in her day for her service as a Provost's Guard. She was fierce and law-abiding and loyal, my son. All that I want for you. And she was doom on lawbreakers, particularly thieves. Steal, and you shame her."

"Yes, Ma," George said quietly.

"Remember her," I told him, giving his shoulder a little shake. "*Respect* her. Respect *me*."

He put his arms around my waist. "I love you, Mother," he said. Now he talked perfectly, as he'd been taught. He helped me to clean up from the medicine making and to make supper.

It is only in writing about this day that I realize he never said anything about thieving.

No, he will obey me. He is a good boy. And I will make an offering to my Goddess to guide him on Rebakah Cooper's path.

READY FOR MORE ADVENTURES IN TORTALL?

MEET